My Life as a Whale

My Life as a Whale

Dyan Sheldon

AVON BOOKS  NEW YORK

AVON BOOKS
A division of
The Hearst Corporation
1350 Avenue of the Americas
New York, New York 10019

First Avon Books Trade Printing: June 1993

AVON TRADEMARK REG. U.S. PAT. OFF. AND IN OTHER COUNTRIES, MARCA REGISTRADA, HECHO EN U.S.A.

Printed in the U.S.A.

OPM 10 9 8 7 6 5 4 3 2 1

For Buckwheat

My Life as a Whale

1

Born to Be Ordinary

My name is Michael Householder. I'm an ordinary, average kind of guy. Asked to describe myself I guess I would say I was nice. A nice, normal guy—in an ordinary, average sort of way. Except for an unfortunate juvenile habit of keeping small animals and reptiles imprisoned in cages and aquariums, I've always been a nice guy. And I've always been pretty ordinary. Average. Nothing special. When I was a kid I was Junior So-So. Junior So-So, who grew up to be Mr. Not-So-Bad. No special talents, no secret sins. Other men have always liked me. Women have always found me both attractive and sympathetic. Mothers (with the occasional exception of my own) have always loved me. Fathers (including both of my own) have always been fond of me. Except that I can't swim, look Italian in a slightly sinister way, and have an allergy to apples, I've always been what you might call an all-American boy.

That's me in kindergarten, sitting in the middle of the middle row, saying "Cheese."

That's me with my Little League team (I'm the one wearing his helmet), fifth from the end, smiling right at the camera.

That's me, standing at the back of the grocery store in chinos, a flannel shirt, and old sneakers, my hair not too long and not too short, my clothes neither too stylish nor too schlumpy, trying to choose between Shredded Wheat and Raisin Bran.

When the police question you about who else was on the subway platform at the time of the robbery, I'm the guy you can't remember. "I think there was someone else there," you say, "some guy over by the candy machine, but I can't really remember him. He was sort of average, I guess. No, I'm not sure what he was wearing. No, I'm not sure what he looked like. Just average, I guess. I'm not sure, I think he must've gotten on the local."

When your friends ask you who you met at dinner, I'm the one whose name keeps slipping your mind. "He was a nice guy," you say. "Sort of . . . kind of . . . not unattractive . . . not stupid or anything. . . . Jesus, I wish I could remember his name."

At the time my story begins, I was thirty-four years old, made a pretty good living as a literary agent, theoretically owned my apartment and a late-model gray Ford, and went to the gym every Wednesday night to de-stress and keep time on my side. Like millions of other guys in Manhattan, I worked hard, worried about cholesterol, and had my suits and shirts done by the cleaners around the corner from where I lived. Like millions of other guys in Manhattan, I had a squash racquet under my bed, a ten-speed Italian racer in the hall, and a yogurt maker at the back of the closet. I bought my home-baked cookies (nothing at all like mother used to make) and hand-packed New England ice cream from the store across the street. If I wasn't eating out in the evening and didn't feel like cooking, I'd order Thai or Malaysian or Japanese from down the block. I shaved once a day, drank too much specially blended fresh-ground coffee, and had strong liberal tendencies (most of which I have by now managed to overcome).

But though I was, in most respects, an average Joe, as ordinary as a doughnut, there was a time there when I was, in my own small part of the world, and in my own small way, as popular as Michael Jackson, as hunted as the finback whale. For I did have one small attribute that made me special. One rare quality that made me stand out among my peers like a scarlet ibis in a flock of penguins. "And what was that, Mike?" I hear you ask. Did I possess artistic genius? Intellectual brilliance? The character and personality of a Mother Teresa? Had I inherited forty million dollars and a suit once worn by Elvis Presley? Won the lottery? Discovered the Fountain of Youth or a cure for cancer or the meaning of life?

The answer is: No. None of the above.

The answer to the question "What was it that set you apart from other metropolitan men of similar education and socioethnic background and gave you a notoriety and appeal usually reserved for rock stars or serial killers?" is: I was single.

As of the summer of 1986, some stockbroker in the Village and I were the only two fully operational, healthy, solvent, heterosexual males within, say, a seventy-mile radius of New York City whose sell-by date had not yet expired, who had no severe bad habits (like a tendency to violence or a toxic dependency), and who were not married, about to be married, or as good as married. And because of that one simple—and in most societies unnotable—fact, in the years that have followed 1986 as surely as the honeymoon the wedding, my entire life has been turned around and upside down.

No longer am I thirty-four, carefree and happy, as trusting of the future as an infant of its mother. No longer do I drive out to Long Island for the weekend in a car that looks just like every second car you pass. Three secretaries sublet my apartment, and my racer is being ridden by a young woman who was a Cherokee chief in a former life. My mother has my yogurt maker, which she doesn't use either. The everyday stresses of contemporary urban living—do I have a good job? am I doing well in it? will I get one that's better? is the new man in the office going to be promoted over me? am I going to be fired, robbed, mugged, or hit by a cab in the near future? when does debt really become a threat? have I drunk too much water with aluminum or lead in it? breathed too much air from New Jersey? did that salmon taste a little funny? what about those clams? am I putting on weight? losing my hair? showing my age? what are the chances that that blonde, what's her name, the one I slept with after the Wasserman's Fourth of July party in 1976, has given me some fatal disease?—no longer affect me as once they did. I laugh at them. Hah hah. I have gone to the edge of the abyss, looked over, not liked it particularly, and (miraculously and not a moment too soon) been hauled back by my heels. That sort of experience changes a man. Puts things in perspective, much like coming back from the dead. "What's it like being dead?" everyone asks you. "Was it dark? Was it light? Did you see James Dean? Was Marilyn happy? Jim still writing poems? Was it hard to breathe?"

And you smile enigmatically and say, "Well, I'll tell you one thing. I'm not worried about being impotent anymore."

In fact, there's only one aspect of my life that hasn't changed. I'm still single.

And, as my mother would say, therein lies the tale.

2

In Ways Too Subtle to Recognize at the Time, the Beginning Begins

To be totally honest, I don't really remember all that much about the summer of 1986. Not detailwise, that is. I couldn't tell you what the rainfall was, or if it was a scorcher or unseasonably cool. I don't remember what the craze of the moment was, or even exactly how things were going at the office. It may have been the summer I had the twenty-four-hour flu and thought I was going to die without having made a will, or it may have been the summer it poured every weekend and I reorganized the spice rack (rather cleverly changing from an alphabetical arrangement to placing the jars by frequency of use) and invented three new stuffings for mushrooms. It may have been the summer everyone who invited you to dinner served walnut pesto and arugula salad, or it may have been the summer everyone who invited you to dinner served sun-dried tomatoes and olive bread.

I can't even recall if it was during that summer that some psychopath first started leaving bits of women in garbage cans along Broadway, or if he'd actually begun the winter before. But despite the ease with which the summer of 1986 has melded with thirty-three of its predecessors (only 1966, the summer I fell in love with Alma Huttenmeyer, remains on its own, vivid and clear), it was one of the most important of my life—perhaps even more important than the summer of hell I spent in 1966, trying to get up the courage to ask Alma Huttenmeyer for a date. For three things happened that fateful summer that were to have far-reaching, not to say catastrophic, effects on my peaceful and pleasant existence.

The first was personal. One Friday night in late May, Marissa Alzuco, my lover for the past two years, dumped me.

I was in the kitchen, preparing supper, when she arrived for the weekend. I had the DO NOT DISTURB sign on the kitchen door, but I heard her enter the apartment, walk down the hall, and go into the bedroom. She was in there for some time, but since it always took Marissa a good forty minutes to change from the clothes she wore to work (not because she was so meticulous about her personal appearance—Marissa never brushed her hair more than twice a day —but because she could never decide what to change into; and once she'd decided, she could rarely find it), and since I was involved with the meal and relieved that she hadn't ignored the sign and barged in as usual, I didn't think anything of it.

I was just spooning the gougère onto the baking sheet when the kitchen door opened and, from the doorway, Marissa said, "Michael."

If I hadn't been at that tricky stage in the operation when if you don't get the shape just right you wind up with what looks like a football, I might have noticed a certain tenseness in her voice. But I was and I didn't. "I'll be with you in a couple of minutes," I replied.

"Michael," she said, "Michael, we have to talk."

"What's the matter?" I may have asked. "Didn't they have the rioja I wanted?" Sometimes, even if I wrote down exactly what wine would go perfectly with what we were eating, Marissa would come back with something else. Something Australian or Bulgarian because she thought "it might be nice to try something different for a change." It used to drive me crazy.

"Michael," she said again. "Michael, it's not about the wine. I have to talk to you. Now!"

It wasn't enough that Marissa never seemed to think that the DO NOT DISTURB sign was meant for her ("Who do you think it is meant for?" I would ask reasonably. "The busloads of tourists who come marching through my apartment? For God's sake, Marissa, I live alone!"), but she insisted on discussing things when I was busy.

"For God's sake, Marissa," I hissed. "Don't scream, will you? You'll ruin the pastry." And that was when I turned and saw that she was still wearing her jacket and had her hand on a loaded luggage trolley. Tears were dripping down her cheeks. Her lower lip was trembling.

"Michael," said Marissa in a choked voice, "Michael, I'm really sorry about this. I really, really am."

I can remember looking from her to the gougère, weighing my options. And I can remember thinking, Why don't they ever time these things better? "Do you think you could just hold on one second, Marissa?" I asked. "Just till I get this into the oven?"

In case you think that my reaction to this drama was a little cool, let me mention here that Marissa was always threatening to leave me. Every few weeks she'd talk to her mother or one of her girlfriends, and she'd decide that she was tired of waiting for me to suggest that we take that fatal step and she give up her apartment (or, more accurately, that she was tired of waiting for me to give in and take up her suggestion that she permanently park her racer in the hallway behind mine). Her biological clock was winding down. Everyone thought she was wasting her life. She wasn't getting any younger. Her mother's one wish was to live to see her grandchildren. I couldn't expect her to go on forever without some sort of commitment. Her friends were all married and starting families. She wanted more from a relationship than someone to play backgammon with and the best stuffed artichokes west of Tuscany. She wanted more than shared vacations and a guaranteed date for New Year's Eve. She deserved more.

This was the first time, however, that Marissa had actually packed up her things. And it was also the first time that Marissa had decided that "more" was a tattoo artist named Hewitt Monserrat who lived on a houseboat in Florida.

I didn't try to persuade her to stay. After all, her mind was made up, and somewhere in the swamps of the Sunshine State there was a man with *Marissa 4ever* tattooed on his arm, waiting for her to rock his boat. What was the point of arguing?

"I want you to be happy," I told her as we waited for the elevator. I handed her my handkerchief. She hadn't stopped crying since she'd begun, but, being Marissa, she'd run out of Kleenex. "I just hope you know what you're doing," I added.

"Me?" She stopped sobbing abruptly, and her voice in the quiet of the hallway sounded a little loud. Like a gunshot in a library. "You hope *I* know what *I'm* doing?"

I was sure I could hear Mrs. Sontag in 8A, our early-warning system and gazetteer, shuffling toward her peephole, anxious not to miss anything.

"Marissa!" I hissed. "You want to keep it down, please? You're going to have the whole floor out here in a minute."

But Marissa didn't want to keep it down. "Michael!" she bellowed. "Michael, have you been listening to one word I've said?"

I adjusted the strap holding her suitcases onto the trolley. "Of course I've been listening," I answered, calm and collected. "You don't want to spend any more time in the waiting room of life. You want to climb onto the main stage. You want a home and family. You want someone to grow old with. You want a man who has a bison head tattooed on his inner thigh."

"Michael!" I heard the click of a door being surreptitiously opened behind me by a seventy-year-old woman with excellent sight and hearing for her age. "This isn't just about me," Marissa wailed. "It's about you, too! About you ending up a lonely, unfulfilled old man, unwanted and unloved!"

"Marissa," I pleaded, "please give me a break." By now, I reckoned, Mr. Sontag had joined Mrs. Sontag at the door, and they were probably

calling the doorman to get everyone else in the building to come to
the eighth floor and see the show. "Wait'll you catch a load of this,"
they were telling him. "It's better than *The Dating Game!*"

"Michael!" shrieked Marissa, unconcerned that we were attracting
an audience. "Michael, you've got to take chances sometimes. You
can't plan every moment of your life, every detail. You can't really
live if you refuse to confront your human needs and emotions."

Mrs. Sontag's brain was like a professional tape deck; I was sure
she was getting down every word. "Marissa!" I whispered. "Marissa,
for the love of God . . ."

"Aren't you human, Michael?" screamed Marissa. "Can't you see
what you're doing to yourself? You're turning into some sort of freak!"
She grabbed hold of my arm. "Open your eyes before it's too late,
Michael!" she roared. "Reach out and seize the day!"

I reached out and seized her. I shoved her into the elevator, dragging
her luggage in after us just as the doors closed.

"You don't have to come down with me," Marissa sniffled, wrench-
ing the trolley from my grip. "We've already said our good-byes."

"Don't be silly," I protested, always the gentleman. "You can't wait
for a cab by yourself. There's a murderer loose on the streets."

"You're the murderer, Michael," Marissa announced as the doors
opened.

Mr. Sontag, a bag of groceries in his arms, stood before us, tipping
his hat.

We struggled past him, each of us trying to drag the trolley.

"Evening," I said.

Marissa honked.

I tried to help her to the front door, but she kept pushing me off.
As we came out onto the street she turned to me, her eyes shimmering
with tears. "It's true," she said in a choked voice, pulling the trolley
over my toes. "You are a murderer. You murdered my heart." Marissa
always was a little melodramatic.

After I'd put her into a cab, I went back inside. Hector, the doorman,
was watching me over the top of his paper. I gave him a smile. "Her
grandparents came from Russia," I explained.

Hector nodded. "That's too bad," he said.

And, surprise of surprises, Mrs. Sontag was polishing the brass on her front door when I got back upstairs. "Don't tell me this one left you too," said Mrs. Sontag, my surrogate mother.

"How's the circulation?" I asked with a neighborly smile.

Mrs. Sontag shook her head. "Things weren't like this in my day," she informed me.

Well, they certainly were in mine.

And so Marissa Alzuco departed for the sunny shores and low taxes of Florida. She left behind a pink-and-maroon chenille bathrobe with crocheted roses down the lapels, a rather temperamental African Gray parrot named Gracie, and, of course, me.

I put the robe at the back of the closet; I ate the gougère, sans rioja, by myself; and then, because the apartment seemed a little on the quiet side without the sound of female weeping, I brought Gracie's cage into the living room so she could watch the news with me.

And, after a day or two, things went back to normal, as things used to do. Losing Marissa was sad, I'm not saying it wasn't, but it was not the end of the world. I knew I would miss her (though an uninspired, even mediocre, cook, she was a terrific person, a good friend, and a sensitive lover), but the miss would be a dull ache, not a sharp, bleeding wound. Once you've passed the age of fourteen or fifteen, losing a girlfriend is not the most traumatic thing that can happen to you. It is not, for instance, as traumatic as losing an arm. It is not as catastrophic as being declared bankrupt or discovering that you have only six months to live. It isn't anything like being in a plane that's about to make unexpected contact with the Atlantic Ocean. Experience had taught me that you lost a girlfriend and the sun still came up in the morning, the stars still came out at night, and triple chocolate mousse could still make you smile. Life would go on. Only dogs and dolphins, experience had taught me, ever died for love.

That, the first significant event of the summer, was met by my mother with a failure to feign either sympathy or indifference.

"I knew this would happen," said my mother.

It was a Saturday, and I'd taken her to lunch at one of those sidewalk cafés where the waiters forget about you as soon as you sit down, but where your mother's voice can't travel quite as far as it can in an enclosed space, to tell her the news.

"I don't know how you could have known it when I had no idea," I said.

It's my experience that most mothers have this slightly smug smile they employ right before they tell you that they told you so.

"It's a pattern, isn't it?" my mother opined. She broke a roll in half. She smiled. "If you ever listened to anything I said," said my mother, her knife pointing right at my heart, "you'd know that. I try to advise you, but do you pay any attention?" Crumbs bounced across the table. "No, you don't pay any attention. I give you all those books to read, but will you read them? No, you won't read them." Her knife clinked against the butter dish. "You were always stubborn," said my mother, "even as an infant."

I peered over her head, trying to catch the waiter's eye. "Mom," I said, waving toward the slender figure dressed in black trousers and a white shirt who was standing at the far end of the patio, staring into traffic, "Mom, this is not a pattern. Things just didn't work out, that's all. Sometimes they don't."

"With you they never do," said my mother.

I waved again. One or two people, none of them employed by the restaurant, smiled back.

"I knew this would happen," my mother repeated. "The first time you brought her to the house, I knew this is how it would end. I said to Barry, 'Mark my words, honey, this is going to be another of Michael's dead-end relationships. Either she's more interested in her career than in getting married and having a family—' "

"Mom, please," I cut her off. I was half standing by then, hoping our waiter would see me as he came back through the door. "I'm the one who didn't want to get—"

" 'Or she's going to stay around for a while, and then go off and marry someone else or live with a woman like all the rest of them did.' " She bit into her bread. "I'm only surprised she lasted so long," said my mother. "Isn't a year something of a record for you?"

"Two," I corrected her. Other waiters saw me, but they weren't any more interested in serving us than our waiter was. "And no, it's not a record. I don't know what 'all the rest' you think you're talking about."

My mother began to count on her fingers. One. "First there was that Sophie Lumbucco," said my mother, digging far enough into the past to qualify as an archaeologist. "Then there was Alison." Two. "Amber." Three. "Georgina." Four. "That big Norwegian girl, ate like a horse, what was her name?"

There are moments in a man's life when what he wants more than anything—more than love, or money, or global peace—is another vodka and tonic. I signaled with my empty glass, desperately. "Orysia."

"Orysia. Patricia. Ellen." Fivesixseven. She picked up her knife. "And God knows who else that you never even bothered to introduce to me." She gave me a look. "Or didn't have the time to." She gave me another look. "Ships in the night." She picked up her drink. "You're not getting any younger, you know," said my mother. "Time's running out."

"I'm thirty-four, Mom. Thirty-four is not old. Not in this day and age. I've got plenty of time." I was surprised to notice that I sounded a little on the loud side.

"Is there?" asked my mother. "Your father was thirty-two when you were born." The couple next to us looked over. "What do you think would have happened if he'd waited to settle down, Michael? What if he'd told himself he was in no hurry to get married? What if he'd thought, Oh, I'll wait till I'm forty, that's not old?"

"Mom," I said in my most reasonable voice, "Mom, I've told you. I don't want to start thinking about children and lawn mowers until my career is better established. I'm just not ready yet. Once I've got my partnership—"

"He was dead by thirty-nine," boomed my mother. A woman two tables away shook her head sadly.

"Mom, real—"

"If he'd waited to have you till he got his promotion," said my mother in clear, resonant tones, "you'd never have been born." A passing waiter, not ours, gave me a wink.

Had I known what maniacal fate lay in wait for me, I might have said, "At least that would have been the soft option." But, of course, I didn't know. On that bright summer's day, I was still unreservedly glad that my parents had decided to have three children and not stop at two. So what I said was "Mom, do we really have to discuss this now?"

"And when do you think would be a better time?" my mother inquired, not merely of me, but of the other seventeen people sitting on the street with their empty breadbaskets and unfilled glasses as well. "When you're fifty-five? When you're sixty? When I'm already dead?"

I stood up straight.

For some reason, she stood up too. "Don't you think Barry and I would like to live long enough to see our grandchildren?" my mother wanted to know of the world at large. Several passersby stopped with inquisitive, even helpful, expressions on their faces, as though prepared to try to answer her question. "The rate you're going," my mother shouted, "Methuselah wouldn't have managed that."

My best friend, Jerry, was in analysis for most of the 1970s. Jerry told me that the one really valuable thing he learned from it was the concept of nonparticipation. "The people who drive you nuts," said Jerry, "they can only drive you nuts if you let them." Jerry said that just as it takes two to tango, it takes two to have an argument, or to have a serious and meaningful discussion about life and how you're failing them. If you won't argue or won't discuss, said Jerry, then the other person is left arguing or discussing with herself. Instead of an emotionally draining, blood-pressure-raising scene, what you end up with is a nonevent. "You should try it sometime, Mike," Jerry always used to say. "It might stop you from going bald."

I moved to walk away.

My mother's voice, more familiar to me than any other single thing on the planet, rang through the crowded, pulsating streets of Manhattan. "Michael," it said, "Michael, I'm talking to you. Where the hell do you think you're going?"

I knew that I should nonparticipate. I knew that I should answer, "Home." I knew that I should say, "Mother, I'm warning you, unless you promise that we're never going to have this discussion again, especially in a public place, I'm going to the gym for the rest of my life." I picked up our glasses. "I'm going to get us another drink," I said.

Not long after that first event came the second, which was as impersonal as an act of God. One otherwise unremarkable week in June, *Newsweek* ran a cover story with the title "The Marriage Crunch." "The Marriage Crunch," complete with sobering scientific statistics, was something of a cautionary tale for the liberated, independent female human (of whom, I suppose I should mention here, in my liberal days, I used to think of myself as something of a champion). Not only did this article claim that a thirty-year-old college-educated woman, single in 1986, had less than a 10 percent chance of ever finding a husband, but it also claimed that by forty this same unfortunate had more chance of being shot by a terrorist than of ever wearing a slender gold band on her left hand. "You see?" *Newsweek* seemed to be saying. "You should have stayed home and married your high school sweetheart instead of becoming a nuclear physicist, just like your mother told you."

I myself didn't usually read *Newsweek*. Nor did I ever read anything with a title like "The Marriage Crunch" unless I was in the dentist's waiting room and there was nothing else to do but guess which patients were there for dentures and which for root canals. So the odds were pretty much against my happening upon this revolutionary information. But my mother read *Newsweek*. And she especially read anything—articles, recipes, scientific papers, photonovellas, picture books, absolutely anything—that had the word "marriage" in the title.

My mother was on the telephone only minutes after that momentous issue hit the stands.

"Look, Mom," I said. "I've got a meeting with an important author in a few minutes, so why don't I call you back later in the afternoon?"

"Have you seen *Newsweek*?" asked my mother.

There was a no-nonsense knock on the door, and Elizabeth Beacher, a highly successful writer of adventure romances featuring tough, willful, but drop-dead-gorgeous heroines, stepped in. I motioned to her to sit down. "My mother," I whispered. She rolled her eyes. Although this was something I hadn't previously suspected, it seemed that Elizabeth had a mother too.

"*Newsweek*?" I repeated. Maybe all that hormone therapy was having some sort of adverse effect. "Mom, look, I really have to go now. I'll phone you later."

"I knew this would happen," said my mother. "But would anyone listen to me? No, of course not. No one paid a blind bit of attention. They never do."

I tried again. "Mom," I said, "Mom, I'll—"

"This is what comes of being too smart for your own good," continued my mother.

It seemed unlikely that she was referring to me.

"You can't cheat Mother Nature, you know," said Mother Householder Taub. "If you go around demanding everything, you end up with nothing. That's what I've always said. Not that anyone's ever listened."

"Mom? Are you all right? Can I call you back in a little while?"

"It's good news for you, though," said my mother, her voice instantly sounding chirpier. And then, slipping into Barryese, the language used by my entrepreneurial stepfather, she added, "It's a buyer's market."

"Don't go out," I ordered her. "I'll call you back before lunch."

Elizabeth looked up as I put down the receiver. "Trouble?"

"Mothers." I pulled my chair in. "She's all wound up about some article in *Newsweek*."

"Oh," said Elizabeth. She rested her elbows on the desk, looking at me with an expression other than her usual one, that of a star player greeting her coach. "That must be 'The Marriage Crunch.' "

If I'd thought about it, I might have realized that Elizabeth was giving me the same inscrutable smile her heroes employed right before they pulled the knife from their boots or took the heroine into a rugged embrace. But I didn't think about it. I was still an innocent then. Elizabeth had come to talk about her new novel (in which Tamara Wintermeer brought a South American drug baron to justice and won the love of a renegade CIA agent), and that, I knew from years of experience, was all she could be expected to think or care about. When a writer is geared up to discuss her new book, Cuban troops taking over Lincoln Center wouldn't catch her attention, let alone the reading material of her agent's mother. So what I thought was that, uncharacteristically, she was trying to be polite.

"Let's not talk about my mother," I said. "Let's talk about this fantastic book."

Elizabeth smiled, one of her normal, straightforward, I'm-always-happy-to-talk-about-myself smiles. "I think I've solved that little continuity gap in chapter six," she said.

I was enthusiastic. "That's great."

But then the new smile reappeared. She leaned forward. "Michael," she said, slowly and almost delicately picking up the picture frame from my desk and turning it toward her so she could see the photograph. It was of my mother and Barry, dressed up for a masquerade party as Tweedledum and Tweedledee—as close as I came to the photo cubes filled with dribbling infants and gap-toothed children that most of my colleagues favored. "Michael, you never told me you weren't married."

The third event of that summer occurred a few days after the *Newsweek* article appeared, and managed to combine the personal and the impersonal in much the same way as a psycho killer.

I stared at the manuscript on my desk: *How to Get Mr. Right to Pop the Question: Making Love Work for You*. In only 358 pages, Suzanne Lightfoot, expert on men, love, romance, and sexual politics, told the women of America how to take control of their lives and their potential for love.

"Ladies," Suzanne Lightfoot wrote in her introduction, "we are almost in the twenty-first century. We have microwaves and computers, we have fuel-injected engines and liposuction, and yet our ideas about love and courtship are as old-fashioned as the horse and cart or the whalebone corset. It's time we brought romance and marriage into our hi-tech world." Chapters included: "How to Separate the Mr. Wrongs, Mr. Disasters, and Mr. Married-to-Somebody-Elses from the Mr. Maybes and the Mr. This-Could-Be-Its"; "How to Find Men"; "How to Make a Man Interested in You"; "How to Keep Him Interested"; "How [as the book's title so subtly suggested] to Get the Right Man to Marry You."

I looked up, smiling that noncommittal but interested smile that agents have. "Oh, um," I said. "This looks like a project with a lot of potential."

Suzanne Lightfoot, elegant, efficient, shrewd, smart, and attractive in a try-not-to-mess-up-my-makeup kind of way, smiled back. More the sort of smile that makes you wonder what she'd do if she decided that she hated you than the sort of smile that makes you wonder what she'd be like in bed, but a smile nonetheless.

"I like your style," I said, "informative but informal, direct but intimate."

Her smile locked. "I feel very strongly about this."

I tapped the typescript. "I can see you do. I can see you do." I shuffled a few pages until I found the table of contents. "I really liked the chapter about meeting men." I shook my head. "And the one on getting a man to notice you . . . fascinating, absolutely fascinating."

She leaned forward in the earnest way that authors do. "I hope you're taking this seriously, Mr. Householder," she said simply, and threateningly.

I looked surprised, almost shocked. "Of course I'm taking it seriously. I—"

"Because this happens to be a very, very serious issue at the moment."

"Oh, yes, yes," I tried to say, "I do appreciate how timely it is. My mother has mention—"

"I'm telling you," Suzanne Lightfoot told me, "there's a real gap in the market for a book like this. Women are crying out for guidance."

I tried clearing my throat. "I know. My mother says tha—"

If she'd leaned any farther across the desk we'd have banged heads. "Do you have any idea how few good men there are available right now? Do you have any concept of the enormity of the shortage and what this means for thousands upon thousands of intelligent, attractive and loving women?"

"Well . . ." I tried clearing my throat again. "My mother has said—"

She tapped one long silver-tipped nail against the title page. "I'm telling you, Mike." She smiled as the sun shines over the Sahara—relentlessly. "You don't mind if I call you Mike, do you?"

"Of cour—"

"I'm telling you, Mike, this book is going to be big. And if you'd like to handle it . . . well, Elizabeth says you're the best agent in town."

Good old Elizabeth. "I'd love to take it on," I said. Which at least was true. I knew a good commercial idea when it landed on my desk. And, also, my mother had been right when she said that the hula hoop would pass. Right when she said that flares would never stand the test of time. One hundred percent correct about Sophie Lumbucco. Chances were that she was right about this male drought thing, too. "I think I know the perfect publisher."

"You won't be sorry," said Suzanne Lightfoot. "This book is going to be mega—mark my words."

The Oracle had spoken.

And only half lied.

3

Count No Man Happy Until He Is Dead

One of the most striking similarities between a life-shattering event and a charging rhino is that they both start slowly. The animal, like the event, just stands there for a while, looking at you. You look back. Nothing to worry about. You can handle this. Not, of course, that there is anything to handle. There's just this rhino standing there, munching on his lunch. Then, almost as in a dream, you think you see his ears twitch a few times. Are his ears twitching? Your expression becomes one of puzzlement. Why are his ears twitching? You rub your eyes. His ears aren't twitching. Probably just a trick of the light. The rhino looks as if he's about to doze off or shuffle over to a new patch of grass. You start thinking about your lunch. Lunch and maybe an afternoon nap. Feeling one with nature, you glance toward the rhino again. He's pawing the ground.

Another striking similarity between a charging rhino and a life-shattering event is that in both cases it's almost inevitable that you wind up dropping your gun and climbing the nearest tree.

It is no reflection on Marissa or our time together if I say that in those first few months after she left me I considered myself a pretty happy man. Not that I was made of stone or anything, you understand. No matter what Marissa may have said in the heat of the moment, I was human. I missed those companionable times when we'd watch a late-night movie together or she'd give me her opinion on the sauce for the linguini. I missed the shared jokes and her inspired imperson-ation of Mrs. Sontag discussing anything ("You think it was like this in my day?" Squint of the eye, shake of the head, finger in the chest. "I'll tell you for nothing, it wasn't like this. It wasn't like this at all"). I missed having someone else around who was driven nuts by my mother. I missed the internationally renowned Alzuco back rub. And I guess I must have missed the sex—there were days when I certainly thought I missed the sex. More than that, though, I think I missed the really intimate things we did together, like brushing our teeth and turning the mattress. But on the whole, I'd have to say that there wasn't really that much difference between life without Marissa and life with Marissa.

I went to work. I went to parties and dinners and expeditions to the theater. I saw my friends for drinks and meals and overrated movies. Jerry and I went to the gym every Wednesday. And as for the weekends, there was always plenty to do. Aside from the usual weekend things—cleaning, running errands, doing those household chores, trying out new recipes—I started going for long walks and runs, enjoying the total solitude and anonymity that you can find only in a city of over ten million people. My life, you can see, was more full than ever.

If there was a difference, it was that without Marissa things were easier.

No more sixty-five-minute discussions on how to boil water or cook an egg.

No more nights when I couldn't use my own phone because she hadn't talked to her best friend in sixteen hours.

No more coming home from a hard day of stoking the furnaces of hell and having to be cheerful and pleasant and interested in someone else and whether or not she had a tension headache or cramps.

No more having to pretend that I didn't mind eating soggy rice or refrigerator rolls.

No more not being able to find my razor, or the painkillers, or the grapefruit knife.

No more uncapped toothpaste tubes or unfilled ice-cube trays.

No more having to turn down free tickets to a game because I'd been to a game the night before.

And I'll tell you another thing I didn't miss. I didn't miss the tears and tantrums that had marked our relationship more and more toward the end. Life without Marissa was not only easier, it was considerably more peaceful, too.

Now and then, of course, one of those lonely moments that everyone experiences might suddenly sneak up on me. Moments when you find yourself staring into the mirror, wondering where all the time and keratin have gone. Moments when you're walking down the street and everybody you pass is with someone else (and for some reason not arguing). Moments when you catch yourself smiling soppily at a father pushing his grimy child through the supermarket, talking about breakfast cereals. Moments when, after twenty long and full years— and for no reason at all—you discover that you're gazing into space, thinking about Alma Huttenmeyer and how different things might have been if you had been taller and had gone out for football.

But those blue moments were few and far between. And I did have Gracie. I might have lost a lover, but I'd gained a parrot. A not inconsiderable acquisition.

Previously, Gracie and I had had a relationship best described as nonexistent and bad. Though I might occasionally pass her a piece of fruit or let her out of her cage, Gracie was Marissa's. I wasn't even sure how she had come to reside in my apartment. One weekend she arrived with Marissa, but for some unexplained reason, and unlike Marissa, Gracie never left. The bird who came to dinner.

But after our abandonment, Gracie became mine. My little feathered friend. I will admit that once upon a time I'd been a little concerned that Gracie might attract mice and carry disease. Her habit of impersonating a car alarm at odd moments of the night had disconcerted me. I wasn't really comfortable with the way she would hang upside down from the bottom of her cage and just stare. I took her playful nips as personal assaults. I never really cared for her feet.

However, as the weeks passed, those feelings disappeared completely. She was really kind of cute. And smart. She was small and she had feathers, claws, and a sharp little beak, but she had a lot of personality as well. I began to enjoy her company. I talked to her and she talked to me. At the end of an imperfect day, Gracie was never distant or preoccupied. She would listen sympathetically to the longest tale of woe. She'd rub her head against my chin. We'd share a bag of nuts. We'd sing along to the radio together.

"Gracie, I'm home!" I'd call when I entered the apartment in the evening.

"I'm in here, honey," Gracie would shout back. "How was your day?"

We started spending hours in the kitchen together, while I perfected my pasta puttanesca and my enchiladas Householderas, and Gracie learned relevant culinary phrases. "Sgetti! Sgetti!" she would cry as I brought out the pasta machine, "Al dente! Al dente!" as I brought the water to a boil. At her first sight of the tortilla press she'd usually burst into a chorus of "Down Mexico Way."

While I read manuscripts I'd brought from the office, Gracie would perch on the back of the sofa, watching the quiz shows and the Spanish-language soaps. "We did it! We did it!" she'd shriek. "Go for it! Go for it!" Or she'd lean her head against my ear. *"Te quiero, te quiero, amor de mi corazón."*

With Gracie's help, I caught up on all those back issues of *The New York Times Book Review*. "Uh oh," she'd say, "another bad review." With Gracie as coach, I started doing my morning exercises again. "Feel the burn!" Gracie would shout. "No pain, no gain!" I got some games for the computer, and she'd sit on my shoulder while we played. *"Beep. Beep. Beep."*

I started coming home earlier from the office because I didn't want to leave her alone any longer than I had to. I began picking up little treats for her whenever I did the shopping. I even repapered the bedroom in a jungle motif. It was a little extreme for my personal taste, but I thought it might recall her roots. "What do you think, Gracie?" I pointed out the giant pink and yellow flowers, the swinging monkeys, and the toucans peeking through the trees. Gracie, of course, was nobody's fool. I'm sure she knew that if I really wanted her to feel at home I should have decorated the bedroom to look like a pet store. And yet, loud and flashy as it was, I felt it had a weird kind of charm. It reminded me of being nine. "Remind you of anything?" I asked her. "Cocoa Puffs," said Gracie. Either she agreed, or she was definitely watching too much TV.

And every night I'd carry her cage into my room and put it on its stand. "Say good night, Gracie," I'd tell her.

"Good night, Gracie," Gracie would say.

"I love you, toots," Gracie would say.

And after a week or two I started to say "I love you, toots," too.

By the end of the second month, I had several pictures of Gracie in the photocube on my desk—one extremely fetching one of her hanging upside down from the bottom of her cage with a piece of spaghetti in her mouth.

If anyone besides my mother was concerned that my life might be incomplete, my nights empty, my heart on hold, the little red light flashing furiously, they gave no indication during those first happy months.

Two, maybe three, months of relative bliss. Bliss, except for my relative.

She telephoned me every day and twice on Sunday. Sometimes the first thing she said to me after "Hello, dear" was "Have you started dating yet?" Sometimes she waited fifteen or twenty minutes into our conversation, until my guard was down, and then she'd respond to something I'd said about the terrific deal I'd just made or the unhappy world situation with a snappy "And how about you, Michael? Have

you met anyone interesting lately? Have you started dating again?"
Other times, pacing herself like the born strategist she is, she'd wait
until I was about to hang up, and then she'd break into my relief-
filled good-byes with a sudden "Are you sure you don't have anything
else to tell me, Michael? Are you sure there's nothing new?"

She became more nosey and obsessive than usual.

"It's not natural," my mother said, upon learning that Jerry and I
were going camping for a few days. "You're a grown man. You should
be raising a family, not carrying on like a Boy Scout."

"Jerry has a family," I pointed out.

"That's exactly what I mean," said my mother.

Everyone at my cousin Caren's wedding thought it was unbelievable
that I was still a bachelor. "They all thought I must be joking," said
my mother. "And you know what your aunt Peggy's like. If she had
one picture of those funny-looking grandchildren of hers, she had a
hundred."

I laughed. "So what?" I chortled. "Aunt Peggy's the mother of a
man who's in more debt than Nigeria."

"He has a wife and three children," said my mother.

I was still laughing. "That may be so," I answered, "but his children
look like Cabbage Patch dolls and his wife was once an extra in a
soft-porn movie."

"Everything's a joke to you, isn't it, Michael?" said my mother.
"Thank God your father died so young. This would have broken his
heart."

Her interest became more active.

"Do you ever read the personals?" my mother inquired. There was
a rustling of pages. "Listen to this: Attractive, vivacious, young thirty-
year-old, with a good income and many interests, owns own apartment and share in beach house, loves music, Bengali food, sailing,
and walking in the rain, has kissed a lot of frogs and is now ready to
meet her prince." I could hear her slap the paper flat. "Well?" she
wanted to know.

And once again, joker that I was, I laughed. "She's probably an
ex-girlfriend of mine," I quipped. "I'm probably one of the frogs.
Rititnitit."

"Do you ever go out with women?" my mother demanded. "Or do you stay home all the time by yourself, making chocolate mousse?"

Since I was about four and a half and my mother, catching me gazing at myself in the bath, warned me about what would happen if I ever, even accidentally, put one finger near my penis, her ability to make the most innocent activity seem decadent and/or depraved has never ceased to amaze me. She made "making chocolate mousse" sound exactly like "doing hard drugs."

My mother sighed. "It's not normal. Who ever heard of a man spending all his time cooking?"

"What about Chef Boyardee?" I asked, perhaps cruelly. I once tried to get my mother to write a cookbook: *1001 Family Meals from a Can of Ravioli.*

And then again, perhaps I hadn't been cruel enough.

"Never mind about him," snapped my mother. "It's Friday night. What are you doing? Why aren't you out?"

"I'm making egg rolls," I said. "With two kinds of sauce."

In every life there are events that, viewed in retrospect, make you bury your head in your hands and sob, "I should have known."

The time when you were six and thought you could just help yourself to one more cookie from the jar. How was anyone ever going to find out?

The time you were fourteen and Alma Huttenmeyer kissed you outside the gym the night of the Halloween Hop, and you took that as a good sign. She must like you after all if she let your lips touch hers, right?

The time you were sixteen and borrowed your brother's car without permission. Who would ever know?

The time you were eighteen and asked your best friend to keep an eye on Sophie Lumbucco for you while you went away to college. What made more sense?

The time you were thirty-four and assumed, simply because it was already August and no one else had said anything about reading a fascinating article in *Newsweek* about the shortage of eligible men in America, that no one else had read it.

Two, maybe three, months of relative bliss, and then, ever so slowly, but ever so surely, the killer rhino began to paw the ground—and the women of the greater metropolitan area began to lower the boom.

Thump.

The number of invitations I received to dinners where I was the spare man began to increase just that little bit. I was flattered. Completely forgetting everything Suzanne Lightfoot had taught me in chapter 7, I thought I was receiving more invitations because I was so well liked. I imagined the couples of my acquaintance turning to each other while watching television and saying in unison, "Hey, you know what great guy we haven't seen in a long time? Michael. Michael Householder. Why don't we invite him to dinner on Tuesday?" I pictured these couples leaning over the guest list for the patio picnic or the theme brunch and saying, "Hey, wait a second, we can't leave out Michael Householder. What social occasion is complete without him?"

Thump.

My boss, Vanessa, and her husband invited me out to the Island for their famous Labor Day barbecue. Gracie or no Gracie, I couldn't refuse. I assumed it had something to do with my partnership. She was testing me out. She wanted to see how I floated in the high social seas. So I attached a little flag to Gracie's cage, and she came too. Vanessa introduced me to her niece, Jemma, who had heard so much about me. Now I was sure I was there because Vanessa was finally going to offer me the partnership. I let Jemma beat me at volleyball. I told her I'd be happy to show her how to make pierogis sometime, if she was really as interested in my recipe as she seemed. Everyone thought Gracie was adorable. Almost every woman there told me that a liking for animals was a sign of sensitivity in a man. And I didn't once point out that Gracie wasn't an animal, she was a bird. I was floating like an empty can.

Thump.

Women started talking to me on checkout lines. They would start with something neutral but topical. "Oh, where did you find the crackers that are on sale?" or "I've never tried that tea, is it any good?" And then, after a little chitchat about the inefficient layout of the store or loose tea versus bags, they might move on to something a little more personal. "Your wife away?" they might tease, or "Isn't your girlfriend lucky to have someone to do the shopping for her."

Then it began to happen while I was waiting for my number to come up in the deli. I'd be standing there, watching the scales, when I'd suddenly smell Opium among the oil and cheese. "What do you think of their Greek olives?" a husky voice would whisper. Or "I don't suppose you have any idea of what Manchego is?"

At first I thought I was getting this extra attention because it was obvious from my shopping cart that I was a serious cook. Then women started winking at me across subway tracks and smiling at me from buses, and I thought the workouts and extra exercise were taking effect. I thought that maybe my hair was coming back. I thought I must be one of those men who get better-looking as they get older.

Thump.

"Jerry," I said to Jerry one Wednesday night. "Jerry, is it my imagination, or are there a lot more women in here today than there usually are?"

We were sitting in the health club's café, recovering from our weekly workout. Like most things these days, our club was not exclusively male. But the reason we'd picked Body and Soul in the first place was because it was one of the few whose ad hadn't featured the grainy photograph of a beautiful young woman in a leotard and sweatband, leaning against an exercise bike and grinning like a flight attendant. I suppose (as Jerry's wife had said accusingly at the time) that we thought that because this gym was male-oriented, it was also more serious. Either that or we thought that, being male-oriented, it would remind us of high school and our disappearing youth.

Jerry put down his mineral water. He immediately became absorbed in checking out the seeds in his high-fiber salad. "Must be ladies' night," he mumbled absentmindedly.

"It's not ladies' night," I reminded him. "That's why we don't come on Thursdays." I smiled back at the woman in hot-pink leggings and an NYU sweatshirt who was smiling at me as though she knew me, maybe even biblically. "And there were at least three women on the weights," I pointed out. In the gym, as in life, women had their places: the aerobics class, the tennis court, the rowing machine, the sauna, the swimming pool.

Jerry flicked a few sunflower seeds from his spinach. "So what? Is there some sort of law that says a woman can't have biceps?" asked the husband of that well-known feminist analyst and writer Lonnie Stepato. "If you ask me, with that psychopath on the streets, any woman who goes out after dark needs biceps. Biceps and an Uzzi." Just two nights before, someone had found a severed hand, arranged rather like a crown roast with paper frills, in a plastic lunch box on Sixty-ninth Street. People, especially female people, were getting jumpy. The press was talking about the Butcher of Broadway.

"Oh, come on, Jer," said the agent of that well-known feminist analyst and writer Lonnie Stepato. "There's always some guy running around murdering and mutilating women, but you never saw this place so full before." I started counting in my head: two, five, six, ten, thirteen, sixteen.

Jerry shrugged. "So maybe it's just a sign of the times. You'd be amazed, Mike. We even had a couple of women applying for repair jobs." Jerry owned No Problem, a computer maintenance outfit ("No fault too big or too small"). He shook out a lettuce leaf. Jerry was an easygoing guy, but he had an almost pathological dislike of sesame seeds. "There are even a few at Cooper's nowadays." Cooper's was Jerry's lumberyard. He didn't own it, but he had an almost proprietary interest in it since he'd spent a small fortune there, doing up his loft (at long last scheduled for completion on December 31, 1986). "I guess it's a good thing," said the man who shared his loft bed with the author of *The Better Half: A Study of the Contemporary Marriage*. "But in all honesty, Mike, I have to admit that it gave me a shock the first couple of times." He speared a tomato. "Sort of like finding stockings hanging in the men's shower room."

"I guess sisters really are doing it for themselves," I said. I nodded back at the two women who had just sat down at the next table.

"And about time, too," said Jerry, who had come off very well in his wife's study.

I passed the napkins to our fellow keep-fitters. They were very appreciative. I turned back to my best friend. "I don't know, though, Jerry." I shook my head thoughtfully. "I can't help thinking that it reminds me of something. Maybe something I've read recently . . ."

We got up to leave.

"I'd invite you back for a drink," said Jerry as we pushed in our chairs, "but Lonnie's got her yoga group tonight. They've had to move to our place because the woman who used to hold it is splitting up with her husband, and he's keeping the apartment."

"Say no more," I said. The last thing I wanted was to walk in on six women bending their legs behind their necks, drinking herbal tea together, and complaining about men. "That's one of the great advantages of being single," I said. "You can call your home your own." I nodded "so long" to the woman who was waving her napkin at me.

Now, as I recall that long-ago, innocent conversation, I see it not as a normal man-to-man talk after a workout, the informal interfacing of two guys who have known each other since elementary school and are used to sweating with each other, but as an omen. A clue to the new direction things were heading in with maniacal urgency.

Thump.

Elizabeth Beacher came back from Acapulco.

This in itself was not a particularly surprising or significant event. She telephoned me the day after she returned to tell me that she'd brought me a souvenir. "Wait'll you see it, Michael," she breathed into the receiver, her voice as warm as the Mexican sun. "It's so *you.* I just know you're going to love it."

In the five years I'd been Elizabeth's agent, she had often gone to Acapulco—or someplace like Acapulco—and she had always come back. But she had never telephoned me the next day, not even if I'd left twenty urgent messages on her machine. And she had certainly never brought me a souvenir from her travels before. I'd counted myself pretty privileged the year she sent me a postcard from Barbados, even though the message had been *Having a wonderful time. Hope my check's come in.*

"Why don't we have lunch tomorrow?" Elizabeth continued. "I can't wait to see your face when you open your gift."

For some reason, the image of an iguana lumbered through my mind. Me opening the box in Elizabeth's favorite Vietnamese restaurant ("At least one good thing came out of the war," Elizabeth liked to say) and finding myself eyeball to eyeball with a grumpy-looking reptile with flaking skin who wanted nothing more than his prickly pear cactus. It seemed like the sort of thing a woman might give her agent: personal but not intimate.

I flipped through my appointments book. "Christ, I'd really love to, Elizabeth, but my lunches are taken for the rest of the week. How about next Wednesday?"

Elizabeth had this habit of clicking her teeth whenever you disagreed with her. It was never a good sign. Her teeth started clicking like castanets.

"How about supper tomorrow night?" she countered.

Having weathered (and lost) more than one teeth-clicking war over things like plot, character, dialogue, and whether or not a woman could experience multiple orgasms while hurtling over a hundred-foot waterfall in a torn raft and being shot at by savage drug dealers, I knew it would be unpolitic to say no. And anyway, why should I have said no? I was flattered. I thought these new overtures of friendship must mean that she'd finally forgiven me for making her rewrite four chapters of *Under Cover of Dark.*

"Great," I said. "I'll pick you up at eight."

"This reminded you of me?" I asked, trying to sound both credulous and pleased.

Elizabeth picked up a spring roll with her chopsticks. We were in her favorite Vietnamese restaurant. I'd already complimented her on her tan and her hand-embroidered peasant blouse, and she had already commented that the fried fish toasts, while they certainly didn't justify My Lai, did make it all just a little more bearable. She was eating. I was staring at the present she'd brought me from Mexico. It was not an iguana. It was a detailed replica of an Aztec ceremonial knife.

Elizabeth's foot touched mine beneath the pink-clothed table. She lowered her chopsticks. "They used it to remove the still-beating heart," she said softly, seductively.

I turned the knife over in my hand. Something intimate without being personal. One of the more obvious differences between this knife and an iguana was that an iguana has a great deal of charm. I tried smiling. "Did they?"

Elizabeth's foot, which had somehow managed to escape its shoe, seemed to be polishing the toe of mine. "Rather like love, don't you think?" she drawled.

Not bloody exactly, I wanted to say. Remove the still-beating heart, my ass. What had she been doing down in Mexico? Taking peyote? What I did say, however—trying both to sound like her agent and to diplomatically get my feet out of reach—was "Well, yes, I guess you could describe it that way, couldn't you?" I attempted a small, professional laugh. "You certainly have a real gift for imagery."

For the only time I could remember, Elizabeth Beacher didn't want to talk about her real gift for imagery. She reached out and stroked the knife's handle, slowly, gently, oh-so-warmly. "You do like it, don't you?" she asked. Her voice had the same thick, sighing quality that characterized the voices of many Elizabeth Beacher heroines. "The minute I saw it I thought of you."

I didn't like to ask why. Even if I had liked to ask why, I probably wouldn't have been able to. At the time I was struggling with two powerful but conflicting emotions. On the one hand: terror, total and abject. God help me, I was thinking, this woman is going to eat me alive. On the other: lust, equally total and abject. God help me, I was thinking, I'm going to show her where to start.

Until that moment, sitting at that small cane table, temple music playing softly on the tape machine, wind chimes tinkling in the breeze of the air conditioner, the traffic wheezing in the street outside, I had never thought of Elizabeth Beacher as a woman. To me, she had always been a difficult author first, a difficult person second, and somewhere well behind those first two categories, a girl. I knew she was attractive, just as I knew that Jerry was attractive. But not to me. At that moment, however, my tastebuds tingling from the lemon grass, the chili, and the unaccustomed piquancy of desire, all I could think of were her hips and breasts and smooth, smooth skin.

"It's stunning, Eliza—"

"Lizzi."

She had fantastic cheekbones. "Lizzi. It really is. I've never seen anything quite like it." That was certainly true. "I can't tell you how plea—, how touched I am that you thought of me." And, if her novels were anything to go by, she could do a lot more with a jar of honey than spread it on toast.

"I like the idea of you being touched," she didn't so much say as mouth. Her foot relocated mine. "But, Michael," she said, lowering her voice even more, so that I had to lean forward to catch her words, "you must know that I think of you all the time."

I resigned myself to the fact that there was no way I could keep my feet away from hers without actually sitting on them. "Well, um, Eliza—, Lizzi . . ." I turned my attention to dinner, keeping my eyes on my spring roll as I tried to lift it from the plate with two sticks of plastic and Elizabeth started to pry my left shoe off with her toes. "I do think that I . . . um . . . well, it's just that there's something that maybe I should make clear to you right now."

She leaned forward too. "And what's that, Michael?"

The spring roll fell back on the plate. My shoe thudded to the floor. Terror got a headlock on lust. I took a deep breath. I met her eyes. They were almost violet in the subdued subtropical lighting of the Little Saigon. Thank God we hadn't invaded Iceland. "Elizabeth, it's just that I think you should know that I have a firm policy of never getting romantically involved with a client. No matter how much I might, as a man, want to break that policy, I think it would put the real interests of my authors in jeopardy." There, that hadn't been so bad. Maybe honesty, as my mother had always assured me, really

was the best policy. "You know," I further explained, "it's unpro-
fessional. My stepfather has always said that business and pleasure
don't mix."

She touched my knuckles with her chopsticks. There was something
sticky and sweet on the ends. "Well, I'm certainly happy to hear that."
She smiled.

Lust threw terror to the ground.

"You are?"

She was?

"And I couldn't agree with you more." She laughed. She winked.
She blushed. "I probably shouldn't tell you this," she told me, "but
Suzanne hasn't been able to stop talking about you since you met. I
was a little worried that you might have come on to her or—"

"I never . . . Did she say that? She didn't say that, did she?"

". . . vice versa. I mean, if she thought you were available . . ."
Elizabeth lifted my spring roll with her chopsticks. She popped it into
my mouth. "After all," she said softly, "Suzanne is not only rather
pretty despite her nose, she is the expert, isn't she?"

But, of course, the most attractive thing about Elizabeth Beacher at
that moment wasn't her good figure, or her nice complexion, or her
high cheekbones, or even her money and fame. The most attractive
thing about Elizabeth Beacher was the fact that she wanted me.
Clearly. Openly. A lot.

My all-cotton socks glided over her real silk stockings. Electricity
shot through my groin. My penile member began to ache. My toes
slid past her ankle. Terror passed out.

"But not the only expert." I smiled back.

Thump.

Elizabeth Beacher returned from hungry Mexico (or returned from
Mexico hungry), and Betsy Shopak took up residence in 8A.

I came home one evening to find several stocky young men in T-
shirts and bandannas singing rock songs and lugging bison heads and
pagoda lamps down the hall. Standing in the center of all this activity
was a very tall young woman in bubblegum-pink slacks and a white

cotton blouse, sobbing her heart out in a subdued but noticeably hysterical way.

I stopped the thug with the trunk on his shoulder. "Is she all right?" I whispered.

It had been my experience that men who could carry footlockers on their shoulders while singing "I've Got My Mojo Working" weren't overly sensitive, but there seemed no one else to ask. He looked over at the woman as though he hadn't been aware of her before. He shrugged. "She comes from Cincinnati or someplace like that."

Cincinnati? What other place could be like Cincinnati?

"That's why she's crying?"

"Nah." He shook his head. "She just split up with her old man." He gave me a conspiratorial look. "You know what it's like."

I nodded manfully. Who, after all, knew better than I, the world expert, according to my mother, on being dumped and left alone?

"These things affect everybody differently, don't they?" he continued conversationally. "Me, I was drunk for two months after my wife left. I never cried, but I sweated Jack Daniels."

It's funny, isn't it? I didn't usually bare my soul to men who wore earrings and dirty bandannas, but there is something about openness that encourages openness in return. Or perhaps I was caught so off guard by hearing another man talk about being lonely that I spoke without thinking. "I perfected the stacked Swiss-cheese-and-spinach enchilada," I found myself confiding. "It took three and a half weeks."

One of the other movers stopped to examine the door he'd just come through. "Hey, lady," he called.

The woman in the pink slacks wiped a few thousand tears from her eyes with her shirt sleeve and stared at him blindly.

"Lady," he said affably, tapping the door, "if I was you I'd get a decent lock on here. They just found some chick's tongue near Twenty-third Street." At least he had the courtesy not to mention that it was sliced and on a bed of lettuce.

The guy with the trunk started walking. I turned to my own well-locked door. The woman in the pink slacks started making the sounds of a sink backing up. I crossed over to her and introduced myself.

"Hello," I said. "My name's Michael C. Householder. I live in 8C."

"My name's Betsy Shopak," she snuffled. "I'm moving into 8A."

There was a rumble and a clank, and Mrs. Sontag stepped out of the elevator. She froze with her key in her hand, surveying the scene before her. The burly bodies. The smell of sweat. The sound of sniffling. She nodded to me and Ms. Shopak. Her eyes fell on two young men who were heaving an enormous credenza through the stairwell door. "Don't drop that!" she warned them. "You're going to scratch the finish."

The singing became louder.

I invited Betsy Shopak in for coffee.

"They're usually crying when they leave, not when they move in," Mrs. Sontag announced as I shut my door behind us.

4

Squelching Towards Bethlehem

On the first Thursday of September, *How to Get Mr. Right to Pop the Question* was rushed into publication. Its editor (coincidentally a single woman pushing the age of terrorist targetdom) decided there was no time to waste. And autumn, of course, is always a good time for self-help books. The vacation season (when travel guides, thrillers, sweeping sagas, and chunky romances are popular) is over and, booted out of frivolity, people begin to reassess their lives. They return to their shrinks, their yoga classes, and their assertiveness-training sessions. They need something to read on the way to work. They start thinking about Christmas gifts.

The launch party for *Mr. Right* was attended by several thousand women, circulating like crazy, and a handful of men, huddled together by the drinks table like compulsive eaters at a smorgasbord trying to decide whether to go for the pickled fish or the potato salad first. While the women argued among themselves about whether there really were fewer men around or if women had simply become more discerning, the men discussed what sort of women they found most attractive. I can still remember that the majority favored slender blondes with firm breasts, narrow hips, and good legs (of which there were a remarkable number present), though there was also a vocal minority that liked them dark and full-bodied. ("You mean like Guinness," I joked, and someone hissed back, "Shhh, not so loud.") I can also still remember that the men were as excited as schoolboys getting their first glimpse of the naked female form. All those women—and they all liked us again! "Remember the seventies, when they thought we were scum?" asked the literary editor of one of the dailies. The publisher's publicity manager grinned. "I feel like I've died and gone to heaven," he whispered.

It wasn't long, however, before I began to feel that, though I had died, heaven was not where I'd gone.

Mr. Right hit the bookshops, and it instantly became apparent that Margery Householder Taub, the inventor of the ravioli pie (two cans of Chef Boyardee with cheese and one stack of saltines), and Elizabeth Beacher, author of *Love on the Run*, were definitely not the only women to have read that timely piece of journalism "The Marriage Crunch." I think I can safely say that it was read by at least 78 percent of the women between twenty and forty-seven—married, single, or in the middle of a painful divorce—on the Eastern Seaboard, and by one in Texas. And that each of those women took it to heart. Each one slapped her forehead and cried out loud, "My God, it's a male drought!"

The married ones put aside their worries about housekeepers and baby-sitters and started thinking instead of their unmarried sisters and friends, drifting toward the bushes of middle age, where the terrorists lurked. They rushed out and bought Ms. Lightfoot's equally timely book.

The single ones put aside their worries about their next career moves and where they'd go skiing next winter and started thinking instead of themselves, of their biological clocks, of what life was going to be like at fifty-five if nobody gunned them down before then. They rushed out and bought Ms. Lightfoot's book.

The soon-to-be-available put aside their thoughts of homicide, of revenge, or of how much more pleasant life was when there was no one to leave the toilet seat up, and instead started thinking of all those long nights and longer weekends, of stretch marks and gray hairs, of the younger women their exes would be dating. They rushed out and bought a copy of Suzanne's book too.

By the end of November I'd met more single women than I had in twelve years of public school.

What separates man from the beasts? His superior intelligence. His ability to reason and to think.

What separates modern man from his more primitive forebears? His more superior intelligence. His ability to think and to reason better.

For modern man is no longer the prisoner of superstition and instinct. He is no longer the pawn of violence and fear, or a slave to his own hormones. He is free. He is liberated. He is grown-up.

For instance. Only a few short decades ago, man still believed that woman was inferior to him. Man believed that woman existed almost solely for his sexual gratification. Now man knows better. Sophisticated, educated twentieth-century man knows that sex is not an end but a means. I knew that, too. He and I know that women are not mere sexual objects, but people just like us. He believes that they are deserving of respect and should be treated with dignity. So did I. He doesn't have to be told yet again that women are not playthings or just some warm, convenient place to put his penis when it gets tired of hanging out in his pants, and I didn't either.

But rub away society's fine veneer, and what do you discover? The Neanderthal within. Scratch the surface of this mature, intelligent, cultured gentleman, and what do you find? You find the twelve-year-old boy who used to jerk off in the bathroom while he ogled the *Playboy* centerfold and wore his sister's dirty bra over his head.

Or better yet, don't rub at the polish; don't scratch him. Make him wanted. Make him the object of desire. Surround him with intelligent, attractive women, all of whom want to invite him back for a drink. Set his phone to ringing. Give him invitations to Scrabble tournaments and after-theater get-togethers. Don't let a Sunday go by that he isn't invited to brunch, lunch, or soccer in the park. Don't let a Saturday night pass that he isn't sitting at some well-laid table, eating fettucine and being asked his opinion of Philip Roth by a thirty-year-old lawyer (a Virgo who likes sailing and walking in the rain) who hasn't found the right man yet. Don't have a party without him, whatever you do. In these troubled times, as Suzanne Lightfoot would be only too happy to tell you, one single male is worth two dozen single females. Let him know that, in subtle ways. Preface every conversation with "Michael, there's someone I really think you should meet." Preface every other conversation with "Have you met my cousin Jocelyn yet, Mike?" Massage his ego. Say, "Oh, please join the Trivial Pursuit team, Mike, we really need a man. None of us know anything about sports." Say, "I was wondering if you could give me a little advice . . ." Say, "Why don't you shut up and kiss me instead?"

I'd never been so popular before. I'd certainly never had so many women after me. If any. Never had so many women hormonally humming my song. My usual limit was more like one every four or five years. I think I knew that I wasn't really interested in any of them. I'm pretty sure I knew that I wasn't about to fall in love with any of them. Deep down inside, I even knew that none of them were really interested in me. They just thought that they should be. *Newsweek* and Suzanne Lightfoot had warned them that they'd better be. "Who cares if he wouldn't be your first choice," they'd said. "He beats being mowed down by some guy with a stocking over his head." It wasn't like being Moby Dick, obsessively pursued by Captain Ahab. It was like being a dolphin caught in a tuna net. But in the beginning it didn't seem like that, of course; in the beginning it seemed like I was the best thing for women since the battery-operated dildo. What the hell, I told myself. I'm only human. If they can't resist me, how can I be expected to resist them? You're only young once, as Margery Householder Taub was always telling me, why not enjoy it?

Elizabeth Beacher had handed me a ceremonial surgical knife and cut loose the stud within.

He was shy at first, shy and a little tentative. But not for long.

I can't honestly say that I managed to keep Elizabeth Beacher at arm's length, but I did at least succeed in staying out of her bed—and in keeping her out of mine. We'd go to the theater together, and we'd wind up in a clinch in the back of the cab on the way home. "Why don't you come up for a nightcap?" Elizabeth would breathe into my ear. And I'd say, "Oh, Elizabeth, you know I'd love to, but I really don't think that would be a good idea." I'd escort her to a signing session or a luncheon, and we'd wind up in a clinch in the stockroom or a broom cupboard, her tongue in my mouth and my foot in a pail. "Why don't we go back to your place?" she'd whisper. And I'd say, "Oh, Elizabeth, you know I'd like nothing better, but I really don't think it would be a good idea." To my credit, I knew it wouldn't be a good idea. But seduction is seductive. Cab drivers wink at you. Bartenders whisper words of encouragement. Your buddies nudge each other and chuckle under their breath. Women watch you in a new way. It makes you feel powerful. It may play havoc with the crease in your trousers, but it makes you feel loved.

I knew it would be suicide for me to sleep with Elizabeth, no matter how persuasive her case—and no matter how often she presented me with it—but that didn't mean I couldn't sleep with someone else. Or someone elses, if it came to that.

In the beginning, just to test my skills, I toyed and dabbled. I invited Vanessa's niece, Jemma, over to stuff pierogis. I went with Suzanne to buy a new computer. While Suzanne was using the rest room, I showed a woman who was being ignored by all the salesmen how to copy a disk. While Suzanne was selecting fonts, I flirted with the cashier. After I dropped Suzanne off, I went back to the bar where we'd stopped for a drink and a quick game of footsies and asked out the waitress. On the way back to my place, I stopped a rather attractive dog-walker to ask her what breed her dog was. He was a beagle; she offered to show me his papers. As I was thanking one of the city's most aggressive editors for a lovely lunch, I let her adjust my tie. "Most women don't do ties very well," I confided. "It's not the only thing I do well," she replied. The only woman I purposefully ignored—with the exception, of course, of my mother—was Mrs. Sontag.

That is, I ignored her as best one can ignore a large elderly lady, fragrant with the aromas of furniture polish and baby powder, who has decided to stand guard over the eighth floor. Of course, the reason Mrs. Sontag was always in the hall or hovering at her door may simply have been that, after more than fifty years of marriage, she'd had enough of Mr. Sontag. Or it may have been that I was spending a lot more time in the hallway—seeing women in and seeing women out—and the fact that Mrs. Sontag always seemed to be there as well was only a coincidence. Or maybe not.

If I was alone, she would start talking as soon as she saw me, undeterred by the fact that I didn't stop moving. "Going out again?" she might say, noticing my coat and the decisive way I called for the elevator. "My, you certainly are busy. In my day young people couldn't afford to go out all the time, they had families to support. Mr. Sontag and I never went out when we were your age, we had to meet our ends." Or "Did you read about that breast they found wrapped up like a fancy cake on Sixteenth Street?" she might ask conversationally. "Cellophane and silk ribbons, can you imagine that? Yellow cellophane, the papers said, and pink paper roses. It makes you wonder about people, doesn't it? He wouldn't've gotten away with it in my day, though. The police would have put a stop to him by now."

But if I was with someone, someone who wasn't Jerry, for whom she always had advice on raising children, her usual garrulity would vanish. "Good evening, Mr. Householder," she might say, her laser eyes peering over the rims of her glasses. "That poor bird was lonely again. I heard him calling for you through the wall." "Good morning, Mr. Householder," she might say, her lips pursing. "Have you heard from dear Marissa lately?"

I grew more confident and bold. I showed Leona Fisher, the stock-

broker I met at the second Halloween party I attended, how to season
her wok. I took Emerald Plodchuk, the set designer I met at the
Bledsoes' divorce dinner, to Jersey to watch the sun rise over Manhattan. I let Mary Jane Kilpatrick seduce me in the bathroom at her
roommate's birthday bash. I went off with the waitress in the Brazilian
restaurant the night of the launch of *Women in Latin American Fiction:
Myth and Reality*. I invited one of the women I'd met at the gym, the
one whose sweatshirt said *Single and Loving It*, to come over and use
my chest expander.

Mrs. Sontag took to standing on tiptoe at her peephole for evenings
on end.

By the end of November, this little Neanderthal was pretty exhausted.

"What are you saying?" said my mother. "That you'd rather go somewhere else than come to your own family on Christmas?" I'd been
lying on the sofa, listening to Leon Redbone sing "Somebody Stole
My Gal," with a cold compress on my forehead, recuperating from a
strenuous weekend of two brunches, one sit-down dinner, one ethnic
buffet, and a night at the opera with my regular bus driver, when the
telephone rang. This was before I stopped answering the phone.

So now I was lying on the sofa, a lukewarm washcloth in my hand,
listening to my mother sing the "But We're Your Family" song.

"That's not what I'm saying, Mom," I said. "All I'm saying is that
I've had fourteen other invitations this year." I tossed the washrag
onto the coffee table. "I'm spoiled for choice. Roast duck and wild
rice with my boss, or canned ravioli shaped like a turkey with you."

"Very funny," said my mother. "No wonder they all leave you,
with that sense of humor."

Gracie landed on the back of the couch. She put her head near the
receiver. "Hello, toots!" said Gracie.

In the old days, Gracie had sounded exactly like Marissa; now,
when she wanted to, she sounded exactly like me.

"Hello, toots!" she repeated.

"Michael?" shouted my mother. "Michael? What are you doing?"

Gracie sighed. "Wait a minute, Mom," said Gracie. "Wait a minute, Mom."

I shoved her away. I sighed. "Mom, don't worry, I'll be there, all right?" To be totally honest, I was looking forward to having a meal with people whose lips wouldn't be saying "Please pass the succotash" while their eyes were wondering whether or not I had a tendency toward sodomy or domestic violence. "I'll even do the cooking if you want."

"I don't want you to do the cooking," snapped my mother. "What would everyone think? A grown man making Christmas dinner."

"Who's *everyone*? There isn't going to be anyone there but us." I looked over at Gracie. She cocked her head. "Is there?"

I knew from the slight change in my mother's breathing that she was squeezing her lips together and looking at the carpet. It was exactly how she'd responded when, at seven, I asked her why I had to tell her what I wanted for Christmas when I'd already written to Santa Claus. "You never know," said my mother. "Someone might drop in."

I sat up. "Drop in? Who might drop in?"

"No one you know," said my mother. "Just someone."

Gracie bobbed over and stuck her head under the receiver.

"Just someone who wears a bra?"

"Michael!" roared my mother.

"Mom!" cried Gracie.

"Are you mocking me, Michael?" screamed my mother. "Is that what you're doing? Because if that's what you're doing, I want you to know that I don't like it. I don't like it one little bit."

"Okay, good-bye," said my little feathered friend, in my voice. "Okay, good-bye."

My mother hung up.

I collapsed back on the couch with a heavy sigh. Jesus. It wasn't that I wasn't enjoying myself. Of course I was enjoying myself. How could I not be enjoying myself? I had the sex life of a teenage boy's dreams. And all the attention! Wasn't that what we all craved, attention?

The telephone rang again.

Gracie rang.

I lifted the receiver. "Hello?"

"Hello?" said Gracie.

"Michael?" said my mother. "Michael, Barry and I talked it over, you know, about Christmas?, and he thinks you should bring the pecan pie, it's better than what we buy around the corner."

"And how are you?" asked Gracie politely.

"Michael," said my mother, "Michael, are you talking to someone else?"

"No, Mom, just you."

"Just you."

I could hear my mother shaking the phone. "There's some sort of echo."

"It's okay."

"It's okay."

She shook the phone again. "And the other thing, Michael," my mother shouted. "If you do bring the pie, I think it'd be better if we pretended that we got it around the corner. You know what people are like."

I joked about my new popularity with Jerry.

"I tell you, Jer, it's like the whole world's just sitting out there, organizing my social life. They're sipping their juice in the morning, and they're thinking to themselves, Hey, Cynthia is single; Mike is single. Cynthia eats supper; Mike eats supper. Hey, what the heck, let's get them together and see if they click!"

"Maybe you're going to come into a fortune or something," said Jerry, "and everybody knows but you."

We were sitting on the floor, watching a game. It was halftime. I switched channels to a better commercial. I took my beer from the coffee table. "And to think," I laughed, "it was you who was voted most popular boy of the senior class." I shook my head. "It was you who was the varsity sex machine because in the twelfth grade you slept with two different girls in the same month."

Jerry picked up the popcorn bowl with a thoughtful expression. "Did you ever think that maybe everybody just feels sorry for you, Mike?" he asked. "You know, almost middle-aged and still all on your lonesome." Jerry can toss a fistful of popcorn in the air and catch most of it in his mouth. It's something he perfected in elementary school. "You know, Mike," he continued, "if you think about it, your life really is kind of sad. I feel for you, man, I really do. Here you are, all by yourself, able to watch a game on a Sunday afternoon without getting in the way of the rebirthing class, never having to feel guilty because you didn't get home in time to read your son *The Paperbag Princess* for the four-hundredth time." He tossed another handful into the air. "Sometimes, you know, when Ethan's throwing a fit because someone moved one of his animals a quarter of an inch, and Lonnie's throwing a fit because I forgot to do something she asked me to do when I was doing something else she'd asked me to do, and my father-in-law starts nagging me that we never go fishing together anymore, I think of you, Mike. I do. I think, That poor sonofabitch, all by himself in that quiet apartment, watching whatever he wants on TV, listening to whatever he wants on the stereo, doing his push-ups without someone jumping on his back and whacking him over the head with a stuffed giraffe, not being forbidden lamb and onions, two of his favorite things, because his wife's toying with vegetarianism and his child won't eat anything white." He finished off his drink. "And all these women after you, day and night! Jesus H. Christ." He squeezed the can in half. "How can you stand it? Sleeping with someone who hasn't timed how fast it takes you to come and wants you to extend your foreplay by ten minutes, whether you're tired or not?" He tossed the can into the wastebasket. "I swear to God, Mike, I don't know why you don't just shoot yourself."

"You're right," I agreed. "It's probably pity."

Jerry flipped a couple of kernels in my direction. "Anyway, I guess it's just as well we're not having our New Year's Eve party this year. You probably wouldn't've been able to make it."

I switched back to the game and leaned against the armchair. "What are you talking about, you're not having your New Year's Eve party?

This is the first time I've heard of it. I thought it was going to be the official unveiling of the Finer-Stepato total living environment. I was going to make a speech about Mr. Finer builds his dreamloft."

Jerry said, "Does it look to you like Marino's limping?"

"I feel like I've lived through every nail, every two-by-four, and every can of stain myself."

"He is," said Jerry. "He is limping."

"How come you've canceled the ceremony? I mean, it's an important occasion, isn't it, finishing your home? Your home and the bank's."

"It's not quite done," said Jerry, not moving his eyes from the screen. "Ethan's unit isn't flexible enough."

"Not done? Jer, you've been working on this thing for forty-four years, man and boy. How can it not be done?"

Jerry moaned. "Jesus Christ, he's never gonna last the quarter."

"Have we changed the subject or something?"

Jerry slapped his head. "Christ, I knew I should never've made that bet with you."

I got up for two more beers.

Christmas was bad, even by my mother's standards. Stuffed celery and fruit cup for the appetizer, her famous Desert Turkey (dry and visually uninspiring) and instant mashed potatoes for the main course, and Angie Lombardi, daughter of Mrs. Lombardi from downstairs and a visitor to our fair city from Amarillo, Texas, for dessert. Bad. But not as bad as New Year's Eve promised to be.

Vanessa, my employer and Jemma Wyte's favorite aunt, had invited me to satisfy my masculine need for preening at a gala celebrity-studded champagne disco to benefit world famine relief. "I understand you haven't met Jemma's parents yet," said Vanessa. I couldn't face it.

Elizabeth Beacher had invited me to satisfy my masculine need for adventure by going midnight skidooing with her in Maine. "Just try to imagine the ice in your lungs," said Elizabeth. I couldn't face it.

Suzanne Lightfoot wanted to satisfy my masculine need for adoration by spending a quiet, intimate New Year's Eve with her in Barbados. "You'll realize you've never seen moonlight before," said Suzanne. I couldn't face that either.

I had nine invitations to large parties. By then I'd stood at the doorways of enough parties, smiling determinedly as the well-coiffed heads turned in my direction, to know how the seal pup feels as that dark figure moves toward it from the other end of the ice floe. I passed on all nine.

My mother was having open house. Open to every unmarried daughter of every woman she had ever talked to on a bus or bumped into in the supermarket or sat next to while she had her roots done. There was no way I could face that.

I don't know, I was having a good time, but a certain weariness had set in. How on earth do rock stars keep it up? I decided to stay home with Gracie.

I was just coming back from buying Gracie a bag of Tropical Fruit and Nut Mix and myself a bottle of champagne when I happened to glance into Just Like Mom's, the cookie store. There, standing at the counter, dressed from head to toe in canary yellow and pointing to the peanut butter chocolate chips, was Betsy Shopak. There was something about the expression on her face that tugged at my heart. I went in. "Hey, Betsy," I said, "what are you doing?"

"Oh, Mike!" said Betsy. And in one smooth movement she threw herself into my arms and burst into tears.

Strange as it may seem—given her taste in clothes and home furnishings, and her fondness for store-bought desserts—Betsy Shopak and I had sort of become friends. One day I was telling her where to go in the neighborhood for the best mascarpone (having first, of course, explained what mascarpone was and why she should want it), and the next day I was listening to her tell me how Nils Shopak had scorch-earthed her heart.

I guess she just wept her way into my life. Since that first evening, when I'd found her hysterical among the movers and invited her over to sob into one of my coffee cups, the sight of a tearstained Betsy

Shopak had become a familiar one. So familiar, in fact, that Gracie and I had a nickname for her. Betsy Wetsy. The doorbell would ring, that snuffling sound would be heard in the hall, and Gracie would shout out, "Betsy Wetsy! Betsy Wetsy! Better get the Kleenex! Uh oh! Here we go!"

Betsy cried when she watched sad movies. She cried when she watched scary movies. She cried when the movie had a happy ending. She cried when the refrigerator defrosted itself unexpectedly. She cried when she'd had a bad day and came home to a dark and empty and lonely apartment. She cried when her mother phoned her from Cincinnati. She cried when Nils the Pills phoned to see if she was still alive. She cried when Nils didn't phone. She cried on any day that could be counted as either a special occasion or a holiday. She cried anywhere. She was the first person I'd ever seen weeping her eyes out in Birdland, holding a cuttlebone in one hand and a plastic ball in the other.

And so this friendship had sprung up between us. I'd become her confidant. When work got her down, when the guys at the office wound her up, when she had a date with some cretin in loafers, when her half-slip fell off while she was waiting for the D train, I was the person she talked to. I was her buddy. When she wanted someone to listen to her new Dwight Yoakam album with her (I'm a better friend than you might think), when she wanted someone to help her select her dress for the theater, when she ran out of lightbulbs, I was the person to whom she turned.

And she'd become my confidante; my pal. I went to Betsy when I was worried that Gracie seemed a little under the weather. I went to Betsy when the soufflé fell. On nights when our voices seemed to echo in the apartment, Gracie and I would both go to Betsy. I told Betsy things. Ever since I'd started dating, way back before my voice changed, women had been the ones I poured my heart out to (okay, maybe not exactly poured, maybe dropped a hint or two to). That, I'd been given to understand, was one of the things that women were for. But the women I traditionally confided in were always the ones I was involved with. The trouble was, the women I was with now weren't women with whom I felt involved.

But I was involved with Betsy. She was probably the first real female friend I'd had since I was five or six. She was the only woman of my present acquaintance who didn't make me feel like an endangered species. We did things together. Shopping. Walking. Watching game shows. We'd go to the late movie together on a Friday night. I'd make the fudge and we'd watch *The Attack of the Killer Tomatoes* together on my video. She'd bring me homemade cookies (largely inedible) to cheer me up at the end of a bad week. I'd bring her homemade raviolis to cheer her up at the end of one of hers. She'd give me her opinion on my experiment with pickled vegetable empanadas, and I'd try to hang her blinds. She'd wanted me to go to the Ice Capades with her, but I'd begged off, explaining that I'd gone when I was nine, and that as far as I was concerned it was, like circumcision, one of those once-in-a-lifetime experiences best gone through when young. Betsy was the one woman I could have a good time with without wondering what she wanted from me—or what I wanted from her. In short, Betsy Shopak was the only female I felt relaxed and comfortable with who didn't molt.

"You're kidding, right?" I was practically choking on my margarita. "Guys don't really do that kind of thing, do they?"

There were several reasons why Betsy had started crying in the cookie store. The first was that it was New Year's Eve and Nils was back in Cincinnati, having a great time with his new girlfriend, and Betsy was in New York, all alone. The second was that the Butcher of Broadway (the Gourmet Killer as the press had even more affectionately begun to call him because of his inspired dressing and presenting of his victims' severed parts) had struck again—an ear and a lock of hair in a burger box off Thirty-first—which made Betsy feel vulnerable as well as lonely. The third reason was that it was five and a half months to the day since her divorce had become final and she had fled from her old life in search of a new one, which made Betsy feel like shit. The fourth was that Nick Minusci, the specter that haunted Perfect Words, where Betsy worked, had rubbed up against her at the coffee machine that very afternoon, promising her a good time—"Feel that, Bets?" he'd whispered. "Don't you think I could show you a real good time?"—which made Betsy feel like puking. She'd been planning to get into bed and eat two dozen peanut butter chocolate chip cookies while she cried herself to sleep. I'd suggested Mexican food, several dozen killer margaritas, and a night of accordion music and singing in a foreign language as a viable alternative. "What the hell," I'd said. "I'll give Gracie her Tropical Mix early, wish her a Happy New Year, and she'll never know the ball hasn't fallen in Times Square yet."

Betsy shook her ponytail. (One of the things I liked best about Betsy was that she was thirty years old and still wore her hair in a ponytail. Another was that here we were, out having a wild time in one of the most sophisticated cities in the world, dining in a restaurant where everyone went to prove how ethnically hip they were, and Betsy was wearing a sweatshirt with poodles on it. The eyes and collars of the poodles were made of rhinestones. I don't know, there was a time when I might have found this a little gauche—I had this dim memory of refusing to take Marissa to a publishing party once because she insisted on wearing a kilt; I think I may have accused her of trying to sabotage my career—but now I found it oddly endearing. Either I'd been dating too many sophisticates lately, or I was getting soft.) "No, Mike, I'm not kidding." She licked salt from her fingers. "They really do. I swear it. He tells you he's single and that he never met anybody like you before, and then, after you've given yourself to him, you find out he's got a wife, three children, and four bantam hens in Connecticut."

I also loved the way Betsy said things like "given yourself to him." It was not a phrase most women of my acquaintance used.

"The bastards," I said, taking another slug of my drink. "I can't believe anyone would lie like that."

"Oh, come on, Mike, don't be naïve." She helped herself to another nacho. "It happens all the time." She put mustard on her nacho, musingly. "You know," she said, "sometimes I really wonder if there are any good men left. Present company excepted, of course," she added.

"Of course," I agreed.

"Like this girl I work with?" Betsy continued. "She was going out with this guy, this salesman, you know, who commuted back and forth between the coasts?, for eighteen months—eighteen months, can you believe it?—she took him home to meet her folks, she introduced him to all her friends, she let him pick the color for her living room, and then all of a sudden, just when she was thinking of coming off the pill, she found out that he wasn't staying in a hotel in Frisco at all. He was staying with his wife and their baby and their Weimaraner."

I did feel that it was incumbent upon me to defend my sex, but nothing convincing came immediately to mind. "Jesus," I said. I refilled our glasses. "You women don't have an easy time of it, do you? We're either lying to you or hacking you into bite-sized pieces."

Betsy stared into her margarita for a second. Then, her eyes still on the crushed ice bobbing gracefully on the surface, she said, "What about you, Mike?"

There was too much lime in the drink. "What do you mean, what about me? I've never dismembered a woman in my life. Not even a small one."

But Betsy was in an earnest, not a humorous, mood. "What do you tell all these women you go out with?"

I raised my glass. "I tell them exactly what you tell all the guys who are after you. I tell them I've just come out of a relationship and I'm not ready to start a new one yet."

She picked up two nachos at once. "I wasn't trying to pry," she said.

I hadn't realized that I'd raised my voice. "I know you weren't, Betsy," I said, my voice no longer raised, perhaps, but even to my ears slightly shrill. "But you've got to understand, I don't pursue them, they pursue me. I don't seduce them, Betsy, they seduce me. I'm innocent in all this, Betsy. I'm the innocent victim. It's like blaming the cow for becoming a hamburger."

She leaned across the table and put her hand on mine. Her cuff went in the salsa. "I'm not accusing you of anything, Mike, I just can't help wondering why you don't want . . . you know . . . more . . ."

I removed her cuff from the salsa. "More women? What are you, out of your mind? One more woman and I can open up my own YWCA."

She snatched the napkin I was passing her out of my hand. "Why do you do that?" she wanted to know. "Why do you always do that?"

"Your sleeve was getting wet."

"Not that." She threw the napkin at me. "Why do you always make jokes when I'm trying to be serious? You never want to discuss your feelings, Mike, you've got a real male thing about it."

I drank down half my margarita, so what if it had too much lime. Something that might have been thought or might have been emotion was doing a fast fandango through my mind. "There's nothing to discuss."

She reached for my hand again. "I know you think I'm being too pushy, Mike, but it's just that, well, I don't think you know how much I worry about you—"

The fandango slowed down. "Me?" I smiled the smile of a man about whom it would be a waste of time to worry. Worry about Don Johnson. Worry about Bruce Willis. But don't worry about Michael C. Householder. He's doing fine. "Don't worry about me, Betsy, I—"

"You look so haggard lately."

Haggard? I?

"Haggard and lost." She shrugged her shoulders and the poodles sort of winked. "I don't know, I just have this, you know, this feeling that you're not having a very good time."

The fandango stopped completely. "Of course I'm having a good time," I screamed. "I'm having a great time!"

Three Puerto Rican guys wearing sombreros climbed onto the tiny stage and the people at the next table stopped looking at us and looked at them. The guys in the sombreros started to sing "Volver." The room was beginning to blur around the edges. This little voice in my head, this little voice that was absolutely smashed on tequila, was saying, "She's right, Mike, you know she's right. Not only are you dicing with death, fooling around with all these women, but you're hating every minute of it. This isn't you, Mike. She's right, this isn't what you want from your life: three dates a night. You do want more." Fortunately, before I could put this little voice on the loudspeaker, the waiter hove into view with our chilaquiles. I pulled myself together. "I'm having a good time now," I said truthfully.

She clinked her glass against mine. "I always have a good time with you, Mike," said Betsy. "You really are a nice guy."

"Me, too," said I. This seemed to be true, too. "So are you."

I took a tentative taste of my chilaquiles. The cheese was wrong. I took another taste. They'd used jalapeño peppers instead of poblano. I looked up at Betsy. She hadn't touched her food but was sitting there, staring at me with a concerned expression in her big blue eyes. "Betsy," I pleaded, "Betsy, will you please stop worrying about me? I'm all right. Really."

"Oh, it's not that," said Betsy. "I was just waiting for you to tell me what's wrong with the meal."

We staggered home together, arm in arm, singing "Blue Eyes Crying in the Rain."

"Blue eyes crying in the rain, in the ladies' room, in the hallway, and in the cookie store," I sang as we pitched out of the elevator and slammed into the wall.

The door to 8B flew open. "I thought you were my husband," said Mrs. Sontag. She was wearing a luminescent blue party hat decorated with ostrich feathers and a silver star. And then, perhaps judging from our faces that more of an explanation was called for, she added, "He went out for more ice."

"We're not husbands," I informed her. "We don't look like husbands. We don't act like husbands." I turned to Betsy. "We don't even like husbands, do we, Betsy?"

Betsy said, "Michael . . ."

I answered my own question. "No," I said, "we don't. We hate them."

Mrs. Sontag turned to Betsy. "Happy New Year, dear," she said. She shut the door.

Betsy started to giggle. We bounced off the wall. "I have a bottle of champagne in the refrigerator," said Betsy. "You want to see the New Year in?"

I looked at my watch. It's one of those modern watches, with no numbers on it. I had no idea what time it was. "Sure," I said. "Why stop now?"

She fished several used tissues, a paperback, a fork, a couple of packets of gum, three tiny tubs of strawberry jam, a flashlight, her old cheerleader's whistle, and her keys from her bag. "You know what else I've got, Mike?" She winked. "I've got two dozen peanut butter chocolate chip cookies."

"With champagne?"

"It's only eleven," said Betsy. "We can have dessert first."

"I'll go home and get the coffee," I said.

I made the coffee while Betsy got out the cookies. I plugged in my electric grinder and filled it with beans. I whistled as I worked. I was feeling good. This was better than discussing my plans for the future with Jemma's parents. This was better than standing by the cheese ball with some strange woman, learning all about her exercise regimen. This was an improvement on debating the pros and cons of mixing love and work with Elizabeth Beacher. This was a significant step up from being lectured by Suzanne Lightfoot on building a relationship. I was feeling happy. It occurred to me as the pleasant whir of the grinder filled the kitchen and Betsy asked how I felt about rum raisin ice cream with peanut butter chocolate chip cookies, that this was the happiest I'd felt in months. I put the coffee into the caffetiere. You know, I thought, this is the happiest I've felt in months. Since Marissa, maybe. Relaxed. Easy. Friendly.

"So, Mike, is rum raisin okay, or is there some reason why you can't have it with chocolate chips?"

"It's okay, Bets."

Without realizing it, I'd missed having a woman I really liked around. Going out on dates and being sized up over the tortellini wasn't the same thing.

"But no Hershey's, Betsy. Hershey's does not go with rum raisin."
I turned around.

She was looking guiltily at the can in her hand. "Oops." She
grinned. "Back home we . . ."

But I missed what happened back home (back home they probably
couldn't eat rum raisin ice cream without three gallons of Hershey's
and a couple of quarts of marshmallow fluff on it), because another
tequila-induced thought had suddenly occurred to me. If I had never
slept with Marissa, we'd still be friends. If we had never been lovers,
she wouldn't have vanished from my life with such finality. We'd still
be arguing about Saul Bellow and having corny-joke competitions. I
wouldn't be giving my best lines to a small gray bird.

Betsy was still talking. "Come on, Mike," she was coaxing, "open
up. Just one little taste."

I opened up. Something warm and cold and sweet slipped between
my lips.

"There," said Betsy. "That wasn't so bad, was it? I bet you'd really
like it if you gave it a try."

Betsy was wiping syrup from my chin with her finger, but as sometimes happens when your nervous system is partially paralyzed by
alcohol, it didn't really seem to have anything to do with me. I was
still thinking about Marissa. Suddenly I knew that my whole relationship with Marissa had been like a faked orgasm. There's the guy,
pumping and sweating and grunting away, having a great old time,
all by himself. And there's the woman, lying there with her eyes closed,
making the right sounds and the right movements, and looking forward to going to sleep. That had been Marissa and me. She'd been
on her side of our relationship, thinking that one thing was
happening—thinking we were getting more and more serious, thinking we were going to end up getting married and moving to Connecticut and learning about natural childbirth together. And all the
while, I'd been on my side, making all the right movements and all
the right sounds—and thinking of no such thing.

Betsy was reaching past me for the bowls. Her ponytail brushed my
lips. Her ass just grazed my waist. She smelled like garlic, tequila, and

lime. If I'd been a nuclear reactor, I'd have been going into meltdown.

"You know, Mike," Betsy was saying, "you know, I think this has been the best time I've had since me and Nils split up." Her voice was cold and warm and sweet. "You know . . . it's really been fun."

As it was, I was having a lot of trouble standing up. She turned so that her back was against the counter and the bowls were against both our bodies and her smile was on me.

I smiled back. "Yeah, Betsy, it's been a great night."

And in that instant I knew that I wanted to sleep with her.

She slid the bowls onto the counter behind her. "You know, Mike," she said slowly, "you never really told me what happened with you and Melissa . . ."

And that she wanted to sleep with me.

"Marissa."

And that what had happened with me and Marissa was that I had never really loved her. It was that simple. I'd liked her. I'd admired her. I'd respected and cared for her. But it wasn't love. No fool to passion, no hopeless romantic I.

"Marissa. Right. It's just that, well, you're so kind and warm, and you'd . . . you know, you'd make such a great father, and . . ."

Betsy and I wanted to sleep together because we'd had such a good time. Because, I guess, we were both a little lonely. Because we were friends. And when a woman and a man are friends, they start to think that there must be another step. But there isn't. Jerry was my friend and I'd never wanted to sleep with him; why should I want to sleep with Betsy? Why did that seem like the next thing to do?

". . . the first time I saw you, even though I was still so upset about Nils and I didn't think I'd ever be interested in anyone again as long as I lived, even then I noticed you. I said to my mother, there's this really nice guy across the hall . . ." She took the little plastic container of ground coffee from my hand and put it next to the bowls.

And I knew that I wasn't in love with Betsy either. If we did sleep together we'd wind up more apart than if we'd never met. Because we might go through all the motions, but we'd never end up in Connecticut or even Bayonne together, not in a million years. Betsy and I weren't one kiss away from the magical mystery tour; we were one kiss away from never speaking to each other again.

"Jesus!" I pulled away so suddenly that we both nearly fell.

"Mike!"

I shook my head. I ran my hand through my hair. "I just remembered something." I looked urgent. Urgent and upset. I'd left the bathtub running. I'd left the iron on. I was going to be sick.

Betsy was concerned. "Mike, Mike, what is it?"

Maybe if I'd been sober I'd have handled it more like an adult than a two-year-old. Or maybe not. I started for the door. "I've got to go, Betsy. I'm really sorry about this. I'll talk to you tomorrow."

She trotted after me. "Mike, Mike, is it something I said? I didn't mean to . . . I . . ."

I gained the safety of the hall.

"Mike, you don't have to . . ."

I fumbled with the lock. I stumbled into my apartment.

"Happy New Year!" Betsy shouted through the door.

Should auld acquaintance be forgot, and never brought to mind? Should auld acquaintance be forgot, and auld lang syne?

Betsy burst into tears.

I passed out on the couch.

5

Retreating in Haste, Repenting in Leisure

After my encounter of the third kind with Betsy Shopak, I dreamed about Alma Huttenmeyer. She was as she had been (a bright-eyed, shining teenager); and I was as I was (dulled by age and fading fast). It didn't seem to matter. She came up to my shoulder. Her hair was straight and her skirts were short. Her lipstick was the pink of bubblegum. She didn't call me Householder, as she had in school, but Michael.

"Michael," Alma Huttenmeyer whispered in my dream, "Michael, why don't we go away somewhere? Somewhere where there aren't any telephones, or parents, or teachers. Somewhere where no one wants anything from us." She put her head on my shoulder, her arm around my waist; she slipped her tiny hand into the back pocket of my jeans. She blew in my ear. We kissed. She slid her chewing gum into my mouth. "Michael," Alma whispered, "Michael, we can go all the way if you want."

She loved me; she loved me in exactly the same way that I had loved her. Totally, unquestioningly, irrationally, each contact a small explosion. In my dream, Alma Huttenmeyer stood on tiptoe, and I leaned down to meet her lips. Unlike the one kiss she had permitted me in real life, the kisses of my dream were full of passion, saliva, tongue, and, of course, gum.

"Michael," Alma whispered while I slept, "Michael . . . Michael . . . Michael . . ." We rode a roller coaster. We stood at fast-food counters. We strolled along a moonlit beach, writing our names close to the tideline. "I'm so glad we met in English," she told me. "When love is so simple." We chased each other through the soft white sand. "Michael . . . Michael . . . Michael . . ." She laughed as I caught her. "Wait'll I get you!" I shouted. "Wait'll I get you . . . get you . . . get you . . . !" I woke up feeling weak and kissed. And as if the contents of several parrot cages had been dumped in my mouth.

I took a good long look at myself. I've seen kitchens after a two-day party that pleased me more. All New Year's Day I shuffled around the apartment nursing a rather severe hangover and a distinct feeling of self-loathing. I didn't answer the telephone. I didn't go to any of the several celebrations I'd been invited to. I kept my distance from the door.

Loyal beyond human understanding, Gracie stayed by my side. She followed me into the kitchen for juice. She followed me into the bathroom for painkillers. She followed me into the bedroom, where I took the box I kept old photographs and letters in down from the closet.

"What are ya doin'?" she asked, cocking her little head to one side to study me as I lay groaning on the sofa. "What are ya doin'?"

"I'm bemoaning the past," I told her. "I see now all the mistakes I've made. How wrong I've been."

"It's salsa time!" cried Gracie. "Amigo, let's dance!"

"That's part of my problem," I admitted. "I've never wanted to dance. I've never wanted to just trot out onto the dance floor of life and let go. I've been too cautious. I've been too cold. I've let my head rule my heart."

"Breaking my heart," sang Gracie. "Breaking my heart."

"And that's my new problem," I informed her. "I've been callous and insensitive. I've been self-centered and egotistical. I've let my penis rule my head." I thought of Jemma. I thought of Suzanne Lightfoot and Elizabeth Beacher. I thought of that well-seasoned wok. I thought of what it feels like to have a hot water faucet pressed against your spine. I thought of all the women I'd been with once or twice and would never be with again. My justification for sleeping with women I had no intention of ever opening a joint bank account with had been that they'd asked for it. Asked for it? They'd practically reached out and grabbed it. But what they'd wanted, of course, was not simple animal gratification. What they'd wanted was love.

"I've been pushing my luck," I admitted. The mingled aromas of garlic and lime assaulted my memory. I saw Betsy standing in her kitchen with a spoonful of rum raisin ice cream dripping with chocolate syrup in her hand. "I've been acting like a real shit."

"What, no capers?" chortled Gracie. "What, no capers?"

I thought of Alma Huttenmeyer. Love was what I wanted, too. That feeling of oatmeal in the solar plexus and galaxies in the groin. "Oh, where is love?" I moaned. "Where is love?"

"Look in the cupboard!" squawked Gracie. "Look in the cupboard!"

But instead of looking in the cupboard, I decided to lock myself in one. I was going to beat a retreat from the cutthroat world of dating. I was going to lie low and mind my own business.

But as any mediocre military tactician could tell you, when the enemy begins to crumble is precisely the time to bring in the heavy artillery. As I retreated, the armies of the dinner date advanced.

"So you see," Betsy was saying, "the trouble with me and Nils wasn't that we were incompatible. The trouble was that he had this Attila the Hun complex."

"Now you've lost me, Bets," I said. It was a balmy Sunday morning in early spring, and I was kneeling on the floor of Betsy's kitchen with my back to her, staring into the washing machine.

Gracie and I had just been discussing what to have for breakfast—a baked omelette with fresh herbs (my choice) versus dry Cheerios (hers)—when Mrs. Shopak's only daughter, tearful and distraught, had come banging on the front door. "Uh oh," Gracie had said, "Betsy Wetsy. Get the Kleenex."

After the New Year's Eve fiasco, I apologized profusely for my behavior. I blamed the tequila. I told her that I loved her like a sister, but I wasn't ready for anything more. I told her that I didn't want to jeopardize our friendship on what might be merely a passing physical attraction. She understood. She blamed the tequila too. She still wasn't over Nils. She wasn't ready for a new relationship either. She valued our friendship and wouldn't want to do anything to ruin it. She wouldn't want to take advantage of me by grabbing me on the rebound. So things between us, though not quite the same, had more or less returned to normal. We were a little more self-conscious when we were together, but I still turned to her when I'd made too many blintzes or there was an old Jimmy Stewart film on the late show. And she still turned to me in times of stress and danger.

That morning's panic had been caused by the fact that water was pouring out of Betsy's washing machine and the kitchen looked "like Lake Michigan." The kitchen looked less like Lake Michigan than like the wading pool in the park, but I'd pulled out the plug (just about expending all of my mechanical abilities in one swift movement— Jerry might be Mr. DIY, but I am Mr. Call-the-Super) and helped her mop up. And now I was looking into the washing machine, the way men do. Why do they do it? There's nothing to see. I got to my feet. "What are you talking about, Attila the Hun? Nils is a biochemist not a barbarian."

Betsy made a Betsy kind of face. "Yeah, I know he's a biochemist, Mike. But he has this bossy side to him. You know? Everything always has to be his way. He's always right. He doesn't understand about boundaries or other people's space or stuff like that." She dumped the mop pail out in the sink and faced me with her hands on her hips. "Can you believe it?" she wanted to know. "Nils and I once had a sixty-minute argument over the right way to boil an egg! Sixty minutes! Can you believe it? It doesn't take that long to lay one, for Pete's sake."

I didn't say that I could believe she and Nils had a sixty-minute argument over boiling an egg because Marissa's and mine had lasted sixty-five minutes. I said, "Well, I guess that does seem a little incredible, but scientists are like that, aren't they?"

Betsy picked up a book from the counter. "I did the quiz on What Type of Man Is Your Man, and that's what it said: Attila the Hun."

The jacket of the book she was holding was white and gold with tiny red foil hearts dancing in and out of the lettering. I recognized it immediately. A person would have had to have spent the last six months on K2 not to have recognized it. Every other woman riding public transportation was reading that book. Every other woman eating by herself in crowded restaurants, or sitting by herself on a park bench, or waiting for the dentist to call her in was reading that book. Talk show hosts never tired of asking guests their opinions on it. Radio DJs never tired of asking their listeners their opinions on it. Even the first lady had been photographed with a copy in her hand.

"Oh, come on, Betsy," I laughed. "You don't really believe in all that garbage do you?"

"Now you," Betsy was saying, "you're more the Peter Pan type."

This may surprise you, but I had heard that before. "Betsy, pl—"

"No, really Mike. I'm not criticizing you or anything, I'm just stating the facts. You don't want to commit yourself to a permanent relationship because you don't want to grow up. You're afraid to take responsibility. You don't want to admit that you're going to die."

I leaned against the refrigerator. There had been more than one moment in the last few months when death had seemed like the easy option. I looked at Betsy, intense and serious, squinting myopically at the opened page. Where was my fun-loving pal of yesteryear? The Betsy who had a sense of humor about life? The one who wasn't obsessed with getting another husband?

I sighed. "Betsy, for Chrissake, you're an intelligent person, how can you fall for all this nonsense?"

She sighed. "It's not nonsense, Mike. Everything Suzanne Lightfoot says in this book makes a lot of sense."

"Everything?"

She tilted her chin in a way that must have driven Attila the Bio-chemist nuts. "Yes, everything."

I grabbed the book from her hand. I started reading from the contents page. " 'Where to Go to Meet Men.' 'How to Strike up a Conversation.' 'How to Get a Man Interested in You.' 'How to Keep Him Interested.' 'What Sort of Women Do Men Really Go For?' " I shook the book at her. "You can't be serious, Bets. Where's your dignity and your sense of pride? Is this what women chained themselves to the gates of Parliament for? Is this why women have suffered imprisonment, ridicule, insult, and injury in order to champion their sex? Is this what the struggle to be treated as full and equal people has been about? So that they can be told how to flatter and pander to men? So that when some jerk asks you why you've taken up white-water rafting you can tell him it's because you're looking for love? Can't you see this is crap?"

"Whew," said Betsy, pretending to fan herself. "You sure are defensive."

She was right, I was overreacting. But then the opening months of 1987 were destroying my nerves. I got a hold on myself. "I'm not being defensive, Betsy," I explained more calmly. "I'm merely stating the truth."

"No, you're not," said Betsy. "You're being defensive. Because in case you didn't know it, Michael C. Householder, this book is a best-seller. It's affected the thinking of millions of American women."

Now, that was news.

She snatched the book back from the infidel. "And I'll have you know that following Suzanne Lightfoot's advice—"

I buried my head in my hands. "Not you, too," I moaned. "Don't tell me you've been accosting strange men in drugstores and delis. Don't tell me you've been hanging out at racetracks and in men's stores."

There was still enough of Cincinnati left in Betsy that she blushed. "Well, no, I'm a little shy for the more advanced tactics. But I have been taking some night courses in auto mechanics and karate."

At least those things were useful.

"And you've met dozens of wonderful, eligible men?" I pushed.

The Shopak cheeks grew a little pinker. "Well, no, no, I haven't. To tell the truth, the only men in either of my classes are the instructors, but—"

"You see?" I sneered. "Crap, the whole thing, from beginning to end."

Betsy drew herself up to her full six foot one. "It is not crap," she said firmly. "It just so happens that I think I've met a very, very nice man through using this book."

"You have?"

Her ponytail bobbed. "Yes, I have."

But I couldn't let go. "Oh, yeah?" I sneered some more. "Where did you meet him? At a wrestling match?"

"At the police station."

Suzanne Lightfoot, egalitarian that she was, recommended military bases, sports training camps, and prisons and police stations as great places to meet men. "At the police station?" I was trying not to hoot.

"Yes," said Betsy stiffly. "I thought someone was following me home the other night, and it was right after that nose was found in the burger box on Seventy-second Street, you know, with the radish and the sprig of cilantro?, so I went over to the police station. And that's where I met Jesus."

I could hold back the ripples of mirth no more. "You met Jesus at the local precinct house?"

Betsy glared at me. "Yes, I did. And whether or not you believe it, Mr. Know-It-All, Suzanne Lightfoot's book has already started to change my life."

I stopped laughing. These days I jumped whenever some woman tried to attract my attention on the street. I'd stopped answering the phone and was declining all invitations, be they for dinner, hang gliding, or a funeral. I was taking the bus everywhere, because when I took the subway there was always some woman falling into me or pressed up against me, apologizing profusely at first and then asking me where I worked. I'd stopped riding my bike because I'd gotten tired of being whistled and shouted at by women waiting for the lights to change. Those female truck drivers were the worst. I'd actually had one snatch my cap from my head and refuse to give it back until I promised her a date. If I forgot to bring coffee into the office (my secretary, Linda, did not *do* coffee, nor did she go out for a cup, no matter how desperate a person might be), I had to go without, because the counterwoman in the deli downstairs had taken to flirting and making suggestive jokes. Oh, I believed Betsy, all right. After all, Suzanne's book had certainly changed my life.

At first, Jerry was totally, one might even say callously, unsympathetic.

"You agents," he said when I complained about being accosted on the bus line by a woman who was sure we'd been to college together, "you never quit, do you? Everything's always a big deal."

"Jerry, for the love of God, this is not some figment of a feverish imagination, you know. I can't even stop for a drink after work anymore. Just sitting by yourself is an open invitation for every woman with nothing better to do to put the moves on you."

Jerry waved one hand dismissively. "They're only being friendly, Mike. What are you getting so worked up about?"

"Hah!" I replied. "Friendly, my ass. That's exactly what they say, Jerome. But they're not being friendly. They're being aggressive and demeaning."

One Finer eyebrow rose. "Aggressive and demeaning? What are you talking about, Mike? You sound like Angela Dworkin."

"Well, maybe Angela Dworkin has a point, Jerry, did you ever think of that? You have no idea of what I go through every single day, just doing the most ordinary things. Shopping, Jerry. Do you know what doing the week's shopping is like? It's like that strip joint we went to in Jersey."

The eyebrow went down, but the lip went up. "What strip joint in Jersey?"

When Jerry's partner, Morgan, was getting married, we decided to take him to this bar in Jersey for his bachelor party. It was one of those one-story places built out of cinderblocks, like something the army would put up. And, also like something the army would put up, the windows were black and had neon signs in them for Bud and Miller and Johnnie Walker and Girls! Girls! Girls! I can't remember now why we thought this was such a great idea. I guess it just seemed like the thing to do. The kind of thing men do. You know, one guy says, "Hey, where should we take Morgan for his stag night?," and instead of suggesting the theater or a charity concert, somebody else says, "Hey, I know, why don't we go somewhere where we can shout and whistle and drink beer while we watch women take off their clothes? That'll be fun!" The next thing you know, there you are, sniffing the glasses and watching another human being shake gold tassles from her nipples to an old rock song. I do remember that we were all pretty heyheyhey about it at the time. But if you want the truth, I don't think any of us really enjoyed it. Morgan claimed that he passed out in the john. Jerry fell asleep at the table. I went outside for some fresh air (already a risky enough thing in Jersey) and wound up sitting in the car listening to country music till it was time to go home.

"You know, Jer, where we took Morgan that time."

His look became concerned. "Mike," he said, "are you comparing The Men's Room in Newark to Sloan's? Is that what you're saying? That buying half a gallon of juice and a couple of tomatoes is like taking off your clothes to 'Mony Mony'?"

I nodded. "Yes, that's exactly what I'm saying." It had struck me suddenly one Friday night as I was wheeling my cart down Rice and Pasta, watched by at least seven women with pocket calculators and "hi there" smiles, half of me feeling pretty pleased with myself (what a guy! what power! what appeal!) and half of me wishing I didn't have to eat. All at once this image had come into my mind of a woman walking across a bar top in some of her underwear, all these guys grabbing at her with their eyes, and I thought to myself, Jesus Christ, so this is what it feels like. "More or less."

"I don't know, Mike." Jerry shook his head sadly. "I'm really getting worried about you. The next thing you're going to tell me is that buying a newspaper is like being a whore."

"Jerry, I swear to you, I'm not joking. I even dream about shopping.

Nightmares, Jerry. Nightmares about being trapped in Fruits and Vegetables."

"Maybe there's a book in it," he joked. "You know, sexual harassment and the single boy."

"I'm not a boy, Jerry, I'm a man," I snapped back, sounding a little defensive even to myself. "And anyway, it's a book that's caused this whole mess." The personal computer is mightier than the sword.

Jerry sighed. "Mike," he said patiently, "Mike, you can't blame all of this on Suzanne Lightfoot. If I remember correctly, you were getting pretty paranoid before her book came out." He sighed again. "If you ask me, Mike, you need a vacation. You're becoming obsessive."

I refrained from telling him that since the weekend I'd spent in Woodstock (arriving there only to discover that with the exception of my host—well guarded by the hostess—and the dog, I was the only male among a houseful of unattached females, all of them pathologically interested in my views on poison ivy, charcoal lighters, and the sounds the woodland makes at night), I was also pretty terrified of going on vacation. "Paranoid?" I repeated with a certain amount of incredulity. "Paranoid? Me?"

"Yeah, Mike. Paranoid. You. Anybody who thinks everybody he knows is in some kind of conspiracy to get him married is paranoid."

"Jerry," I inquired politely, "Jerry, is the finback whale paranoid? Is the African elephant overreacting? Do you think there's something neurotic about the giant panda's fear of men with guns?"

But then, one Wednesday night in the spring, Jerry's attitude began to shift.

We had both missed a number of workouts by then (I because I was too weak or too tired to face the woman in gold and black, the Bee Lady, who was always inviting me to check out her deltoids; he because he had to work late, or go to Brooklyn to find this certain kind of handle for Ethan's storage complex), but we hadn't yet abandoned the club in favor of a more obscure venue.

"So what do you think, Mike?" Jerry called from the next shower stall. "Do we risk a mineral water?" We decided to risk it.

The woman dressed in the colors of the Steelers was just paying the cashier as I led the way to a corner table for two. I made sure I got the chair facing the wall so she couldn't catch my eye.

"You know, Mike," Jerry said as we sat down, "I've been thinking lately. Maybe there is something in all of this endangered species stuff of yours after all."

I was cool. Unsarcastic. "Oh, really?" I heard a chair scrape behind me. Bee Woman alighting. "And what's brought about this sudden change of heart?"

With a look of concentration, he poured out his drink. "Oh, I don't know . . ." He shrugged. "I was just sort of noticing that there do seem to be a lot of women in places where you never used to find them."

I looked curious but kept my silence. Vibrations were assaulting me. Someone was staring at the back of my head, wondering about my astrological profile.

"Well, you know . . ." He shrugged again. "Here for instance." His eyes darted behind me. "And at games. You know, there always used to be a few, but they'd always be with men." He stirred his water with his straw in a contemplative manner. "Hardware stores, Mike. You can't walk into a hardware store these days without tripping over some woman asking your advice on toggle bolts. And Cooper's." He groaned.

Jesus Christ, was he going to cry? I hadn't seen Jerry Finer cry since George Geronski beat him up over Christina Lilly in the eighth grade.

And then, more or less apropos of nothing, and more or less addressing his slice of lime, he went on. "Cooper's, Mike. Cooper's. It's not really fair, you know, a guy doesn't stand a chance."

I myself had been taken to Cooper's several times over the long years of Jerry's domestic construction. It was one of those places where men are men—where they speak a language and live by a code of their own and don't take too kindly to outsiders or amateurs. You didn't wander into Cooper's lightly. They'd laugh in your face if you said you wanted "a couple of screws" or "a handful of nails." They'd throw you out if you asked for "a not-too-big piece of wood." Going into Cooper's always made me feel like a greenhorn hosiery salesman walking into the bar in Dodge City and ordering a sarsaparilla. But watching Jerry's face, I had this sudden image of Cooper's, overrun with women in plaid shirts and baseball caps, buying up all the best cuts and asking personal questions.

Jerry continued to stare numbly into his glass. Where was he? His body was next to me, but his mind was somewhere else. Somewhere dark and distant where the lighting wasn't soothing and the decor wasn't pleasant and the steady rhythm of female conversation didn't drown out the background music. And then Jerry looked up at me. For one second, I thought he was going to tell me something more. Maybe tell me where he'd been.

"Jerry," I said, "what's wrong?"

But the second had passed.

"Nothing." He ripped the wrapper off his sesame snack. "Nothing's wrong. I was just thinking, that's all."

"Well," I said, "I guess it's nice that you've finally decided I'm not losing my mind."

But Jerry, like so many of my new admirers, wasn't interested in my mind.

"Mike," he said, "you know all these women you're always meeting . . ."

I stared at the crumpled wrapper on the table between us. "Jerry," I said, "Jerry, you're eating sesame seeds." Things really must be bad.

He leaned toward me, his eyes on my chest. "Do you ever . . . have you . . ."

"Jerry, you don't eat sesame seeds. You hate them."

If I'd been wearing a tie, I think he might have grabbed me by it, but I wasn't, so he threw the sesame-seed-snack wrapper at me instead. "Well, I do now, all right? Somebody made me try them and I found out they weren't as bad as I'd always thought. Are you happy now, Mike? Can I go on with what I was asking?"

He certainly was getting touchy. "Yeah, sure, Jerry. Sure."

He took a deep breath. He focused on something over my head. "Mike, do you sleep with these women?"

"Not anymore."

"Not anymore?"

I shook my head. "Uh uh."

"But you did?" His voice had an eager, hopeful quality to it. He reminded me of an author whose novel has been turned down but who still calls up to ask if you at least liked the title.

"Yeah, Jerry, I did. However, recent studies have shown that sex is a very serious business. I no longer take it lightly." I sipped my water. "In fact, I no longer take it at all."

"You don't?"

"No, I don't."

"Oh," said Jerry, and went silent again.

But as we got up to leave, sidling toward the exit so as not to catch Bee Lady's eye, he said, "You want to come back for a drink, Mike?"

"I thought Wednesday night was yoga night."

He glanced at his watch. "Yeah, it is, but Lonnie said they'd probably be finishing early."

"Oh, right."

He zipped up his jacket. "Lonnie said it seems like ages since she's seen you."

"She does?"

"Yeah, she's always after me to get you around more."

"She is? Lonnie? Really? Lonnie wants to see *me*?" Lonnie and I had always gotten along, but not with anything resembling overenthusiasm. It wasn't the way it is in the movies, where the guy and his wife and his best friend are so close you can't always tell who is married to whom. It was more the way your mother treated your best friend when you were a kid: she didn't hate him or anything, but he wouldn't have been her first choice.

Jerry almost looked me in the eyes. "Yeah," he said, "she's always liked you, you know that." And then he said, "But, Mike, I'd appreciate it if you wouldn't mention to Lonnie that I didn't see you last week."

"Why not?" I asked, impelled by some force greater than fear to take a quick look back just before we left the café. Bee Lady waved. Politeness forced me to wave back.

"Oh, you know, I don't want her to know I went all the way to Brooklyn for those handles. She thinks I'm becoming obsessive about the house."

"You are becoming obsessive about the house."

"Mike . . ."

"Sure, partner, my lips are sealed."

As we walked through the door a woman in red satin shorts and a matching top squeezed past Jerry. She winked.

"We're going to have to meet somewhere else," said Jerry. "This place is getting too crowded."

"Really?" I asked. "Gee, how come I never noticed?"

So that was the night Jerry admitted I was right about being hunted, the night we decided not to meet at the club anymore, and the night I went by Jerry's for a drink, because Lonnie's yoga class was ending early and she felt she hadn't seen me in ages.

Only the yoga class hadn't finished early.

"We were just going to heat up some chili and open a couple of bottles of wine," said Lonnie. "Won't you gentlemen join us?"

I looked over at Jerry, expecting him to say, "That's okay, honey, me and Mike will grab a beer and go watch the news." But instead he just stood there, smiling at nothing in particular.

Lonnie was looking at me. "Mike?"

I looked at Jerry.

Jerry looked uncomfortable.

"Well, um . . ." I mumbled. "Yeah, sure, that'd be great."

One of Lonnie's classmates, Angel, the dietician, appeared at my elbow. "So," she said, "you're a literary agent. That must be fascinating."

"I'll say," said Bobbi, the teacher. "I'd love to hear all about it."

"Me, too," said Elaine, the artist.

"I'll be back in a few minutes," said Jerry, the Judas. "I want to see how the grout's drying in the bathroom."

The next time I saw him to speak to was at one in the morning. Angel, Bobbi, and Elaine had offered to escort me safely home, and the three of us were saying our good-nights.

"Now, remember," said Lonnie as she hit me with one of her near-miss kisses, "dinner a week from Saturday, okay? Don't disappoint us. Ethan's been asking for Uncle Mike."

It was then that Jerry emerged from the bathroom with a trowel in his hand. "See you, Mike," he said. "I'll phone."

When I got home, there was a message from my mother on my answering machine. She wanted to know if I'd ever called the daughter of the woman she'd met at the hairdresser's, as I'd promised I would.

That night I dreamed about bumblebees. Bumblebees dressed in leotards and leg warmers, practicing their yoga around a hive.

Not long after that, Barry Taub, embodiment of the entrepreneurial spirit that has made this country great and stepfather to the three Householder siblings, invited me to lunch.

I said, "Me?"

Barry said, "Yes, you. Is it that unusual for your old dad to want to spend a little quality time with you, man to man?"

The answer to that question was, of course, "Yes." Barry had been an excellent father. He was kind, upright, and cheerful. He paid the bills, he gave me money to go out with my friends, and, except when my mother made him talk to me, he left me alone. But he'd always hated all the things that fathers and sons are supposed to do together in order to bond, and he'd never pretended that he didn't. He fell asleep at games, he threw a ball like a girl, he got seasick just visiting the Aquarium, he was a pacifist and a vegetarian, and the one time he went camping with me and Jerry, it took him five hours to get the tent up (he was too proud to ask the help of ten-year-old boys, and we were too embarrassed to offer) and it fell down on us during a storm in the middle of the night, soaking and nearly suffocating us at the same time. And we never talked. I'm sure that when he and my mother were alone they discussed everything under the sun, from the domestic problems of the famous to the destruction of the ozone layer, but when Barry and I were together he had only three topics of conversation: money (how to make it, how much he'd made, how much more he was going to make); the incredible new thing he'd just bought or was going to buy with some of his money; and money (how to invest it in your future).

"Well, no," I lied. "It's not that, it's just that I know how busy you are . . ."

"Not too busy to see my son," said Barry.

I had a bad feeling about this. And not only because I was sure I could see the heavy hand of Margery Householder Taub, flat against his back and pushing hard. I had stopped going out to lunch with men toward the end of January. Having lunch with a woman was one thing (it worked more or less on the principle of riding into Apache territory with an Apache), but I'd finally given up lunching with men the afternoon I took the humorist to that mediocre Cajun place and a woman at the other side of the room called us on her cellular phone. The humorist had seemed distinctly interested—this had never happened to him before—but it had happened to me before, on four separate occasions, and I'd found the whole thing deeply humiliating. Humiliating and insulting. We were adult men, conducting business; not teenage boys at a pick-up bar hoping to get lucky.

"Lunch?" I asked.

"Lunch," said Barry. "My treat. You pick the restaurant."

"I don't suppose there are any places left that exclude women," I ventured.

Barry thought I was joking.

We went to a Japanese restaurant I knew of where every table was secluded by paper screens. I relaxed. Barry ordered sake. He relaxed. We ate our seaweed and pickled turnip (which weren't too bad) and chatted about taxes. We drank our soup (a little weak for my taste) and chatted about the interest rate. We started on our sashimi (not quite as confidence-inspiring as when you prepare it yourself), and Barry ordered some more sake and cleared his throat.

"Actually, Mike," said Barry, lowering his voice and looking shifty, "actually, I really invited you to lunch because I wanted to have a little talk with you."

I feigned surprise. "With me?" I asked. "What about?"

Barry poked at a piece of tuna. "About the future."

Mutual funds and preferred stock. I sniffed a slice of salmon and tried to look interested.

He poured us each more wine. "You see," said Barry, gazing paternally not at me but at the cup in his hand, "your mother and I are very concerned about you, Mike."

He made eye contact. And in that instant, I knew that I was both right and wrong about the subject of today's discussion. It was about investing in my future. But it wasn't about unit trusts and equity shares. It was about taking life seriously. About finding my center. About not drifting on year after year with nothing to give my life purpose and substance.

"Mike," said my stepfather, "when are you going to settle down and put some meaning in your life?"

"I have meaning in my life," I answered.

Barry shook his head. "Do you, Mike?" he wondered aloud. "Do you really?"

I explained. "I like my job," I said. "And I'm good at it. It gives me a lot of satisfaction."

"Your job?" Barry laughed. If he'd been in an Elizabeth Beacher novel, he would have laughed hollowly. Being in a Japanese restaurant in midtown Manhattan, he laughed softly. "A job is not satisfaction," said Barry, a man who had been known to shout out in his sleep, "Oh, my God, we're down two percent!" "A job is just work." He leaned forward. "A family is meaning," said Barry. "A family is satisfaction."

I switched to the vegetable sushi. "A family is several deductions," I joked.

Barry didn't smile. "Until I met your mother and you kids," said Barry, emotion catching in his voice, "I didn't even know what a sad and lonely man I was."

I was about to say that I did know what a sad and lonely man I was, but having seen his look during union negotiations, I could tell that this was not the time for levity. There even seemed to be a little moisture on those chiseled cheeks. "Really, Barry," I said hastily, "you don't have to worry about me. I have a lot of friends. I have a lot of interests."

"Friends," Barry muttered gloomily. "Interests." Again he shook his grizzled head. "Mikey, friends can't always be there when you need them. Having a hobby isn't going to keep you company in your old age."

I accepted another thimbleful of sake. "I'm only thirty-four," I pointed out.

"Thirty-five in three days," said Barry. "Time goes faster after you're thirty-five. It's like sliding downhill on mud."

"Barry, really, I have a very full life."

"You just think you do," said Barry. "But it's an empty fullness, Michael. Believe me, it's empty. Until you've found a partner to struggle up life's steep and rocky slope with you," he intoned, not bothered that a few seconds ago I'd been going down, not up, and that the way had been smooth and fast, "you can never know real fulfillment or happiness."

I helped myself to more sake.

Barry stared at his chopstick. "Michael," he said, kindly, fatherly, searching for the words to reach out and communicate with his youngest son, man to man, "is there . . . um . . . is there any special reason why you don't want to get married?"

Once upon a time, the answer to that question would have been "I don't know." But now I did know. I'd known since New Year's Eve. I wasn't afraid of anything (well, death, poverty, the Internal Revenue, and imprisonment in Morocco, maybe, but those were pretty standard fears), I just hadn't found her yet. The woman of my dreams. Love. That was what I wanted: love. Real, lunatic love. I wanted to feel the way I had when I was fourteen and just the sight of Alma Huttenmeyer filled me with a frantic joy. Alma hadn't been the prettiest girl I'd ever known, or the brightest, or the funniest, or the nicest, or the kindest, or the most trustworthy and reliable, but I'd loved her all the same. She smiled and the sun broke through the clouds. She punched me in the arm and my day was made. I knew it was irrational, but love is, isn't it? And I'd gotten close. But never close enough. Love comes, if it comes, maybe once or twice in a lifetime. Love comes when it will. It can't be created. It can't be summoned on demand. Like faith, luck, and health, love is something you either have or you don't have.

"Mike?" asked Barry, shy and tentative and, I deduced from the peculiar color he'd turned, extremely embarrassed. Probably the most personal question Barry had ever before asked me was about jock itch. My mother must have had him wired for sound. "Mike, did you hear me?"

Here was a man who, meeting my mother in the housewares department at Macy's, had immediately known that she was the one. He didn't say to himself: I hope she's sweet and quiet, like I am. He didn't say to himself: I hope she doesn't want a family, like I don't. He didn't say to himself: I hope she's interested in the stock market and solitaire, just like me. No. He said: I love this woman with the double boiler in her hands. Even when he discovered that she had a stubborn streak as long as the Mississippi, a serious temper, and three young fatherless children, and fell asleep at the first mention of stocks or shares, he still didn't flinch. "Marry me," he pleaded. "Please."

"Actually, Barry," I said, feeling that in my stepfather I had found a person who might understand, "actually, there is a special reason."

Barry breathed.

I stared at the teardrop of wine at the bottom of my cup.

"Yes?"

The teardrop of wine stared back.

"I haven't met anyone I really love," I said simply.

"You what?" said Barry.

I looked up. "Love," I repeated. "I haven't fallen in love."

Barry reached for my cup. "Don't worry about love, Mike," said Barry in the same voice he used to advise me on investments. "Just find someone you can stand to be around all the time and muddle through like everyone else does."

I crept home quietly, almost stealthily, that evening. I ordered something from the local Chinese, where I knew all the delivery boys. I had neither the heart nor the strength to cook. I took Gracie out of her cage and put her favorite show on for her. I poured myself a stiff drink. I stretched out on the couch and switched the answering machine to Playback. There was one heavy breather, and one obscene caller. The first sort of moaned until the machine cut her off; the second told me everything she was doing, in detail. But they weren't that bad.

What was that bad was Sara Cooper, an ex-girlfriend.

"Hi . . . ? Mike . . . ? Mike? Um." She cleared her throat. "Hi. It's me . . . Um. Just called to see how you're doing. How're you doing?" Her voice was warm and friendly, genuinely concerned, not unlike the voice of an insurance salesperson. "Alex and I were just talking about you yesterday, and we almost at the same moment said to each other how long it's been since we've seen you. So we thought maybe you'd like to come over for supper on Friday . . . I mean, I know you're busy, but we won't take no for an answer. And also I wanted to say how sorry I was to hear about you and Melissa . . . well . . . um . . . both of us were really, really sorry. I'm always saying to Alex, Mike's such a nice guy, really, it's a shame things never work out for him, and she agrees, you know how much she likes you, well, we both do . . . Um. If things were different . . . well things might have been the other way around, right? So if you can come on Friday, we're having a couple of other friends over . . . you remember Sam? the marine biologist? . . . you liked her, remember?, she and her husband and this friend of Alex's from Columbia, who is so terrific, I really . . . um, well, you know how much I hate talking to these machines, they're so impersonal, aren't they? Let's just say it's going to be a really great night. So we'll see you Friday, okay? Between eight and eight-thirty, ciao, Mikey."

Mikey. When the women who left you for other women and the women they left you for begin matchmaking, you know you're really in trouble.

6

Desperate Measures for Desperate Times

As events go, I was looking forward to Sara and Alex's dinner party only slightly more than I would have anticipated my own hanging.

Not that I wasn't fond of them. I was fond of them. It was I, in fact, who first brought them together. "Sara," I'd said, "you'll love Alex." "Alex," I'd said, "you'll love Sara." Of course, I hadn't expected them to take me quite so literally. (My mother often cited this as a classic example of what she diagnosed as my self-sabotage syndrome. "You don't want things to work," my mother determined. "You go out of your way to make sure that they don't.") Nonetheless, the three of us had remained friends. And even though neither of them could cook and it was a good policy to have a snack before you got to their apartment, I always enjoyed seeing them. But having a pleasant if poor meal with people you like and being hauled to the dinner table like a slave to the auction block are not the same thing. I'd been hauled to the block often enough by then to know that.

You arrive for what has been described to you as "just having a few friends over." You arrive punctually. Your host opens the door to you. "Mike!" he cries. "We're so glad you could make it. Come on in." You ask him how he's doing; he asks you how you're doing. He leads you into the living room. The living room looks like Grand Central Station at five-thirty on a Friday night. Except, of course, that most of the people packed into the living room are not commuters but couples. You know that most of them are couples, because you immediately spot the one other person present who is not. She is sitting on the sofa, seemingly talking to a man who is either a psychiatrist or a sociologist, but she is darting glances at you. It is obvious from the kind of glances she is darting that she has already heard a lot about you, including the fact that your lovers always marry someone else. Here you were, hoping the main course was going to be baked ziti, and instead the main course is you. "Come on," says your host, deliberately guiding you away from the sofa (a clever tactic designed to get you to drop your guard). "I'll introduce you to a couple of people." He introduces you to a couple of people—to a couple of couples as it turns out—all of whom nod their heads and smile and ask you what you do and tell you what they do and then get distracted by the smoked almonds. And then, much to everyone's surprise, there you are at the sofa. Now how did you wind up there? The two individuals already sitting on the sofa stop talking immediately. "Natasha," says your host, "I'd like you to meet Mike." He gives you a tiny push forward. "Mike, Natasha." You smile; she smiles. "I think you two will find that you've got a lot in common," your host continues, already beginning to sidle away. "Oh, really?" you say. The psychiatrist excuses himself. Without any movement on your part, you find yourself sitting on the couch, learning how much Natasha has already heard about you (a hell of a lot more than you've heard about her) and why your host thinks you two have so much in common (either it's because she studied English at college and you're a literary agent, or it's because you once lived in Barcelona and she's learning Spanish). Coincidentally, you and Natasha are seated next to one another at dinner. By the time the evening's over, it is taken for granted that you and Natasha will share a cab home, unless she lives in the same building as your host and hostess, in which case you will be asked to walk her to her door, she knows it's silly, but a woman can't be too careful these days, can she?

To give them credit, Sara and Alex's dinner was not run-of-the-mill. For one thing, when I arrived no one else was there. No Sam the marine biologist and her husband; no other couples, squabbling over the details of a story they were both trying to tell. Just Sara and Alex, and Snow Lazarro from Columbia, an important figure, I assumed, in Women's Studies. For another thing, Sara and Alex were nothing if not direct. There was going to be no game-playing or observation of social conventions here. Everything was going to be open and straightforward.

Sara and Alex both met me at the door. They were glad to see me. They said so. They each gave me a kiss. They each took an arm. They marched me right into the living room and over to the couch where a rather tall, striking woman all in black, silver, and purple (black leggings, black T-shirt; silver earrings and bracelets; purple eyes) was watching me cross the room. I walked tall. Like Sara and Alex, she was open and direct. She didn't act as though she were surprised to see me. Her lips twitched. She seemed almost amused.

"Snow," said Sara, "this is Michael Householder."

Alex squeezed my arm. "And Michael, this is Snow Lazarro."

Snow smiled and the room brightened—almost as though someone had turned on the overhead light.

I'd never met anyone named Snow before. "I'm surprised your last name's not White," I said.

She responded as though I hadn't spoken. "Michael," said Snow, not extending her hand. "It's so nice to meet someone with an ordinary name for a change."

She smiled some more. The overhead light was on a dimmer; someone cranked it up.

"All the men I meet lately seem to be called Damian or Redfang or something like that," she explained, though not to me.

This was not the kind of opening conversational gambit I was used to. I couldn't think of any reply. What was she saying? Was she saying that one look had told her how obviously ordinary I was? Was she implying that she hung out with men who were dangerously fascinating and anything but ordinary? Was she letting me know that she'd lost interest the second I tripped over the carpet? Did she have any idea of the effect her smile had on obviously ordinary people?

Sara nudged me. Galvanized into action, I smiled too—a flashlight next to her klieg. "That's New York for you," I said, "no sooner does one wave of immigrants begin to assimilate than the next one arrives."

The three women glanced from me to one another and back again.

"How about a drink?" asked Alex brightly.

I said that sounded great.

Snow gestured to her half-filled glass and said she was fine.

Alex went to get more wine. Sara said she'd found that article she'd been telling Snow about. She went into her study to get the article.

That left Snow and me alone for nearly three full minutes. I stared at the side of her head; she studied my shoes. I noticed that one of her earrings was a silver skeleton; she may have noticed that my shoes had a spit shine. Though an articulate and skilled conversationalist, I somehow couldn't think of anything to say. I'd never actually spoken to anyone who dressed like this before. Desperate, I said, "So, going anywhere interesting this summer? Mexico? Greece? Rhode Island?"

She met my eyes. "What I really want to do is walk across the Himalayas again," she said. She flashed me an understandably rueful smile. "But I'm so busy at the moment that I don't have the time." The skeleton danced. "If I'm lucky I might get in a little white-water rafting in Maine."

I decided she must be kidding. Who in their right mind would think that being pounded against the rocky shore of a raging river was a fun way to spend their vacation? "Abseiling in the Himalayas, body surfing in Maine . . . you certainly aren't the sort of woman who likes to sit on the terrace and sip Bloody Marys," I kidded.

"No," she said, no smile, rueful or otherwise, disturbing her lips. "No, I'm not."

Sara returned and we started to chat about quantum mechanics.

That is, Snow and Sara started to chat about quantum mechanics.

"You see," said Sara, leaning over Snow to point out some faulty reasoning in the article, "what he says here just doesn't make sense, not in light of recent work. He doesn't even seem to have heard of chromodynamics."

That made two of us.

Alex came back with a fresh bottle of wine and an almost-clean glass for me. I didn't even stop to give it a sniff.

While I chugged my Chilean red, I watched Snow's movements, the expression in her eyes, the set of her firm and angular jaw. She was what my mother would have called a tough cookie. I listened to her, the steadiness of her voice, the clarity of her thoughts, the wide range of her knowledge. She was what Lonnie Stepato would have called an intellectual ballbuster. But Snow was not just incredibly intelligent. Despite a too-large mouth and too-large eyes and legs that went up to her armpits, she was attractive as well. In a take-no-prisoners sort of way. She was stunning, though definitely not my type. I began to feel more and more ordinary. Why had they wanted me to meet her? Couldn't Jack Nicholson make it?

"Oh, right," said Snow, speed-reading, "I see what you mean."

Alex, who had obviously heard all of this before, got to her feet. "You two and your black holes," she laughed. "I'm going to see what's happening in the oven."

Normally, I would have been a little curious myself to see what was happening in Alex's oven, but I was reluctant to leave the room. This was not the way these evenings were supposed to go. Snow was supposed to be interested in me, not in leptons and gluons. She was supposed to be asking me questions about myself, talking to *me*. I was a little worried that if I left the room she might forget about me completely. When we finally sat down to dinner, she'd look over and say, "So who's this guy? Where'd he come from? Don't tell me he's been here all along!" She'd reach across me to get the sea salt. "I bet he doesn't have a very interesting name," she'd say. She'd wink at Alex. "Boy, is he ever ordinary! I bet he's never even flown over the Himalayas in a plane. I bet he vacations on Long Island and he never goes in the water because he's afraid of jellyfish."

"Michael!" Sara was saying. "Michael!"

I'd been trying to think of something I could talk about that wouldn't make me sound incredibly pedestrian or ill-informed, something that might get me into the conversation—something that might change the bloody conversation. I jumped. "Yes?" It was all right, Sara was going to get me into the conversation.

"Michael, what *is* that you're humming?"

"It's the theme song from *The Twilight Zone*," Snow answered. More light radiated through the room. "I think maybe Michael's a little bored."

Sara laughed. "Oh, no, not Michael." She'd always had a rather harsh laugh. "Michael's like a dog. When he starts to get bored he just falls asleep."

Like a dog? Falls asleep? Had she invited me here to meet this woman because she thought we had a lot in common, because she wanted to give her friend a few hours of cheap light entertainment, or simply to completely humiliate me in front of her? I made an effort to pull myself together. "Excuse me, Sara—"

"You know, Michael," said Sara, "Alex and I are always telling Snow she should write a book." She turned to Snow. "Michael's Lonnie Stepato's agent," she told her.

For the first time since I'd arrived, Snow looked at me as though I hadn't wandered in by mistake. As though, dressed down and re-named, I might pass for human. "Really?" she said, too honest to hide her astonishment. "Lonnie Stepato? Are you really her agent?"

Sara turned back to me. "You wouldn't believe the life Snow's had. She's traveled and done so much . . . And the work she's involved in now . . ."

So she hadn't invited me because she thought Snow and I would hit it off. She hadn't invited me because Broadway tickets were so expensive. She hadn't even asked me over to humiliate me. She'd invited me because Snow needed an agent. Someone with a feminist track record.

Snow waved the idea away with one perfect hand. She laughed, glass bells tinkling on a clear spring day. "You're exaggerating, Sara. I haven't done much more than anyone else."

Sara, who was always living in pup tents on ice floes and things of that ilk to further scientific knowledge, rolled her eyes. "Oh, sure . . ."

I, who over twenty years ago had spent two summers at Camp Shining Water, and who once, in a madcap moment, took a day trip to Tijuana, tried to look as though it seemed likely that Snow's life was no more adventurous than mine.

"And anyway," Snow continued, "I'm sure poor Michael doesn't want to hear about my job."

Truthfully, the last thing poor Michael wanted to hear about right then was the inside story on Women's Studies, the treachery of male academics, and the recent discovery of a new Mother God among primitive hill tribes in Afghanistan, but he smiled manfully. "Oh, no," he said, "I'm sure it's fascinating."

More bells, these of fine silver, tinkling over a pure mountain stream. "It's even more boring than the unified field theory." She winked.

Alex appeared in the doorway, looking a little wild-eyed. Whatever was going on in the oven wasn't good. "Sara?" hissed Alex. "Sara, do you think you could give me a hand?"

Poor Michael cleared his throat. He had to start improving on the first impression he'd made. He had to prove that he was neither ordinary, stupid, nor uninteresting. And that he wasn't poor. He was rich in humor, wit, sensitivity, intelligence, culture, and imagination. He sipped the last drop of wine in his glass. He cleared his throat again. "So," he said, "what sort of book were you thinking of writing, Snow?"

But Snow didn't want to talk about the type of book she was thinking of writing. She didn't like the way we all categorized everything. "Especially you book people," she said. "Everything has to have a label on it, doesn't it? It has to be crime. Or it has to be romance. Or it has to be a thriller."

So we talked about the role books play in establishing our ideas on gender identities instead. We agreed, but Snow said that my agreeing with her was hypocritical, as well as meaningless, because I belonged to a literary establishment that encouraged sexual stereotyping. I poured us each more wine. Then we talked about the ghettoization of Women's Studies. We agreed, but Snow said my agreeing was offensive, as well as meaningless, because I was part of an industry that encouraged this ghettoization through its dependence on categories and labels. Snow poured us each another glass. To prove her several points, she asked me what my most successful book had been in the last year. "And don't tell me it's one of Lonnie Stepato's," she warned.

It wasn't. I told her what it was.

She leaned forward. "What?" she asked. "I couldn't hear you."

I told her again.

She was so close that I could see that the tiny silver skeleton dangling from one of the five holes in her earlobe had movable joints. What would they think of next?

"Did you say *How to Get Mr. Right to Pop the Question?*"

"Yes," I said. "I did."

"Is that a joke?"

"No," I said. "No, it's not."

She frowned. I could tell that she was looking at me in a new light. Before she'd merely been uninterested; now she was beginning to dislike me. "Are you sure you're Lonnie Stepato's agent?"

I emptied the bottle.

It was at that point that Alex returned to the room with a distinct odor of charred flesh in her wake. "Everything okay?" she asked hopefully.

"Fine," said Snow politely. "You two need any help in the kitchen?"

"Oh, no, no," said Alex quickly. She gave me a hug. "We like to keep Michael out of the kitchen if we can. He's so bossy." It was her turn to wink. "You know how men are." She laughed so I'd know she was kidding. The smoke alarm went off. Supper was nearly ready. Sara started hollering for Alex to hurry back. "Why don't you tell Mike about your trip to Mali?"

Snow told me about her trip to Mali, where the men sit around drinking all day and the women do all the work.

"You might as well have stayed home," I quipped.

Usually, during this kind of evening, the other party would laugh at my jokes from time to time, whether she thought they were funny or not. Snow Lazarro, however, felt no such obligation. She knocked back her wine, then looked me straight in the eye. "You know," she said evenly, "I never fully trust a man who thinks he's a feminist."

Jesus. Were we on *Candid Camera*? Or had they paid her to come here and give me a hard time?

I knocked back my wine. What the hell. I winked. "Neither do I."

At last, the smoke alarm went off for the second time. "Soup's on!" called Alex. Snow and I stood up. She was even taller standing than she had been sitting. I sat back down. Alex appeared in the doorway. "Michael," she snapped. "Michael, what are you doing? We're eating now."

I chuckled. "Oh, right," I said. "I forgot."

Even this has to be better than the predinner sparring, I told myself as we sat at the table. I stared at my plate. God knew what it was, had been, or was supposed to be. I sniffed it. Still no clue. I prodded a bit with my fork.

"Wow," said Snow, sounding more excited than she had since the conversation turned away from subatomic particles, "this looks great." She helped herself to some dead lettuce. "I don't know how you two do it," she said. "I just hate cooking. It's enough for me to open a can. Remember in Home Ec when you had to make things like baked eggs and macaroni and cheese? God, I hated that. Why didn't the egg ever get cooked?"

Sara smiled in my direction. "Mike's a great cook."

"My cooking's even worse than the stuff in the college snack bar," said Snow.

Alex moaned. "Oh, no, nothing this side of Alpha Centauri could be that bad."

I took a small forkful of whatever it was that was covering the pattern on my plate. She was wrong; there was one thing.

"Lots of people think he should open his own restaurant," said Sara.

Snow turned to Alex. "God," she sighed, "did you taste that spaghetti last week?"

Sara gave up. "It can't be worse than the junk they feed us," she said. Sara worked at NYU.

They chatted happily for a few minutes about the frequency of food poisoning in the institutions of higher education in and around Manhattan, and then, one thing leading to another, someone mentioned the lips that had been left with an order of home fries in a barbecued-chicken bag near 110th Street the day before.

"It'll be a uterus next," said Snow.

I gagged. Why did they always want to talk about things like that at meals?

She made a face reminiscent of one often employed by Margery Householder Taub to display scorn and contempt. "You can be pretty sure that if some psycho were going around castrating men and snipping off their body parts, there wouldn't be any of this 'another dead end' and 'insubstantial clues' shit. The cops would have found him by now if they had to call in the Mounties and the National Guard to do it."

"You bet your life," said Sara.

"Exactly," said Snow. "That's exactly what we are betting, our lives." Illustrating her own words, she took a second helping. "And we're losing. We're losing because the violence, contempt, and hostility men feel toward women is so deep-rooted and so endemic that it's difficult even to prove that it exists."

"Well, to be fair," said Alex, who always was, "the police have been trying very hard." Casually, she picked something yellow and plastic out of her dinner and laid it on the table. "I mean, it can't be easy. And they are under a lot of pressure."

Another woman might have squealed in indignation, but not Snow. "Pressure!?" She spat the word into the air. "Pressure?! Alex, they've found pieces of eight different women in the last twelve or thirteen months, and they've been working on the case day and night for at least nine of those months. And what do they have to show for it? Nothing, that's what. Absolutely nothing."

"Well, they have put together a psychological profile of the killer," said Alex. "At least now they know what sort of man they're looking for."

"They're looking for a psychopath!" howled Sara. "You don't need a score of cops and psychiatrists working for over a year to come up with that."

"They know more than that," defended Alex. "They know he's educated, and sexually repressed, and has a highly developed sense of irony; that's why he presents the pieces as though they're food."

"And they know he's afraid of women," snarled Snow, with a quick glance at me. "Well, that narrows it down a lot, doesn't it?"

"Oh, come on, Alex," urged Sara. "Admit it, Snow's right. They have nothing to show for all that time and money."

"They have quite a good collection of food containers," I chipped in.

Snow gave me the first long, hard look she'd given me all evening. It lasted for an entire nanosecond; then she turned back to Alex. "If the police force weren't dominated by men, they would have solved this case by now, and you know it. But the truth is that the Butcher is practically a metaphor for the male attitude toward women."

"Oh, hey," I said, "don't you think that's a little harsh?"

"No," said Snow Lazarro, articulating her words very carefully, "I do not think it's a little harsh. You probably haven't noticed, but in our society, women are treated as hunks of flesh to be ogled and displayed and eventually consumed. All the Butcher's doing is underscoring that fact."

"Maybe the Butcher's not a man at all," I suggested. "Maybe she's a feminist trying to make a point."

Even Alex glared at me. "Michael," said Sara, "just shut up and eat."

How could someone so intelligent, so interesting, and so beautiful be so hostile and humorless? So incredibly annoying? So unrelentingly antagonistic? What was it with her? I didn't expect every woman I met to fall madly in love with me—not even in these desperate days—but most women liked me at least. They appreciated my many fine qualities. I felt like interrupting her monologue on the subconscious collusion between the NYPD and the Butcher of Broadway to tell her that. "Hey," I felt like saying, "you may not have noticed

because you've been too busy putting me and my sex down all evening, but I'm a really nice guy." I swallowed a couple of lumps of
something whole. Not chewing seemed to help. You could still smell
it, but you couldn't actually taste it.

Suddenly I heard my name.

I looked up. Not one of them was looking at me.

"What?" I asked.

"Here," said Sara, "have some of this, it's got this weird Cuban
dressing on it." She passed me the salad. It smelled like Vicks. "I was
just saying to Snow that of all the men I've known, you're one of the
few who has never showed any sign of harboring any violent or hostile
feelings toward women."

I smiled. "Except toward my mother." I glanced quickly at Snow.
"And maybe one or two others."

Alex kicked me under the table. "Be serious, Michael. It's true, your
feelings about women are exceptionally clear and positive."

Snow stabbed a slice of cucumber. "And yet Michael here's a con-
firmed bachelor, isn't he?" Her eyes met mine—not curious but chal-
lenging. "Aren't you?"

"Uh uh." I winked. "I'm not Catholic."

Sara and Alex rolled their eyes and groaned.

"Was that a joke?" asked Snow Lazarro.

Not surprisingly, Snow did not need to share a cab home with me.
Nor did she live in the building or offer me a ride. I barely persuaded
her to let me walk her to her bike. "I'd feel totally responsible if it
were your lips they found in a chicken bag tomorrow," I argued.
"Would you want me to live with that guilt?"

"It wouldn't matter to me," said Snow, a practical woman if ever
there was one. "I wouldn't know about it, would I?"

"But we would," said Alex. "And we'd feel awful."

Snow relented.

"I have a bike too," I said as we strolled uncompanionably into the
warm Upper West Side night, she on one side of the pavement, and
I on the other.

This information brought her a good six inches closer. "Oh, really? What kind of bike do you have?" Except for Lonnie and the question of my real attitude to women, this was the first thing about me that had aroused her interest all night.

Not for long, though.

"It's a racer."

"Oh," she said, flatly, "a racer."

But I was not to be discouraged. I pressed what I took to be my advantage. "Yes," I went on, "it's a ten speed. What kind of bike do you have?"

She came to an abrupt halt and dropped her bag on the ground. "This is my bike." She opened her satchel and removed a helmet. Her bike looked like something you'd find under a Nazi stormtrooper.

"Oh, right," I said, "that kind of bike." I was too embarrassed to ask what it was.

Snow snapped on her helmet. She straddled the saddle. She started the engine. She extended her hand. "Nice meeting you, Michael," she said politely.

God knows why, maybe it was some sort of reflex reaction, but I shoved my card into her open palm. "Here," I said. "It's my card. You know, in case you decide to write that book."

She looked down at the small rectangle of cardboard beneath the street light. "Michael C. Householder," she read. She grinned. "What's the *C* stand for?"

In ten years, no one had ever asked me that before. Chump, I should have said. Chucklehead. Coward. Coldfish. "It doesn't actually stand for anything," I answered at last. "I just thought, you know, a middle initial sounded more, you know . . ."

It wasn't often that you heard a woman in a neon-green motorcycle helmet laughing like that.

C as in jerk. As in imbecile. As in pretentious jackass.

She tucked the card into her jacket pocket. "Thanks," she said. "I'm sure it'll come in handy." She roared into the dark.

Defying death, I decided to walk all the way home. The combination of alcohol and lack of conversation was playing havoc with my central nervous system, and I thought the warm night air, packed as it was with hydrocarbons, might clear my head. I began the march downtown.

In the months since Marissa's departure, I had felt many different emotions. Hurt. Bewilderment. Relief. Loneliness. Affection. Terror. Fear. Exhaustion. Paranoia. Parrot love. But this was the first time I'd felt real rage. Fury. Anger fueled by a great sense of injustice and humiliation. Who the hell did Snow Lazarro think she was? Just because I was a man didn't mean I wasn't entitled to a little courtesy, a little basic respect. Just because I was a man didn't mean I didn't have feelings. The evening replayed itself in my mind as I stalked along. I skirted a small community of people in boxes. I roughly shook off a guy wanting to sell me several old grape jelly jars and a Duke Ellington LP. They had deliberately excluded me from their talk most of the evening. When Sara or Alex had made any effort to include me, the result had been patronizing and embarrassing. When Snow had acknowledged my existence, it had been with chagrin if not actual regret. I crossed Broadway against the light, mumbling to myself. Because of the way they'd treated me, I hadn't said one truly intelligent thing all evening. I'd made stupid jokes when she was being serious. Instead of revealing the sensitive nature of my heart and soul, I'd shown myself as crass, cynical, and chauvinistic—though not, if anyone was being honest, as chauvinistic as Snow Lazarro. She had questioned my relationship with my mother. She'd wondered that I could make light of something as serious as mass murder. She'd practically come right out and accused me of misogyny. She'd been appalled that I refused dessert. My footsteps echoed in the quiet of the sleeping city. Just let someone try to mug me tonight—they'd be sorry. "That bitch!" I found myself saying out loud. "For two cents, I'd call her up and give her a piece of my mind!" I kicked a beer can into the gutter. She'd come only because she'd already known I was the agent of New York's leading feminist thinker. She was just as crass, opportunistic, and grasping as anyone else. "That duplistic cow!" Pretending that she didn't want to talk about her book, let alone write it! Give me a break! Sirens wailed in all directions. I strode eastward. "We'll see who has the last laugh!" I muttered as I stepped over some guy holding his hand out to me. Unless Sara or Alex told Snow that the reason I was Lonnie's agent was Jerry, she'd be calling me within a month to beg me to take her on. But I wasn't going to. Let her go elsewhere with her humorless, fanatical, misandric writings. I'd be damned if I was going to help her. Not after the contempt and indifference she'd lavished on me!

I reached my building, still muttering to myself. I stomped through the lobby. The night doorman nodded. I got into the elevator and pressed the button. At the eighth floor I got out. For a few seconds, I just stood there, still furious, but now disoriented as well. There were two strangers in the middle of the hallway, kissing each other in a rather unbridled way. I was on the wrong floor. There was no way Mrs. Sontag would permit behavior like that in our hall! I reached behind me for the call button, lost my balance, and banged into the wall. Passion's playthings pulled apart. I looked the other way.

"Michael!" cried a familiar female voice. "Michael! We didn't even hear you. Did you come up the stairs?"

I turned. I stared. It was Betsy Shopak. Betsy Shopak and an extremely large, sullen-looking man in a worn denim jacket and a green baseball cap that had *End It Exterminators* and a dead cockroach embroidered across the crown.

"Michael," said Betsy, dragging her companion toward me. He seemed vaguely familiar. "I want you to meet Jesus."

I smiled. Of course he looked familiar. This was the guy Betsy met at the police station. I'd probably seen his picture in the post office at least a hundred times.

Jesus flexed the corners of his mouth.

"Jesus," said Betsy, squeezing his arm, "this is the Michael I've told you so much about."

He looked at me, and I looked at him.

"Michael," Betsy continued, clearly in a state that she would have described as happy as a basket of fluffy ducklings, "Michael, this is Detective Jesus O'Brien."

I hid my surprise at the news that he wasn't a hardened criminal after all. Without any enthusiasm on either side, we shook hands.

"Nice to meet you," I lied.

More honest, or just more tired, he nodded slightly but said nothing.

"Well," said Betsy.

"Well," said I.

"Good night, Mike," said Jesus.

I took the hint.

Sara had already left a message on my machine. Snow liked me a lot, said Sara, but even though she thought I was pretty smart and a very nice guy, she didn't think I was really her type. "If you want to know the truth," said Sara, with no reason for thinking that I did, "you're a little short." There was a honking sound in the background, which meant that Alex was laughing. "Well, what she really said," spluttered Sara, "was that if her name was White, you'd be one of the Dwarfs." Honkhonkhonk. "But also," she continued, "also you're maybe not, well, you know, not spectacularly good-looking enough. You should have seen her last boyfriend. He made Tom Cruise look plain."

Though I had never thought of myself as an especially vain or emotional person, I called Sara right back. I got her machine. "What are you talking about, 'short'?" I screamed down the receiver, still a little tipsy from all that wine on an empty stomach. "What are you talking about, 'not spectacularly good-looking enough'? I've never heard so much crap in my life! Mature, intelligent adults do not go around judging other people on their appearances! They don't decide not to give someone a chance just because he's not a basketball player or a male model! What is this? I thought you guys were liberated thinkers. I thought you were whole human beings! And anyway," I bellowed, "just for your information, I wouldn't go out with that rude, conceited Amazon if she were the last woman on earth!" I slammed down the phone.

"What are you talking about?" called Gracie from the bedroom. "What are you talking about? Short?" she screeched, sounding a little like me and a little like Marissa. She imitated the sound of a telephone receiver being banged into place and badly chipped.

I went into the bedroom and wrapped the special cover I'd bought her to make up for the wallpaper—a moon and stars over the New York skyline—around her cage. "Good night, toots," I told her. "Sweet dreams."

"I love you, toots," said Gracie. "Sweet dreams."

Jerry understood about love.

"Am I crazy or something?" I asked him. "Holding out for love?"

"Of course you're not crazy," said Jerry. This big guy with a skull and crossbones tattooed on his neck gave Jerry a friendly shove as he made his way to the bar. Jerry pulled in his chair another inch. His tie dangled in his draft beer. "Love is . . . love is . . ." He was staring at his hands. His shoulders heaved. Someone put the jukebox on; WASP doing "F**K Like a Beast." Jerry's words were buried beneath the bass line.

"What?" I shouted. "Jerry, I can't hear you. What did you say?"

Jerry leaned close to my ear. "Well, you know, Mike, love isn't something you can control, is it? It just takes over everything, doesn't it? Reason. Ideals. Principles. Everything."

It seemed to me that my problem was that love wasn't taking over anything, but I decided to let it slide.

Owing partially to Jerry's preoccupation with wall paneling, and partially to my still-complicated social life, our nights out together had become even fewer and farther between. Fewer, farther between, and located downtown in Jo Jo's Bar and Grill.

Jo Jo's was a bikers' hangout, and the only bar I'd ever been in that made the streets of Manhattan look safe and had Megadeth on the jukebox. Where else would two middle-class white guys who thought playing Space Invaders while drinking Wild Turkey was the height of excitement go for a little privacy?

Nowhere else, that's where. We couldn't go to Jerry's because Lonnie and one of her groups would be there. We couldn't go to my place because the telephone never stopped ringing. We couldn't go to the gym anymore. We'd tried regular bars—you know, bars where people who drove cars and had day jobs hung out—but there was always someone trying to pick you up in them. Restaurants, snack bars, and fast-food chains were also out. Suzanne Lightfoot had told the women of America that men went to sports events, grocery stores, barbershops, pool halls, and garages, so they were all out too. We'd even tried the train stations, but there it was the homeless who wouldn't leave you alone. And then, one dark and stormy night, we stumbled upon Jo Jo's, its neon sign glowing over the door like a beacon of hope. "What do you think all these bikes out front mean?" Jerry had asked as we stood on the threshold. Still smarting from dinner at Sara and Alex's, I'd been thinking, almost hopefully, that they meant that Snow Lazarro would be inside and I'd have my chance to tell her what I thought of her. I'd pushed him through the door. "That nobody in here is looking for love."

"My point exactly," I said to Jerry. "You can't force someone to fall in love. You either do or you don't."

"A man is helpless against love," said Jerry. "I mean, the way it makes you feel . . . you can't just turn your back on it, can you?"

We tossed a coin to see who was going for the second round. The other patrons of Jo Jo's tolerated us. At first I think they thought we were tourists. Then they thought we were either feds or writers. But once they'd been assured that we were none of those things, they seemed happy enough to leave us alone. They probably thought we were nuts—nuts but harmless. I couldn't help feeling, though, that hanging out in Jo Jo's was a little like living with lions: you could never be sure that they wouldn't suddenly turn. Tails. I lost.

"I'm not wrong, am I?" I asked as I got to my feet as unobtrusively as possible. "It's worth waiting for, isn't it? I mean, you and Lonnie, you've got something special together, don't you?"

"Love," said Jerry, "what else do we strive for? What else are all our finest thoughts and dreams about? What is art for? Poetry? Moonlight? The skyline at night?" He handed me his glass. "Of course it's worth waiting for, Mike," he said somberly if not completely soberly. "Don't let anybody tell you different."

Besides Barry, both Lonnie and my mother were telling me different.

"Mike," said Lonnie, ever logical and rational, "Mike, you've got to be realistic. It's time you sorted out your priorities. Everyone needs to establish a home for himself." She smiled at Jerry, who looked as though he was about to choke on a piece of garlic bread. "Although some people do carry it to extremes." She laughed, slamming him affectionately on the back. "By the time Jerry finishes our home we'll be shuffling off to a retirement village." She patted his hand, also affectionately. "Talk about obsessive!" She laughed again. "He no sooner gets the storage units right than he decides the floor's all wrong or the lighting should be changed." Then she turned back to me and all affection and humor dove for cover. "You're not a kid anymore, Mike, you know. You're not getting any younger."

"I know that, Lonnie," I replied evenly, too vain to point out my bald patch and my ever-increasing number of gray hairs. "I do know that." Too vain, also, to joke that I wasn't getting any taller, either.

"Then why do you act like a kid? Skulking around, waiting for Cupid to shoot you through the heart?" Boy, did Jerry Finer have a big mouth. "For God's sake, Mike, romantic love is just a fiction created to sell Valentine's Day cards and cheap novels. You, of all people, should know that." She pointed a breadstick at me. "A truly meaningful relationship doesn't just happen, Mike, it has to be worked at, like anything else in life." She turned to her husband, the obsessive worker. "Isn't that right, Jer?"

Jerry dropped his fork.

I was a little surprised that she didn't seem to have heard Jerry's speech about love being the most important thing in the world. I pointed my breadstick at her. "I know that, too, Lon," I said. "Only it seems to me that if you don't start with love you're not going anywhere. If you don't love this person who's stuck in this ship with you before you leave the harbor, then you're not going to be willing to put all this work into it, are you? You're both going to end up drowning at sea."

Jerry bent to pick up his fork, and slammed his head against the table.

We were having pasta salad, red wine, and a postmortem on the last blind date that Lonnie, having moved on from introducing me to her self-improvement groups to doing a little agenting of her own, had arranged for me. The pasta was overcooked, the wine was a little heavy, and my behavior had been "paranoidal and juvenile" (were you the wife of my oldest friend) and "boorish, rude, and defensive" (had you happened to be with me on the date).

Lonnie plonked her elbows on the table and leaned toward me in that earnest way of hers. "And how are you going to know if you love someone or not if you never give anyone a chance?"

I can look pretty earnest too, when I try. "What are you talking about, 'never give anyone a chance'? I've given plenty of people a chance."

"Not Cheryl Takuboku you haven't," said Lonnie.

The way I had come to view the world, God created the land and the water, the trees and the flowers, the birds and the fish and the animals, music, laughter, and black bean soup. And Satan created the blind date. He must have laughed himself stupid. "This'll give them a taste of what they're in for," he chortled. "And they think fire and brimstone are bad!" The lower devils rolled in the aisles. "What a mind!" they gasped. They nudged each other. "Who but a genius could think of something so simple yet so effective?"

Blind dates, like snowflakes, are each of them different. Sometimes the datee is someone whom, in different circumstances, you would find perfectly acceptable. Sometimes the datee is someone you would never find acceptable, not even if she was the one who dug you out of the rubble after the earthquake. Sometimes you and the datee just don't click. Sometimes it is fear and loathing at first sight. Whatever the particular character of each individual date, however, they all have one thing in common. If you worry about time going too quickly, if it seems to you that your life is going by so fast you can barely catch your breath, then the most effective way to put the brakes on is to start dating blindly. The night that is usually over before it's begun will last a week. "My God," you'll say to yourself, glancing at your watch as the two of you sit having coffee after the show, discussing her decision never to have children, "how can it still be Friday?" The afternoon that usually lasts no more than a few hours will last two months. "Of course we have time to do the postmodernists," she'll giggle. "It's not even two o'clock yet." Even as little as one blind date a week can extend your life by several years.

And blind dates, unlike the fountain of youth, are easy to find. Your friend's wife corners you one evening and says she knows someone you really should meet. You say, "Lonnie, I'm sure she's a wonderful woman . . . any friend of yours, you know . . . but I'm really not interested."

Your friend's wife says, "Michael, I'm not saying she's gorgeous, she's not gorgeous. I'm not saying she's an Einstein, she's not that either. But Michael, I am telling you, if you don't meet this woman you'll regret it for as long as you live." She touches her heart. "Trust me, Michael, I have this feeling, call it woman's intuition, call it professional judgment, call it what you want, but I have it very strongly about you and Cheryl Takuboku."

"Whatever happened to the days when a woman needed a man like a fish needs an umbrella?" you wondered out loud.

"It was a bicycle, not an umbrella," said Lonnie, a little sharply. "And, in case you haven't noticed, Michael, the times have changed."

The other thing Lonnie didn't say about Cheryl Takuboku was that she was boring. (Which is not, of course, to be confused with boorish. You, because of a crack you were eventually driven to make about artificial ears, were boorish.) Though it did, to be truthful, take a little while before you realized just how boring Cheryl Takuboku was.

You entered the bar where you'd agreed to meet. She was sitting at a table by the window. You went over and introduced yourself. She introduced herself. So far, so good. She seems pretty nice, you told yourself. She's got teeth and everything. She doesn't sound like Minnie Mouse, like my last blind date. She doesn't look like she's going to offer to do my chart or help me paint the kitchen. You weren't too sure about the cycling shorts or the earrings that looked like bunches of grapes, but where would we be as a species if everyone favored conservative clothes in muted shades of brown and gray? You asked her if she'd like another drink, and she said she'd love another orange juice, thank you so much. Standing at the bar, you glanced back at her, and she was looking at you. You smiled. So far so good. You brought the two juices back to the table.

"Well." You laughed.

"Well." Cheryl Takuboku laughed.

"This is sort of embarrassing," you said. "I mean . . . well . . ."

"Oh, I know," said Cheryl. "It's so awkward, isn't it?"

You exchanged another smile, this one slightly more than sympathetic. My God, you thought to yourself, don't tell me Lonnie's finally making up for the egocentric journalist. "Oh, it is," you agreed, "it's very awkward."

Cheryl took a dainty sip of her drink. "Of course," she said, "even though it is awkward, it's a good way to meet people, isn't it? You know, so you don't get in a rut."

You decided to pass on that one. You said, "So, what was it Lonnie said you did for a living?"

She sipped daintily. "I'm in prosthetics."

"Excuse me?"

She smiled. This had, perhaps, happened to her before. "I make artificial noses and ears."

"Oh, really," you said. "Artificial noses and ears. That sounds fascinating." You soon found out, however, that it wasn't nearly as fascinating as it sounded. Like the journalist's tales of scoops and counter-scoops and drunken nights in Hong Kong, it got less and less fascinating as the seconds shuffled on. You began to wish you'd had something stronger than orange juice. Tequila, maybe. Or morphine.

"See, if you're making two ears, that's no problem, right?" said Cheryl Takuboku.

You nodded. "Of course." You could grasp that.

She started drawing diagrams on a napkin. "Because you can do what you like, really, I mean, within the existing framework, you know. But if there's one ear intact, then you've got your work cut out for you."

You nodded again.

But somehow she knew that you had no idea of what she was talking about.

"Because you have to match them up, see?"

You dug your nails into the palm of your hand. "Oh, right, sure. You have to match them up."

"You have no idea how difficult that can be," she said. She decided to remedy that situation.

You interrupted a monologue about the problems often inherent in lobes to suggest that the movie would be starting soon.

"Oh, sure," said Cheryl Takuboku, not missing a beat. "But that's nothing when you compare it to nostrils."

It was here that you made the first unfortunate joke about ears.

Crossing the street took a little of the sting from her reply.

And the movie itself did prove a peaceful lull in the continuing saga of Cheryl Takuboku's fraught and demanding work life. So peaceful, in fact, that you fell asleep. You woke up with a start when a sharp object (later identified as a Takuboku elbow) dug into your ribs and someone tried to grind your toes into the floor. "What the hell?" you said, perhaps a trifle loudly.

"You were snoring!" she hissed.

There was a chorus of *Shhhh*s.

But you, still half asleep, didn't heed them. "What are you trying to do," you inquired of your companion, "cripple me?"

She said, "Yes," a hint, mayhap, that she was beginning to find your behavior both boorish and rude. Not to mention defensive.

The two of you, being adults, and having been assured by Lonnie Stepato that you were meant for each other, tried again after the film. You went to a sushi bar she knew. It was there that you discovered that Cheryl Takuboku, unlike the journalist, and unlike the woman who sounded like Minnie Mouse, had more than one topic of conversation. The journalist had only herself. And Minnie Mouse had only her family. But Cheryl Takuboku had both plastic organs and Elmore Patterson.

"This is the table me and Elmore always used to sit at," she announced as you reached for your menu.

Your mother (though you don't always make it obvious) raised you to be polite and well-mannered. "Elmore?" you queried. You should have known better, but you didn't. "Who's Elmore?"

Cheryl shrugged. "Oh, he's just this man I used to go out with."

You smiled at the menu. "Oh."

"Well, actually, we didn't just go out, you know, we lived together."

You smiled again, convinced, all of a sudden, that you could read Japanese. Didn't that say rice? Didn't that say pickled turnip?

"Well, actually, we were married for a while."

That definitely said sake.

"We were married for twelve years."

"Twelve years?"

Her voice sounded a little huskier than it had when she was talking about nostril hair. "Uh huh. We got married right from college."

"Twelve years, huh?" That said beer. Not a doubt.

"He was the first man I ever loved."

And that had to be winter melon.

"Oh, but you don't want to hear about Elmore," she snuffled.

And she was right. You didn't.

"So," you said cheerfully, "what do you recommend?"

But she didn't hear your question. She heard you say that you were dying to hear about Elmore. Every detail, no matter how small. She started by telling you how they met. Then she told you about their second date. Then she told you about the time they went camping in the Smoky Mountains and the tent blew away in a storm. Hours passed. The waitress fell asleep at a back table. The chef and the barman started playing cards in a corner. It was then that you made your second unfortunate wisecrack of the evening. You said, "Boy, if Elmore didn't have rubber ears when you met him, I bet he did when he finally left."

But it wasn't until the cab ride home that you really began to get defensive. She asked you who the first person you ever loved was, and you said, "My mother."

"You know what I think your problem is, Mike?" asked Lonnie as Jerry, silent through most of our conversation, thinking, I imagined, of roller cupboards, began to clear the table.

"No, Lonnie. What do you think my problem is?"

She looked into my eyes. "I think you're becoming gynophobic."

I turned to Jerry, but he had his back to us. " 'Gynophobic'? What's that mean? Afraid of gynecologists?" Not an unreasonable fear at all.

Lonnie's look was one of pity: you poor fool. "Everything's a joke with you, isn't it, Mike? Nothing's ever serious. A perfectly wonderful woman confronts you with a little real pain and emotion, and you make a joke. A true friend tries to help you face the shallowness and emptiness and selfishness of your single existence, and you think it's funny."

Jerry turned back from the sink. "So what's it mean, 'gynophobic'?" he asked with a nervous laugh.

"Tell him," ordered Lonnie.

I told him. "Fear of females."

And she was going to blame me for that?

My mother, an older and more experienced woman than Lorraine Stepato (and one never deflected from her maternal mission for even half a second by the siren call of women's liberation) was more subtle. She answered the personals for me.

Using Barry's home computer and my name, my mother wrote to The Girl You Wish You'd Married When You Had the Chance. She wrote to Vivacious, Ambitious, Multi-talented but Warm and Giving. She wrote to Exceptional Woman Seeking Exceptional Man. She wrote to Wait Till You Taste My Stuffed Peppers. She wrote to I'm Lonely and So Are You.

"Mom," I pleaded, "Mom, you've got to stop."

"This is how people meet each other nowadays," explained my mother. If I'd been her mother I would never have taught her to read. "The world is too big to rely on being introduced in the usual way. When the globe is a village, you can't just expect to bump into someone in the candy store. You've got to spread your nets wide."

"Mom, please, it's so calculating. It's like a meat market or something. It's like being a pork chop and advertising for someone to eat you."

"Don't be ridiculous," my mother snapped. "It's nothing of the kind. It's a way of meeting people with similar interests."

"But that's what I mean," I reasoned. "What does it matter if you have similar interests or not? That has nothing to do with love. You and Barry don't have similar interests, do you?" Alma Huttenmeyer and I had had nothing in common but English class. We weren't even in the same homeroom. I became passionate. "It doesn't prove anything, except that you probably never had to go to all the trouble of taking out an ad in the first place. You would probably have bumped into each other walking in the rain anyway. And you're going to hate each other, because you're too much alike!"

"When did you become so cynical?" asked my mother.

"Promise," I begged her.

She promised. And then she went home and wrote to Muscle Mad. She wrote to Arnie Fan. She wrote to If I've Only One Life to Live Let Me Live It Outdoors. She sent my photo and telephone number to Aerosmith Rocks My Body But Only You Can Rock My Heart.

"Jesus," I said to Linda, my secretary, "can you believe she gives them my work number?"

Linda slowly stirred one sugar into my coffee. "Don't worry, Mike." She smiled, my friend, my confidante, my ally. "I'll screen all calls."

I was still rattled by the letter I'd received from I Don't Care What You're Into As Long As I Can Get You Into Me. Was my mother totally losing her mind? "But what if one of them turns up in reception?"

Linda put the coffee on my desk. "She'd still have to get past me," said Linda. "Don't forget, Mike," she said gently, "my hands are lethal weapons."

As though anyone who'd seen her stun that football player for making a pass at her could forget. "Oh, I haven't forgotten." I took a sip of my coffee. It was perfect. "Linda," I said, "you're really a pal. I don't know what I'd do without you."

"Oh, Mike, please . . ."

"No, really. If there's anything I can do, you know, I owe you a couple."

"Oh, Mike, really . . ." She paused in the doorway. "Well . . ." She smiled. "Do you mean it?"

"Of course I mean it."

"Well, I was kind of wondering if . . ."

"Wonder no more," I said, gesturing expansively. "A few extra days off? I don't know about a raise right now, but I might be able to wangle a little bo—"

"Oh, no, no . . ." She shook her head. "No, it was just that, well, this friend of mine, Denise?, she's really terrific?, she almost went to the Olympics?, well, Denise, she's been meeting nothing but androids since her boyfriend disappeared off the coast of Africa, and I was telling her what a honey you are . . ."

The coffee turned to gall on my lips. I suddenly understood why I hadn't had to make it for myself the last few days. "Don't tell me," I said, hollow as a drum. "You want me to ask her out."

"You want me to get her on the phone for you?"

I nodded, too numb to speak.

"You'll love her, Mike." Linda smiled. "I just know you will."

And then, just when it didn't seem that things could get any worse, my mother invited me over for a family supper to celebrate her and Barry's wedding anniversary. "I've forgiven you for embarrassing me in front of Mrs. Grancoolie's niece by leaving in the middle of dessert last time," said my mother, "so I don't see why you should hold a grudge."

"No," I said, "you wouldn't."

"Chuck and Elinor are coming," threatened my mother. "Don't you want to see your brother?"

In the old days, I would have lied and said that of course I wanted to see Chuck, we shared a room for sixteen years, how could I not want to see him? But the new me was beyond hypocrisy. "Not particularly."

"Your sister and Matt and the baby are coming," persisted my mother. "You haven't seen Trixie since Christmas."

Trixie. Who names a kid Trixie? When she was first born I thought the name was a little strange but kind of cute. Trixie, pixie—like a little doll. Now I knew that if I ever had a daughter of my own I'd name her Penthesilea and teach her how to shoot.

"Has she stopped puking all over everyone?"

"Michael," said my mother curtly, "are you coming or not?"

"All right," I capitulated, "I'll come. But I don't want to be hassled, you hear me?"

"Of course I hear you," snapped my mother. "The whole neighborhood hears you, the way you carry on."

It started out normally enough. My sister and my mother had a disagreement about how long the roast should be in the oven. Barry and my brother had a disagreement about Japan. My mother and Barry had a disagreement about where they'd met and who'd said what at the time. Then there was champagne and a toast to the happy couple. Barry put "Moon River" on the stereo and he and my mother danced. We opened more champagne. Trixie had brought her family of hippos with her, and that kept us pretty occupied. Chuck and Elinor started telling a story about their recent vacation in Italy, and both his version and her version, though conflicting, were mildly amusing.

"Mike," said my sister, suddenly appearing in the door to the kitchen. "Mike, you want to help me bring out some more snacks?"

I looked down at the little lilac bow just beneath my chin. "But I'm holding Trixie."

Candace, who is very much like her mother, tapped her foot. "Well, give her to Barry."

I looked at Barry. He was already a little drunk. He had clumsy, meaty hands. What did he know about babies? The youngest child he'd ever dealt with had been eight—and look what had happened to him. I glanced at my niece, who was trying to gum my own slender, artistic fingers to death. "Trixie's happy where she is."

"Mike," said Candace, "give the baby to Barry or to Matt, and come out and give me a hand."

My mother was in the kitchen, lifting a tray of mini–egg rolls from the microwave. She smiled at me as though she hadn't seen me in a while.

"I don't see why somebody else couldn't have done this," I grumbled. "Trixie was having a good time."

My sister looked at my mother.

My mother looked at my sister.

"I don't see what you need me for. Can't anybody else open a jar of peanuts around here?"

My sister looked at my mother.

My mother looked at my sister.

"So?" I said. "What is it you want me to do?"

They both looked at me.

"Mike," said my sister, turning her back to me as she started to busy herself with a bowl of corn chips. "Mike, your mother has something she wants to ask you."

I felt as if someone had just handed me a telegram. I didn't want to open it, but I knew I was going to have to.

I looked at my mother. "What?"

My mother looked at my sister.

My sister handed me a bowl of guacamole and a bowl of bean dip (both from jars). "Go on," my sister goaded my mother. "You're the one who wants to know. Ask him."

"Ask me what?"

My mother looked at my feet. She cleared her throat. "Michael," said my mother. She cleared her throat again. She raised her head level with mine and her eyes to the cupboard handle above my head. "Michael," said my mother, "Michael, are you gay? Is that what the problem is?"

"What?"

Candace was looking at the corn chips, but my mother, finally, was looking at me, if warily.

"You know," said my mother, her eyes darting toward Candace for support that wasn't exactly forthcoming. "It's fine if you are. I mean . . . it's . . . no, it's fine, as long as you're careful . . . it's fine with Barry, too . . . but if you are, well, if you are, we'd really like to know."

I slammed the guacamole down on the counter. "I can't believe I'm hearing this," I said, a little loudly. I slammed the bean dip down next to the guacamole. "It's none of your business." I was not a little loud now, I was shouting. "You have no right to ask me whom I do or do not sleep with. I don't ask you if you and Barry like to tie each other up, do I?"

There was a sharp intake of maternal and sisterly breath.

"None of your business," I repeated. "Not unless I volunteer the information of my own accord. Which I haven't." And then I stormed from the room, the door swinging behind me.

"See," I heard Candace hiss. "I told you he'd react like that."

But after I'd composed myself, and Trixie and I were rearranging the hippos, I suddenly realized how Lee must have felt after Atlanta. I was going to lose. Just as Lee had been no match for the economic superiority of the North, I was no match for the fearsome forces of matrimony on the march. I gave Trixie a hug. They wouldn't give up until I surrendered. Short of having myself thrown into a Moroccan prison, I had no way out. I looked at Chuck and Elinor, correcting each other's memory of Livorno. I looked at Candace and Matt, feeding each other corn chips. I watched my mother slip her hand into Barry's and receive a warm little squeeze in return. And then I heard a voice in my head whisper the one piece of military strategy I'd totally forgotten. "If you can't lick 'em, join 'em," it said. I kissed the top of Trixie's head. The little voice was right: there was only one thing to be done if I was to survive any longer against the ruthless forces of domestic bliss.

I was going to have to get married.

And pretty damn quick.

7

Single No More

Some marriages are made in heaven. Some marriages are made in hell. Some marriages are made in the computer of the Love 'Em, Don't Leave 'Em Dating Service. Mine was made in Jo Jo's Bar and Grill, Fine Food and Beer, during Happy Hour.

It was a Saturday night, ribs night, and very crowded. Regulars like us always shared tables when the place was that packed, and Jerry and I were sitting with Bongo and Charley Ray.

"So then she asks me if I'm gay or not," I said to Jerry.

Our tablemates, who had been sipping their beers in companionable silence, looked over.

"I'd kill anybody who said that to me," said Charley Ray.

Bongo's narrow eyes narrowed a little more. "What're you saying?" he inquired. "Are you sayin' you're queer?"

"No, no," laughed Jerry, that champion of free speech and the Bill of Rights, "he's not saying that." Jerry explained about the male

drought. He explained about his wife trying to set me up with her
friends. He explained about Suzanne Lightfoot and her book. He explained about my mother. He offered to buy them a beer.

Charley Ray moved over to Jerry's seat while Jerry went to the bar.
"Don't think I was eavesdroppin' or anything," he said to me, "but
it's hard not to listen, and I want you to know that I hear what you're
sayin'." He shifted toward me. "I had the exact same problem myself."

I looked at Charley Ray, hoping my smile was something like normal. If the bison could breed with the Centurion tank, and if the result
of that union were, somehow (or to some small degree), human, then
the result of that union would probably look a lot like Charley Ray
on a good day. "You did?"

He shook his great shaggy head sadly. "You got it. They were all
over me like flies around a corpse. I didn't have a minute's peace."
He slurped up some foam. "There were days when I gave a lot of
thought to committin' some small, you know, insignificant sort of
felony and going inside for a while." He laughed. "Just for some
peace."

Thus is man united by his nightmares as well as his dreams. "It
wouldn't've worked," I pointed out. "Not only would they write to
you all the time, but visitors' day would be hell."

"I don't get it," said Bongo. "Why does everyone think you're queer
if you're not?"

"Shut up, Bongo," ordered Charley Ray.

I rested my elbows on the table and leaned closer, not wanting to
miss a single word. "So what did you do?" I asked. "How did you
get them to leave you alone?"

He smiled, but it was not a smile of unadulterated joy. "I did what
you said you're gonna do. I did what everybody does in the end if
they don't die young and happy." His smile turned to a grimace of
resignation. "I joined the institution."

"But it doesn't make sense," Bongo mused. "If you're not a faggot,
why would anyone think you was?"

I passed him the peanuts. "It's very complicated, Bongo. But the
thing is that it's not just anyone. It's my mother."

"Oh," said Bongo. "Your mother." Watching understanding settle on his face was like watching a flashlight beam cut across a starless Nebraskan night. "Why didn't you say it was your mother in the first place?"

I turned back to Charley Ray. "And getting married, it worked, right? It solved all your problems?"

He smiled again. "It solved that set of problems." He took the beer Jerry was handing him with a nod. "It shut my folks up. And it stopped chicks from always wantin' to introduce me to their friends."

"You see?" I said to Jerry as he sat down and slid my mug to me. "It's the only way."

Charley Ray stared down at the knuckles on his left hand, across which was tattooed the word *D-O-O-M*. "But it gave me some other problems, Mike, if you know what I mean." He sighed. "Chicks. They're very complicated, aren't they?"

"Yeah," I agreed, "they have their dimensions." I leaned so close to him that I could distinguish the various motor oils that had soaked into his jacket. "But you're missing the point, Charley," I explained. "You see, I don't really get married. I just pretend that I do. You know, I set it up so everybody believes that I'm married, but really I'm still all alone."

"I don't get it," said Bongo. "Isn't that like pretending to eat?"

But Charley Ray was gazing at me with new admiration. "You mean, you don't even hafta shack up with anyone?"

My grin was gleeful. "Nope. I keep right on living with my parrot."

"What kind of parrot you got?" asked Bongo. "What's it's name?"

Charley Ray's smile, despite the missing teeth, was a beautiful sight to behold. "You mean you don't really lock the chain? You just make up this wife?"

"Bingo!"

"You mean you don't hafta go shoppin' with her and shit like that? She isn't always jumpin' all over you and makin' you do things? You don't have to have her friends over or go fishin' with her father?"

"Hey," said Jerry, "do you have to go fishing with your father-in-law, too? Isn't it the pits?"

"I don't get it," said Bongo. "What happens when she meets your mother?"

"It's beautiful," sighed Charley Ray. "Simple but beautiful."

I couldn't help a little rush of pride. I'd never had a man with serious muscle definition and a gold hoop in his ear look up to me before. "I know."

"Hold on a minute," Jerry interrupted. "Bongo's right. What does happen when your mother wants to meet her?" He groaned. "What happens when Lonnie wants to meet her?"

Charley Ray reached over and clapped me on the shoulder. "Don't you worry about Mike here," he said. "He's a smart guy. He'll think of somethin'."

I was such a smart guy that I thought of several things.

The first thing I thought of was that I had to go slow. I had to plot and plan this as carefully as one would engineer a million-dollar heist. My scheme wouldn't work if one day I simply announced on the back page of the *Voice*: "Michael Householder has wed. His mother, his secretary, his best friend's wife, his neighbor across the hall, and every other woman in the greater metropolitan area can now get off his case." I had to be fiendishly clever and diabolically thorough. I could leave nothing—not one thing—to chance. I had to take every possible contingency into consideration before I committed myself to any course of action. I had to create my make-believe soulmate with all the care and precision and attention to detail that had gone into the creation of Disneyland. I had to allow for my local surveillance network—Betsy Shopak and Ida Sontag. I had to allow for my mother. I had to allow for Lonnie. I had to make the newest Mrs. Householder so real that the only thing missing would be the body—and no one would even notice that.

"Subtlety and care are the key words here," I said to Gracie. The kitchen table was spread with papers, color-coded for efficiency. I was making charts, diagrams, lists, and outlines for Operation War Bride; Gracie was making a mess. While I slaved, trying to create the blueprint that would save our happy home, she shred corners, dropped sunflower seeds, and made pooh. "Cut it out, Gracie," I said as she tried to pull the pen out of my hand. "Can't you see that this is serious?"

"Don't take it serious, it's too mysterious," sang Gracie. She'd been listening to Mrs. Sontag's easy-listening station through the bedroom wall again. "Don't take it serious, it's too mysterious . . ." She had an accident on item A.3.a. (Planting the Seeds; Simulating Reality; at home).

I balled up the page and tossed it across the room at the wastebasket. I started again. "Think, Gracie," I urged her. "How can I create the illusion of sexual preoccupation?"

Gracie looked at me. She bobbed her head. "Go, go, go," sang Gracie.

Clever and subtle.

I asked myself this question: How would you behave if you really had fallen in love?

And then I answered the question: Like a man on drugs.

So I started keeping irregular hours. I came home late from work. I came home on time and then went out, not returning until even the whores were beginning to call it a night. Sometimes I didn't return at all, but staggered back to change my rumpled clothes just as Betsy was leaving for work or Mrs. Sontag was emptying the vacuum.

"Gosh, Mike," Betsy would say. "You look awful. You're not just getting home, are you?"

And I would smile the smile of a man whose sex life is killing him—smug, proud, shamelessly triumphant—and I would say, "Oh, hoho, you know how it is."

"Burning the candle at both ends again?" Mrs. Sontag would ask, calculating the exact number of hours I'd been wearing that shirt, how long it had been since I'd changed my socks.

And I would smile the smile of a man who would never be so old that he preferred a pint of chocolate chip ice cream to a five-minute fuck—conceited, self-congratulatory, condescending—and I would say nothing but I would wink volumes.

The other person I frequently ran into was Betsy's boyfriend, Detective O'Brien. Sometimes we passed as I was going in and he was coming out. We'd eye each other. We'd nod. "Night," I'd say. "Night," he'd say. Or "Morning," he'd say. "Morning," I'd say.

Other times, we'd arrive together, materializing in the lobby from the dark outside at some nebulous hour between supper and breakfast, he from his battle with the forces of evil and I from my workout with love. By then, of course, I'd figured out why he looked so familiar the first time I met him. Jesus was in charge of the Butcher of Broadway case. Which is another way of saying that he was the man being blamed for allowing the "Gruesome Gourmet" to "Terrorize Our Streets." The press were having a field day with him. Every day they called him something else. "The Silent Detective: Jesus Refuses to Give Press Conference." "The Duped Detective: Following a Trail of Carnage, but No Nearer to the End." "The Daunted Detective: O'Brien Prays for a Miracle." When five fingers were found in a bread basket on Sixty-seventh Street, wrapped up in a handkerchief like profiteroles in a serviette, the headlines screamed: "The Dieting Detective: O'Brien Says He May Never Eat Again." Usually we'd ride up to the eighth floor in the strained silence that occurs when you know someone too well to ignore him but not well enough to know what to say (or, in our case, just well enough to know that you don't want to say anything). Once in a while, though, we'd make small talk. "How's it going?" I'd ask as we soared heavenward, both of us looking at the little light moving along the numbers. "Okay," he'd say. "How about you?" "Not bad," I'd say. "All right."

And where was I all these nights when I was supposed to be reinventing the *Kama-sutra*? The combination of lack of sleep, comfort deprivation, and physical exertion simulates perfectly all the symptoms of love. I was riding the subway. I was riding the ferry. I was biking across Staten Island. I was watching midnight movies. I was sleeping on the couch in my office. I was hanging out in bars, reading manuscripts by the light of a twenty-watt bulb. I'd drive out on Long Island, I'd stop for a meal or walk through a mall, I'd park by a view and listen to the radio, and then I'd drive back. Sometimes I'd take a train because it took longer.

I didn't miss a trick.

Casual. Once I'd established a new behavior pattern on the home front, I set about introducing my love into the rest of my life.

"Gee, Mom," I said with a regretful sigh, "I'd like to come to dinner Wednesday, but I have a date."

Be cool, I told myself, let her drag it out of you, make her suspicious.

"A date?" asked my mother. "A date with who?"

"Oh, just this woman I met."

"Do I know her?" asked my mother.

"You don't know her, Mom. How's Barry?"

"She isn't one of your lesbians, is she?"

"I don't even know her, Mom. I only just met her. We're going out on a date."

"Who is she?"

"She's just this woman, Mom. You've never heard of her."

"Is she single? Has she ever been married? Does she have any children?"

"Blood type O."

"Very funny, Michael, hah hah," said my mother. "Just answer me this, if it's not too much to ask. Is this thing serious?"

I groaned. "Mom, I just met her, Mom. We're not engaged yet." I winked at Gracie.

Gracie blinked back.

Thorough.

"You look different, Mike," said Lonnie. "I don't know, more relaxed. More at peace with yourself. Don't tell me you finally got that partnership."

"No, no"—turning shyly away—"no partnership yet. You know, it's just . . . well . . . let's just say that things are looking pretty good at the moment . . ."

"Mike," breathed Lonnie, "don't tell me you've finally met someone?"

"Well," I mumbled, cautious but pleased, not wanting to jinx myself but unable to suppress a rapturous grin, "there's nothing . . . I mean, it's very early days yet, you know, I don't want to jump the gun or anything . . ."

"Mike!" cried Lonnie.

"I can't wait for you two to meet . . ." I lied.

Jerry, about to enter the room, turned around and walked back out.

Under normal circumstances, Lonnie Stepato only hugged me on national holidays, my birthday, and when I'd closed a good deal for her, but she hugged me then. "Well, Michael . . ." She grinned. "This is really wonderful. Tell me all about her. Where did you meet?" She started to laugh. "Look at me! I'm asking you all these questions and I don't even know her name. What's her name?"

"Alma," I said. "Alma Huttenmeyer."

"Alma," Lonnie repeated. "What an unusual name."

Painstaking.

I sent Alma flowers to my apartment. Outrageous bouquets with scented cards covered with purple prose. *To the Light of My Life. For the Flower of My Heart. Darling, Every minute without you is like an eternity in hell.* I signed myself Hopelessly in Love. Your Obedient Slave. Your Lovesick Fool.

I taught Gracie some new phrases. Instead of saying "Hello, sailor," the way she used to, she learned to say "Hello, Alma." I'd come home at night, switch on the light, and Gracie would shriek, "Hello, Alma. Hello, Alma. Wanna dance?" I'd go to the fridge, get out an olive (Gracie has a thing about black olives), and Gracie would bellow, "Olive, Alma. Olive, Alma. Thank you very much, toots."

"Where's Alma?" I'd ask Gracie as we sat together on the sofa, watching a movie (Westerns were her favorites), sharing a bowl of grapes. And Gracie would cock her pretty little head and her beady little eye and she'd say, "Where's Alma, Michael? Where's Alma? Alma want a muscatel?"

I'd be dancing around the kitchen, preparing supper, Gracie on my shoulder, probably dancing too, and I'd say to her, "When is Alma coming home, Gracie? When is Alma coming home?" Depending on her mood, and what was on the evening's menu, Gracie would either repeat, "When is Alma coming home? When is Alma coming home?" (loud enough for Mrs. Sontag, in her kitchen, to hear), or she'd bob her head or stretch her neck and she'd say, "I don't know, honey. Let's eat."

I made a tape of a woman laughing (Linda reading an Elizabeth Beacher novel on a lazy afternoon), and now and then, when I returned to the apartment, I'd play it just before I shut my front door behind me. "Oh, come on, sweetheart," I'd say, in a voice that was coaxing but that also carried across the hall, "you know you don't mean that," and then I'd press the On button, and a woman's warm, loose laughter would surround me. Me and Betsy and Mrs. Sontag, and everyone else on the floor.

Gracie and I rehearsed a few basic dialogues between me and Alma—dialogues made just a little bit difficult to overhear clearly by the radio, the stereo, the television, the vacuum cleaner, the hair dryer, the washing machine, and/or running water—that we could slip into whenever we knew Mrs. Sontag was waiting for the elevator or Betsy was dumping the entire contents of her bag on the floor of the hall because she couldn't find her keys.

I'd whisper Gracie's lines to her in a falsetto, to encourage her to use Marissa's voice. For instance, in my normal speaking voice I'd say, "Shall we go to that party, honey?" And then I'd prompt softly: "What do you think, darling?"

"What do you think, darling?" Gracie would pipe.

"Oh, I don't know, darling, what do you think?" I'd say. (Then I'd give her her next sentence: "Sweetheart, please, it's up to you.")

"Sweetheart, please, it's up to you . . ." Gracie would parrot.

"But if you don't want to . . ." I'd say, loud but sensitive.

("Don't be silly," I'd hiss.)

"Don't be silly . . ."

"You know I'll do anything you want . . ." ("Of course I do, darling.")

"Of course I do, darling . . ."

And so forth.

Matter-of-fact.

"Don't put any calls through after four-thirty," I told Linda. "I've got to get out of here early tonight."

"Don't tell me you've got another date," said Linda. She eyed me over her steno pad. "Not with that same woman?"

I smiled my most enigmatic smile. "How late is that florist downstairs open?" I asked.

Confident.

"Alma Huttenmeyer?" repeated my mother. "Is that Jewish? Where does she come from?"

"Wisconsin." Somebody must come from Wisconsin, right? It's certainly not a place you'd go to.

My mother digested this information. "Wisconsin," she said. "I hear it's very nice out there. Very healthy. No drugs or anything." I could hear the scratching of a pencil. She was probably writing down every detail so she wouldn't forget anything when she started calling her friends. "So what did you say she does?"

Still on inspirational overdrive, I gave Alma a job that entailed working long, irregular hours and a lot of travel. A job that would explain an eccentric personality and any tendency toward temperament or reclusiveness. "She's a writer," I said. What made more sense?

"Have I heard of her?" asked my mother, a woman who thinks a book is the thing you put in your suitcase next to the sunscreen.

"She writes travel books," I said. I was possibly a genius. I would certainly have made a great politician, being able to lie on my feet like that.

"What kind of travel books?" asked my mother. "You mean like Esso guides?"

Maybe even president. "For women on their own."

"Well, I can't believe there's much of a market for that," said my mother.

I was brilliant.

"I'd really like you and Jesus to get to know each other better," Betsy said to me one June evening as, having unexpectedly found that we were both home and alone, we strolled to the ice-cream store together. "I think he was a little jealous of you at first, but he's gotten over that." She slipped her arm through mine. "You'll never guess what he said to me the other day," she sort of tittered.

From our minimal acquaintance, I knew that the mind of Jesus O'Brien was as closed to me as a book written in Sanskrit. "He didn't ask you to try on his handcuffs, did he?"

Betsy gave me a playful shove. "No, silly," she laughed. "He said he never would have pictured you as a ladies' man. You know, because you're so sh—, because you're so self-reliant." A faraway look came into her eyes. "He's so sweet. You'd think that someone in his job would be really worldly, but he can be so naïve . . ."

I remained noncommittal. "Naïve" was not the word I would have chosen.

"Oops!" She came out of her reverie just in time to avoid something unpleasant on the pavement. "It's one of the things that make him so endearing," she informed me.

I didn't mention that I found nothing about Jesus O'Brien in the least bit endearing. He gave me the creeps, the way he looked at me. "Lady," I protested instead, "not ladies. This time there's only one."

Betsy bounced through the door before me, not listening to a word I said. "But I explained to him about your Peter Pan complex, you know?, and he said that made sense."

"Betsy," I further protested. "Betsy, how many times do I have to tell you? I do not have a Peter Pan complex."

We stood at the counter, staring up at the menu. "Chocolate?" asked Betsy.

"Chocolate's fine. Did you hear me, Bets? I do not have a Peter Pan complex. And I do not have ladies."

"Which chocolate?" asked Betsy. "Chocolate plain, chocolate dark, chocolate ripple, chocolate with nuts, chocolate with chips, chocolate peanut butter, chocolate with toffee, chocolate mint, chocolate . . ." On the day of creation, did God realize that he was giving life to a creature that would eventually invent one hundred and forty-six different flavors of frozen cream, half of them chocolate?

"Betsy," I shouted, "Betsy, will you shut up for a minute? I think I'm in love."

"Mike!" She swung around so fast she nearly took off my ear. "Why, Mike, that's wonderful! When did this happen? How did you meet? When are you going to introduce us?"

"In the supermarket," I said. "By the fresh herbs."

There was a rap on the counter. "Next! Do you two know what you want?"

"It's so romantic!" sighed Betsy. "In the supermarket! It's just like *Mr. Right*!" She gave me a hug. She turned to the salesperson. "We'll have a pint of Death by Chocolate," she decided. "To celebrate!"

"Make it a quart," I chimed in, high on success.

Alma and I were married exactly six weeks after our encounter over the basil and thyme. We were married suddenly and exceedingly quietly, in a very small, very private ceremony (the justice of the peace, his dog, his wife, and us) in Las Vegas. We hadn't expected to get married that weekend, but I'd had to fly to Vegas to talk to a client of mine (a showgirl who was writing her memoirs—that part, as it happens, was true), and Alma, in L.A. at the time, discussing a video project, had hopped over to see me, and, well, Las Vegas is that sort of place, isn't it? The romance just takes over, makes reckless and restless the most sober of hearts. Of course, the way we'd visualized it when we'd talked about it as dawn cracked the sky over Manhattan, we'd both wanted our friends and families to be at our wedding, but we were love's toys, and it wasn't to be. One minute we were sipping champagne and playing roulette, and the next thing you knew, I was slipping my father's college ring on her finger and kissing the bride.

As Charley Ray had said, the whole thing was beautiful in its simplicity.

I'd thought of almost everything.

8

Me and the Wife Settle Down

"Have you done something with your hair?" I asked Betsy as we walked to the bus stop together one crisp autumn morning, hoping to steer the conversation away from me and mine. Since the announcement of my marriage, I'd been avoiding Betsy, but this morning she'd caught me as I was sneaking to the stairs. "You look different." I gave her an appraising look. "I know what it is! I can see your ears. What happened to your Walkman? I thought you never went out without Hank Williams."

Music blared from passing cars, traffic roared, the harried work force surged past us. She lowered her voice. "Jesus says it's too dangerous," she informed me. "You know, because of the Butcher."

"Is this a secret?" I asked.

Her voice shimmered down to a whisper. "He could be anywhere," she breathed. "I wouldn't want to bring attention to myself. Jesus says the psychiatrists think he's about to peak. You know, go really nuts?"

It was difficult to imagine what really nuts could be for a man who had already established the first catering firm for cannibals in the history of the city, but I nodded as though this made sense.

"They can tell because they know so much about him now, you know, because they've been studying him night and day," said Betsy, bending down so I could hear her. "Jesus says he's gotten away with it for so long that by now he thinks he's really clever, you know, that they'll never catch him, so he's bound to give himself away. It's only a matter of time."

I refrained from mentioning that the Butcher wasn't the only one who thought he was so clever. My opinion—and that of just about every other layperson in the metropolis—was that the only way the police would ever catch the Butcher was if he gave himself up. There'd been a cartoon in the *News*, a Norman Bates–type caricature standing in front of Lieutenant O'Brien's desk saying, "How many New York cops does it take to catch a lunatic? Yes, of course it's a joke."

"So a girl can't be too careful," summed up Betsy. "Jesus says you want to hear what's coming behind you." She gave me a look. "You should tell Alma," she said at normal volume.

We had come to a corner. I glanced to the left and then to the right. "I will."

She gave me another look. "Jesus said he rode up in the elevator with Alma the other night," said Betsy, switching from the tone of a conspirator to that of an inquisitor without a blink.

My wedding ring glinted in the sun. I couldn't help smiling to myself. The Butcher of Broadway wasn't the only one who could fool the good detective. "Oh, really?" I answered casually, as though I, in my Alma Huttenmeyer pastel track suit and fashion sunglasses, had not counted every floor of that journey as though it were an hour on the gibbet. "I don't think she mentioned it." We started across the road.

"He said she was taller than he thought she would be," said Betsy, in what I took to be an uncharacteristic dig at my height. I quickened our pace to make the light. "He said she seemed very shy."

"Writers," I said. "It's a lonely existence."

"I thought you told me she was away," said Betsy. "Working on one of her books."

"She came back unexpectedly." I gave Betsy a wink: *lucky me.*

"So does that mean I'm finally going to meet her?" asked Betsy. "Maybe you two would like to come to supper tomorrow night. If Jesus isn't working he likes to have tamales on Fridays."

I tried to imagine what a tamale made by Jesus O'Brien would be like, but he was a man far easier to picture in an abattoir than in a kitchen. "Tamales? O'Brien makes tamales?"

"Really, Michael . . ." She rolled her eyes. "They come in a can."

Slightly more appealing, but not much. "Gosh, Bets," I said, "that would've been great, but I'm afraid Alma's had to go off again."

Her head swiveled round as we reached the stop. "Already?"

"It's country fair season," I explained. "It keeps her hopping."

"If she hopped any more she'd be a kangaroo," said Betsy.

I ignored her sarcasm. "Life's not easy for a boy in love with a professional globe-trotter." I sighed.

Webster's New World Dictionary defines the intransitive verb "settle down" as follows: "**settle down 1**. to take up permanent residence, a regular job, etc.; lead a more routine, stable life, as after marriage **2**. to become less nervous, restless, or erratic **3**. to apply oneself steadily or attentively."

Like most couples, Alma and I had settled down quickly. That, after all, is what marriage is all about, isn't it? No more late nights and poor eating habits. No more partying and carousing. No more wondering what your life is about, where it might be going, or what you'll be likely to do when you get there. To settle down is to cement yourself into society's great wall. To shun the chaotic and ritualize the mundane.

Although Alma, as Betsy had noticed, was away a great deal of the time, when she was home we were as domestic and predictable as any other young marrieds. Alma had her days to take out the garbage, and I had mine. She had her nights for coming home late, and I had mine. She shopped, when she shopped, in the deli and the health food store; I shopped in Sloan's and The Universal Bean. She showered in the morning, while Mrs. Sontag and I exchanged greetings as we took in our papers. I showered in the evenings, while she worked out with Jane Fonda. On Fridays, when Betsy and Jesus were tucking into their can of tamales, we ordered from the Szechuan place around the corner—hot and sour soup and General Tso's chicken for her; fried seaweed and garlic shrimp for me. Most Mondays we had a large pizza delivered, half artichoke and eggplant, half sausage and mushroom, diet soda for my honey and mineral water for me.

Unlike most couples, however, Alma and I didn't find that applying ourselves steadily and attentively to settling down lessened our restlessness or jittery nerves. It was getting harder to keep Alma out of town as much as I had. But it was getting even harder to keep her in. I was running out of reasons why Alma and I couldn't dine with my parents, couldn't go out for Italian with Jerry and Lonnie, couldn't pop by Betsy's for a drink. It was becoming trickier and trickier to make her presence known but keep her unseen. The whole bloody business was making a wreck out of me.

It is a dark night and raining. More than raining. Teeming. Pouring. Storming. The few frail city trees bend roughly in the wind. The thunder rumbles over the traffic. The lightning is brighter than the HOT FOOD SALADS COLD BEER sign in the deli. It is late. Buildings are dark. Except for the occasional late-night shopper or workaholic hurrying home, or the occasional homeless person huddled in a doorway, the streets are deserted. But in one midtown office, a light still burns.

There, on the twenty-third floor, while the Nicaraguan cleaners sing along to their Walkmans as they mop out the rest rooms and vacuum the halls, a lone figure still lingers among the file cabinets and personal computers. She is small and compact, neat and trim. Her head is covered in dark brown curls. Preparing to depart, she checks her lipstick in the mirror, adjusts the hem of her skirt, picks a piece of fluff from her sweater. Satisfied, she sits down and puts on her pink-and-white trainers, tying the pink-and-white laces into a neat bow.

She stands up again and slips into a hooded raincoat. She is taller than she seemed at first; at least five foot eight. She places an oversized pair of rhinestone-studded sunglasses over her eyes. Barely breathing, she opens the office door and nervously surveys the empty corridor. The coast is clear; though the broken lyrics of what may very well be a familiar rock song can be heard at the end of the hall, the cleaners are out of sight.

A large leather shoulder bag bangs against her hip as she darts down the corridor and into the elevator. With a nod to the night watchman, she scurries through the foyer and out into the treacherous night. This is the part she hates most.

Once upon a time she could stride through these streets with confidence and ease. She'd delighted in the edgy movement, in the textured weave of sight and sound, in the third-world charms of New York after dusk. Once upon a time she might have walked home, enjoying the anonymity and freedom of the metropolitan night. But now, as she moves through the dark alone, her footsteps echoing, her heartbeat loud, she is wary, not to say terrified out of her wits. She has come to realize that a woman never knows what might suddenly reach out and grab her—a hand, a look, an ominous smile, the sound of loudly smacking lips or lascivious slurping, some guy in a car with Jersey plates wanting to know if she takes American Express.

Mindful of the warnings of the embattled enforcers of law and order, she enters the subway and stands in the lighted Waiting Area with two college boys smelling of beer, a middle-aged man in a suit and Burberry, and a young punk couple in tartan and leather with rings in their noses. She stands near the punks. Men with women are always safer than men on their own, a lesson she learned the night the very pleasant-looking gentleman carrying a jacket and *The New York Times* exposed himself on the downtown platform. It is unlikely that she will ever view the male form in quite the same way again.

No one looks at anyone else. Every scudding shadow causes an intake of breath: is it a rat? a mugger? the Butcher himself? The train finally comes and she hurries on board. Her pulse slows down. She's going to make it home safely after all. At the next stop a dozen teenage boys get on, higher than Mars. Then again, maybe she's not. Shouting and laughing, the boys strut through the car. "Fuck you," they say to each other with all the exuberance of youth. "Fuck you, you cunt," they shout with all the arrogance of manhood. They drape themselves over the seats. They rip ads for foot doctors and computer dating from the walls. The air goes taut. The women bury their heads in their books. The men go to sleep. She keeps her eyes on Elizabeth Beacher's *No River Too Deep*, engrossed in chapter 8, in which Arielle Savage finds herself in the harsh but hypnotic embrace of the man she has sworn to kill. The boys ask rhetorical questions. "You know about pussy?" they howl. "You know about pussy? It smells like fish but it tastes like chicken!" She gets out at the next stop and takes a cab the rest of the way home.

At last, having refused the cabby's offer of a night of jazz in Queens, she stands in front of her building. With a deep breath and a slight lowering of the head, she pushes through the street doors, marches through the lobby, nods casually at the doorman at his post and mumbles a hurried "Hello." He is flicking through a photography magazine. He nods and mumbles back. Though helpful to women with heavy shopping bags and strollers filled with children, he really notices only those in lycra leggings or short skirts.

Unlike most of the tenants, she takes the stairs. This—as much as the lonely walk to the subway and the long ride downtown—is also a dangerous part of her journey. At the eighth floor she stops. She presses her ear against the stairwell door. She holds her breath. Can she hear someone waiting for the elevator? Can she hear the elevator itself, bringing a neighbor safely home? Is a door about to open? Is someone peering through a peephole, checking for sounds? She takes her keys from her bag. She closes her eyes. *C'est la vie*, she tells herself. She opens the door as soundlessly as possible, and walks briskly, purposefully, but not suspiciously, across the hall. Once inside, she snaps her bolts and, not bothering to so much as hang up her dripping raincoat, staggers into the kitchen for something alcoholic.

"Hi ya, honey!" called Gracie.

Dropping my scarf and glasses on the kitchen table, I picked up the scotch I'd just poured and went into the bedroom to greet my parrot. "Hi ya, honey," I answered, opening the door of her cage. Then I put my drink on the bureau and sat down on the bed.

Gracie perched on her doorway. "Have a nice day?" she asked.

I kicked off the trainers. In the beginning, to look taller, I'd worn an old pair of Marissa's dress shoes that I'd found in the closet, but I quickly came to the conclusion that they must have been designed by a rapist, since it's virtually impossible to walk in the damn things, never mind run. And, anyway, I caught one in a grating and snapped off the heel. That's when I thought of trainers with lifts. Height and comfort, in colors to coordinate with your leisure wardrobe. I removed the wig. I put both safely away in the closet.

"So-so," I said. "And you?"

"Give me a smooch!" cried Gracie. "Come on, baby, give me a smooch!"

"Give me a second to stop hyperventilating," I answered, and collapsed on the mattress.

This little "Bride of Householder" charade was something I performed a couple of times a month, and only under cover of darkness and bad weather. And since I'd run into Jesus in the elevator that time, though I'd still stop at the deli or the health food store in my disguise, still race out to the stairwell with the trash at one in the morning in my wig and Marissa's chenille robe, I'd become more cautious than ever. Was it any wonder that I was shattered? Being Alma Huttenmeyer was way up there with Presidential Adviser and Head of General Motors in the megastress league.

"So why do you do it?" Jerry was always asking. "You're looking for trouble, Mike," Jerry, supportive as ever, was always saying. "Even if you don't get attacked on the way home, one night Betsy's going to catch you before you can get into your apartment, and then you're really going to be up the Mississippi without a paddle."

Why did I do it?

I did it because I had to. Though Alma's name was on the mailbox and the bell, I had suddenly understood that that wasn't enough. I wanted the woman on the seventh floor with the poodle to be able to say to Betsy Shopak, "I saw what's-his-name's new wife, you know, the one across the hall from you? I saw her come in in all that rain last night. What's she like?" I wanted Betsy, too embarrassed to admit that they had never met, to lie and say, "Oh, she's very nice." If my mother stopped by on one of her routine tours of inspection and said to the doorman, "So, I guess you've seen my new daughter-in-law," I wanted him to be able to say yes. "Yes, Mrs. Householder, she's a great little lady."

Gracie hung from the roof of her cage, pecking at the bars. "What's for supper, honey? What's for supper?"

I sat up, reached for my drink, and drained off half without pausing for air. "Garbage first, Gracie," I said, not one to let catastrophe alter his structure and system. "First the garbage, and then we eat."

Why did I do it?

I did it because—as Margery Householder Taub had always warned me I would one day do—I had bitten off a hell of a lot more than I could chew.

Not that it was completely my fault. The way I saw it, I was a man of my times. A victim, even. I had been raised in a culture dedicated to instantaneous personal gratification. I had been trained to expect quick results and simple solutions. You want a baked potato now? You don't want to wait an hour for it? Put it in the microwave. You want a million bucks so you can buy a microwave and go to Hawaii? You don't want to have to figure out a way to earn it? Get yourself a ticket for the lottery. You want a good night's sleep? Take a pill. You want to lose weight? Drink diet soda. You want to talk to someone at three in the morning? Dial this number.

Know what you want, and you can have it; get it, and happiness is yours.

I'd known what I'd wanted: I'd wanted a wife. A no-fuss, no-bother spouse.

There's an old Serbo-Croat saying that goes: A man should be careful what he wants, because he might just damn well get it. A little bit of rustic wisdom that might seem, to some, old-fashioned and out of place in a world such as ours. "Oh, hey," we say, "what could be bad about getting what you want?"

But what the advocates of getting what you want, ignoring centuries of Serbo-Croat experience and knowledge, fail to consider, of course, is that the baked potato will probably be lukewarm in the center; that everybody you have ever known will want a part of your winnings; that you'll become drug dependent, lose your job, your wife, your children, your home, and have to go to the Betty Ford Clinic and appear on Phil Donahue; that just as you're congratulating yourself on being able to appear in public in a bathing suit it will be discovered that there are certain side effects to your artificial sweetener, one of the more pleasant of which is death; that those phone calls are costing you four bucks a minute.

Because—as Margery Householder Taub and any Serbo-Croat worth his or her salt could have told you—the get-what-you-want advocates overlook the fact that every form of refuge has its price.

And that's what I was thinking on that stormy night as I prepared to take the garbage out to the stairwell. Every form of refuge has its price, I thought. Nothing is free in this world, as my mother also often said. You buy your ticket and you take your chances.

I tied up the black plastic bag.

And further combing through the files of folkloric philosophy, I remembered an old Oglala Sioux saying that goes: If you wish for snow, make sure you've got a warm cloak, dry feet, and plenty of meat put away.

I'd wished for snow. Wished, prayed, danced, and finally seeded the clouds. I'd thought—as many a poor bastard has thought in the past—that once I was married all my troubles would disappear. I could go back to my peaceful, quiet life and start answering the phone again.

The temperature dropped, the leaves fell from the trees, the geese flew south, the days grew short, the lake froze over, the snow grew high over the tepees. Then, and only then, huddled in a corner, rubbing two sticks together to try to get a fire going, did I realize my mistake. I hadn't checked my winter wardrobe. I'd forgotten to get in a couple of pairs of fur-lined boots. I was clean out of dried bison.

I am not—though it may be less than obvious at the moment—a complete idiot. I had appreciated the fact that if I claimed to have a wife, there were certain people who were going to expect me to produce her eventually. I knew that. I knew that Lonnie would be anxious to meet her. I knew that my sister would want to ascertain her maternal instincts. I knew that my mother would expect to buy more ravioli and set another place for family occasions.

I peered through the peephole. The corridor was clear. The garbage and I bolted for the stairs.

I might be afraid of running into anybody in my rudimentary Alma Huttenmeyer disguise, but I was even more afraid of running into Betsy Shopak as myself.

I dropped my bag beside the others and paused to catch my breath.

I'd known all that, but I'd still believed I could create the illusion. It was only now becoming clear to me that I couldn't keep this up for ever, or even for long. The question was: How much longer could I keep it up? Here I was, over four months later, still sneaking in and out of my own home, still jumping when the telephone rang, still afraid to run into anyone I knew. I'd managed to evade the hounds of matrimony, but only to wind up having to avoid busloads of curious tourists with their faces pressed against the windows, hoping to get a glimpse of my spouse. Worse. Now I had to watch every single move I made. Now nothing could be left to chance. I constantly had to build up my story, keep track of my lies. I had to remember if I'd told Barry that Alma was in Europe or that she was visiting her mother in Madison. I had to remember what the last excuse I'd given Candace for not coming to dinner was, and what my last three reasons for breaking a date with the Finer-Stepatos had been. I couldn't even afford to forget which cashier in which supermarket I'd told that my wife loved peanut butter cups, and which I'd told that she hated sweets. No longer could I just call up a pal and say, "Hey, you want to go to a game?" or "You want to meet up for a drink?" Because if it wasn't the week I was claiming that Alma was in town and we wanted to spend some precious time alone, it was the week I was claiming she was in Toronto and I had to hang around in case she called. I made no statement to my mother that I didn't immediately write down. Half the time, I had to pretend I wasn't home.

I listened at the door to the hallway. I could hear the jingle of keys and a slamming door. Someone was going for the elevator.

No more dropping by Jerry's on a Sunday morning with a bag of bagels. "Where's Alma?" Lonnie would want to know. "How come you never come over with her when she's around?" No more dropping by my mother's on a Thursday night when she always ordered Japanese and I had nothing else to do. "Where's that wife of yours?" my mother would want to know. "What kind of woman isn't anxious to meet her mother-in-law? What kind of marriage is this if she's always away?" No more going to the movies with Betsy Shopak on restless Friday nights. Betsy Shopak, right across the hall, was the enemy within.

The elevator doors slid open. Someone said, "Hi. Still raining out?" The elevator doors crunched closed.

Before, when I was an eligible bachelor with prospects, the questions and the attention had been a source of annoyance and frustration. But now the questions and attention that came with my altered state only drove me further and further into the isolation and loneliness of the secret life. With whom could I relax? Whom could I trust? What friend might not betray me? No longer a whale, I had become a double agent: 000.

Quiet had descended on the eighth-floor hall. I inched the door open so as not to make a sound, and stepped stealthily onto the polished blue tiles—and smack into Betsy Shopak.

"Hey! Betsy!" I cried, hoping my smile concealed the horror in my heart.

"Mike! I was just coming over to you."

Wellwellwell, what a pleasant surprise.

"What do you know about that?" I grinned. We both looked at my door. "What a piece of luck!"

"I really appreciate this, Mike, I really do," Betsy was saying in her earnestly grateful way as I ushered her in. "You're a lifesaver."

Physician, heal thyself.

"Don't mention it," I said, leading the way through the foyer—where, as part of the new marital decor, a woman's hat and sweater (donated, along with the raincoat, the skirt, and the trainers by Jerry from a box of things he was dropping off for the day care center's rummage sale) were hanging—through the living room—where Marissa's robe was casually flung over the arm of the sofa and her bowling shoes were strategically placed so that you had to see them or break a bone tripping over them—and into the kitchen, where the news was on the radio and the red pesto sauce was already simmering on the stove. "I—We have plenty of sugar."

"Flour," said Betsy. She smiled, though, to be honest, it was not one of her most effusive smiles. Since the morning I'd informed her of my hasty marriage ("Hey, Betsy, guess what?"), the teeth ration in her smiles had markedly decreased ("I'm very happy for you, Mike, I really am").

She looked around my orderly kitchen, where she had stood so many times before, borrowing a handful of fresh cilantro, asking my opinion on whether or not she should dye her hair, crying. "Gee," she said (noticing, I hoped, the mirror and the lip balm on the shelf over the sink, the woven basket hanging with the aprons, the plants huddled together at the window—inspired touches, if I said so myself), "it seems like ages since I've been in your apartment."

I opened the cupboard. It had been exactly four months, one week, and three days, since the night we went out for ice cream together and I told her I thought that I'd fallen in love. Two weeks and four days later, a mad honeymooner, I'd barred her entrance when she wanted me to show her how to work the timer she'd just bought on sale. "I'm really sorry, Betsy," I'd stammered, looking awkward and embarrassed (and feeling pretty awkward and embarrassed, the more complex bits of my scheme suddenly becoming clear to me as Betsy peered over my shoulder and sniffed the air), "but I'm kind of busy right now." "Oh, sure, Mike," she'd replied instantly. "Sure, Mike, I understand." After that I'd started being even busier. I bought perfume, and every now and then I'd spray a little in the hallway, just so Betsy would have no doubts as to just how busy I really was.

"I know what you mean," I said, lifting down the flour jar. "Time really does fly, doesn't it?" I winked. "When you're having fun."

Betsy picked up a bobby pin from a dish on the counter. (There were days when I couldn't help wondering if I wasn't, after all, some kind of genius. "Mike," I'd say to myself as I sprinkled bobby pins around the apartment, stuck another toothbrush in the holder next to mine, made space between canned goods and spices for low-calorie soups and salad dressings and a box of artificial sweetener, filled the drinks rack with diet cola and the freezer with Weight Watcher's meals, dumped a bag of makeup on top of the dresser, "you really would have made a great spy.") She looked toward the window, at the view of the alley, now obscured by three sprightly spider plants.

"I thought you hated houseplants," said Betsy.

"No," I said, shaking my head in a thoughtful manner, "no, I don't think I ever said that. I know I objected to them dropping things in my food, but I never said I hated them."

"Yes, you did," said Betsy. "You said they breed bugs."

I measured out the flour. "Oh, well." I laughed, just a little nervously. Experience and instinct told me that it was probably time to change the subject. We might be arguing about whether or not I'd once said something disparaging about succulants now, but we were about one step away from arguing about whether or not I had ever said I would never get married. ("You said you weren't ready," Betsy would say. "No, I didn't," I'd say. "Yes, you did," she'd say. "You said you weren't interested. You said you just wanted to be friends. You said marriage was an unnatural way for people to live." "I never said that," I'd say. "I've always had an open mind on the subject." "Oh no, you haven't," Betsy would say. "You said you'd rather be dead." "Betsy," I'd say, "I think you're exaggerating." "Oh no, I'm not," she'd say. And then she'd start to cry.) I leveled the flour with the back of a knife. "I guess maybe I've changed a little."

Betsy gave me this look, half shrewd, half hurt. "I guess maybe you have," she commented. "You're certainly not the person I used to know."

I couldn't quite bring myself to say that of course I wasn't, I had less hair. So I dumped the flour into a plastic container and said, "Tempus really does fugit. Hehhehheh."

Betsy twirled the bobby pin between her fingers for a second, in that hesitant, musing way that women do when they have a speech to deliver that they've been rehearsing for the past few weeks. And then she said, "You know, Mike, I promised myself I wasn't going to say anything to you, but after the other morning, when we walked to the bus together?, well, it was sort of like old times, and after that I started thinking it over, and I decided I owed it to myself to talk to you."

"Carpe diem," I muttered, as I wiped a little spilled flour from the counter.

The bobby pin fell back into the dish with a hollow ping. "I guess you don't realize it, but I was really upset that you didn't ask me to your wedding," said Betsy in a rush. "I know Jesus has changed things between us, well, that's what happens, isn't it?, but I thought you and I were special friends, that there were some things that wouldn't change."

It was this, of course, and not my wily ways, that explained why Betsy no longer turned to me when she needed a jar opened or ran out of conchigoliette or wasn't sure how to shell a walnut. This, and not my cleverness and skill at evasion, was why she hadn't been in my apartment in so many months. Beautiful in its simplicity.

"Betsy," I said, already sounding like the father my mother was hoping I might soon become, "Betsy, we are special friends. But the wedding was in Nevada, Betsy. Nevada's a long way to go for a glass of cheap champagne."

She picked up another pin and dropped it on the floor. "I know that, Mike," she said rather waspishly. "I meant when you got back here. The party you had when the two of you got home. You could've asked me and Jesus to come."

I snapped the lid on the flour. "What party?"

"Oh, come on, Mike, you know what party. I'm not stupid. Don't tell me you didn't have some kind of celebration." She lifted one small pearl earring from the dish and held it about an inch and a half in the air, her expression immaculately blank.

I plonked the container on the counter beside her. "For Chrissake, Betsy, what do I have to do, get down on my knees and swear it? There wasn't any damn party." Telling the truth, I have found, often makes a person sound peevish and devious. "Betsy, be reasonable.

Would I have a party and not invite *you*?" But oh the warmth and sincerity of a lie.

She let the earring drop. Plink. "Well, no, Mike . . . I guess . . . I mean, oh, I don't know, I'm so confused . . ." She was confused? "It's not that I really thought . . . it's just . . ." Betsy shrugged; Betsy's smile shrugged. "It's just that I miss you, you know? I don't see you at all anymore. You haven't even introduced me to Alma . . . It's almost like you're trying to avoid me."

Trying?

I shuffled uncomfortably under this new weight of guilt. Until about ten minutes ago I hadn't been trying, I'd been succeeding brilliantly. "Well, you know," I muttered, "things have been pretty hectic."

"This is what usually happens when somebody starts up a new relationship, isn't it?" There was something in the way she was staring out the window, something in the tilt of her chin and the tone of her voice, that made me feel as though we were in a movie. "All of a sudden they have no time for their friends."

I couldn't quite name the film, but I was sure it was in black and white and that both Bette Davis and Joan Crawford were in it. It seemed likely that some poor guy was shot at the end.

"Oh, come on, Betsy," I reasoned. "You would have acted just the same, if Jesus didn't spend most of his time looking through garbage cans."

"No, I wouldn't," said Betsy, truthfully. "I would never dump you the way you dumped me."

"I didn't dump you, Bets," I protested. "It's just that—"

"What, Mike? It's just what?"

"It's just that I've—we've—it's been a very busy period."

"Busy?" asked Betsy Shopak. Her laugh echoed. Her ponytail whipped through the air. "Michael, the president of the United States is busy, but even he finds the time to introduce his friends to his wife."

What had I really thought when I started all this? It's kind of hazy now, but I assume I thought that if I could keep the mothers, sisters, Lonnie Stepatos, and Betsy Shopaks of this world at bay long enough—for six months, say, or even a year, a not impossible feat,

I'd clearly convinced myself—then they'd sort of forget about Alma and the fact that they'd never met her. You know, kind of like when you start going bald. The first day you become aware of it, you panic. You can think of nothing else. Every time you pass a mirror or a window you check to see if another follicle has given up the fight. You're afraid to wash it. You're afraid to brush it. Your secretary asks you a question about rising payment schedules, and you say, "Thinning on top." The waiter asks you what you'd like to start, and you say, "Hair." Every time you pass a department store you nip in and buy another hat. You read all those ads in the papers that say, "Why Be Bald?" You secretly watch those hour-long testimonials for The Hair Center on late-night television. You sit shivering in the tub long after the water's drained away, counting those fine, limp strands caught in the plug hole. But after a year or two, you forget about it on a minute-to-minute basis. You don't touch your head the first thing upon waking in the morning. You don't jump every time light breaks behind you. You're surprised when you see old photographs in which you have a full head of hair. "Gee," you say, "so that's what I looked like."

So I guess that's what I thought would happen—that everyone would come to accept the fact that they'd never seen my wife, and that that would be that. What a jerk, right? You'd think I'd arrived with the morning rain.

"It's Alma's schedule, Betsy," I said, an anguished young husband who doesn't see enough of his bride himself. "It's inhuman." You might almost say fantastic.

Betsy's lip curled. "I thought you said she was a writer, not an astronaut."

And then one of Gracie's favorite songs came on the radio, and all at once the clear sweet voice of Marissa Alzuco singing "Living on a Prayer" could be heard in the bedroom.

Betsy's ears pricked up and her eyes peeled. "What's that?"

I said, "What?"

"Is that her?"

Deceit is the bag of potato chips of life. You open the bag, you say to yourself, I'm just going to have one and then I'm going to put it away—and then you eat the whole thing. Even when you're about to go out for an excellent and expensive meal. Even when you know they're going to make you sick, or the salt's going to play havoc with your blood pressure, or the fat's going to go straight into your arteries and turn to cement. You still end up with only six crumbs left, and all of those are scattered down the front of your shirt.

So it happened that, although it would have been both truthful and a hell of a lot easier to have said to Betsy, "What, are you crazy? Of course that's not Alma. It's Gracie—you remember Gracie, Betsy, it hasn't been that long," I didn't. Even though saying yes was to risk giving Betsy Shopak the opportunity to race into the bedroom and come face to face with Alma Huttenmeyer—small, gray, bright-eyed, and beaked—I didn't say no. I can see now that it was too late. I was already halfway through the bag by then, and there was no turning back. If I was thinking at all (which does seem unlikely), I was thinking that this would do it once and for all: Betsy wouldn't actually meet my new life's partner, but she'd think that she had. Another six months of never catching a glimpse of the new Mrs. Householder wouldn't make her suspicious. "After all," she'd assure herself, "this is a big city, people go for years without ever seeing the person who lives next door. I know she exists. I heard her singing in the bedroom."

I picked up the flour and thrust it into her hands. "Yes," I said, trying to look as though just the thought of my wife was giving me an erection that couldn't wait on social courtesies. "That's Alma."

Betsy turned toward the bedroom, and my heart did a somersault —even though, as far as I know, Betsy Shopak does not come from Krypton and can't see through walls. She put the flour back on the counter. "So can I meet her, Michael?"

I looked pained. "Gee, Betsy," I said, metaphorically stuffing another handful of chips into my face. "I know she's dying to meet you. I talk about you all the time, but she's got to catch a flight to Albuquerque in a couple of hours. There's a special Mudhead masked dance she has to see."

"I won't stay," said Betsy. "I just want to say hello."

How could someone who used to be so pleasant, agreeable, and amenable have become so insensitive and so stubborn so fast? New York City had a lot to answer for.

But a child raised in the Himalayas will know something about mountain climbing. A child reared by Arab nomads will not find Jones Beach sandy. I had been raised by a woman whose tenacity, resolution, obstinacy, and bloody-mindedness were legendary. I had suckled at the breast of a woman who had never once been brought to heel by a no-return-on-sale-goods policy. By a woman whose favorite phrase throughout my formative years was "Oh yes you will." Whose own first words, my grandmother had informed me, were "Oh no I won't." I was not the son of Margery Householder Taub for nothing.

I touched Betsy's shoulder, lightly. "I'll tell you what," I said. "Why don't I just tell her you're here?" Scattering potato chip crumbs in every direction, I dashed out of the kitchen. I opened the bedroom door. "Darling," I called, in clear, bell-like tones. "Darling, you're not going to believe who just dropped by. Betsy. That's right. Betsy from across the hall."

"Uh oh, Betsy," said Gracie, also in pretty clear, bell-like tones. And then she added, so there could be no doubt about her meaning, "Betsy, uh oh."

I entered the bedroom and shut the door behind me. "You've got to come out and meet her," I shouted at the wall between the room where we were and the room where Betsy waited. "Didn't I tell you how much you'll love Betsy? You two are really going to hit it off. I know you're in a rush, honey, but just come out for one minute."

"Betsy Wetsy," screamed Gracie. "Betsy Wetsy, get the Kleenex!" reviving our old in-joke. "Betsy Wetsy! Whatever you do, don't let her in!"

Everyone knows that the walls of your average Manhattan apartment are as thin as paper. If someone sneezes in Apartment C, someone blesses him in Apartment B. And so I could hear, almost as though it were happening beside me, the sound of an uncapped plastic container of flour being thrown against the spider plants,

and then the front door slammed so hard that a print fell off
the wall.

I looked at Gracie, who was sort of tilting off the roof of her cage.
"Shit," I said.

"Shit," said Gracie. She jumped onto my shoulder.

The telephone rang. Gracie and I both looked at it. "Let the machine
get it," I told her.

"*Ringringclickbeep*," said Gracie.

Ever since Lonnie made a crack about my not letting Alma answer
the phone, I'd put a new tape on the answering machine.

"I'm afraid neither Alma nor Michael can come to the phone at the
moment," said a husky, rather attractive female voice. "If you care
to leave your name and number after the tone, we'll get back to you
as soon as we can."

"Michael?" said Lonnie. Her voice sounded a little thick. "Michael?
Are you there?" She turned away from the receiver. "It's the machine," she said. "He has the machine on." I could hear voices in the
background, and then she shouted into the phone, "Mike? Mike? I
know you're there. I'm in the Village, at my women's group. I was
telling everyone how I still haven't met Alma but she goes with you
and Jerry to the gym all the time, and they agree that you're trying
to alienate us because we're women."

Jesus Christ, that was all I needed. What was wrong with Jerry,
telling Lonnie that he hung out with Alma? "What are you doing?"
I'd screamed at him. "Have you lost your mind?" "I'm trying to make
it believable," he'd argued. "You know what Lonnie's like. She'll get
really suspicious if neither of us ever meet her." It was good to see
that after all those years of marriage he knew her so well.

"I'm not taking no for an answer anymore," shouted Lonnie. "I
don't know what you and Jerry think you're playing at, but I'm
coming by." She slammed down the phone.

I started pulling on my shoes and putting out the lights. She could
come over, but I didn't have to be here.

The telephone rang again.

Gracie rang.

Feeling overwhelmed with regret, I picked up the receiver. "Five-five-five-four-five-nine-one," I said in the flat, lifeless voice of a man who can see that the writing on the wall probably includes his name.

"Michael?"

"Oh, hi, Mom," said Gracie, sounding just like me.

9

Mrs. Householder
Goes Public

If worse came to worst, I told myself (though it isn't easy to say now just what I thought "worst" might be), Betsy Shopak, Mrs. Sontag, and Lonnie Stepato could easily be handled by the simple expedient of moving. That's all, an old-fashioned moonlight flit. All I had to do to get them off my back once and for all was pack up everything and go somewhere else: a different building, a different street, a different borough, a different state, another country, an unexplored galaxy—it wouldn't be that hard. "No sweat, Gracie," I assured my tiny coconspirator. "Maybe we can even find someplace with a tree. You'd like that, wouldn't you? A tree of your own?"

"Where'd you put the gun?" asked Gracie, who had, perhaps, been watching too many movies with me lately. "Where'd you put the gun?"

But you can never move away from your mother.

Remember when you were a little kid, and you thought that if you did things in secret that you knew you shouldn't do—you know, like finishing off the chocolate cake or reading your sister's diary—God would never find out? Remember what a downer it was to discover that you were wrong? That He knew things you were thinking even before you thought them? Well, your mother is just like God. She knows what you're thinking before you think it, and she can always find you if she really wants to. Don't even contemplate changing your name, dying your hair, having a nose job, and becoming an insurance salesman in Utah. It might fool the Mafia or the FBI, but your mother would know. No matter where you go, even if you move to the Bronx, your mother will track you down. She'll run into somebody in the deli who saw you on a bus that morning. She'll just feel like a little drive down Pelham Parkway, and there you'll be. She'll remember the name of your dentist. You'll send her a card at Christmas and she'll trace you through the postmark. Pressed flat with guilt, you'll phone her for her birthday, not realizing that, expecting this, she's had the phone tapped. Your mother wouldn't be put off by a move to Bulgaria or Jupiter.

"You're moving to Bulgaria?" she'd say. "Fine, I'll be over next month. Make sure you dust under the bed."

"You're moving to Jupiter?" she'd say. "I'll be there for Christmas. Do you want me to bring my fruitcake?"

And as far as my mother was concerned, worse was coming to worst pretty quickly. Her patience, never great, was visibly wearing thin. How many times could Alma be away? How many times when Alma wasn't away could we be so busy or so tired that we couldn't make the short train ride to visit her? How many times a year could I count on my parents going on a Caribbean cruise for a month? How often could I meet my mother and forget to bring any photographs of my wife? How many times could my mother drop by unexpectedly and find no one home?

"Are you hiding something from me?" asked my mother, in the voice she had used to ask that question for as long as I had lived.

"Hiding something?" I echoed. "What are you talking about, 'hiding something'? What would I hide?"

From behind her, in the depths of the Taub homestead, I could hear Barry calling, "For Pete's sake, Marge, leave the boy alone."

It has never been part of my mother's code to leave the boy alone.

"You're the one who was so good at English," said my mother. "You know what the verb 'to hide' means. Is there something about Alma that you're keeping from us, Michael? Something about her that you think we wouldn't understand?"

"You mean like is she a Jehovah's Witness or does she wear a nose ring?"

"You know what I mean, Michael. You know exactly what I mean. And Barry and I want you to know that we're very hurt by your attitude. You should know that the last thing that concerns us is a person's age, religion, or ethnic background."

"I know that, Mom, and I'm—"

"That's not it, is it, Michael?" she interrupted. "She's not a Jehovah's Witness, is she?"

Something would have to be done about my mother. And pretty damn quick.

"Alex," I pleaded, "you have to help me."

"Don't do it, Allie," said Sara. "It's a stupid idea."

"It is not a stupid idea," I protested. "It's a brilliant idea." I made my expression stern. "Alex, listen to me. If you hadn't stolen Sara away from me in the first place, none of this would ever have happened. I'd be a happy man today, with three kids, a Land Rover, and a playroom in the basement."

Alex looked at Sara. Sara looked bored.

"A Land Rover?" sneered Sara. "Get real, Michael. You can't even drive a stick shift."

"I think you owe me something, Alex," I persisted. "I really do."

"Don't listen to him," warned Sara. "Nobody stole anybody away from anyone. He's full of shit, and he knows it."

"I don't know it," I said. I grabbed Alex's arm. "Alex, I'm begging

you. You're my only hope." Which, indeed, she was. My mother
would remember Sara. She'd liked her. She was always asking after
her. "How's that nice girl you turned into a lesbian?" my mother
always said. "You like me, Alex," I reminded her. "Don't forget how
much you like me."

She shoved me out of her way and turned her attention to the salad
she was casually murdering. "Mike, please, of course I like you, but
you really are behaving like a child."

"A very small child," qualified Sara.

"I know this must all sound a little crazy—"

"A little crazy?"

They hooted in unison. And derision.

Sara, always a little on the cool, overrational side, if you want the
truth (and not really the type to provide children with toys to scatter
all over the house), recovered first. "A little crazy, Mikey? Mikey,
that's like saying the neutron bomb is a little dangerous."

Alex shook her head sadly. I could tell that, unlike Sara, she was
touched by my plight and not unsympathetic to my request. "I'm
really beginning to worry about you, you know."

"Once, Alex. Just one time. A few short hours to save a man from
a miserable life. Or death."

Alex shook some bottled dressing over the salad. "I don't
know . . ."

She was talking to me, but she was looking at Sara. She shook quite
a lot of bottled dressing over the salad.

"Don't let him get to you with those big brown eyes," said Sara,
dumping what looked suspiciously like a jar of crunchy peanut butter
over the chicken. "Michael thinks that all he has to do is look sad
and you'll do whatever he wants." She slid the poor chicken under
the broiler. I wondered if it was too late to suggest eating out.

"I don't think that, Alex, I swear I don't. I'm asking you as another
human being. As one kind and sensitive person with liberal tendencies
to another. Please, Alex, do this for me and I'll never ask you for
another favor again as long as I live. I might even forgive you for not
defending me against Snow Lazarro."

Sara groaned. "I knew I should never have told you she thinks you're too short. You're so vain."

I bridled. "You should never have told me she thought I was a dwarf," I said.

Alex patted my shoulder. "But I did defend you," she assured me. "I told her what a great guy you are." She winked. "I told her I didn't see what size matters when you're lying down."

Sara threw a couple of shrubs of parsley (her idea of an attractive garnish for chicken drowned in crunchy peanut butter) at me. "It wasn't our fault you two didn't hit it off, you know. You're the one who came over as stuffy and fussy."

Me? Stuffy and fussy? "Stuffy and fussy? Now what are you talking about? Not only did she treat me as if she thought I was pond scum, *you* told me she thought I was physically unacceptable."

Alex shot Sara a look. Sara shrugged. "I was trying to spare your feelings."

What would she do if she wanted to save my life, shoot me? "Thanks a lot, Sara. That certainly cheers me up."

"And it wasn't really personal that she treated you like pond scum," said Alex. "That's just the way Snow is. She was shy."

Sara took her other idea of an attractive garnish, a stale jar of paprika, from the spice rack. "If it's any consolation, Mike, she really did think you were short, too."

She was sidetracking me. She was deliberately winding me up so I'd forget my mission. I turned back to Alex. "Look at me, Alex," I pleaded. "Look at me. Wives aren't the only people who can be battered and emotionally scarred."

Alex stared at the drooping lettuce and butchered tomatoes and the less than youthful cucumbers, all of them miserably sinking in something pink. "I don't know, Mike . . . I really don't think . . ."

"Wait a minute," said Sara. "Maybe we're being a little hasty here." I could hear the change in her voice. She was thinking. She was working out a deal. She shouldn't have been a scientist, she should have been a lawyer. She turned to me, unsmiling and shrewd. "What are you willing to do for us?"

"Anything."

"Anything?"

I was desperate, beyond reason and self-respect. "Anything at all."

"What are you thinking?" asked Alex.

Sara smiled. To look at her, you would have thought that cotton candy wouldn't melt in her mouth. "I was thinking about the s-p-e-r-m."

S-p-e-r-m?

They exchanged a significant look.

"I can spell, you know," I said. "I do know what s-p-e-r-m means."

"My God!" Alex was beaming. "What a brilliant idea! Sara, that's a brilliant idea!"

Sara was beaming. "I know it is. I can't believe I didn't think of it before. It wasn't until he made that crack about children that I had this sudden image . . . You know."

Alex hugged Sara. "This is absolutely the answer to our prayers! I mean, we already know him, and like him and everything."

Sara hugged Alex. "Uh huh. And except that he's short and not extraordinarily good-looking and tends to be a little stuffy and has an attitude about his mother, he's perfect."

What a sense of humor.

"Sperm?" I inquired.

But the deal, of course, had already been struck. In my experience, that's the way it is with women. They make their decisions, and then, if you're lucky, they let you know what they are. My mother's one last wish before she passed on to that great shopping mall in the sky—that I have children—was going to come true. Though not quite in the way she had hoped. What Alex and Sara were talking about was one wife in exchange for one fertilized ovum. They had plenty of ova, but they lacked s-p-e-r-m. And without that, they could never become mothers themselves—and run roughshod over some other poor little bastard's life. I ask you: What chance has love and romance in a world like ours?

"So who's the guy who lives across the hall?" asked Alex. She was sitting on the stepstool in a corner of the room, watching me from a safe distance as I put the trimmings on the broccoli mousse. Safe, that is, from the mousse's point of view. Wife for a day or no, she wasn't going to touch anything in my kitchen.

"Big guy? Sandy hair? Wears a baseball cap with a dead cockroach on it?"

"That's the one," said Alex. She looked over at the cookbooks as though she'd never seen anything quite like them before. Which probably she hadn't.

"He doesn't live there," I informed her. "He just rents the bed."

"He's very sexy, isn't he?"

I nearly dropped the radish rosettes. "Sexy? Are you kidding? O'Brien's the model before the missing link."

She pulled a book from the shelf, skimming through it without interest. "You're just jealous because he's tall and he has a full head of hair."

"I am not," I said testily. "I think the man looks like a thug."

She eyed me speculatively. "A lot of women like men to have a little edge of danger about them, you know," said the professor of women's studies.

"Oh sure," I sneered. "Next you're going to tell me that the Butcher of Broadway would make some woman a wonderful husband."

She put back *Classic Sauces* and took down something else. "I said an edge of danger, not clinical psychosis." She paused thoughtfully. "Women like a little wildness, you know. A little recklessness. Because they're so earthy and have to be so responsible. It gives them balance."

"We're talking about Ms. Lazarro again, aren't we?" That whole evening still rankled.

"She rides with bikers, Mike," said Alex. "I guess it was silly of us to think she might be attracted to a man who alphabetizes his spices."

I put the last carrot daisy in place, and put the mousse into the refrigerator. "They're not alphabetized," I snapped at her. "They're by frequency of use."

"That, too," said Alex.

I opened the oven door. "And anyway, for your information, Ms. Lonelyhearts, I wouldn't want her attracted to me. She's bright and everything, but she's got a lousy attitude." I slid the baking tray onto the counter.

Alex leaned forward. "Umm," she said. "That smells great. What is it?"

"Cheese crackers."

She gave me a disbelieving look. "You *make* your own cheese crackers? Michael, you can buy them in boxes."

"I know you can buy them in boxes, Alexandra. But they're not the same."

Our eyes met for just one moment. I could tell she was wondering what implications this had for her and Sara's child. Maybe they should take their chances with a sperm bank after all. "Michael," said Alex, "it all winds up as shit, you know."

I took the spatula from its hook on the wall with a philosophical sigh. "Doesn't everything?" I wondered aloud.

My mother thought that Alma was even smarter, funnier, more charming, and more attractive than I'd described her. "You know what men are like," said my mother. "They understate everything, don't they?"

"Unless it concerns them." Alex laughed.

My mother laughed too. "Isn't that the truth?" she roared. "You should see Barry when he gets a splinter . . . you'd think he'd had his arm chewed off by rats. And as for Michael . . ." She could barely go on, she was laughing so hard. "Just you wait until he gets a cold . . ."

"If they had to give birth, there'd be no overpopulation problem, you can be sure of that," howled Alex.

With the skill and effortlessness of the true professional, my mother shifted gears. Had she been a racing car driver and not a mother, she would have dominated Le Mans for decades. "And how about you, Alma? How do you feel about giving birth?"

"I feel very positive about it," said Alex. "Michael and I have been talking about it a lot recently. Haven't we, Mikey?"

I tasted the sauce for dill.

"Isn't it time to open the wine?" asked my mother.

My mother liked the feminine touches Alma had brought to the apartment. "Those plants look really lovely at the window," said my mother. "I've always thought there was something too clinical about this kitchen."

"I know what you mean," said Alex. "Everything's so *organized*." She shuddered. "But they're not my plants," she continued, in no danger of completely losing herself in her role. "They're Michael's. You know how he likes to fuss over things."

My mother said she knew. Michael got that from the Householders.

"I am not fussy," I said shortly. I opened the freezer to get out the iced glasses. "Why don't you two go keep Barry company in the living room while I fix the drinks?" I suggested.

My mother sighed. "Because if we go in the living room with Barry we'll wind up talking about small businesses." She turned back to Alex. "Barry's a wonderful man, but his conversation's a little limited. And anyway, he's much happier reading the paper." She looked over my shoulder. "Weight Watchers?" she queried, sounding shocked. "Don't tell me *you're* on a diet, Alma."

"Oh, not me," said Alex quickly, and there was genuine horror in her voice as well. "Those are Mike's. I don't believe in dieting. I think the pressure put on women to conform to an adolescent-male idea of the perfect female body is one of the greatest evils of our society. Who gives a damn what size your hips are?"

For a second there, I thought my mother was going to applaud.

"I can't tell you how good it is to hear a young woman actually come out and say that," said my mother. She took the drink I handed her without so much as an absentminded nod in my direction. "You know, one of the happiest days of my life was when I realized that I was middle-aged and it didn't matter anymore what I looked like in a pair of slacks. And you know what I did? I took myself out for lunch and had the first guilt-free meal I'd had since I was twelve."

"Bravo!" cried Alex. "Bravo!" She threw her arms around my mother. "That's exactly what I mean."

"But Michael," said my mother, returning from the abstract to the concrete without a blink, "now, you're right about him." She reached over and patted my stomach, not, perhaps, as hard and flat as it was in the days when Jerry and I had worked out once a week instead of hanging out in Jo Jo's, eating peanuts and drinking beer. "He should watch himself, you know. His father died of a bad heart."

"Wow," said Barry with a satisfied smile and a happy grin, "that was a great meal." He turned to Alma. "My compliments to the chef."

"Oh, don't thank me," said Alex, not exactly unpleasantly, but in the way you would if someone had complimented you on something that you didn't particularly care to be associated with. "That was all Michael. I just watched." She turned to my mother. "Did you know that he actually *makes his own cheese crackers*?"

"You want to know what's really funny?" asked my mother. "What's really funny is that when he was little, he wouldn't eat anything but canned ravioli." She rolled her eyes. "And I'll tell you another thing," she said (almost, incredibly enough, as though she were proud of the fact). "He certainly doesn't get all this gourmet nonsense from me. I hate cooking." She knocked back her brandy. "Always have. Who wants to spend hours of her life slaving away in the kitchen, chopping up onions and trying to stuff mushrooms—really, Alma, have you ever tried to stuff a mushroom?, the very idea of putting something that doesn't want to be contained into something that was never meant to contain it . . . it's crazy, isn't it?—when they could be doing something useful . . ."

"Girdles," said Alex.

This statement seemed just a wee bit enigmatic to me—and, I could tell from his expression, to Barry as well. But not to my mother.

"Exactly," said my mother, "another male invention." She helped herself to the brandy. I wondered if I should point out that that was a male invention too.

"I'll tell you what," said Alex, getting to her feet without so much as a glance in my direction, without even a second's pretense that she thought that since she had contributed nothing to the evening so far but quite a lot of talk and a few critical comments about cheese crackers, it might be nice if she got off her butt and did something now.

"Why don't we go sit on the couch and give the boys a chance to clean up?"

It was as rare to see my mother speechless as it was to bump into a rock fowl in Central Park, but I missed the moment because I was too busy being speechless myself. What was she talking about, "give the boys a chance to clean up"?

My mother recovered first. "Why, Alma," she said, smiling at her husband and her son, and looking as if her daughter-in-law had just invented the wheel, "now, isn't that a good idea?"

Alex immediately picked up another conversational thread. "It's a lot like housework, isn't it?" she asked as they strolled together to the sofa. "You get everything all clean and neat, and then what happens? You haven't even put the vacuum away and it's all dirty again."

Barry stared over the empty plates and cups and glasses and across the table at me, like a bank teller from New Jersey who has just gotten off the stage coach in Texas and been handed a gun and told he has a duel with Billy the Kid in an hour. You must be kidding, the teller is thinking. This can't really be happening, not to me. The teller knows which end of the gun to hold and which to point only because he's seen other people doing it. Barry knew there was a sink in the kitchen only because it was next to the refrigerator.

"Well," said Barry.

"Well," said I.

"Oh, honey," said Alex. "How about a little more coffee when you have a chance?"

Most of the time, the wife of a literary agent, unlike the wife of a politician or corporate executive, is not expected to have a profile. She is not expected to entertain important clients or open hospitals. She is not expected to talk to the other wives about clothes and children while her husband talks to the other men about money, golf, and crushing the unions. No one cares what her opinions on law and order, the drug problem, or working mothers are. No one cares how much she spends on dresses or how many pairs of shoes she owns. No one wants to interview her astrologer. The literary agent's wife—

like the literary agent's children, dog, and electric drill—is something
he's supposed to keep quiet about and safe at home.

Most of the time. But not always.

Every now and then there comes into the life of the literary agent
an event or function to which the agent's spouse is not only invited,
but which the agent's spouse is actually expected to attend—in neat
attire and sobriety, with a positive attitude and a steady smile.

The event in my life was the party to celebrate the agency's twenty-
fifth birthday.

"Of course you'll be bringing what's-her-name," said my boss.

My smile held firm. "Who?"

"You know . . ." She snapped her fingers. "Your wife. What's her
name again?"

"Oh, right, my wife."

"I did hear that you got married, didn't I, Michael?"

Oh, yes, Vanessa had heard. Even the cleaning crew and the woman
in the snack bar downstairs had heard. (The cleaning crew had wished
me *buena suerte* and the counterperson had made a lewd joke about
honeymoons.) Vanessa had also heard that I'd married someone who
was neither a close relative, friend, nor important client of hers. She
had also witnessed the arrival of three dozen tiger lilies in the office
when Elizabeth Beacher heard, and had read the note attached: "Of
all sad words of tongue and pen, the saddest are these, it might have
been." The fact that my bride was none of the women Vanessa had
been actively backing had led to a certain coolness in the office, a
certain lessening of the enthusiasm with which she greeted me on a
Monday morning, a certain tapering off of the hints that I might be
up for my partnership at last, a complete cessation of social invitations.
All of this meant that when Vanessa said, "Of course you'll be bringing
what's-her-name," it was tantamount to her saying, "Bring her or
think of career retraining."

"Alma." I said the name in something between a whisper and a
bleat.

"What?"

"Alma. Her name is Alma."

"Great." Vanessa smiled and put on her serious, I'm-thinking-of-expanding-the-agency-and-taking-on-a-partner expression. "I really think it would be a good idea if you brought her. Alma." She lightly touched my shoulder. "I can't wait to meet her."

Or she you.

Jesus Christ.

Now what was I going to do?

"For the love of God, Jerry, if I could do it myself, I would."

"It might be a little tricky," said Jerry, "but I'm sure there must be a way—"

"Jerry!" I was groveling and shouting at the same time. "Jerry, you know I wouldn't ask you if I weren't desperate. Totally and completely desperate."

Jerry dropped a shot glass of whisky into his beer. He used to be a Miller man—three cans and a bag of roasted peanuts used to be his limit—but somehow, over the months of drinking at Jo Jo's, his habits had changed.

"No," said Jerry, not for the first or even the tenth time. There was nothing whispery or bleating or indecisive about his tones. "Absolutely, positively no. Why can't you get Alex again?"

"Because Alex refuses." I didn't add that this was a combination of outrage because I had criticized her performance ("If you ask a person to drag you out of the Atlantic, Michael, you don't then tell her how she should have done it!") and genuine affection for my mother ("I'm not going to go on duping that wonderful woman"). "You know what she's like, Jer. She's nice and everything, but she is a little on the selfish side. Self-sacrifice isn't in her nature. That's why she's in Women's Studies."

He chugged down a third of his depth charge. "Self-sacrifice isn't in my nature either, Mike. That's why I'm a guy."

"But, Jerry," I reasoned, "Alex is not my best friend. You're my best friend. You're supposed to stick by me in my hour of need."

He chugged down the second third of his drink. He shook his head.

His eyes met mine. "Mike, my man," said my best friend in the whole world, "sticking by you in your hour of need is one thing. Dressing in drag and pretending to be your wife is something else."

I signaled Lucifer, the barman, for another round. "Jerry, will you listen to me? Just listen, please? It's going to be at night. On a boat. Almost everyone on board will be writers trying to drink as much as they can and talk about themselves and publishers trying to look more important than each other. All you have to do is wave at Vanessa from across the room, and then you can spend the rest of the time in the toilet if you want."

He chugged down the last third. "You mean I can spend the rest of the time in the ladies' room, don't you?" His eyes were cold and hard. "Listening to conversations about late periods and yeast infections."

I ran my hand through the remains of my hair. "Jesus, Jerry, don't be such a sexist dork. You know women don't talk about things like that. They talk about the causes of aberrational male behavior and quantum mechanics."

Jerry stared into his empty glass. "That just shows you how long it's been since you shared your home with a woman, Mike. Where I come from, it's all bleeding, piss, and diaphragms."

"Jerry, I'm your oldest friend. I'm your blood brother, for Pete's sake." I took his hand across the table, not the sort of thing a man does lightly in a place like Jo Jo's. "Jerry, don't tell me you've forgotten how we cut ourselves with our Boy Scout knives. Don't tell me you've forgotten the promise we made. Don't tell me you've forgotten whose room you hid in for three days when you ran away from home that time. Don't—"

"Forget it, Mike. I won't do it."

"But, Jer—"

He shook his hand free. "Mike, I've seen this movie before. And I never thought it was funny the first twenty times I saw it." He raised his eyes to mine. "And I never thought it was convincing. It wasn't convincing when Cary Grant did it. It wasn't convincing when Jack Lemmon did it. It wasn't convincing when Dustin Hoffman did it.

And it sure as hell wouldn't be convincing if I did it." He raised one eyebrow. "Which I'm not doing."

"Yes, it would be, Jerry, it would be convincing. I know it would. Your impersonation of Shirley Bassey used to fool everyone, remember? Everybody said your impersonation of Shirley Bassey was nothing short of inspirational."

His expression turned to one of pity. "Mike, everybody was always shit-faced when I did my Shirley Bassey impression, including me. Who'd know if it was good or not?"

I thumped the table top. "Well, what do you think?" I asked excitedly. "They'll all be shit-faced at this party, too. It'll be dark, we'll be on a boat, and everybody'll be drunk as skunks." I thumped the table top a second time. "And let's not forget," I said, winding up the case for the defense, "you took ballet lessons for years."

"Eight months, Mike. I took ballet lessons for eight months. To improve my game. And I hated every damn minute of it." He pointed an accusatory finger at me. "And I was lousy at it, too. It did nothing for my game but give the other guys something to taunt me with when it was my turn at bat."

So was that my fault?

"And you have a sister," I rallied.

He gave me a look that twenty years or so ago, in what I could see now was the golden decade of our friendship, he would have been incapable of giving me. "Mike," he sighed, sounding as he sometimes sounded when he was explaining something to Lonnie for the third time, "I've got a cat, too. And I used to have a hamster. You think I could get away with pretending to be a hamster, Mike?"

I had to struggle to remember where I was and keep myself together. Men might beat the hell out of each other in Jo Jo's, and they might eat glass, and they might drink twenty-four pints of beer in one sitting; they might throw up on the table, and they might carve someone's initials on their foreheads, but they did not cry.

"Jerry, please. You're my best friend." Not ever. "Jerry, if you didn't steal Sophie Lumbucco from me the minute I turned my back, it's unlikely that any of this would have happened."

Charley Ray looked up from his card game. "I think you should do it, Jer," said Charley Ray, a man of few words but all of them well chosen.

"Me, too," contributed Bongo.

"Oh, yeah?" snarled Jerry. "And why is that exactly?"

Charley Ray shrugged, much as an astrophysicist when asked why he believes in God might shrug, as if to say, "There are some things that are simply beyond our feeble understanding and ability to comprehend."

"Because he's your buddy," said Bongo.

In the end, Jerry did decide that we men should stick together. "After all," he finally admitted, "when you get to the bottom line, who else do we have? Who else can we really count on when the chips are down?"

But this attitude of sticktogetherness did not arise because Jerry and I were buddies. Not because we'd been best friends since grade school. Not because we'd mingled our blood in his bedroom one summer afternoon in 1964 (and ruined his bedspread trying to bleach out the stains with Clorox—boy, was Mrs. Finer mad). It was not because we were once lost together in the woods surrounding Camp Shining Water for thirteen long and primarily dark hours with nothing to eat but a Three Musketeers bar and a package of Hostess Cupcakes that someone who couldn't distinguish the cry of an owl from the cry of a werewolf had stood on.

No, Jerry's reluctant recognition of the loyalty and support a fellow owes his best and oldest pal came about because he'd been having an affair with Connie Schmidmore for roughly a year and suddenly realized that maybe he was going to need a little male support of his own.

Who the hell is Connie Schmidmore? you ask. It was a question that immediately occurred to me as well.

"Connie who?" I said. "Where the hell did she come from?"

Charley Ray rolled his eyes.

Connie Schmidmore came from Brooklyn. She was a divorcée with two small children who, partly to save money and partly because she had read somewhere (the heart to ask if that somewhere might possibly have been *How to Get Mr. Right to Pop the Question* was, I readily confess, not mine) that hardware stores and lumberyards were good places to go if you wanted to meet men, began frequenting Cooper's.

It started out innocently enough, said Jerry—a point that was, of course, guaranteed to gain my sympathy. Who knew more about innocent beginnings than I? She asked his advice about shelves for her little boy's room. Bingo.

In a place the size of a landing field, packed to the rafters with men with pencils behind their ears, nails in their pockets, and car keys jangling from their belts, what made her single out Jerome Finer from all the rest? He is slight and boyish-looking, and therefore approachable and unthreatening from a female point of view. Or, in her own words, he didn't look like his truck was double-parked. His wife had trained him not to treat unaccompanied women as though they were either part of lunch, terminally stupid, or invisible. Or, in her own words, she knew instinctively that he would neither make a pass nor make her feel dumb. So she asked him about cheap but practical shelving, and he told her. The next time she bumped into him, she blushed shyly and admitted that she hadn't had the nerve to use the drill yet, what if it went through a pipe? He gave her some more expert advice. The next time he offered to carry the tiles for the floor of her daughter's room to the car for her. He said he figured he could probably stop by sometime, she wasn't that far from his office, and show her how to use the drill. There was nothing to replacing a floorboard, he assured her, it was all a question of knack. The difference between rawl plugs and toggle bolts? My God, could he tell her the difference between rawl plugs and toggle bolts!

Connie Schmidmore was the reason Jerry never finished the loft. So he'd have excuses for seeing her, he started undoing things he'd already done; redoing things that were perfectly all right. Like Penelope unraveling her weaving by night, Jerry Finer started loosening tiles and unscrewing bolts.

"I don't know," said Jerry, "it just sort of took me over. It was a little like falling off a log. One minute you're sitting there, gazing out at the view, and the next minute you're flat on your back in squirrel shit and there's a pine cone jabbing into your spine."

"But, Jerry," I reasoned, "you're a married man. What about Lonnie? What about Ethan?"

"For Chrissake, Mike, what are you all of a sudden, my mother? I do know I'm married. It just so happens that that's the first thing I told Connie, if you want to know the truth. I said, 'Sure I know what you want. I just finished doing my little boy's room. He's four, too.' "

But what chance did Jerry have against the combined efforts of Connie Schmidmore's loneliness, vulnerability, and charms and his own powerful masculine sexual drive?

It's funny, isn't it? A man can survive months, even years, of imprisonment and torture, starvation, sensual and emotional deprivation, and grueling hardships without buckling or losing his integrity and principles. But put a woman in the same room with him for a couple of hours and his will power, strength of purpose, and inner resolve all become just so much sand being blown across the beach by a wild and steady wind.

"What was I supposed to do?" asked Jerry. "Chop it off? Is that what you would've done, Mike? Chopped it off?"

"You're lucky you're not married to my Chrissy," said Charley Ray. "She'd chop it off for you."

I was more sympathetic. "No, Jerry," I replied. "I can see that that would've been a little drastic. I just don't understand why you didn't ignore her."

"Ignore her? How could I ignore her? Mike, if it hadn't been Connie it would have been someone else. They're all over the place, Mike. Everywhere you go. You know that. That's why you got married."

"I thought it was because you were queer," said Bongo.

"Shut up, Bongo," said Charley Ray.

"Yeah, okay," I admitted, "I do know that, but I still don't understand why you didn't just tell her, 'Thank you very much, Connie, I'm very flattered by your attention, but I'm a happily married man and I have to go home now. Bye. See you around.' "

He looked pained; exasperated. "But, Mike," he whined, "she wanted me. I'm going to be middle-aged soon. Maybe no one's ever going to want me again."

"So what?" I asked. "Look at all the women who have wanted me. I know I had a few flings, but you don't see me jumping into bed with every woman who looks at me twice. You don't see me letting my dick rule my head."

"Yeah, well," said my best friend in the world. "That's you, isn't it?"

"What do you mean, that's me?"

"Yeah, well," said Jerry. "Lonnie could never get over that you iron your sheets. She's always wondered if you didn't have, you know, some latent tendencies."

"Only homicidal ones."

Bongo and Charley Ray laughed.

"So I'll help you," said Jerry, "as long as you stand by me."

"What do you mean, stand by you?"

"You know," said Jerry, "stand by me. You know, a lot of the times I was with Connie, well, you know . . . Lonnie thinks I was with you."

I stared at Jerry. It was the same high forehead, the same sharp cheeks, the familiar gray eyes and lopsided mouth. And yet I felt as though I'd never really seen him before. "You told Lonnie you were with me?"

"Well, I had to tell her I was somewhere, didn't I? She was starting to get suspicious. You know how nosy she is." He appealed to Charley Ray. "You think Chrissy's tough," he told him. "But she's not tougher than Lonnie. Lonnie would disembowel me if she ever found out." His upper lip broke out in sweat. "One time she even found some lipstick on my chin," he gibbered.

My jaw dropped slightly. "That's why you told her Alma was coming to the gym with us!"

He nodded.

What a pal.

I stood up to go to the john. I leaned over the table toward him.

"You'd better start thinking of what you're going to wear." I smiled. "Darling."

He decided to wear this jumpsuit thing of Lonnie's that he found at the back of her closet.

"I'm not so sure," I said, sitting on the bed, appraising him. "I don't think they're wearing them this year."

"Well, I am," snapped Jerry. "It's the only thing I could find that completely obscures my body and has pockets big enough to keep my hands in."

"Do the voice."

Jerry looked agonized. "I don't think I can, Mike. The only thing I ever really did as Shirley Bassey was the old Burger King jingle."

"Try it."

"It sounds pretty funny at three in the morning after a fifth of Jack Daniels, but—"

"Try it."

"Hold the pickles . . ." he half-sang, half-spoke, "hold the lettuce . . . special orders don't upset us . . ."

It was great. I applauded. "You haven't lost it, Jer," I said sincerely. "The old magic lives on."

"Yeah," said Jerry, "as long as nobody asks me about anything but hamburgers I'll be fine." He adjusted his wig. His was a mass of curls and spirals—much darker, fuller, and more stylish than mine—and it managed to conceal a large part of his face. All things considered, it didn't look half bad.

"You know," I said, "except that she's thinner and a little shorter, and doesn't cover up that much of her body unless she's drying herself off after a bath, you look a little like Cher."

"I haven't put my shoes on yet," said Jerry.

It was raining, a fact my new wife took as an omen.

"You see?" she grumbled as we snuck down the stairs. "I'm telling you, Mike, the gods aren't smiling on this venture. We should give it up while we still can."

"It's just raining a little, Jerry. It isn't the bloody Flood."

We stood in the lobby, side by side, or head to shoulder, watching the people of New York duck for cover.

She pulled up the collar on Connie Schmidmore's pink plastic raincoat. "If my foundation's washed away my beard will start to show," she said, softly but firmly.

I took her by the elbow. "So all right, already, we'll take a cab."

"Are you planning to wear those sunglasses all night?" I asked as, arm in arm, we raced toward the boat. "For God's sake, Jer, not only is it dark, but it's pouring. People are going to think I beat you or that you're a drug addict if you keep those damn glasses on."

"I don't care what they think," snarled my beloved. "Waxing my knuckles is one thing, but I'm not plucking my eyebrows for anyone."

This sudden streak of aggressive feminism was a little distressing. "You're not drinking depth charges tonight, are you?"

Even though I couldn't see it, I could tell that the look he gave me was the same one he'd given me the time I lost the league series by pitching Albie Carlsen a home run in the last inning when the bases were loaded and the score was six to six. "Champagne cocktails," he sneered. "Because I like the way the bubbles tickle my nose."

"Great. And you will, you know . . ."

Jerry disengaged his arm from mine and jammed his hands into his pockets as we approached the gangplank. "I will what?"

I wasn't sure what I wanted to say. I looked at Jerry, got up like a police decoy, and I thought of Betsy Shopak, who was roughly his height and build. Something was wrong. It wasn't just the way he walked, or the fact that he had to stay in shadow and talk like Shirley Bassey. It was something more subtle, something I couldn't quite put my finger on. All I knew was that, primary and secondary sex characteristics aside, if Betsy Shopak had been playing my wife, I wouldn't have had a moment's worry or a single qualm; I wouldn't have had so much as the flicker of a second thought. And yet Jerry was smarter and more sophisticated than Betsy. If anybody asked Betsy what she liked to read, she'd probably say, "I really liked that movie about the secretary, but I'm not sure who wrote it." If someone asked Jerry, he'd say, "Updike, Atwood, Pynchon, that guy who wrote the book about the hat." Jerry knew me far better than Betsy Shopak ever could. If someone asked Betsy what my favorite food was, she would say, "Um, uh, well, he really likes chocolate doughnuts, don't you, Michael?" But if Jerry was asked, he'd say unhesitatingly, "Refried beans with green chili sauce and pickled red onions and sour cream, but it gives him indigestion unless it's made with pinto beans." If someone asked Betsy Shopak if we were planning to start a family, she would say, "Well, Michael doesn't really like kids that much," but Jerry, father of my godchild, knew better. I grabbed his arm, as a dank, black terror had suddenly grabbed hold of my heart and lungs. I looked at him hard, hoping I was making eye contact. "Just re-member that we're not at Jo Jo's, okay?"

"What do you think I am?" asked Alma Huttenmeyer. "A barbarian?"

We splashed toward the entryway, Alma trying to stay on her shoes and I lost in thought.

Every cloud has a silver lining, my mother has long maintained. As Alma, having a little trouble with her heels, hopped on deck, I thought I saw what the silver lining in this particular cloud might be. "You know," I said, "if you think about it, this could turn out to be a very interesting exercise."

She stumbled into the wall. "Oh yeah? And how do you figure that?"

"Well, I was just thinking . . . you're going to have an opportunity to discover for yourself what it's really like to be a woman, aren't you? I mean, that's not something that happens to every man, is it? It could be really fascinating. Important even. If this works, you could even do what that guy in *Black Like Me* did."

She steadied herself and straightened out her glasses. "Black like who?"

"Don't you remember that book? He was this white guy who made himself black, and then he drove around the South, seeing what it was like."

"He didn't know what it was like?"

But I was actually feeling a little cheered. Perhaps my fears were no more than stage fright. Maybe I really was on to a good idea here. After my considerable triumph as the agent of *How to Get Mr. Right to Pop the Question*, if something like this really took off I'd be permanently, once and for always, made. I wouldn't need Vanessa, I could set up on my own. I could open a restaurant. "Can't you just see it? You'd actually live as a woman for several months." I could visualize the hardback cover: a monochrome photograph of Jerry coming out of a rest room, and over his head, in bold red letters, *A Woman Like Me*. "It could be an important sociological study."

"Jesus," said Alma, shaking a pebble from her shoe, "you really are a piece of work, aren't you, Mike?"

All was gaiety and good times aboard the *Lady Liberty*. Balloons and streamers hung from the ceilings and fluttered at the doorways, or whatever doorways are called on boats. Although the weather outside was good news only if you were a body of water that was running a little low, inside the only thing that was flowing like water was the wine. There was laughter. There was scintillating conversation. There were reheated hors d'oeuvres. Authors and publishers gathered in small convivial groups, discussing the state of the trade and the latest best-sellers, going over ideas for the ultimate self-help book (*Everything You Ever Wanted to Know about Everything* or *How to Be Godlike with None of the Responsibilities*), congratulating themselves on their shrewdness and talent and ability to spot a trend.

Vanessa waved to us from across the crowded room. I squeezed Alma's hand. "Well, darling," I whispered, "here goes nothing."

"Mike," she whispered back. "Mike, I don't think I can go through with this, I really don't. They're going to see right through me like I was glass."

"No, they're not. Just talk like Shirley Bassey."

"Yes, they are. They'll notice, they'll—"

I tugged her forward. "Just stay out of direct light and act like you're shy."

Vanessa extended her hand. Alma pretended that she couldn't decide what to do with her champagne glass, moving it from right to
left to right again, and the moment of possible skin contact passed.

"Vanessa," I said, keeping myself in the foreground, "this is my
wife, Alma Huttenmeyer. Alma, this is Vanessa Ellis-Smith."

"Delighted," muttered Shirley Bassey.

"So," said Vanessa, smiling her this-is-going-to-cost-you-at-least-
fifty-thou smile, "this is the woman who finally got our Michael to
say those magic words." And this was the woman who made strong
men tremble, who made the heads of the biggest publishing firms in
the world shit bricks. Our Michael? Those magic words?

I said, "Heh heh."

Alma either smiled or winced.

"Well, it's so nice to meet you at last," said Vanessa. Her eyes went
up and down the considerable length of Alma Huttenmeyer and came
to rest on her six-inch coal-black lenses. Alma Huttenmeyer might
have long legs and a lot of hair, but Vanessa's face said that Alma was
not a looker. Vanessa was not impressed. Vanessa, to my surprise,
seemed relieved. "I can tell you, there was more than one broken
heart in Manhattan when our Michael decided to tie the knot." She
sort of tittered. Vanessa Ellis-Smith, known to her employees as Smith
and Wesson, tittered. And then she winked. "Maybe that's why he's
been so quiet about you. We've all been dying to meet you for ages."
She didn't think Alma could hold a candle to her niece. Or to Elizabeth.
Or to Suzanne. She thought that the women with the broken hearts
were going to laugh themselves silly when they got a look at the
woman with the ring. She probably figured that Alma was pregnant.
Or blackmailing me. She put a hand on my shoulder. She liked me
again.

"And I've been dying to meet you," gushed Shirley. "Michael hasn't
been quiet about you. He talks about you all the time."

Vanessa's hand moved to my back. She was not impressed, but she
was willing to be flattered. "I hope some of it was good." She laughed.

Alma laughed too. "I can't tell you how much he admires you,"
she said.

Arnold, whose office was across the hall from mine, materialized out of the frolicking throng. "Don't tell me!" he cried, looking Alma up and down, glancing fleetingly at her ass. "This must be the unfortunate woman."

I formed my lips into the shape of a smile. "Alma, this is Arnold. Arnold, my wife."

"Nice to meet you," said Arnold. I could tell that though he liked her hair (Arnold was on record as saying that he would never date a woman with short hair), he thought she was too tall. Maybe the heels had been a mistake.

Matthew, whose office was to the left of mine, came bustling up, looking worried. "The boat's about to leave and I haven't spotted Mr. B.," he fretted. Mr. B. was a literary giant and one of the agency's biggest clients.

Vanessa waved away his concern. "It's all right, Matty, he's here." She nodded behind her. "He's over by the bar."

"Whew," said Matthew. "That's a relief." Then he noticed Alma. He looked at me. "Hey, don't tell me this is Mrs. Householder!" He looked back at Alma. He thought she was too tall too. And he was disappointed that he couldn't really see her breasts. Matthew didn't care about hair length, but he did like women with breasts.

"Actually," said Shirley Bassey, tilting her head to catch his gaze where it had rested, at about the level of her second button, "it's Ms. Huttenmeyer."

Matthew waggled his eyebrows. "Ooops," he giggled, giving me a poke with his elbow. "You didn't tell me she was one of them, Mike."

The boat began to slip from the pier. The revelers cheered.

Vanessa turned back to Alma. "So," she said, "you must be very proud of Michael." She smiled my way. "He's one of New York's best agents, you know. And this past year, well, this past year he's really surpassed himself." She darted little glances at Matthew and Arnold, neither of whom had really surpassed himself this past year. "I don't think I'm being immodest when I say that to be a highflier in a company like ours is no mean feat."

Alma smiled back. "Oh, I'm sure it isn't," Shirley agreed. "It's the same in my business, of course."

Vanessa was still talking. "We didn't get where we are today by being second best. A lot of people think that there's nothing to agenting, you read a couple of books, you have a few lunches, but let me tell you, Alma, this is no place for the weak or unambitious." She linked her arm through mine. "Is it, Mike?"

"I'm in a pretty competitive field myself," said Shirley Bassey.

"I've never worked so hard in my life," announced Arnold.

"Me neither," Matthew agreed. He rolled his eyes. "Demanding? Whew! Talk about demanding!"

"Well, my company—" Shirley began.

But Vanessa was still talking. "I have a lot of friends who are professionals, you know," she was saying, "doctors and lawyers, that sort of thing? And they all say to me, 'Vanessa, Vanessa, I don't know how you do it. I really don't.' "

Matthew nodded.

Arnold nodded.

Alma started to say, "Well, in my line—"

But Vanessa was already telling her how she did it.

Well, kiss my copy of *Finnegans Wake*, I thought to myself. This is going to be a piece of cake. What had I been worried about?

And a piece of cake it was. Angel food cake. Angel food cake with marshmallow frosting.

I introduced Alma to Linda, my secretary, and Lesley, Vanessa's secretary. Linda said politely that she liked Alma's outfit, which meant that she didn't. She gave me a look that said clearly, "You passed up Denise Harpsmore for this Amazon with the goggles?" Lesley asked Alma if she'd tried the salmon. "It's really good," said Lesley, with a glance to Alma's hips. "And it's not even fattening."

I tried to introduce Alma to Tucker and Sharla. Tucker was a Nam vet turned freight pilot (of what depended to some extent on what he was drinking) turned thriller writer. Sharla, the fourth Mrs. Tucker, was a model who was probably still teething when Tucker joined the Marines.

"Rick," I said, "I'd like you to meet my wife."

Determining in a glance that Alma wasn't his type, Tucker said,

"You know, Mike, Sharla told me I just had to write that story. She said, 'Honey, you've gotta write that story, just like you told it to me. I just know it'll be the best thing you've ever done.' "

"I'm sure she's right," I agreed.

"You know, Mike," said Tucker, "that's what I thought. Women have an instinct for that sort of thing, don't they?" He knocked back his scotch. "It's because they're more in touch with their feelings," he decided. "Men are more intellectual, you know, but women, women think with their hearts."

Out of the mouths of trained killers, as the saying goes.

Sharla smiled at Alma and said, "Hi." Sharla said, "I've always liked silver as a color, but Ricky thinks it's too, you know, ostentatious. Don't you, honey?" Sharla said, "You're really lucky, Alma, Mike's such a nice guy. And I can tell he's really crazy about you." Sharla lowered her voice, though Tucker never let listening interfere with his conversation. Sharla said, "You should thank your lucky stars you're not married to a writer, they're so moody and withdrawn." Sharla said, "I'm a model. What do you do?"

Tucker said, "So, Michael, you get a chance to look at what I sent you yet, or what?"

We ran into Mr. B., one of our nation's most distinguished novelists, at the bar. "Hey, there, Matthew," said Mr. B. "I was wondering where you were."

"Michael," I corrected him as unobtrusively as possible. "That's Matthew over there."

He slapped me on the back. "Oh, Michael, of course. You know I've got no head for names." He tipped toward Alma. "And who is this charming creature? Is this the new publicist I've been hearing so much about?"

I slipped away to do a little mingling while Mr. B. explained to Alma how he'd come to write his first ten novels, and probably, if the rumors about him were true, to grope her ass in a literary manner.

Elizabeth Beacher and Suzanne Lightfoot were standing to one side, checking out the crowd. Elizabeth would nod toward someone and Suzanne would sort of cock her head and narrow her eyes, and then she'd either smile (thumbs up) or flick her eyebrows (let the lions have him).

"Ah," I cooed, gliding up to them, "my two favorite authors." In the end, I had disengaged myself from both of my favorite authors by telling each that I felt our personal relationship was jeopardizing our professional one. Love walks when money talks.

Elizabeth was cool. She gave me a hug, but it was a cool hug. "Michael!" She gave me her cheek, but the cheek was cold. She smiled. The smile an ice cap would give you if an ice cap could smile. "And how has married life been treating you?" she asked.

"Fine, fine." I rocked back and forth. "How's the book coming?"

"You look a little thin," said Suzanne. "And pale." She winked. "Maybe you're spending too much time indoors."

Elizabeth's eyes went to the bar. "And I take it that that's the lucky lady over there," she said, emphasizing the word "lucky."

I smiled. Happy is the bridegroom whose bride is too far away and too busy dodging the curious hand of a Pulitzer Prize–winning novelist to be summoned over for closer inspection. "That's Alma."

"She's very tall," said Elizabeth, looking down at me, her eyes trying to peer behind my smooth and smiling surface to see the soul beneath, the soul of a man who would prefer a giant in aluminum foil to her.

I sipped my champagne. Happy is the bridegroom whose clients are, in fact, totally uninterested in inspecting his bride at close range because they can tell from twenty yards that she is not a patch on either of them. "She's wearing heels."

"I'm sure she's lovely," said Elizabeth, allowing herself one last look at Alma, looming over the bar and Mr. B. like *Apollo X* over its launch pad. Then she brought her eyes back to me. They focused; her voice came out of the conversational mode and into realspeak. "Actually," she said, "I'm just about ready to deliver the new manuscript. I think you're really going to love this one, Michael." She moved just a little closer. "It's set in New York and Mexico."

"Really? New York and Mexico? I thought you were going to set it in Thailand."

"The heroine's sister is brutally murdered by a psychopath," Elizabeth drawled.

I wondered if it were possible to be murdered by a psychopath unbrutally.

"Sounds pretty realistic so far," I commented.

"And she sets out to bring him to justice and they fall hopelessly in love."

"I like it," I said. "It obviously has a lot of topical interest."

"Michael," said Suzanne, who was still staring at Alma and Mr. B. "Do you think your wife would give me a testimonial for the second edition of my book?"

Piece of cake. Nothing to worry about. I strolled through the party, chatting with so-and-so, picking at the caviar with what's-his-name. I watched the other celebrants. The authors, publishers, and agents were all talking away. And the wives of the authors, publishers, and agents were all ears. They were smiling graciously, listening with interest and attention, nodding with understanding and compassion, commenting with humor and charm. Isn't life wonderful? I thought to myself. So balanced, so sensible. Isn't this a great evening? What a piece of cake.

But as the bobbing boat slowly circled the island, and the laughter and conversation grew louder and looser and everyone, too drunk to be cautious, began to eat even the miniature quiches and the baby egg rolls, I began to notice that there was a hard thing at the center of my particular piece of cake. Hard and possibly fatal.

The dark, dank terror returned, squeezing my heart so tightly that I started choking on my drink in the middle of a rather heated discussion about gun control and the Butcher of Broadway.

"Mike?" one of the Bill-of-Righters inquired solicitously. "Mike? Are you okay?"

"Yeah, sure, I'm fine." If I'd had a gun then, I would have shot myself with it.

The hard thing at the center of my piece of cake was Alma Huttenmeyer. Unlike the other wives, Alma was not always to be seen smiling graciously. Shouting something I was happy not to catch, she had stormed off from Mr. B. in what Mr. B. himself, a man with an old-fashioned love of language, might have described as a state of high dudgeon. Again not quite close enough to hear what she said, I did see her wipe the grin from the face of a very popular syndicated columnist while he was in the middle of his monologue. Unlike the other wives, she often looked irritable and bored. I stopped checking to see if she was all right because to catch her eye, dark glasses or no dark glasses, was to catch an especially nasty short-range missile. She didn't seem to be listening too sympathetically, nor asking too many polite questions about vacations in Europe and the paperback trade in Southeast Asia. More than once, I heard Shirley Bassey's voice, fruity but querulous, wanting to know "exactly what you mean by that." Grimacing and glowering, she was being about as charming as a death squad—even someone not in her immediate vicinity, someone like myself, could easily see that. What the hell was wrong with her?

And then Alma Huttenmeyer started to sulk.

I'd just gotten back into the conversation on the right of every American to bear arms and the effects of television violence on real life when I saw my life's partner stalk out onto the rainswept deck with a bottle of California champagne under her arm, and on her face the expression she got when anyone criticized the Yankees.

Through the severe weather conditions the lights of the metropolis twinkled bravely.

"What's gotten into you? What the hell do you think you're doing?" I demanded. "What's everyone going to think?"

"I don't give a shit what they think," bellowed my beloved. "They can all go swim to Jersey for all I care." She took a swig from the bottle.

Still sober and ever rational, I remained calm. "What happened? Did somebody make a pass at you? Is that what this is?" I touched her arm. "Look, I'm sure he didn't mean anything by it. You know what guys are like."

She took another belt, staring at me rather frostily over the body of the bottle. "No, Michael, no one made a pass at me."

"Not even Mr. B.?"

"That wasn't a pass, it was a swipe."

"You're sure?"

"No, I'm not sure. I'm a complete bimbo, so I'm not sure if some jerk was making a pass at me or not."

I put up my hands. "All right, all right, no one made a pass at you. Then what the hell is wrong? Are your shoes pinching or something?"

"No, you idiot," snarled Jerome Finer, "my goddamn shoes are not pinching."

"Well, it can't be PMT, can it?"

He didn't think that was funny.

"Well, can it?"

He continued to glare at me. Silently. Contemptuously. With unconcealed hostility. Maybe he was better at being a woman than I'd first thought.

But maybe I wasn't as sober.

"So what, then? The other girls want to talk about childbirth or something?"

He shoved me against a pole. "Sometimes I really do think you're a complete imbecile, you know that, Mike? A complete and total imbecile."

After twenty-eight years of a friendship that had weathered even the fickleness of Sophie Lumbucco's love (and, I suppose, to be honest, the selfishness of Jerome Finer's and Michael Householder's sex drives), this. All you have to do is give a guy an art deco brooch and a silk scarf, and right away he turns on you. I tried to regain my composure. "So tell me what's wrong."

He leaned against the railing. He tapped his foot. "You don't know?"

He was definitely better at this than I'd given him credit for.

"No, I don't know."

"You really don't know?"

"Alma—Jerry, for the love of God, I really don't know."

"Oh, yes, you do."

Much much better.

I had had conversations like this one before. What man hasn't? You know what's wrong. No, I don't. Oh, yes, you do. You know what you did. No, I don't. Oh, yes, you do. I recalled a conversation with Marissa that began with her saying "Michael, I know you're going to say this is corny, but the simple truth is that you and I don't communicate anymore" and ended with me saying "I don't understand what you're talking about." I even recalled conversations like this with Jerry—but the last one hadn't taken place any later than ninth grade. Looking back now, with my new wisdom and maturity, I realize, of course, that he was right: subconsciously I did know what he was talking about, but I didn't want to know. I wanted it to be all Jerry's fault. I'd been thinking about it from my point of view—and not from his or Alma's. But at that moment, standing against the rail as the rain and wind dumped the toxic wastes of Jersey on our heads, I really did not know I knew.

And I was clearly not nearly as sober as I'd thought.

"I do not know," I hissed. "Read my lips, you turkey, I do not know what you're talking about."

The real Alma Huttenmeyer had been one of those chatty, confident, slightly bossy girls who carry their books against their chest and are always smiling and laughing in the corridor. She was what was called "fun-loving" and "bouncy." She never gave the teachers any trouble. I don't remember ever seeing her when she wasn't sweet as pie. She once did an English project about the building of the transcontinental railway that discussed (at some length, as I recall it) the plight of Chinese laborers, so she was not without compassion either. I don't, of course, know what sort of woman she became, but I can't imagine that, if we had married, the real Alma Huttenmeyer would suddenly have turned on me on the deck of the *Lady Liberty* with a threatening, "You want to know what it's like to be a woman, asshole? Well, I'm going to tell you."

Being a woman, Jerry informed me, was like being twelve years old. "You remember twelve, Mike?" he screamed against the storm. "Huh? Do you?" When aunts still pinched your cheeks and your mother still helped you pick out your clothes. When adults would ask you how school was and then expect you to keep quiet through the rest of the meal. Twelve, when you couldn't assume that anything you thought, did, or said was of any real interest to anyone over the age of thirteen. Men would talk at you, but you couldn't really call it a conversation. Women would talk to you, as long as there wasn't a man around.

Real women, of course, were probably used to this sort of thing. I'd seen my own mother at countless parties thrown for business associates of Barry's, and she was always delightful and delighted, even at times when she must have been bored out of her brain listening to the same stories of takeover bids and hunting trips. But Jerry, of course, was not a real woman.

How dumb can you get? How blind can you be? The thing that had always been wrong with this plan was Jerry. I should have listened to him when he tried to tell me as much. What was wrong was that Jerry was a guy. A husband. A father. A man who cheated on his wife, not a man who identified with her. Betsy Shopak may never have read *The Second Sex*, as Jerry Finer had, but Betsy Shopak had once been a wife, and Jerry Finer hadn't. Jerry Finer could read Simone de Beauvoir till every cow in the universe came mooing home, and it would never make one blind bit of difference.

"I think maybe you're exaggerating just a little, Jer," I shouted back as calmly as I could.

"Oh, do you?"

"Yes, I do. I think you're getting too involved in your role."

"Oh, really? Is that what you think, Michael?"

"Yes, Jerry, it is."

And that was when he decked me.

10

Divorce, American Style

"Well," I said, standing in the bathroom with my *Psittacus erithacus*, "I guess that this is the creek called Shit, and we are without a paddle."

The worst thing wasn't my busted lip (physical violence, after all, is part of being a man). Nor was it the public humiliation of having someone related to you, albeit by marriage, tell one of America's best-selling authors to take his hand off her bottom if he wanted to keep it connected to his wrist (what man hasn't, at some time, been embarrassed by his wife?). It wasn't even the fact that my bride, sounding remarkably like Shirley Bassey, had ended the evening by standing on the rainy deck singing the old Burger King jingle till we finally docked (this must have happened to someone before).

No, the worst thing was that the events of that evening weren't an aberration, a little bump in a life that was otherwise even and smooth.

The worst thing was that they were symptomatic. My life was out of control. Out of my control, at any rate. Things couldn't go on as they were. How could they? I had no love life, no social life, and even my career seemed suddenly meaningless and hollow. I was exhausted from the effort of constantly lying. I was emotionally drained from the exertions of alienating, hurting, or disgusting everyone I knew. Only my parents were happy with me, and they were happy with me only because they thought I was married to this wonderful woman and wouldn't turn into a grumpy old man whose underwear smelled and who had no place to go on national holidays.

Gracie watched me with concern. "What're ya doin'? What're ya doin'?" she queried. *"Brrrngbrrrngbrrrng."*

She might well ask.

It is undisputable, from a purely objective viewpoint, that on this planet at least, the best thing a person could hope to be is a white Western male. We're the guys with the options and the opportunities. We're the guys who can achieve the highest levels of power, fulfillment, and personal success.

I looked closely at myself in the bathroom mirror—very, very closely. Was this the crème de la crème? Was this power, fulfillment, and personal success? Was this the creature every amoeba in the pool was yearning to be? "Michael," I said, "Michael Householder, how have you let yourself sink this low?"

Myself stared back, bemused and bewildered, not knowing either.

Was this the boy who was going to be the white man's answer to Willie Mays? Was this the youth who was going to make Henry James turn over in his grave with admiration and envy? Was this the young dreamer whose heart was pure and passionate, who would settle for nothing less than true love? This? This cretin who went around hurting Betsy Shopak's feelings and making his pals accessories after the fact? This? This lonely, haggard-looking bald man?

I turned to the left. I turned to the right. I put a towel over my head so I looked almost as if I still had a full head of hair. Was this me? This almost middle-aged businessman whose only serious contribution to the well-being of the planet was making a small annual donation to Amnesty International and using an environmentally friendly detergent? Was I mad or something? Had pollutants damaged my brain? Had testosterone overdose destroyed my mental balance? What had happened to my hopes and dreams? For over twenty years I had lived with the image of my ideal love, a fourteen-year-old cheerleader mindlessly adored by every boy in the ninth grade because she had blond hair, long legs, and breasts. Was that smart? Given every chance in the cosmos to achieve what I might, was this the best I could do?

A moan escaped my lips. Why had I come into this world as something as frivolous as a boy? Why hadn't I come into this world as something sane, sensitive, and sensible: a girl? a cat? a border collie? a finback whale? And for once I couldn't even blame my mother.

I straightened up. It was time to grow up and act not like a man but like an intelligent human being. Time to take responsibility for my life. Time to get my apartment in order. "Gracie," I said. "Gracie, I've made a decision."

Gracie, pacing the shower-curtain rod, looked at me with interest. "Hello, honey," said Gracie. "Honey, I'm home."

I sighed.

Gracie sighed.

"Gracie," I said, "Gracie, we're going to have to get rid of Alma."

"Get rid of Alma," mimicked Gracie. "Get rid of Alma."

Just having made the decision lightened my heart. All at once, the world seemed full of possibilities again. Things could change. I could change. My life could be different. "We're going to start all over," I told her. Relief surged through me. Better. My life could be different and better. I could still salvage some of my youthful ideals.

Gracie bobbed. "So long, toots," said Gracie. "Uh oh, uh oh, where's the gun?"

With no undo ceremony, I packed Alma Huttenmeyer off to California—by Concorde—to work on her video travel books.

"I hope we didn't make too much noise this morning," I said to Betsy Shopak's back as we both searched for an empty garbage can to put our tardy refuse in. "Alma had to catch an early plane to L.A."

I lifted a lid and held it aside for her. "We've, uh . . ." I said softly, "we've, um . . . we've decided to live separate lives for a while."

Betsy dropped in her bag with a plop. "How nice for you," she said coldly. Plop plop. Except for a curt "good morning," "hello," "uh," or "nice day" as we passed each other on the street or on the stairs, collided in the hallway, or found ourselves staring at the elevator door together, there had been no exchange between us, friendly or otherwise, since the night she stormed out of my apartment in baking needs and tears.

I touched her elbow. "Uh, Betsy . . . Betsy, I just wanted to say that I'm very very sorry about that . . . you know, about that night you came over to borrow the sugar . . . about what you . . . it wasn't what you thought, Bets, it—"

She pulled away. "Shrank" might be more descriptive. But her voice was loud and strong enough to cause several passersby and a muzzled German shepherd to turn their heads. "It wasn't sugar," she boomed. "It was flour. Can't you even get that straight? Flour! F-l-o-u-r!" She turned toward the west. "And you can take it and fuck yourself with it for all I care!"

"Fuck"? Betsy Shopak had said "fuck"? My God, on top of everything else, I could probably be held responsible for singlehandedly corrupting the fair women of Cincinnati.

"Way to go, lady!" yelled the guy with the dog.

A week or two later I formally announced that Alma and I had— sadly but mutually—agreed on a trial separation. I didn't advertise it in the middle of Union Square or in the *Times*, you understand—but as good as.

"What did you do to her?" asked my mother.

"Mom," I sighed, hoping I sounded at least a little like the injured party, "I didn't do anything." I moved into the "putting on a brave front" mode. "It's just one of those things. You know." I sighed again, manly but in pain. "These things happen."

"To you," said my mother. "They always happen to you." She turned away from the receiver. "She's left him already," my mother informed Barry. "She hasn't even gotten the rice out of her hair, and already she's gone."

"Let me talk to him," said Barry.

"I don't want to talk to Barry," I said hastily. That was all I needed.

"Can you believe it?" asked my mother. "A wonderful woman like that, and it's not even a year. Is she marrying somebody else?"

"Mom, please." There were more rumblings behind her. "Mom? Mom? Mom, I really don't want to talk to Barry."

"He needs to talk to another man," said Barry.

"Barry wants to talk to you," said my mother.

"Yeah, I know, but—"

"Mike," said Barry, "why don't you come over for a drink and we can discuss what happened privately. Just us men. We'll send your mother out shopping or something. You know, Mike, it probably isn't as serious as you think. Women . . . you know . . . sometimes it takes a while to learn how to handle them . . ."

My mother's voice—firm, authoritative, commandeering—rose above the ramblings of my stepfather. "Give me that phone."

"Mom, really, this is a mutual thing. We don't hate each other or anything like that. We haven't had a big fight. We just feel we'd be better off apart. You know. The pressures—"

"Pressures?" snapped my mother. "What are you talking about, 'pressures'? You don't know what pressure is."

I didn't know what pressure was? "Excuse me, Mom, but I think that maybe you're wrong about that. I happen to have a very good idea of what pressure is. I—"

"Let me talk to him again," insisted Barry. "He really needs to talk to another man."

"I do not need to talk to another man. I do not need to talk to anyone."

"You need to talk to Alma," said my mother. "Have you talked to Alma?"

"Oh, no, of course I haven't talked to Alma. I'm waiting for her to come home and find that I've changed the locks and thrown all her things in the hall."

"That's your problem in a nutshell," my mother informed me. "Everything's a joke to you. You're like Nero, making wisecracks while Rome's torched to the ground."

Lonnie took it better. "I'm really sorry, Mike," said Lonnie. "Really, really sorry."

Jerry had had to go to Newark for a special adhesive and Lonnie and I were having supper together. At my suggestion. It was my suggestion because Jerry had actually gone to Brooklyn to tell Connie Schmidmore that it was all over between them. Being Alma Huttenmeyer for just one evening had made him see what an insensitive, exploitative, self-centered shit he had been, abusing the love and trust of not one but two wonderful women (either of whom, he may also have realized, could have shot him dead in cold blood and never been convicted by a jury of her peers). Which means that it was really Jerry's suggestion. I was the moral support. Moral support for Lonnie in case he never made it out of Brooklyn alive. Moral support for Jerry in case he made it out of Brooklyn alive, but not alone. It was, as he said, the least I could do.

"I was really hoping it would work out this time."

I smiled staunchly. "Me too."

She stabbed at an anchovy with her fork. "Of course, I suppose if we'd thought about it realistically, we'd have realized all along that it could never last."

Did I hear a song coming on?

"We would have?"

"Uh huh." The eyes that looked back at me were guileless. But definite. It was a little like standing on line in the supermarket, and suddenly having the small child in front of you shout out, "Mommy! Mommy! Doesn't that very short man have an enormous nose?" Bang go thirty-five years of self-deception and maternal deceit.

"Uh, Lonnie? Why would we have realized that?"

"Well . . ." She seemed surprised that I needed to be told. "You're not really the type to live with anyone on a permanent basis, are you, Mike?"

"I live with Gracie just fine," I defended.

She smiled, but seriously. Fatalistically. As your mother smiled when it turned out that, as she'd foretold, you didn't take care of that puppy as you'd promised, or that you'd failed that chemistry final, just as she'd said you would if you played ball instead of studying. "You know what I mean." She gazed thoughtfully at my plate for a second. "You're so fussy and inflexible, aren't you?"

"Inflexible?" I asked sourly. "Are you sure you don't mean stuffy?"

Lonnie shook her head. "No," she said pleasantly, "I mean inflexible. Everything has to be just so with you. You're incapable of compromise or rashness. You think you're bending over backwards if you let someone else put the soup bowls away. You think spontaneity is deciding to have two cups of coffee after dinner instead of one." She smiled at me kindly, a Little League coach about to disabuse you of your notion that you might ever play professional ball. "And as if that's not enough, you've still got so much neurotic male behavior to get out of your system, don't you, Mike? Even a saint couldn't be expected to put up with that."

Why had she waited so long to tell me all this?

"Alma was hardly a saint," I muttered.

"You're not like Jerry," Lonnie elaborated. "Jerry's home and family are everything to him, but you, well . . ." Even her shrug was kindly. "You're a completely different type. You know . . . more self—well, I guess you'd call it more footloose and fancy free."

I stared down at my spinach salad. She hadn't quite gotten all the grit off. That was me, all right, good-time Michael, dancing down the open road of life without a care in the world. She really should get a salad spinner.

"I'm really sorry I didn't get to meet her, though," said Lonnie, sounding really sorry. "Jerry said she was really terrific. He thought she'd be a good influence on you."

Jerry said that?

"He did?"

What the hell was that supposed to mean?

"Yeah. You know that weekend the three of you went camping, when Ethan was sick and I had to stay home?"

The weekend the three of us went camping and Lonnie had to stay home because Ethan was sick? "Vaguely . . ."

"Jerry said he'd never seen you so happy." A smile steeped in sympathy flickered on her lips: *you poor bastard.* "He said you didn't even complain about her cooking like you complain about everyone else's."

"Lonnie, I do not—"

"He said, 'Maybe this time Mike really is serious, honey. Maybe Mike's finally prepared to be responsible and adult.' "

"That's what Jerry said?"

"His exact words." She gazed musingly at a green olive. Only Lonnie put green olives in spinach salad. "It really is a shame, Mike," she said sincerely. "I am truly sorry."

"Yeah," I agreed, "I'm sorry, too."

Jerry came home while we were dishing out dessert. Sara Lee brownies out of their pan. Lonnie was not only a mediocre cook, she was a below-average defroster.

"I was telling Mike how sorry we are about him and Alma," said Lonnie.

"Yeah," said Jerry, his eyes meeting mine over the top of Lonnie's head. "Breaking up is hard to do."

The gang in the office took it the best.

"Oh, well." Arnold shrugged. "Easy come, easy go, right, Mike? Anyway, she had nice hair, but you have to admit she was a little on the tall side."

"Yeah, and, you know," said Matthew, waggling his hands in front of his chest and making a constipated face, "not exactly . . ." He gave me a man-to-man wink. "Well, she was pretty tall."

Linda, standing beside me while I fixed us some coffee, laughed. Just came right out and laughed. "I figured the way she decked you at the party was a bad sign," said Linda. "She's got a good right hook, though, doesn't she? Maybe you should've tried a little harder to make it work."

"It doesn't really surprise me," said Vanessa, sympathetic in her own special way. "Not one bit. I could tell she wasn't nearly as interested in your career as a marriage partner should be." She patted my hand. "You just let me know when you feel like dating again, Michael," she said, sounding almost as soothing and compassionate as she did when a movie deal fell through and the author was suicidal. "As you know, I am acquainted with some very wonderful women who would give their eye teeth to be with someone like you."

"Well, if you know someone like me, do introduce them," I joked.

Vanessa patted my shoulder again. Thatta boy.

"Well, I'm certainly glad I didn't get that affidavit from her," laughed Suzanne Lightfoot, trying to cheer me up. "And it is good news for the rest of us, isn't it?" she continued, the Pollyanna of the self-help world. She sighed. "Not, of course, that I'm trying to minimize the pain and heartache you're going through, Michael, but it's not the worst thing that could have happened, is it? It's better to discover you've made a mistake in the first year than ten or fifteen years on, when you've got all that property together and she's economically dependent on you because of the kids." There was a pause, and then the no-nonsense voice of the professional relationship-consultant took over. "In fact, if you don't mind me being frank, Michael," it said, "I think I have to confess that I didn't really feel she was your type, somehow. A little too masculine, if you ask me."

Hector, the doorman, consoled me. "Cheer up, Mike," said Hector. "Look on the bright side. Now you've got one ex-wife who hates your guts. But if you'd stayed together, eventually you'd've had a coupla kids, right?"

I said, "Probably."

"And in time they'd've grown up and turned into teenagers, right?" Right.

"So, just about the time when you and your lady were wondering why you ever got married in the first place, the kids would be reaching that age when they couldn't stand the sight of you either. You with me so far?"

I nodded, so far I was with him.

"So what I'm sayin' here is that instead of just one person hating you, you'd've had three or four." He called the elevator for me. "Think of it, Mike. Three or four people who know you deeply and intimately, hating everything about you, from the way you suck your cereal to the way you start up the car. And that's not even counting the rest of her family." He shrugged the shrug of a world-class philosopher. "You hear what I'm sayin', Mike? You got off easy. Am I right or wrong?"

I said he was right.

Someone sent me a bouquet of flowers. I stood at my desk for several minutes, just looking at it. It was only the second time in my life that anyone had sent me flowers, and it was much bigger than my first bouquet. Much bigger. I sniffed. I tidied up a few broken leaves. Then I picked up the card and opened it slowly. *Dearest Michael, Do let me know when you want someone to talk to. You know I'm always available. Don't think all women will let you down just because one has. Love, Lizzi xxxx.*

Linda came into my office with a fax in her hand. "Jesus, Mary, and Joseph," said Linda. "Who died?"

But it was Charley Ray and Bongo who took my marital defeat the hardest.

"Fuckin' hell," said Charley Ray. "I was really counting on you, Mike. I really was."

I sipped my beer. "That'll learn you, Charley Ray. Never count on anyone or anything in this world."

"Fuckin' truth," said Bongo. "You're not safe till you're dead."

I couldn't help feeling a little hurt at the alacrity with which they agreed with me. "Hey," I protested. "I did do my best, you know. I don't think you guys appreciate what it's been like for me, running around trying to keep my stories straight . . . lying to everyone . . . sneaking in and out of my own home . . . always alone . . ."

Charley Ray spit something that had been in his beer onto the floor. "I appreciate it, Mike," said Charley Ray. "I really do. Right from the start, my old lady said you didn't stand the chance of a snow cone in hell. But I said no. I said, 'No way, baby, this guy's got it all figured out.' " He shook his great head sadly. "Goes to show you, right? She always said it was a dumb idea. 'Tell your friend it's a dumb idea,' she told me. 'It'll never work.' "

"Terrific," sighed I. "Maybe you should've mentioned that before."

Charley Ray shrugged his massive shoulders. "You wouldn't've listened. Anyway, I was really hopin' Chrissy was wrong for once." He picked up his glass. "She's a real bitch that way."

"Charley Ray's old lady's never wrong," said Bongo. "It's like livin' with the pope." He smiled. "If the pope rode a Norton," he amended.

I picked up my bottle. "What'd she say exactly? Why didn't she think it would work?"

Charley Ray made this sarcastic face. Godzilla doing Mork from Ork. "Who knows? You know what women are like, they have these different imaginations, don't they? They don't think with the same side of the brain as us." He popped the top off his next bottle with his thumbs and filled up his glass. "Now she says she hopes you can end it so easy as you think."

I passed him my beer to open. "Meaning what?"

"How the hell do I know? You know what women are like, Mike. Nothin's ever simple with them. Everythin's gotta be complicated. She has this idea, you know, that once you start somethin' it isn't always so easy to stop it."

"You mean like one of those train reactions?" asked Bongo.

Charley Ray handed me back my bottle. "You know, Mike, like karma or whatever that stuff is. Chrissy's very spiritual."

But later, when he drove me home, he said, "You know what we were talkin' about before? About what Chrissy was sayin'?"

"Oh, yeah, yeah, I remember." I slid off the back of the bike, clutching my briefcase. I could barely remember my own name by then.

"Well, Chrissy's very fatalistic, if you know what I mean. Women are, though, aren't they? It's because of their wombs. Anyway, she don't think there's any shortcuts in life. She thinks that once you've picked your route, you should stick to it or you'll never get to where you wanted to be."

I looked back at Bongo to see if this little bit of philosophy made any more sense to him than it did to me. He was nodding his head.

"She's right," he shouted over the commotion of their engines. "When she's right, she's very, very right."

"Um," I said. "I'm not sure that . . ."

Charley Ray patted my shoulder. "You think about it, Mike," said Charley Ray. "You just give it a little bit of thought."

In the end, though, other things to think about were placed outside my door.

Twenty-five things, to be more accurate. And left not outside my door specifically, but on the first floor, in the stairwell across from the service elevator.

It was on a Monday morning when I was feeling much the worse for wear, going down in the elevator with Mrs. Sontag from next door and Bobby Byrnes from 10C, that I first heard about the foot.

"Did you hear?" asked Bobby Byrnes as we stepped into the elevator. Excitement fought with horror for control of his voice.

"I was sick when I heard," said Mrs. Sontag, her mouth curled in distaste. "Physically sick, I can tell you."

"What happened?" I inquired politely.

"To tell you the truth," said Bobby, "it kind of turned my stomach, too."

"They say it was wrapped in its own stocking," said Mrs. Sontag.

"I heard it was one of those sheer black jobs with the little rhinestone bow at the ankle," said Bobby, excitement taking the lead.

"What was?" asked I.

Mrs. Sontag shuddered. "Can you imagine?" Her eyes moved from Bobby to me. "What sort of animal could do a thing like that?" she wondered.

"Did you hear how many pieces the foot was in?" Talk about fussy. Bobby Byrnes was a stickler for details. At tenants' meetings he always held things up for hours while he quibbled over points of order. "First I heard fifteen, then I heard twenty, and then somebody else said forty-two."

"Twenty-five," said Mrs. Sontag. "It was on CBS." She shuddered again. "I'm sure I heard something a few nights ago," she said to Bobby. "About three A.M. You probably couldn't hear it from your side of the building." She turned to me. "What about you, Mr. House-holder? I don't suppose you heard it?"

"At three in the morning?"

"Men!" said Mrs. Sontag shortly. "How can you sleep with so much evil in the world?"

The elevator opened. Where Hector should have been there was a policeman drinking coffee from a cardboard cup and eating a dough-nut. Down the hall and through the glass doors of the entranceway, the sun shone over Manhattan.

"Well, I'd better hurry, or I'll be late for work," said Bobby. He sprinted toward the street.

Mrs. Sontag waved him good-bye.

"Uh, Mrs. Sontag," I said as we strolled through the foyer. There seemed to be quite a few cops having breakfast in our lobby. "Mrs. Sontag, what foot?"

Mrs. Sontag blinked. "You mean you don't know?" asked Mrs. Sontag. Ever critical, she shook her head. "Don't you listen to the news?" she demanded. "Don't you even look at your morning paper?"

I was damned if I was going to explain to her that I had a hangover from an ill-spent night at Jo Jo's tavern and had overslept. "What foot, Mrs. Sontag?"

"The one they found in the garbage," said Mrs. Sontag. "A human foot, sliced in twenty pieces not counting the toes."

Jesus Christ. And I thought I had problems. "In *our* garbage?"

"That's right," said Mrs. Sontag. "That nice young man on the second floor, the one with the bulldog, he found it. He was taking the dog for his walk last night, down the stairs, you know? and anyway they got to the first floor and the dog went crazy barking. He thought he was going to have to have her shot."

"Twenty pieces?" I repeated. "The foot was in twenty pieces?"

"Sliced," said Mrs. Sontag. "Sliced and packed in an ice-cream container."

Mrs. Sontag and I stepped into the sunshine. "My God," I said, "I know New York's a rough area . . ."

"He thinks the dog may have to go into therapy," said Mrs. Sontag.

In New York you have to be adaptable, and so, over the months and in our way, we had adapted to the Butcher. We never forgot he was out there, but we'd learned to live around him. The knowledge that he was lurking somewhere, looking for the right container to cradle an escallop of thigh or a cut from the rump, hadn't stopped us from enjoying ourselves. The thought that he was stalking the streets, searching for just the right blonde or brunette to be garnished with parsley hadn't caused our womenfolk to dress in chadors. We'd grown used to his eccentric, very New York sense of humor. Uptown and downtown, vagrants sifted through the garbage of Broadway, not in hopes of finding a half-eaten steak or a loaf of bread, as in more tranquil times, but in hopes of finding some piece of a woman and claiming a reward. Lips, ears, fingers, breasts, nipples, noses, and one small buttock dressed like an Easter ham had all been found, in packaging that ranged from Styrofoam shells, paper bags, and waxed containers to laminated boxes with classy labels and a special basket from Macy's Cellar. Because the psychiatrists said that attention was the last thing this guy needed, the front page stories had been pulled back considerably, but there was always an editorial, or a news special, or some expert on Donahue or Oprah or Johnny talking about sociopaths and their fondness for women. There wasn't a journalist, news anchor, or TV host—especially of the female persuasion—who hadn't done something on the psychology of the Butcher and the incompetence of the police. We had the Butcher with our morning coffee, with our lunchtime sandwich, with our late-night drink. We talked about him at dinner parties and on long journeys. While we waited on the checkout, we read the stories in the sensationalist press: "Butcher Grew Up on *I Dream of Jeanie* and *Galloping Gourmet*" . . . "Is This Fiend the Man Next Door? How You Can Be Sure" . . . "Woman Claiming to

Be Butcher's Mother Says He Loves Children and Dogs." Everyone had an opinion or a theory: he hated women, he hated his mother, he loved his mother but he hated his father for leaving him, he loved women but hated himself for not being able to get an erection, he was repressed, he was afraid of females, he couldn't admit to being homosexual, he was anal-retentive and could express his sexuality only through food. Dozens of people turned themselves, their husbands, their fathers, or their brothers in. The police, their credibility plummeting, assured the public that they were getting closer and closer, and officially advised women to trust no one and to travel in groups (and unofficially to leave their personal stereos at home). And all the while, somewhere in the greater metropolitan area, the Butcher sharpened his bistoury and his boning knife and probably laughed himself to sleep.

But this latest attack—if the discovery of a perfectly filleted foot, topped with its beribboned toes and an almond macaroon, served on a seamed black silk stocking and packed into a quart Death by Chocolate container from a leading gourmet ice-cream store can be called an attack—had stirred things up anew. This was the first time the Butcher had left anything indoors. Not only did it make the threat seem more pervasive and more real, it was, the experts managed to agree, a significant break from pattern. Something was happening in that sick and twisted brain. Jesus O'Brien, as unlikely as it might seem, had been right. The Butcher was losing it. He was bored. He was drunk on his own cleverness. He wanted even more notoriety. The New York City Police Department wasn't getting any closer to him, so he was going to go to it.

On my way to work I picked up one of the dailies, less discreet than my usual paper, and there in inch-high headlines was the news: TROTTER FOUND IN TRASH. POLICE LED MERRY DANCE. CITY OUTRAGED. "It's somethin', isn't it?" asked the guy behind the counter. I agreed. "Whew," said the woman next to me, "don't it make you think?" I said that it did. Everywhere you went that morning, people were talking of nothing else—at the newsstand, on the bus, in the snack bar, on the street . . .

In the office.

"Isn't this your building?" asked Linda as I staggered through reception. She was holding up a newspaper with a picture of the nice young man from the second floor and his bulldog, Peggy, standing in front of a large blond-brick edifice.

I nodded. "It gives you the creeps, doesn't it?" There's nothing like a homicidal maniac on your doorstep to take your mind off yourself. All the way uptown, all I could think of—except for the fact that I would never drink again—was that while Gracie and I were dreaming our dreams, some lunatic had been tiptoeing through our stairwell with this poor woman's foot tucked under his arm. Maybe I'd passed him in the street. Maybe he lived in the building. Just think of it: someone I saw all the time, greeted in the elevator, nodded at in the hallway, made comments to about the weather or the traffic or lead in the water as we checked our mailboxes at the end of the day. Maybe this guy cut recipes out of the Sunday *Times* just as I did. Maybe we'd even stood on line in the ice-cream store together, exchanging opinions on the range of flavors. What if I was the one who recommended Death by Chocolate? "Don't get Chocoholic," I might have advised him. "Death's ten times better."

"Do you think it was someone you knew?" asked Linda, following me into my room.

"Linda, please . . ."

She shook the paper over my desk. "That's what it says here," she informed me. She began to read. " 'Police have believed for some time that the Butcher's parcels were not left casually or randomly, but that locations were chosen with the same deliberateness and thoroughness that marks the murders and gruesome presentations themselves. Although there has been no positive identification of any of the victims, Dr. S. F. Willerbridge, the country's foremost criminal psychiatrist and special consultant to the police throughout their grueling investigations, believes that the Butcher's packages are left close to where the women either lived or worked. "There are some significant differences between this latest murder and its predecessors," Dr. Willerbridge told a hastily called press conference. "But if anything this departure reveals the obsessive and rigid behavior pattern even more clearly." ' " Linda put her hands on her hips. "You see?" she said. "For all you know he lives across the hall."

I rummaged through my desk for the fast-acting aspirin-free pain-killers. "That's the one thing I do know," I said. "He doesn't live across the hall. He doesn't even sleep over occasionally." Although, on second thought, given the sharpness and brilliance O'Brien had so far demonstrated in dealing with the case, I supposed it was possible. Sometime next spring, over breakfast, he might finally turn to Betsy and say, "Honey, who *is* that guy with the locks of hair hanging from his belt who's been sleeping on the couch?"

"What about her, then?" Linda persisted. "Maybe you knew this poor woman herself." Her eyes widened. "Maybe you even dated her!"

Given the odds, I probably had. "Linda," I pleaded. "Let's not dwell ghoulishly on this, all right? Let's carry on with business as usual."

"Aren't you even curious?" asked Linda.

"Linda," I said, "just answer the phone."

That week, my phone and the phone of the chief of police never stopped ringing.

On Monday afternoon, Elizabeth Beacher called to find out everything I knew. "I'm sure I can use this in my novel," she said excitedly. "It's just the sort of real-life detail I need. Can I come over and see the first-floor landing?"

On Monday night the mayor, having just had an hour-long telephone conversation with the chief of police, announced, "We're going to get this bastard, and we're going to get him soon," on the ten o'clock news.

On Tuesday morning, the front page of every paper in the city had an artist's composite sketch of the man believed to be the Butcher, as described by the few possible witnesses the cops had managed to come up with. It was obvious from the sketch that the witnesses had not always agreed. Usually these sketches look either like Cro-Magnon man or the guy sitting across from you on the train while you're reading the paper, but this one didn't look like anyone. The Butcher, it seemed, was average. Not fair and not really dark. Not tall and not short. Not fat and not thin. Average coloring, average height, and average weight. Everyone agreed that the man they'd seen, or thought they'd seen—the man who might be the Butcher, or might not—had a nose and eyes and a forehead and hair, but no features or characteristics that really distinguished him from anybody else.

A little later on Tuesday morning, Suzanne Lightfoot rang to ask me what I thought of her doing a book on male violence toward women and the connection between it and the mother-son relationship.

On Wednesday morning, the police released what they believed to be a detailed and fairly accurate psychological profile of the Butcher. Aside from the obvious—that he had some unresolved problems with women—the police paper described the Butcher as educated and intelligent, a "gentleman," probably a professional of some sort, and almost certainly a youngest or an only child. He was likely to be emotionally controlled, not to say repressed, and to dislike confrontations and change. Physical evidence supported the idea that he was an athlete of sorts, certainly exceptionally fit. He was a man of precise habits and obsessively well-organized. It wouldn't have surprised Dr. Willerbridge to discover that the Butcher of Broadway had an Oedipus complex, was a latent homosexual, or had grown up without a man in the home.

On Wednesday afternoon, Lonnie called to say that she was doing an article for the *Times* on male violence toward women and the importance of a positive male role model for young boys.

On Wednesday evening, two diamond-studded earlobes were found in a takeout Chinese food container in the elevator of a building two blocks away from mine.

On Thursday morning, a source close to the chief of police said that the police were working on some new leads.

On Thursday afternoon Margery Householder Taub phoned to ask me to settle a dispute that had arisen in her Wednesday night Scrabble game. Did I or did I not think that the mother of the Butcher must know who he was? "Catherine and Fernanda think she must," said my mother, "but Ruth and I agreed that since none of you boys tell your mothers anything, she'd probably be the last to find out."

If every cloud does have a silver lining, I thought to myself, what could the silver lining of this one be? It was a good question. I had no idea what the silver lining of this particular giant cumulus cloud, swelling and darkening over the city of New York, might have been for the Butcher's victims (no more worry that they they would never find a husband? no more wondering when the terrorist's bullet was going to hit? no more walking in the rain with men they'd met through a computer?), but by Friday it was clear what its silver lining was for me.

My nightmare was over. No one was interested in me or my marital status at all anymore. I could walk down the street like a regular person again, ride on public transportation, shop. No one whistled at me, or followed me, or made a pass. No one asked about my wife. Now when women eyed the solitary man it was not to spot the wedding ring or guess his star sign, it was to wonder how he arranged his sock drawer or if he still lived at home.

"We've made it!" I congratulated Gracie on Friday night, as we watched *The Great Train Robbery* on video and tossed popcorn at one another. "Peace at last!"

"Pizza pie!" said Gracie. "Double cheese and pickled peppers! Pizza pie!"

I sipped my beer. "I can't believe it!" I sighed. "Light at the end of the tunnel at last!"

Gracie walked up my arm. *"Choochoochoo,"* she said. *"Choochoochoo."*

11

In Ways Too Subtle to Understand at the Time, the End Begins

The Saturday morning after the discovery of the foot was cool and drizzly. Gracie was watching cartoons on the television, and I, still in my pajamas, was making French toast and singing along with the radio, "What a Day for a Daydream," a golden oldie.

That was the kind of Saturday it was, a golden oldie Saturday; dull, ordinary, and not particularly interesting or exciting, perhaps, but homey and comfortable, like an old sock. The kind of day when a man is happy to have a home and happy to be in it, safe and snug, with the book he's reading on the table and the aroma of fresh coffee filling up the kitchen, and his parrot hopping around on the roof of her cage, shouting, *"Beepbeepbeepbeepbeep!"*

There's nothing like that kind of day to make a man believe that life's not so awful after all. He thinks of the plate of hot, crisp, cinnamony toast with pure maple syrup that he'll soon be eating, and a smiling teddy bear of contentment puts its arms around him and gives him a hug. He smiles back. He says to himself, "Well, when you come right down to it, things haven't really turned out too badly. My mother's given up trying to talk sense into me for a while. My boss has offered me a partnership. Jerry's putting the finishing touches on the loft. Lonnie's pregnant. Connie Schmidmore's taking a night course in advanced carpentry. Sure, in time I may have to outmaneuver a few single women now and then, but that's not so terrible. Not after what I've been through. After what I've been through, the life of the hunted whale almost seems like a vacation. Welcome back to the sandy shores of bachelordom! Even Betsy Shopak may come around in time and be my friend once more."

"What's up, Doc?" yelled Gracie. "What's up, Doc? What's up, Doc?"

"I am!" I called back as I poured out the milk. Good Lord, I was thinking to myself, good Lord, but it's great to be alive. Everything's going to be just as it was, I was thinking as I cracked the eggs. I picked up my fork and began to beat. God's in his heaven, I'm in my kitchen, and all's right with the world, I thought. I was just about to dip the first slice of bread into the delicately spiced egg mixture when there was a ring at the door. A happy little feeling zipped through my heart. Who could it be but Betsy? She'd picked up my vibes. She'd been stirring milk powder into her coffee and she'd suddenly been struck by the memory of those long-ago Saturday mornings when we'd sometimes have breakfast together, me squeezing the juice and making the cheese puff, and she bringing the rolls from that bakery on Sixth. She'd stared into her instant beverage, and decided that perhaps she'd been a little hard on me, a little stubborn. She'd wondered if there was any chance I might be making French toast, her favorite. I put the bread down with a light and happy heart. Betsy Shopak had forgiven me at last, I could feel it in my bones. She was ready to make up. You see, I told myself as I wiped my hands on a dish towel, you were right, Mike, Betsy Shopak's on your doorstep bearing the poppy-seed rolls of peace. I grabbed Marissa's old robe from its hook as I went to the door and wrapped it around me. I didn't even look through the peephole. Who else could it be? I unlocked the double lock. I undid the chain. I flung back the door as Gracie, hearing those familiar sounds, boomed out, "Alma! Darling, please come in!" "Hey, Betsy!" was my happy cry. "You're just in time for breakfa—"

But as Chrissy Dupple, Charley Ray's better half, could probably have told me beforehand, it wasn't Betsy Shopak at the door. "Uh uh, Mikey," Chrissy would have said, if only I had had the sense to call her beforehand. "When you open the door on Saturday morning, don't expect a friendly face. Don't expect forgiveness. If you go off the path, the path does not follow you, the path stays where it was and you're on your own."

Bongo would have told me something slightly different. Something Greek. Don't get too cocky, man. You're not safe till you're dead. Unfortunately, I didn't think to call him either.

The face before me on that Saturday morning, despite the fact that it was, after a fashion, smiling, and despite the fact that it was, after a fashion, both familiar and from across the hall, was not friendly. It was blandly good-looking in a rather primitive, physical way, with expressionless eyes. It was about the same age as my face, but it was topped by quite a lot of badly cut sandy-blond hair, and was attached to a tall, broad body, dressed in a nondescript gray suit and a nondescript gray raincoat. It was the face of Lieutenant Jesus O'Brien of the NYPD, or Jesus, honey, as he was often referred to in the eighth floor hallway.

"Michael." He nodded.

I nodded back, not quite sure what to do with the fork that was still in my hand.

I have known conversations—conversations with my mother, for instance—to last as long as fifteen years. And yet a rather thorough conversation with yourself takes no longer than the time necessary for a man to say your name, introduce himself, and reach for his badge.

Why is he dressed like a cop? I asked. Because he is a cop, I answered. But it's Saturday. But he's probably on duty. But if he's on duty what is he doing here? Maybe it's those parking tickets. I'm sure I paid the parking tickets. All of them? Maybe the building has violations. He's not a health inspector, he's a homicide detective. So what's he doing here? Maybe it's about the foot. It can't be about the foot, I already told that sergeant that I didn't see or hear anything. That's true, you did. Well, probably he's not on duty, probably he wants to borrow some milk or something. Then why isn't he wearing his cockroach cap?

"I'm here in my official capacity" he said, calm and businesslike, and ignoring the fork. He flipped the badge open in front of me.

Instead of looking at the badge, I found myself wondering if anyone ever really looked at the badge. Maybe every person suddenly confronted with the emblem of law and order became occupied with the same thoughts: Now what's happened? What did I do? How will I get out of this? I glanced at the bleached-out photograph of someone who might have been a younger O'Brien and said, "Uh." Even if you did look at the badge, how would you know if it was genuine or not?

But of course it was genuine. O'Brien's voice took on its tone of professional insincerity. "I hate to bother you, Michael," he said, "but I was wondering if you could spare a few minutes just to go through a couple of routine questions."

"Routine questions?" I stuck the fork into my pocket. "About the foot?"

He almost smiled. "I see you're one step ahead of me."

"But I've already answered some routine questions," I explained. "Last week. Your sergeant. I told him—"

"Humor me," said O'Brien. "Let me ask a couple more."

Here was a man I'd seen every few days for months. A man I knew in the intimate way that you know someone you've never really had a conversation with but who sleeps with one of your closest friends. A man who, in the terms of this city, almost qualified as a friend himself. "Hahhahhah," I laughed. "What if I said no?"

Almost smiled, but not quite.

"I heard you have a sense of humor," said the good lieutenant, making it sound a lot like "I heard you have a gun"—and making it clear that a sense of humor was not something we had in common. He winked. "Let's hope you don't need it, huh?"

"I take it you're advising me to cooperate." I chuckled.

The cartoons over, Gracie in the living room called out, "Hello, honey! Honey, I'm home! Honey, where are you? Give me a kiss!"

Lieutenant O'Brien didn't flex his facial muscles or make any comment, but his eyes held a question. "You could say that," he said.

I invited him in.

"Nice place you've got here," said Jesus, glancing around the room. He took in the bookshelves, the furniture, the magazines and the Indian fertility goddess on the coffee table, the pictures on the walls, and the parquet floors. "Live here long?"

"About six years," I said, wondering what the etiquette for this sort of situation might be. Should I offer him a seat? Coffee? A slice of toast? Where was Miss Manners when she might actually come in handy?

"And what do you do for a living, Michael?" asked Jesus O'Brien.

I told him. He wrote it down. He seemed unimpressed.

He crossed the room and checked the view.

Gracie, never good with strangers, started swaying back and forth on the door of her cage. "Scared," squawked Gracie. "Scared, scared scared."

O'Brien turned from the windows across the street to her, and from her to me.

"That's Gracie." I explained.

No expression showed in his face, but he held my eyes for a second. "You live alone?"

Gracie started beeping. "Scared," she repeated. "Good night, toots. Want to go to sleep?"

"With Gracie," I said.

He bit his lip in a thoughtful way. "You an only child?"

"No," I said, for some reason taking offense at this. "No, I am not."

"And your parents never divorced?"

"My mother wouldn't divorce my father, so he died," I joked.

"Mind if I look in the bedroom?" asked O'Brien.

I pointed toward the door. "Be my guest," I drawled, my voice was honeyed with sarcasm. O'Brien paid no notice. "Would you like some coffee?"

"Thanks," he nodded. "Instant's fine."

"I don't have instant."

He turned at the entrance to the bedroom. I wished that I knew what he was thinking when he looked at me like that. "That's okay," said Jesus, and he shuffled through the door.

After he'd checked out the view from the bedroom, he followed me into the kitchen. He asked me if I'd heard anything last Sunday night, or any other night within the last week or two; if I'd seen anything suspicious. I said no. He asked me why I was making fresh coffee when there was plenty in the pyrex pot. I said it was cold and I never liked to reheat it, it destroyed the flavor. He said he'd never seen anyone grind the beans himself before. I said they tasted better that way.

We went back to the living room. "Just for an informal chat," said O'Brien. "You'd be surprised how useful it can be. Sometimes people think they didn't notice anything, and they noticed a lot."

We sat across from each other, the coffee table between us, as informal as the president being interviewed by Barbara Walters. We talked about the building and its tenants. We talked about how difficult it was to get around in the city. We talked about restaurants. We talked about biking. We compared gyms. He asked me what I did to relax. If I ever left the city. He asked me where my mother lived and whether or not she'd remarried. How often did I see them? Did we get along?

Tired of chatting informally, he went over for a closer look at Gracie. Gracie bit him. I got him a clean handkerchief from the laundry to stanch the blood. He asked me why the parrot was frightened.

"She watches too many horror movies." I laughed.

He leaned against the back of the sofa. "Alma," he said in his unpleasant monotone. "Isn't that your wife's name?"

"Pardon?"

He was holding a bobby pin in his hand. "When you answered the door, the bird was calling for Alma. Isn't that your wife's name?"

"Oh, yes," I said, sounding as shifty as I was beginning to feel. "Alma. That's her name." Why had he suddenly brought her up?

He dropped the bobby pin back into the dish on the end table. He asked me where Alma was.

"Alma?" I shrugged, a gesture full of regrets. "She's in L.A."

As it turned out, I'd been wrong, he wasn't genetically incapable of smiling. "I thought you said you lived alone."

I looked away. "I do now," I said. "We're separated."

"That's what I heard." He raised one inquiring eyebrow. "But there's still a lot of her things around."

There were? And here I prided myself on being such a tidy house-keeper. I guess the strain I'd been under was beginning to show.

The cold O'Brien eyes flickered over toward the hall, where Alma's hat and raincoat still hung on a peg and Marissa's bowling shoes sat beneath them, ready to go.

Or maybe I'd just grown so used to my marital decor that I'd forgotten to change it.

"It was a little sudden, wasn't it?" he asked, the eyes, glass-blue and obviously the inheritance from some tight-lipped Irish landlord, flickering back toward me.

"Isn't it always?" I answered, one man of the world to another.

"No," he said, in what I would soon come to know as his direct, unironic way. "No, I don't think it is." He picked up a small papier-mâché box, painted with birds and flowers, and turned it over in his hand. "You had quite a few girlfriends before her, if I'm not mistaken."

"Nothing serious."

His eyes stared into mine. Perhaps they weren't handed down from the O'Briens after all; perhaps they were the legacy of some cold-hearted conquistador. "And yet you weren't together for very long," he continued, with less expression than someone reading a stock report.

I made what I hoped was a rueful face. "Marry in haste, repent in leisure."

"Yeah," Lieutenant Jesus O'Brien nodded. "That's what they say."

No one in his or her right mind would deny that men and women are different. They look different. They think differently. Their behavior in most situations might be that of two different species.

If a man is hurt about something you said, or angry about something you did, or bears you a grudge over some imagined slight or cruelty, his response will be direct and to the point. He's not going to sit around for hours, days, or years, moping and brooding, muttering to himself, "Now, how can I get even with that sonofabitch?" A man will act. He will walk up to you in the middle of a party, or in the middle of the Delightful Deli, or on the deck of the *Lady Liberty*, and he'll crack your jaw. He'll beat the shit out of you in the parking lot or the hall. He'll shoot you while you're drinking a beer. He'll smash your car to smithereens with a tire jack. He'll blow up your house. Something like that. Something clear, clean, and uncomplicated. If a man doesn't like you, he'll let you know in an adult, straightforward way.

But not a woman. A woman who feels she's been scorned is like a devil who feels he's been escorted from heaven both hastily and unfairly. None of this, "Hey, you guys, don't you think we should talk this over?" business. None of this, "Okay, Gabriel, let's go out back. Let's just step outside and settle this once and for all." Satan goes into some dark cave to mull it over. He frowns and sighs and stamps the ground. He winds himself up with a catalog of offenses and slights that stretches back well before the dawn of creation.

And thus does a woman dwell both on real and imagined wrongs.

And thus, I reasoned, finally left alone with my golden oldie Saturday in tatters, had Betsy Shopak.

Who else?

For no matter what he said, it was hard to believe that Lieutenant O'Brien, diligent and hardworking though he might be, had gone through the two hundred apartments in my building, informally chatting to everyone about their leisure-time activities and preference in morning beverages. Had he asked Mrs. Sontag if she got along with her mother, or if her son got along with her? Had he asked the Marshalls in 8K, the lindy champions of 1958, whether or not they used their car much? Had he asked that nice young man on the second floor what had motivated him to get a Boston bullterrier and call her Peggy? No, I reckoned you could wager your best shoulder holster, he damn well had not. Routine schmooteen. O'Brien had questioned me because he was suspicious. Of me! One of the nicest, most peaceful, least violent guys you'd ever want to know. Suspicious of what? Of the fact that my wife had left me? Everybody's wife leaves him at one time or another. Suspicious because we'd been together for months and not years? For Pete's sake, I'd heard of couples breaking up on the honeymoon. No, if O'Brien was suspicious of me, it was because someone had put him up to it. Someone had given him a poke and a nudge and sent him sniffing across the hall in his drab gray suit and dark blue tie. And who could that someone be, if not Earl and Willa Shopak's youngest child?

Betsy Shopak, accidentally discovering that, in the privacy of our own home and with no real malice aforethought—with, in fact, genuine affection—Gracie and I sometimes referred to her as Betsy Wetsy, went back to her apartment, and she began to brood.

The scenario is easy to envision, and envision it I did. After O'Brien left, I lay on the sofa, my French toast and my good mood forgotten, envisioning like hell.

I could see that Betsy would have considered it adding insult to injury. Not only had I criticized her eggplant parmigiana, mocked her reading matter, rebuffed her overtures, married someone else, and killed our friendship, but I'd been making fun of her all the time. What a shit. All the good feelings she'd ever had toward me dematerialized as quickly as a quarter inch of snow in heavy rain. "He thinks he can come in here and eat my ice cream and unplug my washing machine and then laugh at me behind my back," raged Betsy Shopak. "Well, I'll show him a thing or two!" How could she ever have considered me a suitable companion for late-night video watching? a reliable confidant? possible second-husband material? She must have been out of her mind! But instead of slapping herself on the forehead and shouting, "My God! What a close call!" and resolving never to speak to me again, she ripped up the photograph she'd taken of me dressed as a miniature bottle of whisky (it's not true I have no sense of humor about my height) the Halloween before, and she flushed it down the toilet, resolving to make me pay, and pay dear. "That bastard!" screamed Betsy Shopak. "I'll get even with him if it's the last thing I do!"

A man would have snuck over to my apartment in the middle of the night and burned it down. But not Betsy. Betsy bided her time.

And what happened? Time, normally on no one's side, was on hers. Time and serendipity.

Gracie walked across my chest and watched me with concern. "What're ya doin'?" asked Gracie. "Wanna dance?"

"No, tootsie," I told her. "I don't want to dance. I'm picturing the moment when Betsy realized how to get even with me."

I saw it as though it were happening on the television screen. Jesus came over after a hard day of being harangued by the press and attacked by every women's group in the city and trying to divine a hidden message from a precisely sliced foot. Betsy fixed him some instant coffee. She tossed a couple of frozen doughnuts into the microwave for him. She rubbed his neck. "Don't worry, Jesus, honey," she whispered, "it'll be all right. You'll catch him in the end."

"My ass is on the line," whispered O'Brien. He wiped powdered sugar from his lips. "All I need is one little break. One little lead," he moaned. "But there's nothing. I've got every crazy in New York confessing, and no real clues." He took another bite of doughnut, wiped more powdered sugar from his lips, moaned again. "You'd think someone would have noticed *something* unusual."

Betsy squinched her nose in distaste. "You mean like him chopping off somebody's ears?" she asked.

"You got another doughnut?" asked Jesus. He shook his head. "No, something more subtle than that. Something tiny. Some guy who always comes home at five-forty-five coming home at six-thirty for no good reason. Some girl from the office suddenly not turning up one day, nobody knowing where she's gone." He dunked his doughnut in his coffee. "You'd be amazed," he told her. "Sometimes just the smallest aberration, the tiniest deviation from the norm, can give us the lead we need."

Betsy's brow furrowed; something was trying to get through. It was like having a word on the tip of your tongue—the name of your first-grade teacher, or the secret ingredient in Aunt Mona's Jell-O-and-marshmallow salad—and not being able to get it, not being able to shout out "Mrs. McGintley!" or "canned fruit cocktail!" "You mean just something a little odd?" she asked, her ponytail bobbing as she passed him the box.

"Yeah," said Jesus, with the patience of a man who has been running in place for the last fourteen months with the hounds of hell and municipal bureaucracy yapping at his heels. "Something a little weird. Something that in any other circumstances would even be insignificant."

Betsy concentrated. She was not, by nature, a mean or spiteful or really vengeful person. She knew that about herself. But she wanted to be helpful. She wanted her lover to break his case so he could spend more time eating doughnuts with her. She tried to think of something a little strange, a little unusual, a little out of the ordinary. Something that in any other circumstances would be insignificant. A quick and sudden separation, for instance. A man who was madly in love one minute—so in love that he couldn't even spare enough time for a drink with a friend—and not in love the next.

It fell off her tongue. "You mean something like Michael and his wife splitting up so suddenly?" she asked.

O'Brien couldn't speak—his mouth was filled with fried cake and confectioner's sugar—but he gave her an encouraging look. "Uh," he said, urging her on.

"You mean something like none of us ever really meeting his wife?" asked Betsy.

O'Brien washed down the doughnut with a slug of tepid coffee. "Yeah," he said, slowly shaking his head. "Something like that."

"You mean something like how, right before he decided to get married, Michael was never home anymore?" she asked excitedly. Betsy, though no political thinker, was beginning to grasp the domino theory: you touched one and the one behind it fell down too. "You mean something like him coming in at all hours, a man who was always so regular and orderly?"

Jesus popped a chunk of doughnut into his mouth. "It's a hell of a lot more like it than the woman who turned in her husband because he'd changed his aftershave." He grinned.

                                     .   .   .

Was I worried? Worried about what? Not only had I not done anything
wrong, I'm a nice guy. A nice, decent, respectable, upstanding guy. I
knew I was. But we can't all be, of course. If everyone is as nice as
he seems, then where do all the ax murderers and wife beaters come
from? The drug dealers and arms smugglers? The thieves and murderers? Who watches the snuff movies, who goes with twelve-year-
old prostitutes, who locks little kids in closets and fries tiny infants
on the stove? No, some guys seem nice, decent, respectable, and
upstanding on the surface, but look underneath and it's like sticking
your face into Pandora's box. If they're not selling guns to the enemy,
they're running around the house in their wife's underwear. But I
actually was as nice as I seemed. There were no skeletons in my closet,
no dark corners in my soul. I was above suspicion. And I knew that
Jesus O'Brien knew that too.

I kissed the top of Gracie's head. I got to my feet. "Let's face it," I
told her. "Right this minute, O'Brien's probably kicking himself for
ever being dumb enough to listen to Betsy."

"Betsy Wetsy," said Gracie. "Uh oh, get the Kleenex."

"I forgive her," I said, not only nice but magnanimous as well.
Gracie and I strolled toward the kitchen, thinking about lunch. "In
fact," I said, "from a certain point of view the whole thing's pretty
funny." I laughed.

Gracie laughed.

"Can you imagine Betsy convincing Jesus that *I* might be the
Butcher of Broadway?" I howled with laughter.

Gracie went off like a car alarm.

"You know—" I choked, wiping the tears from my eyes. "I think
maybe we should invite them to supper next week. Then we can all
laugh about this together."

"Pass the pizza," shouted Gracie. *"Weeoooweeoooweeooo."*

That afternoon, I ran into Betsy in the deli. "I had a nice talk with
your boyfriend this morning," I said conversationally as we gazed at
the salad bar together. I figured she'd blush and mumble some sort

of apology, and I'd tell her about putting the fork in my pocket and Gracie biting O'Brien, and then we'd both start laughing, and then I'd invite them for enchiladas.

"Who?" asked Betsy.

"O'Brien," I prompted. "Big guy? Quiet? Doesn't like to smile?"

"Well, it's nice somebody gets to talk to him," whined Betsy. "He's been working so hard I haven't seen him for a week."

It struck me as odd that she didn't know he'd followed up her lead, but then, as my mother always says, men don't readily volunteer information, they just occasionally answer questions.

"Yeah," I said, steering her away from the fried eggplant, "we had a very interesting conversation."

"Where?" asked Betsy. She pointed to the mushrooms.

I shook my head. "In my apartment."

"In your *apartment*?" She aimed the artichoke tongs at my chest. "In *your* apartment? Jesus went to your apartment and he didn't stop by to see me?"

This wasn't the response I'd expected. "Well . . . I . . . uh . . ."

"I don't believe this," shrieked Betsy. "He visited *you* and not *me*?"

"Bets . . . I—"

"That bastard!" screamed Betsy, shaking artichoke marinade all over the potatoes and the pasta and salami. She drew herself up to her full height and dropped her voice an octave. "I'm sorry, baby," she mimicked, "but I can't see you for a while. I'm really busy with this case." She threw the artichoke tongs in with the bean sprouts. "Just wait till I get my hands on him!"

I looked over at the several people who were standing around the deli, staring at us with amused smiles. I smiled back. Women, said my shrug. What can you do?

I walked home alone, musing. Betsy's apparent ignorance of the lieutenant's movements didn't quite fit in with my theory, but the only other possible explanation was that O'Brien had come to me all by himself, which of course was ridiculous. What would make him suspect me? I wasn't worried.

On Monday morning, I ran into O'Brien himself, waiting for the elevator.

He nodded.

I nodded.

The elevator came. We got in.

"Looks like a nice day," I said.

He said, "Yeah."

"Off to work?" I asked.

"Looks like it," said O'Brien. "You?"

I nodded.

He nodded.

The elevator landed. We got out.

"See you around," I said.

He said, "Sure."

I still wasn't worried.

On Tuesday night, sans Betsy and with no intention of dining, Jesus turned up on my doorstep. I knew it was an official visit, because he was still in the gray suit and the blue tie, although, with a nod toward sartorial elegance, he'd added a gold horsehead clip. "What happened to the robe?" he asked when I opened the door. "I really liked that robe. The roses were a nice touch."

And I'd thought the man had no sense of humor, no sense of style. How could I have underestimated him so?

I smiled politely. "I only wear it on the weekends."

He nodded.

"Well, Lieutenant O'Brien," I said, "and what can I do for you?"

He shrugged, almost giving the impression that this visit was so spontaneous and unimportant that he couldn't actually remember why he'd come. "Just one or two things I forgot to ask you last time."

"Like my brand of toothpaste?" I joked.

"Colgate," he said.

Not worried yet.

"You can ask me in," said Jesus.

I asked him in.

It was just about the last thing that I asked him.

Lieutenant O'Brien was full of questions. He remained standing, wandering aimlessly around the room. Sometimes his eyes were on mine; sometimes he watched the light on the carpet; sometimes he seemed to be staring into space. But always he was asking. Where had I been on this day? On that day? On this night? On that night? On the twelfth? Did I take the Long Island Rail Road much? Where to? Had I ever been to Wyandanch? To Mineola? When was the last time I'd been on the Staten Island ferry? Where had I ridden my bike? How often did I work out? Where had I gone on those weekend walks I used to take? For a while there, I'd been keeping some pretty odd hours. Where had I been? With whom? How many serious relationships had I had? Where did I shop? How long had I been with Marissa? Two years? But he'd heard it was one.

"Well, it seemed like two," I said.

O'Brien said, "Um."

Where had Marissa gone? Did I ever hear from her? Did I have an address? Did we fight a lot? Had I ever been married before Alma? How did I really feel about marriage? Why had I never married before? What sort of terms had Marissa and I parted on? How did I meet Alma? When? Where? Where had she lived? What was my favorite ice cream? How did I feel about being a husband? If I'd spent so much time at Alma's, surely I must remember the address.

"Where's Alma? Where's Alma?" called Gracie.

"That's what I'd like to know," said O'Brien.

"*Beepbeep*," said Gracie, hanging upside down. "Get rid of Alma! Get rid of Alma."

O'Brien gave me a look.

He was back on Wednesday.

"Lieutenant," I half-said, half-chuckled, surprised to hear myself sounding like someone in an episode of *Columbo*. "I didn't expect to see you again so soon." But I still wasn't worried. After all, he had to do something to justify spending the taxpayers' money. He had to go somewhere from time to time. He was like a dog chasing his own tail, that's what he was, a dog chasing his own tail. Fido O'Brien.

"Who's there?" called Gracie. "Alma, is that you?"

"She seems to miss your wife a lot," said O'Brien.

I attempted to keep levity in our relationship. "It's always hardest on the children," I said.

O'Brien attempted to keep it out. "Just a couple more questions," he said, reaching for his notebook. "I've got the memory of a sieve."

"Sieves don't have any memory," I corrected.

He made a face. "I heard you were a stickler for details," he said.

I didn't mention that he was too. He started again with the where-was-I-ons and who-was-I-withs.

"Where were you on the night of the twelfth?" he asked.

"I told you before," I said. "I was at a big publishing party. Over on the East Side."

One eyebrow arched. "No one remembers seeing you there."

"But I told you," I said, wishing he could get things straight. "I sat next to a woman called Alicia, a foreign scout, and Elspeth or Escot or Elplop, something like that, a mystery writer."

He made a face. "Neither of them remembered your name."

He asked how I'd met Marissa. Alma? Who was Suzanne Lightfoot to me? Elizabeth Beacher? Jemma Wyte? Would I consider myself a ladies' man? asked O'Brien, making it clear that he, for one, wouldn't. While he questioned me, his eyes ran over the shelves—the books and the knickknacks and the photographs dotted here and there. He picked up a small bowl but put it right down. "On the morning of the twelfth, at approximately one-thirty-three, one of your neighbors says she heard gunshots coming from inside your apartment."

"You're kidding, right?" This was not a question.

It is no less amazing that someone with an Irish father and a Mexican mother, two nationalities known for their warmth, humor, and zest for living, should possess the wit and charm of a horned frog than it is that a law-abiding person who even as a child always brought his library books back on time should immediately start looking shifty and behaving like a criminal when ruthlessly interrogated by a policeman. I wasn't really worried yet, but I was beginning to consider it.

"No, Michael," said Jesus, "I'm not joking."

My voice was nervous, insecure. My forehead was damp. "It must have been the television." Even I could hear that I was lying.

"I've checked. There was nothing on at that hour that involved a gunfight."

I watched him as he spoke. He had thin, ungenerous lips. "Why are you doing this to me?" I asked.

"Doing?" asked O'Brien. "I'm not *doing* anything, Michael. I'm just asking a couple of questions."

"For Pete's sake," I said, a little more emotionally than I'd planned. "I don't even own a gun."

"Lots of people don't own guns, Michael. You'd be amazed how many poor bastards are killed every day by people who don't own guns."

"Hey." I grinned with relief, reaching into my pocket for my handkerchief to wipe the sweat from my brow. "I know what it must have been."

He barely blinked. "What must it have been?"

"Gracie."

"Gracie?"

But Gracie would not do a gunfight on demand.

"Parrots are really remarkable," I explained to Jesus as I tried to encourage Gracie by humming the theme tune from *The Good, the Bad, and the Ugly.* "People believe that they just repeat things mindlessly, but they don't; they actually think as well."

Jesus leaned against the bookcase, watching. "Well, that gives them an advantage over most humans I know."

"Get the gun!" ordered Gracie. "Get the gun!"

"On the other hand," I continued, "very often they just repeat things mindlessly."

"Uh oh," squawked Gracie, "now you've done it. Now you've done it. *Beepbeepbeep.*"

"On the other hand"—his lips twitched—"you're a pretty intelligent man yourself, aren't you, Michael? You'd call yourself clever, wouldn't you?" I opened my mouth. "I'd call you clever." I closed it again. He shook his head. "You wouldn't be stupid enough to do target practice in your own living room." He knocked on the wall. "Not knowing how thin these things are." He knocked again. "How much you can hear through them . . ."

And so can a statement sound like a threat. "I wouldn't put too much stock in what Mrs. Sontag thinks she heard—" I began.

He moved a figurine. "Mrs. Sontag?" he asked, his eyes on the china angel in his hand. "What makes you think I've been talking to Mrs. Sontag?"

I stared at him, speechless. Something awful was happening in the region of my solar plexus. It was beginning to dawn on me that the reason I sounded as though I were in an episode of *Columbo* might very well be because I was in an episode of *Columbo*. About two commercials away from the moment when Peter Falk bumbles into the closet and comes out with handcuffs, two patrol cars, an arrest warrant, and a story about his wife's uncle.

Lieutenant O'Brien was playing with me. Toying. Teasing. He knew something that I didn't know he knew (which wouldn't have been odd, since it would have had to have been something that I didn't know at all). I'd seen enough movies and read enough novels to recognize the signs. He thought I was the Butcher of Broadway, but he didn't have any hard evidence. He wasn't positive I was the Butcher, but I was his best hope, a long shot, a hunch. He didn't give a shit whether or not I was really the Butcher of Broadway. He didn't like me, and that was that. He didn't like me—he had never liked me—and he needed an arrest before they put him back in uniform and onto the streets, his girlfriend dumped him, and he ended his days as a drunken has-been. He was going to hound me until I cracked. If he broke this case, the press would stop calling him Lieutenant Lame-o. He'd be a hero. He'd make captain. He'd make captain, marry Betsy, and move to the suburbs. Everybody knows that the doughnuts are better in the suburbs. So what if he arrested the wrong man? Arresting me—the wrong man—might make the real killer so angry that he gave himself away, came out in the open, turned himself in. Psychopaths were always doing things like that. O'Brien would be hailed not just as a hero, but as a genius as well. Forget captain, he'd run for the Senate. No one would remember who I was. Nor would they care. "What was the name of the guy they arrested to flush out the Butcher?" aficionados of true crime would quiz one another. "I don't know," would be the reply. "I can't remember."

"You know, Michael," Jesus suddenly observed, not constrained by the niceties of conversational transition as most of us are when wanting to change the subject, "you don't seem very disturbed about your wife's disappearance."

"That's because she didn't disappear, Lieutenant. I told you. She's in L.A."

"Then you won't mind giving me a phone number and an address where she can be reached."

And then I realized what a jerk I was being. What was I doing? O'Brien thought that I'd murdered my wife, and instead of pointing out that I couldn't have murdered her, since she'd never existed, I was carrying on as if she had. Relief shoved worry out of the way. I smiled. I laughed. I may even have slapped him on the back. "Look, Lieutenant," I said, "why don't I level with you? I can clear this whole thing up right now."

He leaned back against the wall, striking a casual pose. "That'd be very nice, Michael," he said softly. "I'd like that."

But he didn't like it all that much.

If I'd made up my wife, then whose bowling shoes stood next to the bookcase? Whose bobby pins were clustered around the apartment? "And I suppose that robe with the roses down the front is yours, right?" asked Jesus O'Brien. "You have slippers that match?"

If I'd made up my wife, whose knickknacks were dotted around the room?

"For Pete's sake," I protested. "Since when is it only women who like to put little decorative touches around the room?"

"And the cover on the bird cage?" asked Lieutenant O'Brien, obviously on to something here. "Any guy I've ever known who had a bird just threw a towel over the cage at night. You telling me that you went out and *bought* that cover yourself?"

"Yes." I said. "Downtown."

The lieutenant's expression became quizzical. "And the bedroom? All those trees and flowers were your idea?"

"It's a jungle," I said stiffly. "So Gracie would feel more at home."

We studied each other in silence for a second. "Michael," he said at last, "are you trying to tell me that you're gay?"

. . .

He was back on Friday.

"We're going to have to stop meeting like this," I joked. "I think Betsy's getting suspicious."

"It's okay," said O'Brien, with a curt nod behind him. "I've got chaperones."

I looked behind him. Now I was worried. How can you open your front door and not notice a gaggle of guys with identical haircuts and the same blank expressions, trampling mud through the hall? I could hear several doors on the corridor open with a soft click.

"Wait a . . ." I said. "What . . ."

He held up an official-looking piece of paper.

"Oh, come on," I exploded, staring at the warrant. "You can't be serious. This has got to be a joke."

Jesus shook his head. "No," he said levelly, "no, Mr. Householder, it's not a joke."

"On what grounds?" I demanded. "You've got to have some evidence for a search warrant. I know my rights. You can't just—"

He touched my shoulder in what was almost a brotherly fashion. "Michael," he said quietly, "Michael, we've got grounds."

I stood in the open doorway, as vocal as a piece of granite, as O'Brien strode past me. The other cops—some in uniform, some also in bad suits—strode past him. They started picking through the apartment like migrants through a field of lettuce.

O'Brien turned to face me. "We're very interested in this vanishing wife of yours," he said. I took this to be by way of explanation.

My human speech patterns, established nearly forty years ago, slowly came to life. "What wife?" I sputtered. "I told you, Lieutenant, there never was a wife. I made her up. She was a joke . . . a gag . . . a—"

". . . kitchen," finished O'Brien.

I blinked. "Kitchen?" I repeated. "What about the kitchen?"

He gestured with his bullet head to the sparkling surfaces of my food-preparation area. "You're telling me there was never a wife in this apartment, but the kitchen is all set up for a woman."

"What are you talking about, 'set up for a woman'? It's just a kitchen."

"It's got cookbooks."

"Of course it's got cookbooks. It's got a stove and a food processor and pots and pans, too. But no microwave," I added. "I don't believe in fast cooking."

He clicked his teeth. "No," he said, "I'm sure you don't. But you believe in plants, right? You believe in diet salad dressing."

I could but stare in disbelief. For a second there, it looked as though his lips were going to forget themselves and bend into an expression of joy.

"Michael," said Jesus O'Brien in the voice of reason, "you've got live herbs in little pots on the windowsill."

Jesus, Jesus. "Is that a crime in New York now? Fresh herbs? You think I'm shooting up basil? You think I'm sniffing chives?"

But O'Brien had made a deduction. "Somebody cooks in that kitchen," he informed me.

"Of course somebody cooks in that kitchen," I answered, just managing not to shout. "*I* cook in that kitchen. I'm an excellent cook. It's my hobby, my interest." I couldn't seem to shut up; logorrhea had set in. "You should taste *my* enchiladas. I could open my own restaurant. I know everybody says that, but I really could. Ask anybody. They'll tell you."

"Don't worry," he assured me, "I will." He stretched those thin lips. He narrowed those deep-set eyes.

I could see a theory working itself out in his mind. I'd been spending my spare time for the last year or so, hacking secretaries and suburban housewives into tiny pieces and littering the streets of Manhattan with them because I hated women. But to disguise the fact that I hated women, and to disguise the fact that I was a latent homosexual with good color sense and an unhealthy fondness for my sauté pan, I had married the unfortunate Ms. Huttenmeyer. It hadn't worked out. How could it? I was afraid of women, because of my mother. I was addicted to ritualistic butchering. I didn't want to love and cherish, I wanted to fillet and serve with potatoes. Maybe Alma had found me watering the plants one evening. Maybe she'd discovered the wok I had hidden at the back of the closet. Maybe she'd resented my herbs. It's hard to tell when you're dealing with a man who has flowers on the walls of his bedroom. She refused to give me a divorce. Or maybe she began to suspect what I was really doing when I said I had to work late. Maybe I hadn't planned to make her one of my victims, recklessly calling attention to myself. Probably we'd had a fight, and in the heat of the moment, at that point in the argument when another man would have punched a hole in the wall or slammed out of the house, I took out my automatic and shot her through the heart.

Cool and in control, Lieutenant O'Brien drifted to the bookshelves. "You've got a lot of books," he said. It was easy to see how he'd made lieutenant.

How was it possible to make such an innocent statement sound as ominous as "I just happened to notice quite a few fresh graves in the cellar"? Could this man be related to my mother? "Now what are you saying?" I snapped. "That only women read books?"

He reached up and pulled down Elizabeth Beacher's international best-seller *Love on the Run*. " 'He knew everything there was about power, about danger and deceit,' " O'Brien read from the back cover, disproving the ugly rumor about illiteracy and the law, " 'but she knew everything about love.' " He put it back and removed another: *Maybe Tomorrow*. " 'Jemima gazed up at the bright white moon, as shining as a pearl. So far he had lied to her. He had cheated her. He had nearly gotten her killed. He had come within inches of hitting her. But somehow she knew that there was more to him than the rough and heartless loner everyone saw. "Maybe tomorrow," Jemima murmured to herself. "Maybe tomorrow I'll meet the man within. . . ." ' " He held the book up, cover toward me. "This is what you read for fun?"

I threw up my hands. "This is ridiculous, O'Brien, and you know it is. I haven't done anything." I was screaming. I was stomping back and forth. "There is no Alma Huttenmeyer! There is no gun!"

"I know there's no gun," said Jesus Joachim Liam O'Brien. Softly.

I'll just call your wife from the sunroom, says Columbo. He goes to the

*door. He pulls it open. Three umbrellas and a hat box fall on his head. Gee,
he says, this reminds me of my cousin George.*

"I'm not looking for a gun, Michael," purred the lieutenant. "I'm
looking for something with a blade."

"You mean like in the kitchen?" My voice cracked. "Everyone in
this neighborhood has a block of knives in their kitchen!"

"I'm not looking for a bread knife," said O'Brien.

I made my voice calm; calm and tough. "Look," I said, "you guys
have been running around for months now, being outsmarted by some
lunatic with a cleaver, and now you've decided to get yourself off by
trying to pin his crimes on me. I can understand your predicament,
Jesus, but it's not going to work."

O'Brien held up his hand, smiling in a way that might have fooled
some people into believing that he was human. "Let me tell you a
little about the man I'm looking for," he said almost conversationally.
He gestured with his hand. "First of all, he's single and unattached."

"You mean, like you?" I shot back.

"Sort of," said O'Brien, still smiling. "But unlike me, he's probably
very attractive to women. Certainly charming, and probably good-
looking."

"I thought you had no idea—" I began, but he cut me short.

"Michael, Michael." He shook his head, as though he'd expected
more of me. "If you're playing poker, you don't throw your hand
face up on the table." He winked. "Also unlike me," he continued,
"my man had a very dominating mother. Probably his father wasn't
around when he was growing up. He has trouble relating to women."

"All men have trouble relating to women. It could be anyone."

"No," purred O'Brien, "not anyone. This is someone who can't
relate to himself as a man either. Someone with a very feminine side.
He's domestic and fussy, almost fastidious. He's controlled and ironic.
He loves women, maybe even wants secretly to be a woman, but he
hates them, too. He's afraid of them. He's afraid they're going to
castrate him, that's why he can't sustain a real relationship. That's
why as soon as a woman gets close to him, he feels threatened." He
looked into my eyes. "Now who does this remind us of?" he asked.

His entire little monologue had been conducted in the tone and volume you might have used to read out the weather. I, on the other hand, shouted. "Come off it, O'Brien. You have nothing but the most flimsy and shallow circumstantial evi—"

"I have witnesses."

"Witnesses?" This was like being in a Kafka short story. This was like being in an Eric Tucker thriller. Any one of seventeen. Why couldn't it be an Elizabeth Beacher novel, where at least all the main participants have an orgasm or two? "What are you talking about, 'witnesses'? Witnesses to what?"

"Witnesses who have met this imaginary wife of yours."

"Look, how many times do I have to tell you—"

"Your parents, for instance. They seem very fond of the late Mrs. Householder."

"What are you talking about, 'late Mrs. Householder'? Look, I told you about Alex. Have you talked to Alex? I explained about my mo—"

"Your friend Alex doesn't seem to be in town at the moment. But I did have very nice chat with your friend Mr. Finer and his wife. Ms. Stepato says she only heard your wife on the answering machine, but Mr. Finer not only says that he met the late Mrs. Householder—"

"She's not the late Mrs. Anybody. She's the Mrs. Never-Was. And Jerry didn't meet her, he was her, he "

". . . he claims to have spent quite a bit of time with the two of you." He consulted his notebook. "Two dinners, a movie, bowling, and a basketball game, several meals, several trips to the gym, a long weekend—"

"Look, look, there's a perfectly logical explanation for that. You see, Jerry, he—"

O'Brien barely missed a beat. "Mrs. Sontag has seen your wife," he continued in his soothing monotone. "The doormen have seen her. One hundred and ninety-eight people aboard the *Lady Liberty* on the night of September eighth saw your wife."

"They didn't see Alma! They saw Jerry. I told you, O'Brien, in order to make her convincing . . ." Mine was a voice in the wilderness, screaming to the wind.

Rustle-rustle-rustle went the pages of Lieutenant O'Brien's note-

book. Plonk-plonk-plonk went my heart. Damn the soul of whatever
fiend had taught him to write. "Ms. Shopak heard and saw this make-
believe wife of yours on numerous occasions." His stubby finger
moved down the page. "She was in this apartment with you and your
wife on the night of—"

I practically ripped the notebook from his hands. "I can explain
that, Jesus. I really can explain everything."

A slow smile spread across his face, like oil spreading across a bay.
"Michael," he said, his voice so low I had to lean into him to hear,
"Michael, *I* saw your wife. I even rode up in the elevator with her."

"That wasn't my wife!" I squeaked. "I can't believe I fooled you!
That wasn't my wife, O'Brien, that was me!"

The oil had settled, its surface slick and impenetrable in the fading
light. "Poker," said O'Brien, as lightly as the breath of a baby. And
then added, even more softly, "I know."

Before I could react to this, one of the lettuce pickers appeared in
the doorway of the bedroom. "Lieutenant?"

O'Brien turned.

"I think we've found a couple of things you might be interested
in."

"Oh yeah?"

"Yeah. We've found quite a few of Mrs. Householder's belongings."
O'Brien nodded.

"We found some papers of Mr. Householder's you might want to
look at, the shoes with the lifts just like you thought, and these." He
held up a large plastic bag. There were two black patent-leather shoes
in it, high-heeled with ankle straps; both were badly scraped and one
had a broken heel. They were the shoes I'd worn when I first imper-
sonated Alma—that's why they were so damaged—but even I could
see that, hanging from the lettuce picker's hands, they looked remarkably like the sort of shoe you'd wear with black stockings with
little rhinestone bows at the ankle.

"Any blood on them?" asked O'Brien.

"Not that we can see."

Jesus turned back to me. "I'm sure you can explain them, too," he
said.

"As a matter of fact—" I bleated.

But the lettuce picker wasn't through. "And we found this," he said, extending something in a small plastic bag to O'Brien.

O'Brien took it and held it up to the light. It was the knife Elizabeth Beacher had brought back from Mexico for me. "Where?"

"It was hidden in an inside suit pocket."

O'Brien's eyes moved from the blade to me. "I can't wait to hear you explain this." He grinned.

12

This Is Your Life

As a boy, I often imagined what my life would be like when I was an adult. I'd be my own boss; I would do as I pleased. No more lights out by eight-thirty. No more canned peas and Chef Boyardee. My mother would never nag, harass, or embarrass me again. I'd live in a big house and drive a big car and have the sort of parties where no one counted the pretzels or the Cokes. I'd be taller.

As I got older, of course, I began to realize that life's path is not as smooth as I had thought. Things could go wrong. Things did go wrong. Illness, heartbreak, and all-purpose doom were ever bopping down the street with you, just waiting to get in your way. Happiness was elusive. Love was evasive. Work was hard. Gas was expensive. Your mother would always nag, harass, and embarrass you, no matter how old you were. Your hair fell out. You never got that tall.

Sometimes, as a mature, intelligent, and well-adjusted adult, I

would lie awake all night long, besieged by anxieties, by visions of
all the calamities that could—and might—befall me. Brain tumors.
Mugging. Stray bullets. Penury. Plane crashes. Car accidents. Home-
lessness. Short-term memory loss. Walking into the liquor store to
buy a bottle of chardonnay to go with the trout in basil sauce and
discovering that you're in the middle of a holdup. Never finding someone to love.

But there was one disaster that I never anticipated. One divine
poleaxing the possibility of which never once crossed my mind. Call
me foolish, call me naïve, but I never imagined being arrested for mass
murder. When I lay awake all those timeless predawn mornings, listening to the futile chirping of the birds and picturing the worst, the
worst that I pictured never included that long ride in the police car
through the black and rain-splattered night, the light going round and
round, the radio crackling, the cops joking about something that had
happened to someone else. It never included the slow-motion walk
into Central Booking, the curious passersby, the prostitutes nudging
each other as I was shoved down the hall, the newsmen stirring like
dogs who, though sound asleep in the living room, smell the steak
hitting the grill on the patio. The pathetic listing of the few things in
my pockets—-handkerchief, wallet, nail file, change, keys, lip balm.
The fingerprinting. The photograph. The bare interrogation room with
the wooden table and the windows too high to be climbed through.
I never, not in a million sleepless mornings, thought I'd ever hear
myself say, "I'm not saying anything till I've talked to my lawyer."

And that is why, when organizing my life, though I had thought
to find out about good insurance deals, smart accountants, reputable
financial advisers, and recommended hairdressers, I never thought,
Hey, I'd better make sure that when I'm arrested for multiple homicide
I know a good lawyer to call.

My usual lawyer did not handle things like serial killings. He handled things like incorporations and house closings and immigration
problems. It seemed reasonable to me that by now Jerry might have
some advice to offer about divorce lawyers, but felonies were a little
out of his scope. My mother was the sort of person who might know

the mother of a good criminal lawyer—from her furniture-repair class or her volunteer work at the hospital or maybe even from the beauty parlor—but my mother and Barry were away for a few days. In the end, in one of those moments of blinding insight that occasionally happen after you've been arrested, I remembered something incredibly sage and sensible that Suzanne Lightfoot said in chapter 3. She said, "Shopping for a husband is like shopping for a cocktail dress. If you want a cocktail dress you do not go to a sports store. You do not go to Daywear. You go to a shop that sells cocktail dresses. Ergo, if you want to meet men, you must go where men are." What could be more logical? I asked myself. The same had to be true of criminal lawyers. If you wanted to find one, you had to go to someone who might have had cause to use one sometime. Someone who was sure to know several people who had used one sometime. I made my phone call to Charley Ray.

He answered on the fifth ring. "Hey there, Mike, what's up?" asked Charley Ray.

Watched by cops, whores, drunks, addicts, petty criminals, and dangerous psychotics, I explained the situation as succinctly as possible. "You've got to help me, Charley," I said. "You're my only hope."

Charley Ray exhibited none of the surprise, shock, horror, dismay, indignation, recrimination, or inquisitiveness that most people—people like Margery Householder Taub, for example—might have shown. He burped. "Shit," said Charley Ray. "This don't sound good."

I hunched over the receiver. "So, can you help me?"

"No sweat, man," said Charley Ray. "Chrissy knows a great lawyer. Fuckin' hotshit humdinger." He took what I assumed was another slug of beer. "Absolutely first class. Don't you worry, Mike. We'll have you out of there in no time."

I'm not sure whether I'd expected to be kept in a holding pen with dozens of twentieth-time offenders with rotten attitudes, or shoved into a back room and beaten with rubber truncheons. As it was, I had the best of both worlds.

"You're a lucky man, Michael," oozed O'Brien, as they hustled me into a small, airless room, where, I was sure, more than one poor sod had begged for mercy. "We're giving you preferential treatment."

"Oh, the benefits of being white and middle-class," I mumbled, cynical, but still a little thankful.

O'Brien winked. "Nah," he said, "it's not that. We can't put you in with the flotsam and jetsam." He chuckled. "Those guys don't like guys who do what you've done."

Given the timeless popularity of violent crimes against women, I was a little surprised to hear this, but I decided to let it pass. "Alleged to have done," I corrected him.

"Yeah, sure," said O'Brien. He settled himself across the table from me. "So we'll keep you in here with us." He smiled, leaning back in his chair. "Until your lawyer shows up."

Now, that was good news.

Periodically, the door would open and someone—a cop, a detective, a cleaner, a delivery boy, someone's husband or wife who'd just dropped off a forgotten set of keys, a casual passerby—would look in and say, "That him?"

And one, or all, of my companions would nod. "That's him."

Sometimes the visitors would roll their eyes or shake their heads or give a thin whistle. Sometimes they would just stand there and stare for a few minutes, as though wanting to remember me in detail, just in case they were asked by the papers precisely how close together my eyes were supposed to be. Sometimes they'd say, "Geez"—*you never can tell.*

Periodically, O'Brien and his alter ego, Bloomfield, would attempt to question me. Bloomfield would start screaming and shouting at me, or shoving pictures of mutilated body bits in my face. "Remember this?" he'd sneer. "Recognize that? Look familiar?"

And then, as though he'd been thinking of something else for a while, O'Brien would suddenly rejoin the conversation. "I'm sure Michael wants to cooperate," he'd say. "Don't you, Michael?" He'd appear bewildered, almost hurt, by my attitude. "We just want to ask you a couple of questions, Michael," he'd say, never tired of repeating himself. "What's the harm in that? Why don't you make a statement

and save us all some time?'' He'd grin. ''Don't hold me in suspense,''
he'd plead. ''You know I'm dying to hear about that knife.''

''I know my rights,'' I'd assure him—again and again—hoping he
didn't realize I was lying, that all I knew was what I'd seen on TV.
''I'm not saying a word until my lawyer gets here.''

It was Detective Bloomfield who had the unpleasant laugh. ''Your
lawyer?'' he'd sneer. ''Your lawyer? I bet you've got some fancy-ass
attorney from Harvard you think's gonna get you out of here, but he
ain't gettin' you out of here.'' He'd lean over me so that I could smell
the raspberry jelly. ''Not this time, you sick bastard,'' he'd growl. ''The
entire faculty of Harvard Law School couldn't get you out of this.''

''Michael,'' O'Brien would interrupt, in what had quickly become
a refrain. ''One or two little bits of information, Michael. What have
you got to lose?''

What a question.

Then Bloomfield would stand with his back to me, gazing up at the
ceiling. ''We know all about you,'' he'd softly intone. ''We know
things about you you don't even know.'' He'd crack his knuckles.
''About your relationships . . . your habits . . .''—turning and whis-
pering into the top of my head—''your wig . . .''

''Michael,'' O'Brien would reason, ''Michael, you can make things
easy on yourself. We can help you. We can get you through all this
fast and clean. We can see that you're treated well. A man like you,''
he'd croon, ''a man who grinds his own coffee, you wouldn't like to
have it too hard, would you? You know how dirty and unpleasant
this sort of thing can be? You know what the food's like in here? Let
us help you, Mike. Just answer a question or two.''

Then Bloomfield would do something endearing, like bite his plastic
straw in half with a snap. ''Wait'll the press get their teeth into you.''
He'd wink. ''You're gonna wish you were a miscarriage.''

''Of justice?'' I kidded.

''Of your mother.''

In that pleasant manner, we whiled away the hours.

And time stood still.

Time stood still. A familiar phrase, a cliché, in fact: Time stood still.

It's not until you're arrested that you really begin to understand what it means. It isn't just that an hour lasts a week, a day lasts a year, as on a blind date. It is that time stops. Outside, you know, the world goes on as it was going on before, but without you. Outside, people are laughing and talking and making love. They're watching television and going down to the corner for a bottle of mineral water or a container of yogurt. They're wondering if they should stay up for the news. But you, who soon will be the news, do nothing, trapped in time.

There's nothing you can do. O'Brien and Bloomfield get tired of harassing you and finally leave. You sit in that dim, airless room with stains on the floor that are most certainly blood, guarded by silent men with guns, waiting to wake up. Reality fades in and out like a wonky light bulb. One minute you know you have nothing to fear— what is this if not the most incredible travesty, the most astounding farce? And the next minute you can see your face plastered all over the papers, hear your name endlessly repeated on the news. One minute you're wondering what to have for breakfast when you get home, and the next you're imagining your mother sitting down to eggs and toast in her Catskills hotel room. Her husband, who gets nervous when away from civilization for too long, switches on the television. "A man suspected of being the Butcher of Broadway has been arrested in Manhattan," says the morning anchorman. "Thank God they finally got that bastard," says your mother. "Hanging's too good for him," your stepfather agrees. "They should stuff the son-ofabitch." Your huddled form, being yanked from a police car flashes across the screen. "Literary agent Michael C. Householder," says the anchorman. Your stepfather starts to cry. "You see," says your mother. "I knew there was a reason he never married."

At about three A.M., it occurs to you that you will never be out of this moment. You will never walk down a street as you used to. You will never sing a song. You will never again know laughter or happiness. You will never grow old. If your lawyer doesn't show up within the next few days, you may very well never move from this room. You think of your parrot, sitting at home by herself, wondering where you are, calling out for you in the dark, "Hello, tootsie, where'd you go?" It's like being dead, but without the oblivion. Every time you hear a footstep in the corridor, you think something's going to happen, but nothing does. "Friday night," says one of the cops. "You couldn't pick a worse time to be arrested." You assure him that you'll do better in the future. "A psycho with a sense of humor," he says. "Wait'll I tell the wife."

But, terrifying as those hours were, I knew, of course, deep in my heart, that they would pass. It was a nightmare, but it was one from which I would wake. O'Brien had no case. And even if he did have some cobbled-together arguments, even if he had enough circumstantial evidence to get me arraigned, he would never get it past the grand jury. I was an innocent man. Someday I would look back on this and laugh. "Hahaha," I'd say to my grandchildren, "did I ever tell you about the time I was charged with first-degree murder? It took Uncle Brook a whole hour to get me off." All I needed was Charley Ray's lawyer—my lawyer, the man who would become my children's and grandchildren's beloved Uncle Brook—to stride in, briefcase locks snapping, and take me home. I tried to imagine Charley Ray's lawyer. Did bikers use the same sort of lawyer as the mob did? Probably not quite that classy. Cheaper restaurants and ready-made shirts. Bloomfield was wrong. He wouldn't be some Harvard wunderkind named Brook or Wesley in a seven-hundred-dollar suit and platinum cuff links who would make me a million suing the cops for false arrest. No, he'd be some sharp, cynical, crafty sonofabitch from NYU named Al or Victor in a seven-hundred-dollar suit he hadn't paid for and a gold watch who'd make me two million suing the cops.

At last there were footsteps that didn't pass. The door opened. A head appeared. "Mr. Householder's lawyer's here," said the head.

" 'Bout time," grumbled one of my guards. "Where'd he come from, Peru?"

My lawyer was here. Relief wrapped its arms around me and kissed me on the cheek. The warmth of hope resuscitated my heart. I gazed at the room of my incarceration. It wasn't such a bad room after all. Not many amenities, not a pleasant exposure, but better than the

Black Hole of Calcutta. Much better, in fact. My lawyer was here. The words danced through my head. Maybe he had been in Peru, having dinner with a drug lord he'd kept out of prison. Maybe he'd been in a business conference in a private plane over Geneva. Maybe he'd just flown in from Washington or L.A. or some other place where cunning defense lawyers are always in demand. It didn't matter. I had had an important learning experience, but now my lawyer was here and I could go home. I smiled at my jailers.

"We won't go too far," they promised. The nice cop, the one whose wife had never heard of a psychopathic killer with a sense of humor, gave me a nod as he left the room.

I made myself ready. I sat up straight. I brushed off my jacket. I ran my hand over my head. My hotshit, humdinger, first-class lawyer had finally arrived. I was on my way!

The door opened again. A tired-looking young woman in faded jeans and a *Help the Earth Fight Back* T-shirt walked in. She was carrying a bright orange parka and a beat-up old briefcase. She was wearing hiking boots that smelled as though they'd recently walked through bear shit in the rain. There was a carved-bone skull hanging from one of her ears.

I blinked and swallowed hard. Clearly, the strain had been greater than I'd thought. I was losing it. I was hallucinating. Maybe there was something besides dishwater in that cup of coffee they'd given me earlier. Peyote. LSD.

"Jesus Christ," said the young woman. "I don't believe this. It is *you.*"

As opening statements go, it wasn't the best, but it was okay, if only because I certainly didn't believe it was her.

I had been dignified during the arrest and booking. I'd been strong and silent during the bullying and badgering. But now my fragile hold on myself began to loosen.

"What are you doing here? How did you manage to get past the cops?" I jumped to my feet and started shoving her back toward the door. "You have to get out," I ordered. "My lawyer's coming." My voice broke. "How the hell did you get in here?"

"Let go of me, Michael," she ordered, pushing back. She was stronger than she looked. "Have you really gone nuts? Get your hands off me."

"Please," I pleaded, "my lawyer's coming, you have to leave."

She cocked her head to one side. She looked me up and down. I could see what she was thinking: short and aggressive. Napoleon, she was thinking. Hitler. Bluebeard.

"Michael," said Snow Lazarro in that painfully patient voice she had, the sort of voice I'd always imagined God using in his conversations with Adam. "Michael, stop acting like a complete jerk and get a grip on yourself. I am your lawyer."

I don't remember it clearly—it had been, after all, one of those nights—but I think I said "What?"

She shook her head. "I just didn't think that when Charley Ray said his friend Michael Householder had been arrested he meant you." And then, unbelievably enough, she smirked. "I guess he forgot to put in the *C*." And then, even more unbelievably, she started to laugh.

I was living through hell, and she was laughing!

"You!" she spluttered. "You! Of all people!" She looked me up and down again. "You really are too much. You're arrested for some of the worst murders the city's ever seen, and you still manage to show up in a suit!"

"At least one of us did," I said pointedly.

She didn't hear me. "Too much," she said again, "just too much."

"Look," I said, my voice rising above her hilarity, "you can't possibly be my lawyer. You teach Women's Studies at Columbia."

She stopped laughing and started looking at me in a way that my mother often did, as though she couldn't figure out where I'd come from. "No, I don't."

"Yes, you do."

"No, I don't."

"Yes, you do."

"No, I don't, Michael. What I teach is a special seminar on women and the legal system." God had had just about enough of Adam. She slapped her briefcase onto the table. "So now that we've cleared that up, let's hear your side of things."

"Are you telling me that you're a lawyer?"

"Michael, will you please try to pay attention to someone else for a change?" The locks didn't snap open, they just sort of went click. "I'm telling you that I'm *your* lawyer."

"There must be some mistake," I said evenly. "You can't possibly be *my* lawyer."

The last traces of humor vanished completely. She looked as though, in her entire life, she had never smiled and never laughed. Not once. Her voice was crisp. "Why not?"

Experience had taught me to be wary of women with abrupt mood swings, but there was nothing I could do but stare back at her in open amazement. At her jeans and her T-shirt, at her short spiky hair and her ears studded with rings and skulls and God knew what. O wad some Pow'r the giftie gie us, To see oursels as others see us! I thought to myself. "A criminal lawyer?"

She pointed a slender finger at me. "Look," she said, "I'm here as a personal favor, right? And not to you. To Charley Ray and Chrissy. So just cut the crap. The last thing I need is any of your chauvinist bullshit."

Until she'd marched through the door, I'd sincerely believed that I'd be home by dawn. Or maybe a few hours after dawn. Police incompetence had put me here, but all it would take was a lawyer to get me out. A good lawyer. A real lawyer. A lawyer who commanded fear and respect. A hard, sharp, jaded sonofabitch with a Porsche. Not a contemptuous postfeminist with a bad attitude. What had Charley Ray been thinking of? People like Snow didn't defend men accused of heinous crimes again women. People like Snow hanged, drew, and quartered them. "Chauvinist bullshit?" I gasped. "Me?"

"Michael," she said, "I don't know how much O'Brien really has here, but there are some pretty serious charges against you." It was almost refreshing to see that working for me hadn't lessened her contempt any. She propped herself on her arms and leaned forward. "We don't have time to play games with each other. Would you like to start discussing how we get you out of here, or would you like me to go home?"

Ten minutes ago I'd imagined that things couldn't get worse. How wrong I had been. I now had, as my savior, a woman who thought I was short, ugly, fussy, stuffy, and ridiculous. A woman who detested and reviled me. That should help my cause. For the first time it really and truly and vividly occurred to me that I might go to the chair. There was not a doubt in my mind that with Snow as my lawyer, I could become one of the greatest victims of the judicial system this country had ever seen. Sacco, Vanzetti, and Householder. "I'd like you to go home," I said. "There has definitely been some mistake. Charley Ray must have misunderstood me."

"Charley Ray didn't misunderstand you," she said. "He rode all the way out on the Island to get me because you needed help."

Help, yes. But having Snow in charge of my team would be like making the fox the coach of the chickens. "I don't," I said quickly. "I don't need help. The police have been a little overzealous, that's all. I'm sure that as soon as they realize tha—"

"What's the matter, Michael?" sneered Snow. "Don't you want me as your lawyer because I wouldn't go out with you, or because I'm a woman?"

I refused to stoop to her level. "Of course it's not because you're a woman," I said evenly. "My dentist happens to be a woman. And as for not going out with me, Ms. Lazarro, I don't actually recall ever asking you to go out with me."

"Well, what is it then? Don't I fit in with your image of a lawyer, Michael? Is that it? Do you think I'm going to show up in court in leathers with a bone through my nose? Do you think I can't be any good because I don't wear shoulder pads and heels?"

I attempted to deny these charges. I said, "Don—"

She shook a finger in my direction. "Well, let me tell you something, little man—"

I attempted to take offense. I said, "Little?"

I thought she was going to punch me. "Little," she repeated. "I use the word metaphorically, not literally. Little man, you are not the only one who has more to him than meets the eye. Why don't we agree that from now on I won't underestimate you if you don't underestimate me."

I pulled myself up my full five feet six and three-quarters inches. "I just really don't feel that I need a lawyer," I explained. "I'm sorry for ruining your camping weekend, but anyone can see that the whole case against me is ridiculous."

"If you say so," said Snow.

If I said so? "Does that mean you think that I'm guilty?"

"It means I think you need a lawyer."

"Well, I'm not guilty," I said stiffly. "And though I certainly appreciate you coming here, I really do not need your help."

She picked up her briefcase, throwing me a pitying, withering look. "Suit yourself," she said. "But just remember that for whatever reasons, O'Brien has kept this quiet so far. He hasn't gone screaming to the media that he's caught the Butcher." She picked up her parka. "But he will. He probably just hasn't had the time. This is the biggest case of his career, and if he's going after you, you'd better believe it's because he thinks you're his man—and because he's got enough on you to justify putting his ass on the line."

"But—" I bleated.

As usual, she talked right over me. "But the point is that within a few hours, you're going to be all over the press. They're probably setting up their camps outside right now." She pointed herself toward the door, but her eyes were on me. "You'd better have yourself some serious representation by the time you're arraigned, Michael, because it's going to be a circus." She made a face. "Unless, of course, you want to go with the public defender."

Somehow, going with the public defender didn't sound like a great idea. "This is ridiculous," I said. "They can't arraign me. I haven't done anything."

"Hohoho," said Snow.

"They don't have a case."

"They have something," said Snow. "They have what they think may be the murder weapon." She started to leave.

I wasn't going to get home by dawn. I was going to be lucky to get home by my ninetieth birthday. "Snow," I said.

She turned. "What?"

"Ms. Lazarro . . ."

She folded her arms across her chest and leaned against the door. If a look were a gun, she was carrying an Uzi automatic. "Let us make one thing clear, Michael C. If I take you as a client I am doing it not because of you but in spite of you. And if you come on to me with any of your tight-assed male ego-tripping arrogance, I'm going right home. Is that understood?"

What a relief that she wasn't underestimating me anymore.

I nodded. "Understood."

She slapped her briefcase down on the table again.

"Snow," I said.

She eyed me coldly.

"Ms. Lazarro . . ."

"What?"

"Do you think you could arrange for someone to feed my parrot?"

"Your parrot?"

How was it that she could imagine me a psychopathic killer but not the owner of a small and charming bird?

"Yes."

"*You* have a parrot?"

"Yes, I have a parrot."

"Don't they molt?"

"Her name is Gracie."

"Gracie. Sure," she said. "I can take care of that. Now can I ask you one question?"

"Sure."

"Did you do it?"

Home before the end of the next millennium.

13

Lonesome No More

The shoe fit. What shoe? Fit what? The shoe whose heel I broke on the grating in front of a liquor store at Twenty-seventh or maybe Twenty-ninth Street, the shoe that I'd thrown into the back of the closet, fit the woman whose foot was in the Death by Chocolate container.

"What is this, 'Cinderella'?" I hissed.

"Shhh," said Snow.

The ancient Aztec sacrificial knife was not just a harmless souvenir-shop replica. It was a real knife, probably early nineteenth century, with real traces of blood, probably late twentieth century, still on it. It could have been the murder weapon.

"That's ridiculous!" I protested.

"Shhh," said Snow.

The handkerchief wrapping the digits done up like profiteroles was identical with the handkerchiefs I always used, three in a box from Macy's.

"For Chrissake!" I screamed. "That's like being arrested because you own a Fruit of the Loom T-shirt."

"Shut up, Michael!" snapped Snow. She jabbed me in the ribs.

The judge refused to set bail.

"What did you expect?" asked my counsel. "It isn't like you're up for tax fraud, you know."

"But jail!" I squeaked. "No one in my family has ever been in jail before."

She shrugged, the lawyer-philosopher. "There's a first time for everything."

"Boy, I'm glad you're working for me."

I was remanded to a maximum security cell on Riker's Island— three visits from outsiders, one phone call a day, food that would make Colonel Sanders wince. No friends, no bail, oh, lonesome me.

"Look at the bright side," said Snow. "We've got a week before we go to the grand jury. If everything you've told me is true, with any luck, you'll be home stuffing mushrooms before the end of the month."

"What do you mean, 'if'?" I asked.

"Please," she warned, "no attitude. I mean 'if'." She winked. "How do I know that you're telling me the truth?"

At least having her as my attorney meant she couldn't be on the jury. "Would you give me a break, please? I'm having a hard time here. I don't know why you dislike me so much, but I'd really appre—"

Her chin went up. "*I* dislike you? I never said I disliked *you*. You're the one who's never been anything but hostile to me."

"*I've* been hostile to *you*? Who are you kidding? You've disliked me from the moment you first set eyes on me. That night at Sara and Alex's you jumped down my throat every time I opened my mouth."

"That's not true. I will admit that I didn't think you were exactly my type of . . . my type of per—"

My frayed nerves snapped. "You mean short, don't you? That's what you mean, isn't it, Ms. ERA? I'm too short to be your type of person."

"Michael, I realize that you've been under a strain, but will you please stop shouting? They're going to take you back to your cell."

I sat down. God, I wished I had enough hair to run my hand through. "I'm sorry," I said. "I guess you're right. I'm overwrought. I never shout in public."

"I don't dislike you," she said, teeth clenched. "I don't even know you. On the other hand, several people whom I value very highly seem to think a great deal of you . . ."

The words "for some reason" shimmered in the air between us. "Let's forget it, all right?" I asked, regaining my composure. "Just tell me what you mean by 'luck.' "

She sighed. "All I mean is that I've got a lot to do. O'Brien's working on the theory that the Butcher knows his victims, that he preys on lonely women who don't have any friends or family, so I want to interview everyone you've dated in the last two years."

"That should keep you busy," I said. "It certainly kept me busy."

"Spare me the ego," she said.

"Life is ironic, isn't it?" I asked. "First he comes after me because he thought I killed my wife. And now he knows I didn't kill my wife, but he still comes after me."

She gazed at me with a certain amount of wonder—though not, I might mention, the same sort of wonder she might have shown had I just pulled thirteen peacocks out of a silk purse. "Michael," she said, almost gently for her, "Michael, try to understand. O'Brien never thought you murdered your wife. My guess is he never for a second believed you had a wife. He just needed something to get him a warrant." She sighed. It was the sort of sigh you might heave if you were watching someone pull the boat away from the dock without untying it first. "And your whole story of why you made her up . . . don't you realize that's the most damning thing he has against you? All that scheming and subterfuge . . . O'Brien thinks it was either just another manifestation of your insanity or camouflage to hide what you were really doing and to cover your trail. Or both."

"He does?"

"Yes," she said. "He does." She leaned forward. "I'm sure he does, and quite frankly, Michael, if you want my honest opinion, I don't think it's going to be that difficult to convince a jury that he has a point."

"But you believe me, don't you?"

She looked me in my eyes. "That you went to all that trouble so you wouldn't have to go on any more dates?" I could see myself reflected in her pupils. I looked very small. She pushed back her chair. "Michael," said the defense lawyer flatly, "Michael, I don't have to believe you. I just have to get you off."

"Jesus."

She relented. "Okay, Michael." If reluctantly. "I believe you, all right?" She sighed again. "The whole thing's so crazy it has to be true." She stood up. "I'll see you in the morning. We've got a lot to go over." She turned at the door. "Get a good night's sleep!"

"Oh, sure," I mumbled.

Perchance to bloody dream.

My first night on Riker's was the loneliest night of my life. I lay on my bed, watching the dark do absolutely nothing, and listening to the faraway sounds of footsteps and doors being opened and closed, coughing and mumbling, something small and light falling to the floor.

It's not as though I'd never been lonely before. Everybody gets lonely now and then. When you leave home. That first night in a new apartment. The birthday all your friends forgot. The day you spent five hours preparing dinner but your guests never came. Those Saturday nights when you're all by yourself with nothing to do. The moment you discover that you talk to the television, talk to the refrigerator, talk to the bathroom mirror, tell your problems to the bird. Sitting in a restaurant on your own, trying to read a book and eat fettucine at the same time, hoping you look not as though you're there because you have no one to eat supper with, but as though you're there because you want to be. Sunday afternoons. Lonely. Lonely as I'd been after Marissa's departure, cooking away the blues.

But this was different. This was the loneliness of the last Indian left in the tribe. This was the loneliness of being ninety-two and all the people you'd ever known already buried in the ground. Of hopelessness. Of exclusion. Of not being loved.

It occurred to me that prison was a metaphor for life. There you are, in your tiny cell, isolated from everyone else, imagining the world outside, inventing what they're doing and saying, remembering—wrongly, probably—the color of the sky, the thickness of the grass, the affection or esteem in which you were held, listening for the sound of another voice, a footstep in the hallway, a jingling key that might unlock your door and take you somewhere else for a while.

I lay on my bed, motionless but moving fast. Thinking. Wondering. Where had I been most of my life? What had I been doing? What had I been after? You couldn't even call it being asleep at the wheel. It was more like being asleep in the trunk.

"So let me get this straight," said Snow. "There were so many women after you that you started hanging out in Jo Jo's."

"That's right."

"You and Jerry."

"Me and Jerry."

She wrote it down in her small, neat hand. "And that's where you got the idea to invent this wife of yours?"

"No, I got the idea at my mother's. Because she was driving me crazy."

"Because she asked you if you were gay?"

"It was the last straw."

She shook her head. "The prosecution's going to love that. It's exactly what they want to hear."

"I should think we could use it in my defense," I reasoned. "Look at history! It's heterosexual males who cause all the trouble."

She almost smiled. "They want sexual repression and confusion," she said. "It backs up their theory." She made another note. "Okay, so you had the idea at your mother's."

"But Jerry and I discussed it at Jo Jo's. With Bongo and Charley Ray." The perfect character witnesses.

She nodded. "I've talked to them," she said. She tapped her pen against the table. "Chrissy says she tried to tell them from the start that it was a stupid idea. You guys"—she pointed the ballpoint in my direction—"sometimes I don't think you have a brain cell between you."

"Thanks," I said. "Maybe we could call you as a witness, too."

"You're going to do a lot worse than me," she said reassuringly. "They've got you down as promiscuous, deviant, transvestite, obsessively methodical, a gourmet, hostile to and threatened by women . . . everyone in the five boroughs has heard you make jokes about your mother . . ."

"Everyone makes jokes about their mothers."

"I don't." She rested her chin on her hands. "The only thing they need is to find a limb in your freezer. Tell me again why you made up Alma?"

"Because I was tired of all the pressure. I was tired of everyone trying to get me married or analyze why I wasn't. I told you, my mother was driving me nuts."

She nibbled on the top of her pen. "That's all?"

"It's not enough? Snow, she answered the personals for me!"

She shrugged in her unbeguiling way. "It's much more common for men to pretend that they're not married than that they are." She made a face. "Most men enjoy being sexual objects."

"No, they don't," I said. "They enjoy treating women as sexual objects." I leaned closer, lowering my voice. "But I didn't. I know you won't believe me, but I hated it. I hated acting like an erection. Only I couldn't seem to stop myself. They'd throw themselves at me and I'd pick them up. That's the trouble with temptation," I whispered, "it's so damn tempting."

She looked down at her notebook, flipping a page. "The prosecution's going to make something of the fact that you spent a lot of time riding back and forth on the Staten Island ferry," she said suddenly. "And hanging out at suburban train stations. They're going to try to prove that your nocturnal wanderings were to dispose of the bodies."

"The bodies?"

"Why else? What other reason would a man have for riding back and forth on the ferry, or taking a train to some suburb where he knows no one, or driving out on the Island and turning right around and driving back again? They have witnesses who have identified you, Michael, who remember seeing you."

"But of course there's another reason," I protested. "I had to go somewhere, didn't I? I was trying to make it look as if I had a lot of heavy dates."

"Tell it to the marines," said Snow. "The prosecution's going to have a field day proving that Alma and everything to do with her was not only you acting out your aggression but you hiding your tracks."

"Deviant?" I asked. "Transvestite?"

She ignored me. "And what about the fact that you fit their description of the Butcher? Slim, dark, athletic?"

"But I'm shorter. I read the papers, you know. I'm much shorter."

"Not with those damn lifts, you're not. And what about the sketches? Even you have to admit that they look a bit like you."

"They don't look like me! They look like anybody—everybody—nobody. For the love of God, they're nondescript."

She leaned on her arms. "Michael," she said, "why did you dress up as Alma?"

Didn't she remember anything I told her? "So everyone would think I really had a wife."

She peered at me over the tops of her glasses. "Michael," she said, "did you really believe that you fooled anyone? Even with the lifts?"

I felt as if I were in one of those dreams where you're walking down the street and you suddenly realize that you're not wearing any clothes. Deviant. Transvestite. "No one?"

She shook her head. "Not the people in your local stores. Not the cleaners in your office. Not your doormen. Not O'Brien. Everybody knew it was you."

"If they all knew it was me, then why didn't they say anything?"

She gazed at me in silence for a split second or two, her face a picture of a woman struggling for understanding. It was an expression I knew well from my mother. "Michael," she said, with a kindness I hadn't experienced before, "Michael this is New York. What do you think they would say?"

Naked *and* stupid.

"Michael," said Snow, "you do realize that the prosecution's going to claim that your transvestism is just more evidence of your sick relationship with women, don't you?"

"But anyone who knows me knows that's not true."

"What? That your transvestism *isn't* more evidence of your sick relationship with women?"

I still couldn't tell if she was kidding or not.

And then I realized I was getting upset for nothing. "Marissa!" I smiled, giddy with relief. "Marissa knows I didn't have a sick relationship with women. Marissa liked me."

"Mrs. Sontag's going around telling everyone she heard Marissa call you a murderer, an inhuman murderer, and that she saw you threaten and manhandle her."

Naked, stupid, and in someone else's dream. "What? An inhuman murderer? Why would Marissa call me something like that?"

Snow flipped through her notes. "The morning Marissa left, apparently." Whatever my misgivings about Snow, she was certainly thorough. "She shouted it at you just before you forcibly dragged her into the elevator."

"Oh, for heaven's sake, that's ridiculous. Maybe she was shouting at me a little, but she was always shouting at someone."

"She was crying."

"She was upset."

"But you weren't upset? You never get upset."

I was upset now. "And I didn't drag her, I probably gave her a little shove."

"Not according to Mrs. Sontag."

"And forcibly? Forcibly! The woman outweighs me by a good fifteen pounds."

"But you were a gymnast."

"When I was sixteen! For God's sake, I also had hair down to my shoulders when I was sixteen!"

"Don't tell the prosecution that. Besides, Mrs. Sontag's adamant."

"Mrs. Sontag's wrong!"

"Stop yelling at me."

"I have to yell at you. It's the only way you listen."

She looked at me archly. "Mrs. Sontag also says you went through women like a weevil through corn."

"Mrs. Sontag said that?"

She shrugged. "Loose translation." She looked down at her book again. "One other small point, though," said Snow. She sort of pursed her lips in what might have been thoughtfulness.

"What's that? Mrs. Sontag saw me leave the foot in the stairwell?"

"Marissa's vanished from the face of the earth."

I laughed, albeit nervously. "No, she hasn't, she's gone to Florida."

Snow pushed her notebook aside. She folded her hands. She stared deeply into my eyes. "Mike," she said. "Just tell me once more why you invented a wife."

"If you'll tell me one thing."

"I don't do deals."

"I'm begging."

"What?"

"Am I not your type because I'm short, because I'm balding, or because I'm not good-looking enough?"

"Because you're so straight."

Even she had to smile.

Betsy Shopak came to call. She brought me three magazines and a bunch of grapes.

"Betsy," I said, "I'm not having an operation, I've been imprisoned for the good of society."

"Oh, Mike," said Betsy. Her lower lip trembled. "I had to come, I just had to come." She tugged at her ponytail. She bit her lip. The small plastic dinosaurs that were hanging from her earlobes bobbed as she talked. "I really feel like this is all my fault."

Victimization was beginning to make me generous. "Don't be silly, Betsy."

"No, really, Mike," said Betsy. "If I wasn't going out with Jesus none of this would ever have happened."

"Well . . . I don't . . ."

"Not the murders, of course. The murders would have happened, but you wouldn't be in jail." The dinosaurs danced. "I just know he only thought of you because of me."

He thought of me?

"What?"

"It wasn't until you told me about him visiting you that I suspected anything," said Betsy. "I mean, I knew he never liked you, but we never talked about you, I didn't even tell him about our, you know, our little fight . . ."

"Betsy," I said, "I'm really sorry abou—"

"Michael, please let me finish." She shrugged. She tugged. The dinosaurs jingled. "He was always a little jealous, you know, because you and I are such pals." She started nervously twisting the brooch on her blouse, two gray kittens curled up in a blue basket. "Oh, Mike . . ." She sounded dangerously near crying. "I felt so bad when I just stopped seeing you like I did, it was so mean, but it seemed like the best thing to do at the time."

I couldn't help myself. "*You* stopped seeing *me*?"

She laughed. "You mean you didn't even notice?"

"Wait a minute. If *you* stopped seeing me, what was that big speech about how I was avoiding you?"

Her look was clear and direct. "You were avoiding me."

"Yes, but . . ."

"Mike," said Betsy, summing up life, "those are two separate things." Everything bounced. "Anyway, I guess you were busier than I thought. But maybe I wasn't paying so much attention anyway, I was so worried about not wanting to get Jesus all upset."

"Take it from me," I said, "you made the right decision there."

"No," she said, emphatically, "no, I didn't. I should have confronted his jealousy instead of ignoring it. I'm just sure that, you know, sub-consciously, it's colored his, what I mean is, I know it's not deliberate, it's just that . . . well . . . you know how guys are."

"I'm certainly beginning to," I said.

"So when you get out we can be friends again?" asked Betsy.

"You mean if I get out."

"Oh, you'll get out," said Betsy brightly. "Who could think that a nice guy like you would do something like this?"

Several people, so far.

Reality, I thought, it's so subjective. You spend so much of your life thinking one thing's happening, when what's actually going on is something else entirely. I cleared my throat. I took a deep breath. "Betsy," I said, "Betsy, can I ask you a question?"

"Oh, Mike"—Betsy beamed—"of course you can."

"Were you . . . did you ever . . . you and . . . us . . . ?"

She started to laugh again. "Are you asking if I was ever interested in you?"

I nodded. "You weren't, were you?" I tried to take this in. All my subterfuge, all my avoidance . . . all for what?

She looked apologetic. "Well, you know, Mike, I love you like a brother and everything, but you're so—so—you're not really my type."

The guard signaled that her time was up.

"Well, I guess I'd better go now," said Betsy happily. She slipped her plastic bag over her arm. "Was that your lawyer I saw when I was coming in?" she asked as she got to her feet. "The tall woman with the motorcycle helmet?"

"That was she," I said.

Betsy winked. "She's cute."

"Cute?" I repeated.

"Yeah," said Betsy. "Cute."

Yet another new concept.

I spoke with Charley Ray on the phone. He wanted me to know that as much as he wanted to see me, and though he and Chrissy and Bongo and all the guys at Jo Jo's wanted me to know that they knew I was innocent and were rooting for me, he couldn't manage a visit. "It's the way some people feel about hospitals," said Charley Ray. "That's the way I feel about jails."

"Like you're going to catch something?" I asked.

"No," said Charley Ray. "Like I ain't gonna get out."

. . .

I'd always thought that firsts were more potent than seconds. The second bite of ice cream is never as cold. The second kiss is never as startling. Surprise and inexperience sharpen intensity and impact. And so it should follow that the second night in jail is not as lonely as the first.

But it was.

If anything, it was worse. With all that time to do nothing but think, I thought. I thought about women. Who would want to be one? was what I thought.

I thought of Betsy Shopak, coming to New York with her hideous furniture and her broken heart, all alone and brave beyond belief. And I did what I'd never done before, I pictured her sitting in her new home that first night, light-years from everything she knew best and loved, listening to the sounds of laughter and music from the apartments all around her, staring out the window at a couple across the way who were trying to hang a poster on the wall.

And I thought of all the women who had brought me here.

The women whose deaths I was accused of. Desolate women, living on the border between nothing and everything, going to work and going home, going to work and going home, every night the same sharp sound as the door shut behind them, every morning the same number of hours stretching ahead. Women with so few connections that they could be hacked up and stuffed into a burger box without anyone even noticing, anyone saying, "But there must be something wrong, we haven't seen her in a week." Women lonely enough to take their chances with some stranger with empty eyes and a masquerade smile who, I guessed, must be lonesome too.

The women I had run from. Women who had friends and work and full lives, but who were still lonely, still looking for love. Women who every day put on their makeup, squared their shoulders, and determinedly marched out into that bright new morning where lovers kissed and mothers wheeled their children in the sun. Women whose loneliness didn't make them want to butcher or defile you, but made them want to fix you dinner, to listen to your stories, to kiss away the silence and the night.

No one in my wing cried in the darkness. Or screamed. Or even shouted in his sleep. It was just as if we weren't there at all.

Christ, I thought to myself somewhere around midnight, it's a good thing I don't have a harmonica.

Life inside is so quiet, so muffled, so cut adrift that there are moments when you almost forget that there is a world outside at all. But the outside world doesn't forget about you. Not if you're an alleged crazed killer. Not if people want to know all about you. Not if they stand in supermarket aisles and parking lots discussing your character and personality, deliberating the method by which you were toilet trained. Not if they talk about you over breakfast, lunch, and dinner. Not if they bet on your innocence or guilt. Not if they speculate in print on the whereabouts of your very last love. IS MYSTERY MISTRESS IN FLORIDA OR IN HEAVEN? Snow couldn't walk out of her door without being besieged by reporters. She couldn't stop off for a sandwich without being surrounded by the ghoulish and curious. But Snow was tough, resilient, professional. Unflappable, unflustered, totally in charge.

Wasn't she human? you ask. Didn't she want to scream and shout? Didn't she want to take their cameras and their recorders and the menus and old electric bills they wanted signed and ram them down their throats? Where did all her fury and frustration go?

That's easy. She took it out on me.

On the third day, for instance, she entered briskly, ignoring my pleasant hello and friendly smile. She said, "Do you know what really infuriates me about you?"

"That I'm stuffy?"

She placed her briefcase on the table. "It's not that."

"That I'm fussy?"

She shook her head. "It's not that."

"That I made up a wife?"

She threw herself into her chair. "No, not that either."

"That I dressed in drag?"

She glared.

I threw up my hands. "Well, what is it, then? There isn't anything else."

She glared some more. "For the love of God, Michael," she shouted, "Why couldn't you be more like a woman?"

I glanced over my shoulder to see if the guard had heard. He had. "Excuse me," I said, keeping my voice down, "but I thought this whole mess started because I behaved too much like a woman."

"No," said Snow, leaning forward in that intense way of hers, "because if you really were like a woman, you'd know where Marissa is. You wouldn't have let her march out the door without getting a forwarding address. The wolves are getting hungry. You really need to find her."

I said, "Me?"

She said, "Yes, you."

I said, "Wait a minute, Snow. Marissa left on an impetuous whim of passion; she wasn't thinking about keeping in touch. And anyway, she had scores of female friends, but none of them got a forwarding address either. Why pick on me?"

"None of them slept with her," said Snow. "None of them practically lived with her for all those months. None of them were in charge of her parrot and her bowling shoes."

I was astounded. "Are you suggesting that I'm callous?" I gasped.

"Yes," she said, "I am. And insensitive. And thinking about nothing but yourself. You didn't even consider getting so much as a phone number, did you? Not even for Gracie!"

"Oh, wait a minute," I said. "Don't you bring Gracie into this. Let's not forget that Marissa abandoned her."

"That's right!" snapped Snow. "Blame Marissa. It's all really her fault, isn't it?"

"I didn't say that," I snapped back. "But you will remember that she's the one who left us."

"You drove her away," she said. "I can imagine what you were like to live with, Michael. Always going around picking things up. Correcting her. Timing how long she spent in the shower."

"Excuse me, Snow, but I don't think that's—"

"Complaining about the way she boiled an egg."

"Who told you that?"

She clapped her hands. "I knew it!" she cried. "I knew it!"

The guard told us to pipe down. "Hey!" he called. "You having a conference or you going nine rounds?"

We piped down. Snow brushed some hair out of her eyes. I picked a piece of string from my shirt. She folded her hands in front of her. I folded mine.

"I'm sorry," she said.

I said, "Me too."

And then, with a darting look in the guard's direction, she leaned toward me. "Well?" she whispered. "You put it in boiling water, don't you?"

"No," I said, "I don't. I put it in cold water and bring it to a boil. What about you?"

"Are you saying that just to annoy me?" asked Snow.

Jerry Finer dropped by.

"This is worse than in eighth grade when Mr. Holbein used to keep you after school every day and I'd stand outside the door to keep you company," he announced, rather fussily dusting off his chair before he sat down. "Lonnie sends her love."

I asked after Lonnie and Ethan, but my mind was on a long-ago autumn. The memory flickered—those short afternoons, that dull green room, the Finer eyes just peering over the edge of the door. "You know, I'd forgotten that completely," I said. I tried to bring back those afternoons, two or three leaves falling outside, the shrill sound of children taunting each other as they rushed from the building and into the streets, me sitting in the front corner seat, looking for a glimpse of Jerry through the glass pane of the door, and Mr. Holbein up at his desk, correcting papers like the Grim Reaper selecting recruits. I knew why I was being held in maximum security, but I couldn't for the life of me remember why I'd spent all those afternoons of the fall of 1966 in Mr. Holbein's English classroom. "Jerry," I asked, "why was I there?"

Jerry settled into his chair, looking around curiously. You can always tell the first-timers. "Because of Alma Huttenmeyer."

It hadn't occurred to me that he remembered the original owner of that name. "Who?"

He checked the walls and the table for hidden microphones. He searched the corners of the ceiling for gun placements. "Alma Huttenmeyer."

"Alma Huttenmeyer?"

His eyes stopped roving and rested on me. "Yeah, Mike, the real Alma Huttenmeyer. You remember."

Oddly enough, though I remembered she chewed Dentyne, I didn't remember being held after school because of her.

"I couldn't believe it when you named your wife after her." He grinned. "God, she was something, wasn't she? She looked like a cross between Howdy Doody and Bucky Beaver, except, of course, that she was built like a flying buttress."

Howdy Doody? Bucky Beaver? "Alma Huttenmeyer?"

"Yeah, Alma Huttenmeyer." He shook his head at the memory. "Cute," he said, "very, very cute. I don't think there was a boy in the ninth grade who didn't have a crush on her—but she was *so* dumb. Remember how dumb she was?"

"Dumb? Alma Huttenmeyer was dumb?" Reality was taking another tumble.

"Oh, come on, Mike, you must remember. She thought that Indians came from India."

"They do."

He gave me a look. "The Cheyenne didn't." He shook his head, smiling to himself. "Don't you remember that paper she wrote on the building of the transcontinental railway? She thought the Chinese all worked on it as cooks."

"Well, some of them did."

He gave me that look again. "Anyway, that's why Holbein gave you detention."

"Because Alma Huttenmeyer was dumb?"

"Because you helped her cheat in a big exam."

"I did?"

He gave me another look. "How can you not remember this, Mike?

You were crazy about her. But she wouldn't look at you because you were short and you got straight A's."

"I can't see that my height—"

"And then she said she'd let you have a kiss if you let her copy off your English test."

"And did she?"

"Of course she did. Holbein caught her practically leaning across the aisle."

"I meant the kiss. Did she let me kiss her?"

"I guess she must've," said Jerry. "She let everybody else kiss her, only she didn't usually charge them."

I talked with my mother.

"This is unbelievable," said my mother. "I go away for a few days, and look what happens. You're all over the six o'clock news! It's true what the papers are saying, isn't it? It's all because your father died."

"Mom," I said. "I haven't done anything."

"Your sister says it's because I always bossed you around. But it was because you were the baby, Michael, and so headstrong. What else could I do? A woman alone . . ."

"Mom," I said, "Mom, I haven't done anything."

"Your brother says it's because I spoiled you. But I don't really feel that I did, you know. He's the one I thought I was going to have trouble with. The day I brought you home from the hospital, he wanted me to take you back."

"Mom," I said, my conviction beginning to wane. "I'm an innocent man."

"Well, of course you're innocent," said my mother. "It's Alma I'm upset about, not that. She was such a nice girl, I was really hoping you two would patch it up. As for the other, everyone knows there isn't a mean bone in your body. I told your lawyer as much, don't think I didn't."

Snow Lazarro and Margery Householder Taub conversing. What a thought!

" 'It's like arresting Santa Claus,' I told her. 'The very idea!' "

"What'd she say?"

"She said, 'Don't you mean Dopey?' " My mother laughed. "She certainly has a sense of humor. Barry says you need one in a job like hers, but I think it makes a refreshing change."

"From what?" I asked. "From all the criminal lawyers you know who don't have a sense of humor?"

"From your usual women," said my mother.

I'd always thought of myself as a nice guy. And, as a nice guy, I couldn't understand how this could have happened to me. Me! A person who had never done anything to set the world on fire, and who never would, was now the talk of the town, if not the nation. What I'd always wanted—and largely had—was a quiet life. No big hassles. No great traumas. No major-league problems. Some people's lives were one long emergency, but not mine. Mine was one long Sunday afternoon when everyone else was out of town. And that was how I'd wanted it. An okay job, an okay apartment, a well-stocked larder, an okay life. Not for me danger and adventure. Not for me the razor's-edge existence of pounding heart and rushing blood. I just wanted to keep my head down and the wolf from my door. I just wanted to get through with a minimum of pain and bother. So what happened?

I, a man who had never dented someone's bumper while parking without leaving my phone number, was accused of murder. I, a man who might have been just a tiny bit of a misogamist, was accused of being a psychotic misogynist who liked to hack women into tiny pieces and toss them around the city for kicks.

And so I spent another sleepless night, humming old blues songs under my breath and asking myself *why*, asking myself *how*. A nice guy like me.

And then, at about the time when, if I'd had a harmonica, I would have been playing "Columbus Stockade," the truth descended on me like acid rain. I wasn't such a nice guy after all. I'd always thought of myself as a decent person, as a liberated man, but the first time women started treating me the way they'd always been treated—

ogling me, pursuing me, asking me how much spaghetti to use for one serving—I went nuts. I carried on as if I were some sort of martyr. Saint Michael of the golden balls. I didn't become kind and generous like Betsy Shopak. Or spirited and outspoken like Snow Lazarro. Or bold and spunky like Elizabeth Beacher. I didn't become passionate and daring like Marissa Alzuco. Or practical and competent like Lonnie Stepato. Or strong and determined like Margery Householder Taub. Oh no, not I. I became a fifth-rate desperado. Not the kind who have ballads written about them, but the kind who end up in cheap hotels in South America in rumpled suits. I pulled the blanket over my head.

My attorney arrived for our next meeting like a sunny day in April after a winter of snow. "Good news!" She grinned. Had I gotten used to that smile, or hadn't I been seeing it very much lately? "Marissa's turned up!"

But I was not as cheered by this information as I once might have been. It may have been spring where Snow Lazarro was living, but in my cell it was still March and the roads were iced over. Prison has that effect on some people; and it was certainly having that effect on me. For Snow's sake, however, I rallied. "I thought she'd vanished from the face of the earth."

"Uh uh. She was in the Keys. Apparently she'd been riding around in a boat and missed the furor. She said she was aware that some guy had been arrested for the murders, but she hadn't heard it was you. As soon as she did, she called your mother."

"Thank God she wasn't shipwrecked," I said.

"She seemed very nice on the phone," said Snow, in a voice that defined the difference between politeness and enthusiasm.

I gave her a questioning look.

"Well, you know," said Snow. "She didn't really sound like your type."

Who did? Following in the footsteps of Alma Huttenmeyer's loafers, I had come to realize, was a long line of unsuitable women.

"And you sound like my mother." I gaped. "I don't believe this. You never even met her. How can you tell if she's my type or not?"

She waved a hand at me dismissively. "It was just a feeling. From talking to her. You know, she seemed kind of vague."

"What do you mean, 'kind of vague'? Couldn't she remember who I was?"

"Oh, no," said Snow. It must have been that she hadn't been using it much, you couldn't take that smile for granted. "She remembered you all right. In fact, she had a lot of good things to say about you. She really likes you, Michael."

I don't know why this seemed like news. "She does?"

"Of course she does," said Snow. "Everyone likes you."

"You don't like me."

"Except for Mrs. Sontag, everyone has only good things to say about you. Your boss. Your secretary. Your clients. Your friends. Your ex-girlfriends. Everyone, Michael. You're a nice guy."

I looked around us. Concrete walls, iron bars, Plexiglas windows, men with cuffs and guns and truncheons. "Snow," I said calmly. "Snow, none of us are in here for being nice guys."

Snow stared at me for a few silent seconds. And then she spoke. She said, "You're wrong, you know. I do like you."

I was in a supermarket. The supermarket was located in a large, open meadow. The shelves of the supermarket were filled with women. Intelligent women, attractive women, women who spoke three languages and made their own butter. I took one off the shelf. I put her in my basket. I pushed her along. She asked me my star sign. I asked her her favorite movie. She told me she liked walking in the rain. I told her I didn't. She asked me if it was true that Indians came from India. I said, "But not the Cheyenne." She became enthusiastic about rum raisin ice cream with chocolate sauce. The more we talked, the more apparent it became. This wasn't the woman for me. She was unsuitable. I stopped suddenly and started to pull her out of the cart. She resisted. "What's wrong?" she demanded. "Is my nose too long? Are my feet too big? Aren't I good enough for you?"

"It's not that," I said, trying to jam her back on the shelf. "It's not that, really, it isn't. It's just that you're not the one."

"Not the one?" she shrieked. "Just who do you think you are, buddy? Who do you think you are?"

This happened a second time. It happened a third. It happened a fourth. I wanted out of this dream, but it wouldn't end. Every time I'd put one woman back on the shelf, I'd take another one off. Pretty soon the women were all screaming. "Stop him!" they screamed. "Stop him! Don't let him kill again."

I started hurrying down the aisles with my cart. "It's not me!" I yelled back. "I'm not the murderer. I'm innocent! I'm a nice guy!"

"No, you're not!" they bellowed. "No, you're not!"

They began to chant. "Guil-tee! Guil-tee! Guil-tee! Guil-tee!"

I started to run.

"Guil-tee! Guil-tee! Guil-tee! Guil-tee!"

I was running and running but getting nowhere.

"Guil-tee! Guil-tee! Guil-tee! Guil-tee!"

And then, all of a sudden, Snow was standing there, right in the middle of Pasta and Dried Legumes. She grabbed hold of me. "Michael," said Snow, "Michael, what's wrong?"

"I'm guilty!" I gasped. "It's true, Snow, I'm guilty."

"No, you're not, Michael," said Snow. I could feel the warmth of her hands through my shirt. "You're a nice guy."

I leaned against her. She smelled like morning. "I'm not," I said. "I'm guilty. Guiltyguiltyguilty."

She pulled away and started to shake me. "Michael," she said. "Michael, wake up!"

In the dream, I opened my eyes. I opened my eyes, and I was on my bed, in my cell, but Snow Lazarro, was sitting beside me.

"It's true," I said, "I'm guilty. Call a press conference. I'm ready to confess."

Snow started to laugh. "Michael, wake up. Guilty of what?"

I leaned against her again. It was a morning in June. Somewhere with a lot of trees and a lake. "I'm not sure, but there must be something."

"Michael," she said, "you're not guilty. That's why I'm here."

I shook my head. "I am," I said. "I am."

She pushed me away and shook me roughly. "Michael," she said. "Michael, are you awake?"

I looked around. "Am I?"

"Michael," she said, "it's five in the morning and we're sitting in a cell on Riker's Island, and you're not guilty."

I leaned my forehead against hers. "I am," I whispered. I could feel her breath.

"Awake?"

"Guilty."

"Of what?" asked Snow.

All my life, I'd been waiting for something exciting to happen, something that made me feel really alive. But nothing ever did. Sitting back and waiting: waiting for my princess to come. She never came. I drifted. I stumbled from one woman to the next. In over thirty years, the only truly active thing I ever did toward creating my own happiness was to invent Alma Huttenmeyer. In thirty years, that was all I could manage. That was me looking for love. "Of doing nothing."

She didn't pull away. "Michael," she whispered, "Michael, listen to me! They caught the Butcher. You're really free!"

Panic made me act. It wasn't sensible, it wasn't intelligent, it was, in fact, bloody stupid, but in some weird way it was the first positive movement I'd ever made toward controlling my own life. In which case, I hadn't gone off the path after all. Not only would it have been impossible for me to go off the path when I took only one small step every thirty-odd years, but the step I took was one I should have taken a decade ago. A step in the direction I'd always wanted. Away from compromise. Away from meaninglessness. And toward love.

I wasn't dreaming. I was staring into the eyes of Snow Lazarro. She shook her head, but a slow smile, brighter than any smile she'd ever shone on me before, began to light up her face.

I couldn't take my eyes from that smile. Or those eyes. I was smiling too.

"Michael," said Snow. "Michael, did you hear me?"

"Yeah," I said, "I heard you."

And then we just sat there, looking at each other for a few minutes, while the universe reshaped itself and fell into place around us.

Her hands were still on my shoulders. "Michael," she said. "You're free!"

"Not anymore I'm not," I said.

In jail one minute, and in love the next.

14

The End of the End

The Butcher of Broadway, driven wild by my notoriety and all the attention I was receiving, struck again. But this time—much to my surprise as well as to his—the police were waiting.

So, all in all, it was a happy ending. Justice was served. Lives were saved. Jesus was a hero. Betsy was the fiancée of a hero. Jerry told Lonnie everything and the Finer-Stepato marriage progressed to a new and stronger level. Alex and Sara got their sperm from a sperm bank. ("It'd be too weird," said Sara. "If we had a kid and you and Snow had a kid, they'd be related.") I decided to leave agenting and open a restaurant on the money I was making from writing my story.

And I'd discovered how wrong I had been. Firsts really weren't more potent than seconds. Not when it comes to love. Only Snow doesn't believe in marriage. "We can live together and have a few kids and see what happens," says Snow.

Chrissy, Charley Ray, Snow, and I went out for a celebratory night on the town.

"There's this great chili house we know in Jersey," said Charley Ray.

I tried not to show my astonishment that anyone would deliberately *go* to Jersey to eat. To eat chili. Chihuahua, maybe, or even Santa Fe, but Paramus? "No kidding."

"You won't believe it, Mike, it'll clear your sinuses for life."

"And the corn bread," Chrissy enthused. "I don't know what they put in it, but I've never tasted anything like it." She jabbed Charley Ray in the ribs. "Ain't that right, honey?"

"That's right," said honey. "And the tamales are pretty good too."

Snow gave me a poke. "Look at Mike's face." She laughed. "He doesn't believe you." She patted the seat. "Mike wouldn't dream of serving chili with corn bread, would you, sweetie?"

"I might," said sweetie. "You know how reckless and keen for adventure I am nowadays."

"You're gonna be okay, Mike," said Charley Ray. He climbed on the back of Chrissy's bike. She started the engine.

Sweetie climbed behind Snow. "We'll race you!" she screamed over the noise from the engine.

"You're on!" Chrissy screamed back over the Norton's roar. "Loser buys a round of beer!"

It was molasses in the corn bread. Molasses and just a little cayenne. The chili was out of this world.

"Hey," I said, "this isn't bad." Not as good as what my place would serve, but not bad.

Charley Ray shoved his plate toward me. "Just take a taste of the tamale, Mikey. You'll think you died and went to heaven."

There'd been a few turns on the way out when that had seemed a likelihood rather than a figure of speech, but on the whole it had been a pleasant ride. A pleasant ride, great friends, good food. I looked around the table. I was a happy man. A happy man who had moved in with a wonderful woman, who was opening his own business, who owned his own motorcycle helmet, and who had had his ear pierced because his girlfriend told him it would make him look sexier. I was headed for a hell of a middle age.

Charley Ray started banging on the table. "I'd like to propose a toast," he announced. He raised his bottle. "To Michael."

"To Michael," said Snow.

"To Michael," said Chrissy.

"Let's hope he stays out of trouble for a while," said Charley Ray, grinning.

"Man, I'll tell you," said Chrissy, "a couple of months ago I wouldn't've given you any odds on Mike coming out of this in one piece. Not with his attitude and everything."

I started to ask her to clarify what she meant by "attitude," but Charley Ray interrupted. "If you think about it," he said, "the whole thing was kind of like kismet, wasn't it? You know, all of us so different and becoming pals."

Snow leaned against me. "It sure was." She laughed.

Charley Ray winked. "It's a real happy ending, isn't it?"

I looked at Snow.

"Yeah," I said, "it sure is."

Harpooned through the heart.

TRADE PAPERBACKS

___ **A Trail of Heart's Blood Wherever We Go** by Robert Olmstead	$11.00 US/$13.00 Can	71548-1
___ **Call and Response** by T.R. Pearson	$10.95 US/$12.95 Can	71163-X
___ **Gospel Hour** by T.R. Pearson	$11.00 US/$13.00 Can	71036-6
___ **The Jewel in the Crown** by Paul Scott	$11.00 US	71808-1
___ **The Day of the Scorpion** by Paul Scott	$11.00 US	71809-X
___ **The Towers of Silence** by Paul Scott	$11.00 US	71810-3
___ **A Division of the Spoils** by Paul Scott	$11.00 US	71811-1
___ **Lights Out in the Reptile House** by Jim Shepard	$10.00 US/$12.00 Can	71413-2
___ **The Bachelors** by Muriel Spark	$9.00 US	71570-8
___ **The Ballad of Peckham Rye** by Muriel Spark	$7.95 US	70936-8
___ **A Far Cry From Kensington** by Muriel Spark	$7.95 US	70786-1
___ **The Girls of Slender Means** by Muriel Spark	$7.95 US	70937-6
___ **Loitering With Intent** by Muriel Spark	$7.95 US	70935-X
___ **The Mandelbaum Gate** by Muriel Spark	$9.00 US	71569-4
___ **Memento Mori** by Muriel Spark	$7.95 US	70938-4
___ **The Lady at Liberty** by Hudson Talbott	$9.95 US/$11.95 Can	76427-X
___ **The Fugitive** by Pramoedya Ananta Toer	$8.95 US/$10.95 Can	71496-5
___ **Failure to Zigzag** by Jane Vandenburgh	$8.95 US/$10.95 Can	71019-6
___ **Girl With Curious Hair** by David Wallace	$9.95 US/$11.95 Can	71230-X
___ **In the Blue Light of African Dreams** by Paul Watkins	$10.00 US/$12.00 Can	71640-2
___ **Calm at Sunset, Calm at Dawn** by Paul Watkins	$8.95 US/$10.95 Can	71222-9
___ **Night Over Day Over Night** by Paul Watkins	$7.95 US/$9.95 Can	70737-3
___ **Winning the City** by Theodore Weesner	$9.00 US/$11.00 Can	71554-6

Buy these books at your local bookstore or use this coupon for ordering:

....

AVON BOOKS